PJ Grondin

Past Sins

PD House Books

PD House Holdings, LLC
910 S. Meadow Drive
Sandusky, Ohio   44870

Library of Congress Control Number: 2024911458

www.pjgrondin.com

pjgron@pjgrondin.com

ISBN: 978-1-7370004-7-1

Dedication

Past Sins is dedicated to the men and women of the United States Marine Corps, both active duty and veterans. These warriors met, and continue to meet, challenges that average citizens would find nearly impossible to face. I speak with Marine Corps veterans regularly when peddling my works at craft fairs and author events. We exchange stories: me about my time on board the USS *John Adams*, them about their time in the jungles of Vietnam, the deserts of Iraq and Afghanistan, and other places less hospitable. Though many say they could not have stood the confinement of a submarine, I assure them that I could not have performed their job. Past Sins is not reflective of any real-life situations. It is a work of fiction. The job of the United States Marine Corps is real and continues day-in, day-out. Along with the other branches of the military, they allow citizens of the United States to live free as they defend our rights and our country.

Acknowledgements

My dear wife, Debbie, deserves much credit for her patience and love. Without her encouragement, I might have decided to listen to classic rock all day, versus making progress on this novel. To my editor, Bonnie Lukcso, your critical evaluation of this work, and my previous works, has helped me become a better, more attentive writer. Because of this, I hope you will not have to work as hard on my future manuscripts. Finally, to all my readers who have told me how much you love my stories; it is your encouragement that keeps my creative juices flowing. When you tell me that you could see the story on the big screen as you read them, that is all the inspiration I need. Thank you so very much.

Past Sins

Prologue

2011 - Sunday, September 11

8:35 p.m.

The remote-controlled drone hovered high out of sight above and to the west of the target with a payload of a single deadly hellfire missile. If successful, the explosive would eliminate two terrorist leaders: a top Al Queda general and a Taliban military planner. The meeting of these two normally opposing factions offered a rare opportunity for the United States to eliminate key principals of the two groups.

Setting the powerful laser in place atop a short, tripod stand, Sergeant Jeffrey Grumen checked his notes, ensuring he targeted the correct building, the objective of the mission. He had just minutes to verify the operation of the laser and communicate with the command center that the drone could launch its deadly payload. Through heat waves from the desert floor, with the sun at his back, the sighting scope on the laser provided a direct view of the targeted structure on the western edge of Kabul. Sweat ran down his forehead into his eyes, a product of high tension and oppressive heat. He wiped his face with a free hand then turned to Rifle Team Charlie leader, Corporal Rayshon Mack.

"Corporal Mack, verify laser is on target."

Mack scooted along the rocky hill, feeling the strain in every muscle in his body. He moved into position, looked through the sighting scope, checked the coordinates on the laser against those on the paper that Grumen held. The laser had been sighted and locked on a building that stood in a tight cluster of other beige structures.

Mack confirmed, "Laser locked on target."

Grumen knew that Mack had no way of knowing if the laser had been locked on the correct target. Mack's only job - confirm that the device worked properly and that the coordinates on the sheet of paper he had been handed matched the laser's digital read-out. He did not have the paygrade to determine whether the correct target had been selected.

Grumen keyed his satellite radio, "Laser is locked on target."

The reply came back, "Laser locked on target, roger."

Within seconds, members of the rifle team heard the unmistakable sound of an incoming missile screaming out of the sky. They were nearly three miles away in the hills to the west of the Kabul neighborhood, well out of harm's way.

The team had provided support for many drone strikes and they anticipated the ensuing destruction. Some team members drew out their field glasses and watched as the missile screeched towards its target from the clear sky.

The tremendous blast sent a fireball into the air, chunks of concrete, steel, and dirt from the once-sturdy structure scattered in all directions. After the initial fireball, a plume of smoke rose above the shattered remains. Several adjacent buildings showed severe damage but not enough to cause collapse. Once the smoke cleared, a crater nearly twenty feet in diameter and six feet deep - surrounded by debris – replaced the building that had stood there just seconds before.

Neighbors spilled into the street, approaching the hole in the ground, women crying, men looking around for survivors, some on their knees near bodies apparently thrown from the building.

Mack saw movement on the hill to the north, just fifty yards from their position. He swiveled to get a better view of Private Randall Parish, a member of Rifle Team Bravo. They were supposed to be securing their position's northern flank. Rifle Team Alpha performed the same job to the south. The approaching Marine ran straight at Grumen, his expression showing distress.

When he reached Grumen, he shouted, "You hit the wrong …"

Grumen immediately shouted, "Stand down, Private." He paused, thinking fast, then roughly pulled the soldier down the hill, away from Rifle Team Charlie and out of line of sight of the city in case anyone looked their way. Grumen glared directly in Parish's eyes and asked, "Are you trying to get us killed, running up here, waving your arms like that?" He paused, looked around at his team members, who were all staring at their sergeant. "We had direct orders from our chain of command and we executed those orders. You will not speak of this again. Understood, Private?"

The Marine started to protest, but he saw the look in Grumen's eyes. "Yes, sir!"

"Now get back with your unit and do your job!"

The Marine turned and ran back the way he had come.

Confident that the strike had accomplished its mission, he switched off the laser, ordered Corporal Mack to secure the laser, prepare his team to move out, and head back to base. He had paperwork to do.

As he was headed down the hill, a member of Rifle Team Alpha approached him, apparently in distress. He mumbled to himself, "Crap, what now?"

* * *

Moska Aziz felt nauseous as she walked out the back door of her friend's home in Kabul. The intense heat only added to her physical discomfort and mental anguish. Her secret became more difficult to hide with each passing day. She had told no one of her predicament, but that would undoubtedly change, inevitable once her belly started to show. She intended to tell her closest friend, but she knew Zahra could not keep a secret and would tell her own parents. They were certain to tell Moska's parents and then the entire neighborhood would know. She would suffer the torment of a community that would view her as a promiscuous whore with no morals. Why else would she be pregnant outside of marriage?

In her entire life, Moska had never seen peace in Kabul or the rest of her country. Prior to the Americans, the Russians had tried their best to conquer the Afghans and install their own puppet government. It had cost the Russians dearly. Now the Americans and their NATO henchmen thought they knew better than the Russians. They wished to improve the lot of Afghan people, to westernize their lifestyle, to unite the tribes of the country. They promised peace and prosperity through democracy. In her eyes, they simply made life harder and her people more miserable. The Americans extended a war that no one wanted in the first place, and there was no end in sight.

As her nausea built, Aslam Sayed, one of Zahra's older brothers, came out the back door and saw her there holding her stomach. He looked at her, puzzled, as he approached.

"Moska, Zahra is looking for you. Why are you out here in this heat?"

She looked at Aslam with contempt. She hoped that he would just turn around and go back inside. She wanted nothing to do with him. A scoundrel and a fraud, he pretended to be politically connected. A narcissist, he believed he would lead Kabul to better times. Little more than an actor, he hoped real leaders would notice him and elevate him to a position of respect. He would never be like his and Zahra's older brother, Amir.

Amir. Moska adored Amir. A man of deep thought and few words, but his words carried weight. At only nineteen years of age, local leaders, both political and religious, listened to him. He had ideas that many hoped would lead Kabul to a brighter future, which included modernized infrastructure, better schools that included education for girls as well as boys, and economic changes that would bring investment into Kabul from other nations. In short, a visionary. But more than that, he dreamed of peace in Afghanistan, something that the country had not seen for decades.

Thoughts of Amir brought Moska back to her dilemma. Being pregnant with another man's child, regardless of how the child was conceived, Amir would never court her, never love her, and certainly never marry her. He would look down on her with the same contempt as the rest of her village. She would be an outcast for the rest of her life, and her child would be branded, a bastard, forced to bear the sins of its mother.

She turned back to Aslam. "I had to get away for a moment. I'm not feeling well."

She felt self-conscious, worrying, wondering if Aslam knew she was pregnant. But how could he know? He could only guess based on seeing her nausea, her mood swings, her diet. But she avoided him as best she could. She should not have any concerns about Aslam. Everyone she knew thought him a fool.

Another wave of nausea began to overwhelm her. She ducked behind a low wall near the back of the property and began to wretch. Just as she did, she heard a loud screeching sound followed by a blast that seemed to explode in her ears. She felt pain along her back as the ground shook with a violence that she had never experienced. The air filled with dust and sand. Her eyes burned. She inhaled smoke with each breath. Lying face-down, the wall next to her had been demolished, a chunk of rock landing near her head. She tried to stand, but could only get as far as her knees.

Trying to remember the moments before the explosion, she shook her head, pain rippling through her neck and back. Then she remembered talking with Aslam. She looked next to her and saw him sprawled on the ground some twenty feet from her. His body not moving, blood covering his clothing. She slowly turned back towards Zahra's house.

Except for pulverized stone and a massive, smoldering hole in the ground, it was gone.

* * *

Captain Charles "Chip" Chandler stormed into Colonel Virgil Vance's office breezing right past Captain Colleen Temple who normally announced any visitors. Chandler was incensed. Private Rusty Parish came to him, distraught, after the drone strike on the Taliban meeting place. Parish had gone directly to Chandler, bypassing his chain of command, which put Parish's career in peril for such a move. He had been given a direct order from Sergeant Grumen to never speak of the drone strike again. He ignored that order and took his grievance directly to his captain, skipping two levels of command in the process. Parish told Captain Chandler that the home of Amir Sayed, a trusted informant and long-time interpreter for the U. S. Marine Corps, had been destroyed by the drone strike.

At first, Chandler questioned why he had not taken his complaint to his team leader or his sergeant. Parish had replied that he did and his concerns were dismissed, that he was ordered to keep his mouth shut. Chandler then questioned Sergeant Grumen who confirmed that he had ordered Parish to stand down. He also denied that they bombed the wrong house. He cited that they had good intelligence and proper orders to carry out the strike.

Chandler confirmed through his Afghan contacts that they did, in fact, bomb the home of Amir Sayed and that there were two survivors: Amir Sayed and a neighbor girl, Moska Aziz. Both were severely injured and taken to a local hospital. Chandler commandeered a Jeep and raced to the hospital where he conferred with the on-duty physician. He said that both Sayed and Aziz were in serious, but stable condition. Further treatment for both patients required treatment beyond what he could provide in Kabul.

By the time Chandler stormed into Colonel Vance's tent, the two injured Afghanis were on a C-130 transport jet headed for the U.S. Military hospital in Landstuhl, Germany. Chandler had arranged the move because they had provided valuable assistance to U.S. forces in the fight against Al Queda and the Taliban.

The deep, no-nonsense voice of Colonel Virgil Vance bellowed out, "Captain, you better have a damn good reason for busting in here like this."

"You bet your ass I do, sir. We just droned one of our most trusted informants. He survived, barely, but we killed his entire family. How in the hell did this happen? Who provided the intel on the strike?"

Vance's brow furled. "Are you sure about this?"

"One-hundred percent, sir."

Vance rubbed the late-day stubble on his face and closed his eyes. He thought about his future. In the Marine Corps, limited opportunities arose to make general and his second chance was approaching. A failure of this magnitude would ruin his chances and torpedo the remainder of his career.

Instead of telling Chandler to quell any talk of the incident, he said, "Captain, write up a report asap and we'll get to the bottom of this."

Skeptical, Chandler wanted to ensure that whoever ordered the strike on the Sayed home paid for their mistake. "You're not going to let this get buried, right Colonel?"

If the question angered Vance, his face and body language did not show it. He replied, "You have my word, Captain."

Chapter 1

2021 - Saturday, September 11,

7:40 a.m.

The Savannah Morning News lay spread out on Peden Savage's office desk in the lower floor of the Bird-Baldwin House on West Liberty Street in Savannah, Georgia. The paper, thicker than on most Saturdays, had an entire section devoted to the twenty-year anniversary of nine-eleven. It was complete with pictures of the burning twin towers, the scarred and smoldering E-ring on the southwest side of the Pentagon, and the eerie arial view of the hole in the ground and debris field at Shanksville, Pennsylvania. The spread included gut-wrenching stories of individual loss, grief, and survival as well as graphic shots of people falling through the air. The grim reminder of the life-or-death decisions faced by many tugged at his heart even twenty years later. He couldn't imagine facing such a decision: either burn to death slowly and painfully, or take the leap and end the pain after a brief feeling of freedom during the descent from nearly one hundred stories high.

The articles gave Peden pause, remembering how he had felt watching repeated videos of the planes as they slammed into the towers, creating a fireball, smoke, shattered glass and concrete, and showering debris down on lower Manhattan. He had been in his early twenties then, having just been discharged from the United States Marine Corps, and a junior agent with the FBI. He considered emotional, gut-wrenching notions of resigning from his new position and re-enlisting, but changed his mind. He had been recruited by the FBI even before the end of his service obligation with the Marines. Peden had accepted a position with the Bureau with idealistic dreams that his new career would make a difference in the lives of everyday Americans, investigating and arresting drug dealers, fighting white collar crime, and catching pedophiles.

Then terrorists destroyed the World Trade Center twin towers, struck the Pentagon, and tried to take out the Capitol building in Washington, D.C. At that moment, he believed he would be assigned to the FBI's anti-terrorist group. He, like most all U.S. citizens at that time, wanted to hunt down the bastards who had attacked the United States in such a cowardly way. But his assignments at the bureau did not change and he had no direct involvement in the actual investigation. He learned details about the attacks through his boss, Special Agent Roland Fosco, who told Peden that if the team required additional assistance, Peden would be up-to-date with at least a background level of information.

As his mind drifted back to the days and weeks after September 11, 2001, a sense of sadness and dread drifted over him. The country, currently in turmoil, still fought a pandemic that had killed hundreds of thousands of his fellow citizens. The economy faced inflationary pressure not seen in four decades. Caravans of illegal immigrants flooded the southern border and made their way to cities across the country. The political climate between the two major parties smoldered; political hacks, major media outlets, and politicians threw gasoline on an already incendiary situation. The President and Vice President polled at the lowest approval ratings in modern history. The only politicians faring worse were members of Congress, whose popularity approached single digits.

The chirping of his cell phone interrupted his funk. He shook his head and looked around his desk, lifting the newspaper and some other paperwork. Finding his cell within arm's reach, he looked at the display but did not recognize the number. He hesitated, believing the spam callers were starting early. He brushed a finger across the red handset, ending the call before it started. He went back to the newspaper and noticed a story about a body found in Screven County near the Savannah River. He scanned the narrative, noting that the Screven County Sheriff suggested the death may have been a drug overdose, but that final determination would come from the Medical Examiner. The decedents name had been withheld pending notification of next of kin.

Peden had just turned the page after scanning two other short stories of local interest when his phone chirped again: same number as before. He thought back to his former partner from the FBI, Megan Moore, telling him to answer all calls because it might be important.

Still annoyed at the interruption, he answered, "Savage Investigative Consultants."

A voice with a mild southern accent said, "Hi Peden. Chip Chandler."

Peden recognized the voice but it took him a moment to place Chandler. Then it hit him. It had been more than twenty years since he last spoke with Chandler. He and Charles "Chip" Chandler had been in the same unit when they deployed to Kandahar Province in Afghanistan. They spent nearly a year together, helping train the Afghan Army with limited success. Even then, Peden believed that these Afghan recruits had little chance of defending their country from any serious threat. The Afghans remained loyal to their individual clans, much more than to the country as-a-whole. Being equipped with military supplies from the United States, both small arms and heavy armor, made little difference. The language barrier alone presented a major obstacle. Army trainers feared being killed by radicals within the ranks. The training had been nearly impossible.

"Chip Chandler. Now there's a blast from the past. How have you been?"

"I've been good, generally speaking. Making a living, happily married. How about you? You and Susan still together?"

Peden leaned back in his office chair and looked up at the

ceiling. He hated to talk about his family. He and Susan divorced after a bitter battle, and his two girls, now both in college, milked him for every penny they could squeeze from his bank account. Plus, all three of them hated the ground he walked on. But he did not want to paint a terrible picture of his situation so he said, "No. Susan and I split up several years ago, but it was for the best. I have two college-age girls. And I have my own business, but you probably know that since you called my business number. So, I take it you're not calling to chat about the old days?"

"You're right." Chandler paused and Peden could hear him taking a deep breath. "Ya know I stayed in the Corps after you left, right?"

"Yeah, Chip. I remember. You planned to make it a career. Did you?"

"No, I didn't." Again, he hesitated. "What I'm going to tell you has to remain between us, at least for now." He did not wait for Peden to answer. "In 2011, I was captain of three regiments in Afghanistan. We were stationed in Kandahar Province, but we had a platoon sent north to carry out an op in support of a drone strike."

Peden's unease ramped up hearing details of a military operation over a non-secure cell phone. If Chandler wanted to keep this private, between the two of them, a face-to-face meeting would be more appropriate. He cut his old friend off.

"Chip, hold on for a second. Where are you right now?"

"I'm at home, in Holly Ridge, just outside of Camp Lejeune. Why?"

"Cause I'd rather we didn't discuss anything classified over the phone."

"Yeah, you're right, but if we can't talk soon, it might be too late."

"What do you mean?"

"One of our guys was just found dead in Georgia. The county sheriff called it a drug overdose, but that doesn't wash. Rusty – he was Private Randall Parish when in the Corps - he didn't use dope of any kind. He drank a lot but he was totally against drugs. His older brother OD'd while Rusty was in high school. He used to tell the story to anybody who would listen. He joined the Corps because he didn't want to end up like his brother. He wanted to learn self-discipline, self-respect. And he was serious about it."

"How did he end up being a drunk then. Alcohol can be just as bad, or worse, than some drugs."

Chandler took a deep breath. "Yeah, true. Rusty was fine when I first met him; never put anything harmful in his body … a real health nut, all based on his brother's death. He was almost like an evangelist for clean living. Then something happened over there. I think it's related to the drone strike."

Peden let several seconds pass before talking again. "When did this alleged suicide happen?"

"The sheriff found his body yesterday morning by the Savannah River in Georgia. Screven County."

"Wait. There's a story in the Savannah paper. They didn't put his name in the paper because they had to notify next of kin. Is that your guy?"

"Yeah, most likely. And they're never going to find a next of kin. His parents were killed right after he joined the Corps. Car accident, both killed, though his mom lingered for weeks before she passed. He was a mess for a long time."

"I'm not surprised."

An extended silence filled the line until Peden finally said, "Could that have been the start of his alcohol problems?"

"It might have contributed to it in the long run, but he was fine for about a year after the accident. Then, kind of suddenly, he started drinking. You and I know, drinking over there, especially off base, is seriously discouraged. You could get court-martialed and booted out if you got caught, and Rusty drank heavily, almost like he didn't care if he got caught. Maybe even trying to get caught. But he made it to his EAOS (End of Active Obligated Service) and got shipped home with an honorable discharge."

"What did he do after that, once he got back stateside?"

"Another guy from our platoon got out about the same time. They were both from South Carolina. Ray Mack. Big black dude - hell of a great guy. He kind of took Rusty under his wing. Got him jobs and tried to keep him off the booze. I'm friends with him on social media and I call him about once a year, just to keep up. But Ray couldn't be with Rusty twenty-four-seven. So, Ray tells me that Rusty didn't come into work at the hunting lodge the other day. When he tried to contact Rusty on Wednesday, Rusty didn't answer his cell. Ray figured that he went on a bender, so Ray let it go. When he couldn't reach him again Thursday, he started to worry and called me, wondering what he should do. I told him that Rusty was a grown-assed man, that he had to face his demons and there wasn't anything we could do about it. We just decided to wait it out.

"This morning I got a call from some woman. I didn't get her name, but she said she was a friend of Rusty. Said that he was the guy in the newspaper article in the Savannah paper. I hadn't read it at that time, so I didn't know what she was talking about. I tried again to get her name and number, but she hung up.

"After I read the story, I called the sheriff in Screven County and tried to get a positive ID. I told him that I suspected it might be Rusty. He didn't want to confirm it until I told him that Rusty didn't have any living relatives. Then he told me it was probably Rusty. Said he had his driver's license on him and a little cash."

Peden thought for a few minutes then said, "Tell me about this op, in general terms. Don't give me any details that could be construed as classified."

"Okay. Three rifle teams were sent to target a location in Kabul because there were some leaders from two different factions meeting at this house. Some intel we got said it was a planning meeting for a strike against U.S. and Afghan troops. We had to set up the targeting for the drone strike. The strike went off without a hitch, with one big problem. We bombed the wrong house, my interpreter's house. He lived there with his entire family. Only two people survived; my interpreter and a friend of his younger sister."

Peden was shocked. "Are you sure your interpreter wasn't also working for these other groups? It wouldn't be the first time guys worked both sides."

Chandler was adamant, "Nope. No way. He hated the Taliban and other splinter groups. He fought every day, with words and deeds, to do something good for his country. He knew we were trying to help his cause."

Peden figured that Chandler had gone this far, he might as well find out all the details. "When was the strike?"

"September 11, 2011, the ten-year anniversary. I'll never forget it. When I found out what happened, I stormed into my commander's office and read him the riot act. I came close to a court-martial, but he promised to get to the bottom of it; told me to write up a report and get it to him asap."

"What did he do?"

"Squat. The bastard buried it."

"How do you know that he didn't carry it up the chain of command and it got buried higher up?"

"Because his aid at the time, is now my wife. She worked directly for the colonel. She handled all the communications into and out of the office. My report stopped in his office. He sent a different report, the official report, proclaimed the strike was a great success. It was a sham. Shortly after that Rusty's drinking got very heavy. At that point, he didn't even try to hide it."

Peden had heard enough to know that something went wrong with the strike and someone had a vested interest in making sure the truth remained buried in the crater that had once been a family home in a war-torn country. Chip's story compelled Peden to look deeper.

"Hey Chip, you've got my attention. I need the names of everyone in the regiment who assisted in the strike and anything else you can tell me. But not over the phone. Send me an email attachment with the names and contact information for the men in your squad. After I dig into this a bit, can we meet half way

between here and Holly Ridge?"
  "You bet. Thanks, Peden."
  "Nothing to thank me for … yet."

Chapter 2

Rayshon "Ray" Mack finished the early morning tour with three hunters at Cedar Knoll Hunting Lodge and Outfitters in the south-central region of South Carolina. The hunters had scored a hefty twelve-point buck and were pleased with Ray's expertise in the woods. They tipped him well after they carried their prize to the hanging rack behind the lodge's main building. Mack should have felt gratified after a job well done, but the apparent disappearance of his friend and former Marine Corps brother, Rusty Parish, weighed heavily on his mind.

The hunt club, a relaxing forty-five-minute drive from his home just outside of Williston, South Carolina, provided the one-time Marine Corporal with easy money. He enjoyed being in the outdoors with clean air, the scent of pine, blooming flowers native to the low country near the Savannah River, and no city noise. He enjoyed his part-time job at the lodge more than anything else he had done since leaving the Corps some nine years prior.

He had tried his hand at a few warehouse jobs, all with the promise of rapid advancement and better pay, but the noise and constant performance pressure drove him crazy. They sent him daydreaming back to his days at the desert base in Kandahar Province in Afghanistan. He hated the sound of heavy equipment and engines roaring, and the constant odor of diesel fuel. He held those jobs for an average three years before he had to move on to something else. He stumbled into a job as a bouncer at a nightclub in Aiken, South Carolina. He liked the atmosphere there: mostly relaxing, interacting with the younger crowd, and in addition to his regular paycheck, getting paid cash under the table. An imposing figure, Mack stood six-feet-six inches tall, with a muscular, chiseled body, and dark black skin. Few people challenged him. Only on rare occasions did he have to use his military skills to break up a fight or expel a rowdy patron from the bar. The bouncer job and the hunting guide schedules never caused a conflict … until now.

Ray should have been at home, sleeping, resting up after a rather long night at the club. A call from the hunt club's owner threw a wrench in that plan. His friend, Rusty Parish, had not shown up for work that morning and they had not heard from him for several days. Parish had been scheduled to guide the group of hunters from a Columbia, South Carolina, company who used hunting for a team building session. Mack felt obligated to cover the shift, mainly because he had recommended Parish for the position. After completing the tour with the club's satisfied customers, he hoped to find Parish and make sure his friend detoxed before his next shift. Parish's binge drinking, at times, became repetitive, his PTSD only made the situation worse. He needed professional help, but had refused to head down that path saying that he would beat it by himself. Mack hoped he could convince his friend to change his mind.

Randall "Rusty" Parish lived in Fairfax, South Carolina, a ten-minute, country-road drive from the lodge. He rented a sparsely furnished trailer on the north side of town on Second Street among a dozen other trailers of the same age and style. With the entire city block where they sat devoid of trees or any other source of shade, the units were difficult to cool in the summer, especially with the under-sized window air conditioners that hung out the sides of each trailer. A single landlord owned the entire block of trailers and, according to Rusty, he was "frugal," code for "*cheap son-of-a-bitch.*"

Mack pulled into Parish's loose-stone drive and parked behind a beat up, rust-red, Ford Ranger. He made his way up to the trailer's door, believing that his friend must be home. The rickety wooden steps swayed slightly at the weight of Mack's two-hundred-forty-pound frame. He knocked on the door, shaking the side of the trailer.

In a booming voice, Mack asked, "Hey Rusty, you in there?"

He waited and listened for several seconds. "You missed your shift at the lodge, man."

Pausing again with no response.

"Rusty. Wake up, man. Answer the door."

No sound came from within. Mack tried the knob and pulled the unlocked door open. Mack took a deep breath and yelled, "Rusty, wake up, man. I'm coming in. Don't shoot me. It's Ray."

A constant rattle emanated from a tiny air conditioner as it strained in a losing battle to keep ahead of the rising heat of the morning. Mack opened the door wide and took two tentative steps into the living room of the trailer, the floor creaking under his massive frame. He looked around the dark trailer, overwhelming heat assaulting him as he moved into the living room.

From his vantage point, Mack could see into the kitchen and part-way down the hall that led to the two bedrooms in the back. Daggers of sunlight pierced the tattered drapes, exposing clouds of dust kicked up with each step. The cheap coffee table nearly sagged under the weight of empty beer bottles. An ash tray sat in the middle of the table loaded with cigarette butts, each burned down to the filter. The overheated air, ripe with the scent of stale beer and burnt tobacco, made it difficult to breathe. Mack shook his head, wondering how far into the trailer he should venture. Should Parish be on a bender, his state of mind would make him unpredictable - and dangerous. Sweat rolled down his temples from the heat and the tension. Pulling his tee shirt up, he wiped his brow. Parish had several guns which he kept on a night-stand near his bed. Startling his friend could be deadly, especially with Parish's acute PTSD, augmented by his drinking.

As Parish's only friend, and a brother Marine, he had to step up and do what needed to be done – get his friend help, no matter the price. He took a few steps into the kitchen, empty, save for dirty dishes in the sink, an overflowing trash can, and the distinct odor of spoiled food. Mack turned and headed down the hall that led to the bathroom and the bedrooms. He stepped into the bathroom, noting the sink, tub, and toilet all beyond filthy. Sweat now poured from his forehead. Mack held his breath as he backed out into the hall.

The first bedroom on the left appeared empty except for a

mound of dirty clothes. Mack noted the camo pants and shirts in the pile, the ones he wore at the lodge. Parish never entertained at the trailer nor did he have overnight guests so the empty space did not surprise him.

Mack headed for the main bedroom, taking slow steps. In a quiet voice he said, "Rusty, you here man? Come on now. It's Ray."

The stench changed to one of dirty bed linens in need of laundering. On the bed, sheets lay strewn all over, the mattress exposed in several places. It had obviously not been made up for quite some time. Dirty clothes had been tossed all around the room, which bothered Mack. He kept his bedroom immaculate, made up perfectly in case he entertained a young lady for the night.

One thing missing from the trailer - Rusty Parish.

Mack backed out of the bedroom and turned towards the hallway. As he reached the living room, the sound of a car door shutting caught his attention. At nearly the same time, his cell phone rang. He reached in his pocket and pulled out his cell. It was Chip Chandler, his former Platoon Captain. He and Chip maintained contact through a social media group called BIAChat – short for Brothers-in-Arms Chat. A member of their platoon had created the group so that the team could keep in touch. Only a handful of platoon members opted to not join. The social media site provided an easy way for old friends to stay in touch: to share good and bad news.

Mack answered, "Hey, Cap, what's up?"

Most of the men in the group called Chandler "Cap," short for Captain, the highest rank Chandler had achieved prior to him resigning his commission.

"Hey, Ray. How's it going? Still at the lodge?"

"No, sir. I left there about twenty-five minutes ago. I'm at Rusty's place, but he's not here."

As Mack spoke, he headed towards the trailer's door to get out into some fresh air. He concentrated on his phone call with his head down and did not notice the two Allendale County Sheriff's Deputies standing by their car with guns drawn, pointed in his direction. As he turned to close the door behind him, one of the deputies shouted, "Freeze! Put your hands where we can see them!"

Startled, Mack did as he was ordered. With his back to the deputies his hands were not visible to them. Without continuing his conversation with Chandler, Mack slowly moved his hands away from his body, his left hand empty, his right hand still with the phone. Mack knew that his size intimidated most people. Being a black man in the south made him cautious during any encounter with law enforcement, of which there were several.

In a loud, but measured voice, Mack said, "Officers, I have a cell phone in my right hand. Don't shoot. I'm just checking on my friend. He's missing. What …"

"Stop talking and very slowly turn around, keeping your hands where we can see them."

Mack precisely followed the deputy's orders so they could clearly see the cell phone. One deputy said, "Slowly place the cell phone on the railing of the porch and put your hands back in the air."

Again, Mack complied.

"Now slowly come down the steps and move away from the trailer. Then get on your knees."

Mack did not like this last order. One of the deputies, the one doing all the talking, appeared to be in his fifties and overweight, but looked somewhat relaxed. His very young, read-headed partner seemed nervous. Mack could see the sweat pouring from his forehead. He also noticed that his finger was inside the trigger guard of his weapon. One nervous twitch by the deputy and he would be a dead man. He slowly walked down the steps, moved about eight feet away from the trailer and in an easy, smooth motion got on his knees.

He said, "My name is Rayshon Mack. My friend, Randy Parish, lives in this trailer. He was supposed to work at the …"

The older cop said, "Mr. Mack, stop. We'll get to all that. Right now, we're going to place cuffs on you for our protection and yours. Please comply. If everything checks out, we'll remove them as soon as possible."

Mack nodded. He said, "Please do me one favor. Have your partner move his finger away from the trigger on his weapon."

The older deputy took a quick glance at his partner, then calmly said, "Patrick, please do as Mr. Mack requested. We don't want any mistakes today."

The young man appeared nervous, the act of moving his finger away from the gun's trigger a monumental task. Mack noticed him take a deep breath as more sweat ran down his face onto his already soaked collar.

* * *

Fifteen minutes later with everyone relaxed, the men chatted like old friends. The older deputy, Walter Aims, an Army veteran had served in Iraq. His younger partner, Patrick O'Dell, had been on the job for only three weeks after finishing several college courses in criminal justice. He apologized repeatedly about his rookie mistake. Mack assured him that he understood how tough the job could be, especially with all the recent anti-cop rhetoric.

Mack explained the purpose of his entry into Rusty Parish's trailer. Deputy Aims said that one of the neighbors had called about a suspicious person entering their neighbor's trailer. He assured Mack that they would keep an eye out for his friend and would call his cell if he heard any news.

When Aims mentioned calling, Mack remembered that he had been on his cell with Chip Chandler. The deputies drove away as Mack tapped Chandler's name under recent calls. He answered before the first ring was finished.

Chandler asked, "What the hell was that all about?"

"Like I was telling you, I'm at Parish's trailer. He didn't show up for work this morning, so I was here looking for him. Somebody mistook me for a crook and called the cops. It's all good now."

Chandler replied, "Well, it isn't all good, Ray. Rusty's dead. They found his body in Georgia near the Savannah River. They're calling it an overdose."

Mack's entire body slumped, "Oh jeez, Cap. Exactly when

and where?"

Chip Chandler told him all the details that he had, which were few. He added, "I called an old friend of mine and asked him to look into Rusty's death. He's a private investigator. I think he might be able to get more information from the authorities than we can. Guy's name is Peden Savage, so if he calls you, you'll know it's on the up-and-up."

"Okay, okay. Geeze, I can't believe he's dead. An overdose? That doesn't wash, Cap."

"I know, Ray. I know."

Chapter 3

Jeffrey Grumen, sitting in the second story office of Davidson Home Construction in Hilliard, Ohio, read the short, three paragraph story a second time, then a third. The article had been copied from the Savannah Morning News. Chip Chandler posted the news clip on the BIAChat group just hours before. No names appeared in the story, but Chandler stated that the dead man was their former Marine brother, Randall "Rusty" Parish. How did Chandler know this? Gruman had no clue. According to the article, Parish had probably died from an accidental drug overdose. Grumen almost smiled, there being no love-loss between him and the deceased man, but he kept his emotions in check. You never celebrated the tragic death of a fellow Marine.

He looked at the time and date displayed on his computer monitor. September 11, 2021: the twenty-year-anniversary of the attacks on the twin towers, the Pentagon, and the crash in Shanksville, Pennsylvania. Also, the ten-year-anniversary of the drone strike in Kabul. He slipped back into his private thoughts about Rusty Parish.

Ever since the day of the strike when then Private Parish had panicked and had put the entire squad in danger, Grumen had no trust that he would keep his mouth shut and just do his job. After Grumen publicly admonished him in front of his peers, Parish had eyed his sergeant with a raging hatred that radiated from every cell in his body. Prior to that day, the two men had been cordial, as much as a Staff Sergeant and a Private could be. That all changed after the strike. Grumen had heard that Parish planned to take his concerns up the chain of command and have his squad leader "taken down a notch." Parish did talk with Captain Chandler, but that complaint had gone nowhere. Parish's fellow squad members convinced him, through talks and threats of physical violence, to keep his concerns to himself.

Over time, the whole incident died down, and Grumen never heard another word about it from anyone. No one had been hurt from Parish's outburst and Grumen suffered no career impact.

Within a year of the incident, Grumen decided he had enough of the Marines. He also knew his marriage could not withstand another four-year enlistment. If he could not make it to at least the twenty-year mark, reenlistment made no sense.

Breaking out of his daydream, the former Marine Corps Staff Sergeant-turned-civilian, looked out the second-floor window of his office. He watched the bright orange glow of the sunrise just to the north of the skyline of Columbus, Ohio, and home to his alma mater, the Ohio State University. Upon his discharge from the Marines, he joined his father-in-law's company, Davidson Construction. That he joined the family business delighted his wife, Cora. It assured her that she would live close to her family.

During Jeff's ten years in the Marines, she had spent much time away from Ohio, which meant time away from her mother, father, and twin sister, Dora. Jeff knew that his wife considered Columbus her home and despite Jeff's repeated conversations with her that he intended to make the Marine Corps his career, he knew that she suffered from a chronic case of homesickness. Jeff and Cora's two daughters had been born at the Naval Hospital at Camp Lejeune during two of Jeff's deployments to Afghanistan. Cora had wanted to go home to Ohio for the births, but Jeff's military healthcare coverage would not pay for the medical bills for a private hospital when a VA hospital was near their home. Cora's mother and her sister made the trip to be with her during both deliveries, but she resented not having her husband by her side during that crucial time in their lives. It made for a difficult ten years every time Jeff came home from a deployment.

Upon his return, almost before he changed into his civilian clothes, she began badgering him about moving back to Hilliard so that she could be around family. Before the girls were in elementary school, Cora would hound him about leaving the Marines and taking up her dad's offer of a position at his home building company. The offer would provide good pay and benefits, and they would be around family. He tried to convince her that the Marine Corps was their new family; that he wanted to make military life a career, at least for twenty years. After his retirement they could move back to Ohio.

The discussions turned into shouting matches, then progressed to shoving; mainly her shoving him. Not knowing how to handle the situation, Jeff made the worst possible decision. Any time Cora started badgering him, he left her alone with the girls and hit the bars with his Marine buddies.

One hot, summer night after a particularly long and nasty argument, Jeff stayed out with the guys at a bar near Camp Lejeune until last call. He came home and passed out on the living room couch after barely making it through the front door. When he woke up just after noon the following day, dead silence filled the house. He expected Cora to start giving him hell for staying out so late. He staggered into the kitchen and found the long note. Cora had packed up the girls and headed for Ohio.

The hangover pounded at his temples as he read the crushing words that left him numb. She decided to move back in with her parents and that he should make up his mind once and for all if he wanted a life with the Marines or with his real family. She made it crystal clear that he could not have both. Worse, she mocked him, writing that he just played soldier, that the Marine Corps was nothing more than a live version of a kid's video game. Her characterization of the Corps enraged him. They had been together since their senior year in high school. How could she have felt that way about his chosen career, his life's passion? He had balled up her note and thrown it across the room, then proceeded to destroy everything within arm's reach. But that only made his head pound even more.

Later that day, he missed muster. Two days later, he missed a scheduled watch. His lieutenant pulled him aside and told him; one more miscue and he would not face court-martial, but he would be dealt with by his fellow Marines. For days after that warning, his squad, his subordinates, would not speak to him or even acknowledge that he existed. That scared him more than anything else in his life, even more than his wife and children leaving him. He needed these guys to have his back and he realized that he had to have theirs as well. All their lives depended on that commitment from each and every Marine. He finally approached his lieutenant and told him that he would do whatever it took to regain his trust and the trust of his fellow Marines. Hard work and dedication put his career back on track.

Over the course of their nearly two-year separation, he kept in contact with Cora and his girls and patched up their relationship. He remained sober and stopped hanging out with the single guys after duty. He agreed with Cora that at the end of his current enlistment, he would leave the Marines and, if the offer from her father still stood, he would join the family business.

And he did.

His thoughts shifted back to the Savannah newspaper article, allegedly about Rusty Parish. Again, he wondered how Chip Chandler identified Parish. He must have made some calls, but what had prompted him to even ask the question? Clearly, someone had contacted him about Parish's issues with substance abuse.

The idea that Parish had overdosed troubled Grumen. Parish never abused drugs. He drank alcohol, but never used any drugs stronger than Tylenol. He remembered Parish talking about the death of his older brother who had overdosed on heroin. When the subject of drug use came up, even in a joking manner, his mood darkened and he preached about the evils of illicit drugs.

But that had not stopped him from drinking, which he did to excess after his parents were killed in a car accident, and especially after the drone strike ten years ago. Booze nearly ended his enlistment early but he had made it to his EAOS. Grumen had heard that one of his friends from their Marine Corps days, Rayshon Mack, had been helping to keep Parish on the straight and narrow. He wondered if Mack knew about his friend's demise. *Maybe I should get in the chat room and see what everyone knows.*

The ringtone of his cell phone brought him out of his dark

thoughts.

"Grumen."

He thought it might be the foreman of one of his building crews calling about some issue or another at the job site. It was not.

A sultry, female voice asked, "Did you hear about Rusty?"

Grumen frowned. He could not put a name or face to the voice, but a twinge of familiarity tweaked his brain.

"Who is this?"

"You know who I am."

The caller hung up. Grumen looked at his cell to identify the caller's number. It read, *Restricted.* Grumen frowned again, trying to place the voice, but it eluded him.

The phone sounded again. This time, he recognized the number for his job-site foreman. He took a deep breath and answered, still wondering about the previous call.

* * *

Major General Virgil Vance smiled at himself in the full-length, bedroom mirror, admiring the crisp, dress uniform that fit him as well now as it did two years before when promoted to his current rank. He looked impressive with the multi-tier string of ribbons adorning the left side of his chest. He had to look good as he attended the memorial service for the victims and those wounded at the Pentagon in 2001.

His thoughts drifted to Afghanistan where he had vowed to lead his soldiers and unleash the power of the United States Marine Corps and take revenge on the groups and the individual leaders who had attacked his country in such a cowardly manner. Something went awry during the execution of the military's very good plan. *Politics*, he thought to himself and frowned. They should have just given us orders and gotten out of the way.

He thought about the botched drone strike that he had personally made sure looked like a victory to anyone on the outside, though he, and a few others, knew the truth. He had worked too hard throughout his career to let one incident screw up his next promotion. The cover-up succeeded with no repercussions. He even received a letter of commendation for the work and he lavished praise on his men.

The John Phillip Sousa march ringtone from his cell phone broke his trance. The screen read *Restricted* so let it go. But when it rang again moments later, he answered in a gravelly voice, "Vance."

The female voice said, "General Vance. I'm sorry to report one of your men has died."

Vance thought for a moment. *If one of my ranks is dead, who could it be? This should have come through proper channels.*

"Who is this?"

"You know who I am, General."

Vance did not take the bait. He simply ended the call without another word. When his phone rang out again, he ignored it. Then he got a text. Annoyed at the calls, anger crept into his head and he tensed. He read the text.

Rusty Parish is dead. That's on you. I know what you're hiding.

The last line sent a shiver down Vance's spine.

Chapter 4

Peden's plans for the day went up in smoke after his phone conversation with Chip Chandler. The sudden change in priorities put his work list literally into the shredder. He pulled out his notepad and started writing. Typically, he used Saturdays as his paperwork and planning day, massaging his calendar for the upcoming week. It helped him focus on the top issue and demote those of less importance further down his short to-do list. Years ago, his father instilled in him that you do first things first and second things only when they became first things. When he received the file from Chip Chandler with the names, last known addresses, phone numbers, and email addresses for Chip's platoon, Peden had his first thing: prioritize the order in which he would contact the men on the list. Then he wondered if he should contact members by rank, starting at the top, or should the most junior members be first?

Peden leaned back in his modern office chair, put his feet up on his early-nineteenth century, hand-carved mahogany desk, and stared up at the brass-colored ceiling tiles from the same era. The tongue and groove pine flooring creaked with each move. He began considering the names on the list and wondered from whom he would get the most truthful, quality information on the drone strike. More importantly, if they knew why Private Parish had gone off the rails after the attack. Who would be most likely to want to leave the past buried where they believed it belonged? Who had the most to lose from the past being exposed? According to some side notes on the list, most from the squadron left military service. Two men were deceased. Just three of the men, two officers and one enlisted man, remained on active duty.

Besides Chip Chandler, he recognized two names: Major General Virgil Vance and Rayshon Mack. Being a Major General meant that Vance had two stars on his lapels.

When Peden left the service, then Major Vance had been promoted to Lieutenant Colonel. Peden remembered him as a tough, no nonsense, gravely-voiced hard-ass. The men in his company had pegged him with a variety of unflattering nicknames, though Peden had not been around long enough to experience Vance's leadership style. He noted that Vance now held a position in Washington, D.C. His title sounded impressive: Assistant Deputy Commandant for Combat Development and Integration (ADC, CD&I). Peden did a quick internet search for Vance and his department. Reading information from the search, the department's mission statement included *development of forward-looking concepts to best organize, train, educate and equip the Marine Corps of the future.*

Peden smiled at the overly broad statement knowing that the changes being proposed by the current administration included training on "equity and inclusion." He wondered if the average, gun-toting Marine would accept this new kinder, gentler, so called "woke" directive. During his time on active duty in the Corps, they learned to immediately follow orders without question and how to effectively, and efficiently, kill enemy combatants. He hoped that this new policy shift had not caused the men heading into combat to lose focus on that objective. He feared he might be wrong.

Chip had said that Rayshon Mack helped Private Parish find a job, a place to live, and cope with civilian life. Apparently, Mack looked out for Parish, like a big brother, teaching him skills needed to cope with his new environment. Mack seemed like the right place for Peden to start. He lived near Williston, South Carolina, about one hundred miles north of Savannah. If his investigation warranted a face-to-face meeting, Williston was an easy two-hour drive.

After scanning the remaining names on the list, Peden made his decision: he would call Rayshon Mack first. He moved his feet from his desk and, as he reached for his cell phone, the funeral march ringtone sounded. He shook his head. He had no time to talk with his ex-wife, Susan.

Rolling his eyes at the ceiling, the hit the red handset, ending the call before it began. He did not have time to hear Susan's whining about needing more money for herself or their two college-age daughters. He could almost recite her routine from memory. She would start by complaining that she could not live on the pittance that the court ordered Peden to pay her each month until their girls graduated from college. He always replied that she could get a job to supplement that income. She would retort that she did not have time to get a job, that her busy schedule would not allow it. He would reply that, with their daughters away at the most expensive private college in the south, how could her schedule be so full that she could not get a job.

On and on it went until they were yelling at each other, neither listening, then Susan would abruptly disconnect the call. Peden would be more cooperative with Susan and the girls if their daughters applied themselves when it came to their classwork. Both girls barely maintained passing grades, a product of their focus on extra-curricular activities like parties, bars, and boys. In short, the girls put more effort into having fun than into their courses. If they attended a community college, he might overlook their attitudes, but the tuition and housing for each semester at Georgia Southern University cost Peden a small fortune.

His phone's ringtone sounded again. He reached for the phone with the intention of answering and letting Susan have an earful, but he realized that it was not the funeral march. He looked at the number. It was FBI Agent Megan Moore. He took a deep breath to calm himself then swiped the green handset.

"Hey, Megan."

"Hi, Peden. You sound tense. Did I call at a bad time?"

"No. In fact, I was just going to call you. I need a favor, if you have some free time."

"As long as it doesn't have anything to do with your crazy ex, I've got a relatively open schedule. What's up?"

Peden told Megan about the call from Chip Chandler

and the apparent suicide of Rusty Parish, describing the drone strike in Kabul, the chaos that ensued, and the controversy with the lack of follow-up from then Colonel Vance. He added that, since his discharge from the military, former Marine Corps Corporal Rayshon Mack had been helping Parish with his transition to civilian life. Megan listened without comment until Peden finished. He could picture the serious, ice-cold expression on her face, knowing that she would follow-up with questions meant to tear the narrative to pieces. He took a deep breath, waiting to engage in a verbal volley.

"So, Pedee, why are you getting involved in this decade-old squabble? The Medical Examiner in – what county?"

"Screven."

"The M. E. in Screven County has ruled this a suicide. What makes you think that it isn't?"

"I'm not making any judgment about cause of death. Chip Chandler said he didn't believe Parish died from an overdose. He and others from their squadron always thought that he would die from some alcohol related incident, like a car crash, liver failure, or alcohol poisoning. It kind of makes sense. Some drunks swear that narcotics are far worse than alcohol, even though many more deaths are caused by alcohol."

"We could argue the hypotheticals all day. What do you need me to do?"

Peden asked, "Do you need Rollie's approval to work on this?"

"Is this an official request or just a casual, off the books inquiry?"

"I think we can keep this off the books for now. Depending on where the information leads, we can always make it official later."

Megan sighed. "Okay. Where do we start?"

* * *

Fifteen minutes later, Megan strolled into Peden's office in the

1838 Bird-Baldwin building on West Jefferson Street in the heart of Savannah, Georgia's historic district. Wearing a light-weight, light gray pant suit and her serious expression, she walked up to Peden's desk and sat in one of the client chairs. She had not said a word, waiting for Peden to start the conversation. They rarely spoke about personal matters. Megan always got right down to business. It used to bother him when they were partners in the FBI's Savannah office, but he soon learned that she just had no interest in wasting time on chatter. It was probably the reason that she never dated or had a serious relationship with a man, as far as Peden knew.

Megan, according to Peden's ex-wife, Susan, was the reason that she and Peden divorced. Back when Peden and Megan were partners in the FBI, Susan accused the two of having an affair. Megan did nothing to assuage her fears, and even antagonized Susan anytime they spoke. Just prior to her filing for divorce, Susan came right out and said to Megan in an f-bomb-laced tirade that she should stop sleeping with her husband, to which Megan replied, "He's too good for you. You don't deserve him." Megan abruptly disconnected the call. While she did not admit to sleeping with her husband, she did not deny it, which only fueled Susan's anger at Peden.

Peden did not help matters when, in open court, he accused Susan of having a carnal relationship with her attorney. He mentioned that she received her representation pro-boner which enraged the female judge hearing their case. She held Peden in contempt and added a fine just to drive the point home that she would not tolerate such talk in her courtroom. After that, no matter what Peden's attorney said, it held no weight with the judge and Peden paid a hefty price in alimony and child support in the form of outrageous tuition and associated bills.

Peden looked up at his former partner and smiled. She stared back, waiting for him to tell her the plan going forward.

"Good morning."

Megan nodded, then remained silent.

Peden lifted the multi-page list of names and said, "I'm

calling everyone on the list that I got from Chip Chandler to see what everyone knew about the botched strike and why the official report touted it as a great success. I also need to hear what they all say about Parish. It sounds like there were a couple events that led to his drinking. I just want everyone's perspective on that."

Megan's face did not change. She said, "Sounds good. What do you need me to do?"

"I'll put the calls on speaker. You listen as I talk with them, then if you hear something that piques your interest, chime in. Also write me a note if you have a question that you want me to ask."

Megan nodded slightly, then asked, "Did you want me doing any background checking on any of these guys? I can do some searches while you ask the questions."

"That's why I bring you in on these kinds of things. You're always a step ahead"

Megan rolled her eyes as if she did not appreciate being patronized. Then she asked, "Tell me about the guy on the top of your list."

"Okay. Rayshon Mack. I told you a bit about him when you called earlier. Chip said he's a good man, conscientious, hard worker. Mack was concerned about Parish when he left the Corps, so he looked Parish up when he received his discharge from the Marines about two months later. He mentored Parish, found him jobs, kept him off the booze as best he could. This is what Chip told me about Mack. Sounds like a stand-up guy."

"You got your questions lined up?"

"Yeah, I think so."

With her blond hair framing her thin, light-skinned face, Megan gave Peden a skeptical look. "You think so? Doesn't instill much confidence."

"You know me. Just be ready to jump in."

"While you're stumbling through your questions, I'll do a little background on Mr. Rayshon Mack."

Megan opened her laptop, started the machine up and

furiously tapped away at keys before Peden could dial Mack's number on his cell phone. Peden put the cell on speaker and listened to the cell phone ring. After five rings, a canned message said something about not having voice mail set up. Peden called a second time, which Mack answered after the second ring.

"Hello."

Peden asked, "Is this Rayshon Mack?"

"Who's askin'?"

"Mr. Mack, I'm Peden Savage, and …"

"Yeah, Mr. Savage. Chip Chandler told me you might be callin'. This is about Rusty Parish, right?"

"Yeah. What can you tell me about Private Parish?"

Chapter 5

Moska Aziz sat across from Aslam Sayed at a table near the back corner of D's Friendly Diner in Statesboro, Georgia. Moska had explained to the hostess that they needed a table away from the crowd, if possible, so they could work on a project without distractions. The recommended table, secluded from the half dozen occupied tables, provided the perfect spot for their meeting.

Moska liked the diner's location in a non-descript plaza in a mid-sized city close to a busy intersection. Many people came and went, some locals, others from rural areas. A few non-residents visited their children at Georgia Southern University, or just spent the day shopping.

She and Aslam would be random faces in the crowd. They would never be coming back to this restaurant and, possibly, never to Statesboro, Georgia, again. There were many similar towns with similar diners and similar people within a one-hundred-fifty-mile radius where they could blend in without concern of being identified by some random passersby. She could smile and be cordial, like the thousands of college students attending one of the local schools, all while enjoying a breakfast of English muffins and jelly with a cup of specialty coffee.

As usual, Aslam appeared uptight, looking around as if he had just robbed a bank. She had tried coaching him on being more casual in a crowd, or even in a less-than-crowded diner like D's. She had said to him many times before, *Look around you. What do you see? No one is paying us any mind. Relax. Smile. Act as if I'm your girlfriend and we're having a nice breakfast before we go off to school.* For reasons that Moska understood, Aslam could not relax. He was afraid that a federal agent would come up behind him with guns drawn and haul him off to some secret prison to be tortured or killed.

Moska believed with all her heart that Aslam had nothing to fear. One face in a sea of humanity in the United States, he stood out not because of his middle-eastern features, but because he acted nervous, guilty, and scared. Worse, he had no reason for these feelings, at least not presently. Aslam Sayed's entire family had been killed in a United States military drone attack exactly ten years ago. It did not matter to him which branch of the military conducted the attack. His family had been murdered by the United States government.

In the ten years since that fateful day, Aslam Sayed planned his revenge. Now that the plan was in motion, his manner resembled that of a trapped animal instead of a predator. He viewed everyone as a potential government spy. He complained to Moska that he felt the eyes of everyone around him staring at him as if they could read the plan off his forehead. She could feel his radiated tension, his nerves in overdrive.

In stark contrast to Aslam, Moska appeared cool, even happy, always smiling, her body language inviting. Her attractive appearance drew appraising looks and more than a few smiles. Her hair, made blonde from a box, but naturally straight, she wore down on her back. The silky strands contrasted with her tan skin. She liked to wear clothes that were on the edge of provocative. Today she wore a loose-fitting tee-shirt with an obscure alternative rock band name, tight-fitting jeans with the front of the legs prematurely worn out, just like the young college girls wore, so that most of her slender legs were visible. With her dark brown eyes and perfect complexion, she stood out even amongst the younger crowd. When people approached her to remark at her pleasant disposition, she merely thanked them and even held light conversations with many.

The reality of Moska Aziz's life could not have been more polar-opposite from her outward appearance. Under her clothes, she bore scars where concrete and debris had damaged her trim body. Ten years-ago to-the-day, she and her unborn child were close to death as doctors worked feverishly to save them both. Her head, face, and arms were spared severe injury, but her back had been pummeled with debris from the explosion that tore apart the Sayed family home, tearing the skin, breaking several ribs, missing her spine and major organs by centimeters. She spent months in the military hospital in Landstuhl, Germany, required four surgeries, and extensive, physical rehabilitation. Once the life-saving surgeries did their job, plastic surgery repaired, or at least minimized, the visible damage on her back. In the end, when she had been declared fully recovered, her back still caused her pain and she had difficulty bending over due to the hardened scar-tissue which remained stiff and less flexible than natural skin.

The physical scars were not nearly as dramatic as the mental damage left by her ordeal. Though no actual brain damage had been caused, the psychological pain inflicted on that day ten years ago would never go away. But she craved the goal of revenge that she shared with Aslam, and hoped that it might lessen the nightmares that deprived her of restful sleep. She lived through the massive explosion that had destroyed the Sayed family home and killed the man whom she had hoped to marry one day.

Moska looked forward to the day when she would leave the United States with her daughter and live a happy life.

She handed Aslam one of the thirteen-by-nine-inch folders that she had brought with her. Their waitress had just delivered their breakfast and retreated to the kitchen. Moska smiled, taking in the aroma of their meal. She looked at Aslam's expression, his eyes nearly as large as the egg yolks on his plate.

Shaking her head slightly, she quietly and calmly said, "Aslam, relax and enjoy your breakfast. This is just a business meeting, or a study session. You have nothing to fear."

He took a deep breath, closed his eyes, and said a silent prayer of thanks for the food that Allah had provided, even if prepared in a diner in the country he feared and despised. He took a mouthful of eggs and hashbrowns, washed the food down with a sip of coffee, then opened the envelope and slid its contents onto the table. The six sheets of paper from the envelope were printouts from a laser jet printer. Three sheets displayed pictures of three men. The other three contained neatly typed data. The name at the top of the first page of data – Virgil Vance. The number "1" had been hand-written in red next to the name.

Moska noted the questioning look on Aslam's face then said. "Vance was a Colonel in the Marines, commander of the unit that targeted your home."

Her eyes glistened as if she might cry, then she shook her head and smiled. "Keep reading. You'll understand why we're here, in Statesboro. He lives in Washington, but, if all goes well, he'll be near here in a week or two, along with the others."

Aslam nodded his head, knowing his partner's planning to be thorough and precise. He began to relax as much as his racing, paranoid mind would allow. He scanned the other pictures and their names – Jeffrey Grumen and Carmine Russo.

Moska Aziz would have been surprised to know that Carmine Russo was just over one mile down the road making a delivery to one of the many Dollar General stores in the greater Statesboro area.

* * *

Except for his time spent in the desert in Afghanistan as a member of Marine Corps Rifle Team Charlie, Carmine Russo could not have felt more out of place than in Statesboro, Georgia. He hated Georgia. He hated the heat, the humidity, the weather in general, the red clay, and the people. He could not stand the twang in their voices when they spoke. He believed the men, and some of the women, from Georgia all thought the Civil War to be an ongoing conflict and that they were winning. He had been in one barroom fight and had several other close calls with young men clad in plaid shirts, dirty blue jeans, cowboy boots, and ball caps with rebel flags proudly displayed.

His boisterous, New England accent stood out anywhere in the south, but especially in eastern Georgia. Russo's voice projected even more with a few Sam Adams lagers under his belt. An extrovert even without a drink, he engaged people in casual conversation on any subject, whether he knew the topic or not. But alcohol quickly eroded his social filter and, before long, he became obnoxious, argumentative, then combative. Not one to back down from a fight, many bar managers had to intervene before words turned to physical conflict.

There appeared to be another point of contention with the southern boys: he loved ogling the beautiful southern women, especially the college-aged crowd. Model-like hotties strutted everywhere in Statesboro and Russo loved to stare at their charms with obvious intent.

Russo parked his FedEx delivery truck near the front door of the Dollar General store on Highway 80 East, southeast of Statesboro, blocking several cars into their parking slots. He had delivered a dozen boxes of store merchandise and picked-up one package. He cared little of the inconvenience it might cause the store patrons if they wished to leave before he completed his deliveries. His stomach growled and he planned to stop at a local sub-sandwich shop and grab a six-inch steak sub for lunch. He hated to eat much while on the clock, but believed his workout at Planet Fitness later that evening would sweat off those added calories.

As he sat in his truck, his mind wandered to the desert ten years ago as he watched a bomb destroy a home that held many secrets. His smile back then had been of joy, knowing that the massive explosion obliterated any evidence of the truth.

The blare of a horn brought him back to the present. He could see two young black children looking out the back window of a white, late-model Cadillac. A woman's arm waved wildly out the driver's-side window, encouraging Russo to move his truck.

Russo yelled out the open passenger door of his step-van, "Hold your horses, I'm moving."

He started the engine, looked around in his side-view mirrors and backed up to the exit. As he headed north towards the center of Statesboro on Highway 80, he thought about Rusty Parish. He had been surprised when he learned that Parish lived in South Carolina, not too far from Statesboro. *He should have died a long time ago. Bastard almost got us killed. He can rot in hell.* Parish's demise may have been a tragedy for some, but not for everyone.

Chapter 6

Midday Monday, with Special Agent Megan Moore in the passenger seat, Peden Savage pulled his dark blue Chevy Tahoe off US Highway 301 onto the south branch of Archadian Road, then headed east. At 11:50, the sun perched high in the sky, almost directly overhead. Even with his sun visor in the full-down position a glare coming off the hood of the Tahoe made sunglasses a must.

The north branch of the road, now blockaded and in total disrepair, had previously connected to an old, decrepit, one-lane bridge over the Savannah River. The south branch of the road, little more than a gravel path, led down to a small boat launch used by local fishermen. Lacking needed road maintenance, the quarter mile trek to the Savannah River challenged his Tahoe's springs and shocks. Peden wondered how much of a beating a small fishing boat on a trailer might endure before making it to the launch.

He and Megan spoke little on the way from his Savannah office to Screven County, Georgia. Both had been lost in their thoughts about what little they knew of Rusty Parish's death. When a person dies from a drug overdose, usually there is little controversy from a law enforcement standpoint, especially when the death appears accidental in nature, and there is no indication of foul play. Many people in law enforcement to whom Peden had previously spoken, described the mental despair and physical anguish of the addict, and the heartache their families endured. Some parents expressed belief that their son or daughter had been beyond help, or that the family had gone bankrupt because of their child's addiction. Others described their attempts at tough love, cutting off the financial stream that would have allowed their son or daughter to purchase their next fix. Most times, the result of their good intentions exposed the folly of such a move. With no other options, the addict turned to theft of either cash, or merchandise they could sell easily to pawn shops or on social media sites. Failing that, the addict succumbed to their body's agony during withdrawal and jumped in front of a train or dove from a bridge or high-rise building. Few people addicted to opioids escaped the clutches of a once highly touted pain killer.

Megan looked at her phone and said, "When you get to the end of the road, just park. There's a path along the river. It's about forty-to-fifty yards to where a couple guys found Parish's body."

Peden asked, "Who found the body?"

"A couple of fishermen. They saw it from the river. Said they noticed the guy hadn't moved for over an hour, so they got closer and realized he was white as a sheet. They called 911 and waited for the sheriff."

Peden pulled onto a grassy patch where the road turned left into a primitive parking area. The humid, sticky, hot air assailed them as they exited Peden's Tahoe. They walked east along the river where the tree canopy blocked direct sunlight. The shade offered only slight relief. A gravel path, in better shape than the incoming road, made walking easy. After twenty-five yards, the gravel ended where an old dock extended out some thirty feet over the muddy waters of the Savannah River. The path continued, now with a floor of red clay, the vegetation closing in from both sides. Mosquitoes swarmed making the trip uncomfortable. Megen appeared calm, ignoring the insects. They did not alight on her while they attacked Peden, who began a constant swiping motion with his hand around his face.

Megan reached into her purse and handed Peden a small pump spray bottle.

"Here, this should keep the bugs away."

Peden looked at the clear, non-descript bottle with no writing on it whatsoever. He asked, "What is it?"

"Don't ask. My grandmother's secret recipe. If I told you, I'd have to kill you."

Peden shrugged his shoulders and sprayed around his face, arms, and hands. The homemade concoction provided immediate relief with mosquitoes backing away, making a wide berth. He raised his eyebrows in amazement then handed the bottle back to his partner. "Thanks."

As they continued down the path, Peden noticed a significant number of footprints in the damp clay and freshly broken limbs on the bushes lining the path. He wondered if they would find anything of value while inspecting the area where the fishermen had found Parish's body.

They arrived at the tree. They knew they were in the right place because the path and the multitude of footprints ended. The twenty-foot-tall tree had barely a five-inch diameter trunk. Vegetation and red clay at the perimeter of the tree had been trampled, a portion of clay flattened, most likely by a body board used by the medical examiner's team to haul Parish's body out.

The sheriff's office had either not put up any crime scene perimeter tape or they had already taken it down completely. No debris littered the surrounding area. Nothing, except for the disturbed soil, indicated to them that there had been a dead body here less than seventy-two hours earlier.

Peden asked, "If he came here to commit suicide, how did he get here?"

"My thoughts exactly. Did the sheriff mention finding an abandoned car in the lot?"

Peden rubbed his chin in thought. "Nope. He didn't say, but I didn't ask."

He reached into his pocket and pulled out his cell. He looked at his recent call list and found the Screven County Sheriff's office and hit the dial button. When the call connected, a robotic voice advised Peden that if he had an emergency to hang up and dial 9-1-1, then began to list the possible departments where his call might be directed. When he heard …*press three…* he looked back down the path towards the parking lot and noticed a tall black man in a crisp sheriff's deputy uniform approaching. Peden disconnected the call and placed his phone in his pocket.

When the deputy closed within about twenty feet, the officer smiled and said, "Hi y'all. I'm Deputy Deshaun Ruffin." He looked at Megan. "You must be Special Agent Megan Moore." He touched his hat and nodded his head slightly. "And you are Peden Savage."

Ruffin extended his hand and gave both Peden and Megan a firm shake. Slight beads of sweat ran down Deputy Ruffin's temples. Peden noticed that the mosquitos did not swarm anywhere near the young man.

Megan, all business as usual, said, "We understand that you were the first law enforcement officer on the scene."

Ruffin, tall and slender, but with an athletic body, apparently felt the no-nonsense vibe that Megan projected and toned down his smile. "Yes, ma'am. Dispatch received the call from the folks, a couple fishermen, who discovered the body at around 10:00 a.m. Friday morning. When I arrived on the scene, it was clear that the victim was dead. He had no pulse, was cold to the touch, and his limbs were stiff. He still had a needle in his left arm. I'd been here for about twenty minutes before the medical examiner arrived. He made the declaration. Said that the man had been dead for at least twelve hours."

Peden asked, "Deputy Ruffin, did the victim drive here, or do we know how he got here?"

Ruffin paused as he thought about his answer. When he spoke, his answer came out slowly, ensuring the accuracy of his answer. "We don't know how the victim got here. There was no car in the lot. We noticed multiple sets of footprints coming from the parking area, but this area has a fair amount of foot traffic. We identified the victim's footprints, but not any of the others. We suspect that he might have been hitch-hiking on 301 and came back here to shoot up. We don't have any other plausible theories at this point."

Megan asked, "Seems like the Sheriff wants to call this a suicide and move on. Is that true?"

Ruffin's answer was even more tentative. "Ma'am, I was ordered to meet you here and answer your questions about what I found. You'll have to ask Sheriff Fleming about his intentions."

Megan and Peden both nodded, acknowledging the deputy's

cognizance of his limitations.

Peden said, "I understand that the victim has been identified?"

Ruffin nodded. "Randall Parish from Fairfield, South Carolina. We notified the sheriff's department up there in Allendale County about Mr. Parish's death."

"Has the next of kin been notified?"

"From what I understand, we haven't been able to find any family yet, but a friend of his from the Marine Corps came forward late yesterday asking to take possession of Parish's remains. The body was taken to the Optim Medical Center in Sylvania. That's where the M.E. has his practice. If they can't identify any relations in the next few days, the body might be released to his Marine Corps pal."

Megan asked, "How was the body identified?"

"We found his driver's license and a veteran's ID card in his wallet. The pictures on both matched his face. He had a fair amount of cash in his wallet, which is unusual for an addict, unless he was dealing to support his habit. At least, that's been my experience."

A call came over Ruffin's radio. He replied that he would respond to the minor traffic accident. When he finished, he turned to Megan and Peden and asked if they had any other questions. They replied no and thanked Deputy Ruffin for his time. After a final look around the spot where Parish's body had been found, they followed Ruffin back towards the parking lot and got in Peden's Tahoe. Peden started the engine and turned the air conditioner on maximum cool.

Megan turned to Peden, "I think we need to talk with the M.E. and get his take."

"Agreed."

* * *

A single-story, light brown brick building landscaped with a few trees and shrubs, the Optim Medical Center on Mims Road in Sylvania, Georgia, provided office space and examination rooms for six doctors and staff. The facility also provided emergency services for the surrounding counties. Peden found an open visitor's space in the small parking lot adjacent to the entrance. The main entrance opened into a brightly lit reception area with white walls and an abundance of fruitwood-stained oak trim. Pictures of the members of the hospital board hung from the wall just to the left of the entrance. He and Megan approached the reception counter and were greeted by an older black woman with a broad, bright-white, toothy smile.

"Welcome to Optim Medical Center. How can I help y'all this lovely day?"

Peden returned her smile while Megan looked around the lobby with her usual stone-faced expression. Peden said, "I'm Peden Savage. Late yesterday, a young man's body was brought in. Randall Parish?"

"Yes, sir, he was, God rest his poor soul. Are you a relative?"

Peden looked at the woman's name tag which read *Shirley* in block letters, and replied, "No, Shirley. We're looking into his death. My partner, Special Agent Moore," he turned and gestured towards Megan, who had taken a few steps away from the counter, "is with the FBI. She is the agent in charge of the case. I'm a private investigator."

Shirley raised her eyebrows, clearly surprised that an overdose death attracted such attention. She said, "What is it that you need?"

Peden replied, "We'd like to speak with the medical examiner. We have a few questions about Mr. Parish's death."

"That would be Dr. Daniel Erin. If you head down this main hall and take a right at the first hallway, you will see another reception desk for his wing. Miss Andrea Wills will assist you."

Peden thanked Shirley, then he and Megan headed down a long corridor, the sound of their footsteps echoing in their wake. When they made the turn, another long counter came into view. Across from the counter, four people sat in a waiting area with more than a dozen chairs and a television tuned to a national news station. An attractive blond woman manned a copier that buzzed away. A mirror on the wall let the woman know that she had clients at her station. She turned with a smile and recited the exact same greeting as Shirley.

"Welcome to Optim Medical Center. How can I help y'all this lovely day?"

After a twenty-minute wait, Andrea ushered them into Dr. Erin's office where the dark-haired physician remained seated with his hands folded on top of his pristine desk. Even from a seated position, he projected a sense of superiority, his nose higher than necessary, his face showing what Peden read as impatience at the inconvenience. The doctor's white lab coat had his name and the official Optim logo embroidered in blue and orange on the left breast. He had a stethoscope around his neck and several pens and a pen light in his coat pocket.

With a deadpan expression and a cultured southern accent, he said, "I'm Dr. Daniel Erin. Andrea mentioned that y'all have questions about Randall Parish. Could I see some ID, please."

After the obligatory display of their credentials, Dr. Erin proceeded with his medical determination on the cause of death being an opioid overdose. All indications pointed to a self-administered lethal dose. He waited for any questions.

Megan spoke for the first time since entering the building. "Did you notice anything unusual about this particular overdose?"

"Such as?"

"Were there signs of addiction, multiple track marks, emaciated body from lack of nutrition, things of that nature."

Dr. Erin hesitated, then said, "No, ma'am. Mr. Parish had none of the hallmark traits of a habitual user. In fact, I did not find anything to indicate drug use at all. His liver had seen better days. I suspect that he drank heavily, but drug use…no."

"If you didn't suspect casual drug use by Randall Parish, why wouldn't you indicate that in your report?"

With a dismissive roll of his eyes, he replied, "Miss Moore …"

Megan cut him off and said, "Special Agent Moore."

With another look of annoyance, Dr. Erin continued, "Pardon me. I meant no disrespect. Special Agent Moore, I record facts in my reports about the cause of death. In the case of Mr. Parish, he died of a drug overdose. There is no room for opinion. Y'all asked for my opinion beyond the report and I gave it to y'all." He paused for effect, making sure that no one challenged his authority on this matter. "Any other questions?"

Megan looked at Peden who smiled and shook his head. Megan turned to Doctor Erin and said, "No. Thank you, Doctor."

As the three stood, Megan handed the doctor her card. When he did not reach out and take it, she dropped it on his desk and said, "Please call if you think of anything else that you feel is important. Even if it is just your opinion."

As they left the building, Peden remarked, "Interesting. Fits with Chip Chandler's recollection."

Megan replied, "Yeah, and it doesn't fit with suicide."

Chapter 7

Chip Chandler ran a successful financial consulting business which he had taken over from his in-laws just one year after leaving the Marine Corps. They decided to retire to Pensacola, Florida after making a small fortune in the stock market. Chandler and his wife, Colleen, immediately moved the business into their home in Holly Ridge, North Carolina. They narrowed their clientele, taking on only those with assets significantly higher than the average American. Their profit-loss sheet proved that they made a good decision with the company near tripling profits over the past three years.

Sitting at his home office desk, Chip had just completed the last meeting of the day. A relatively new customer, less than pleased with his portfolio's performance, pointed to the down-trend in his bottom line. Chip educated the man on wealth management basics. He compared his portfolio with trends in the overall market and his holdings against specific companies within the same sectors. His portfolio, though down overall, fared better than those in Chips examples. He assured his client that the market would turn and that he remained well positioned to take advantage of the upswing, which appeased the man's concerns.

Throughout the meeting, Chandler had a difficult time focusing on his client, his thoughts wandering to Rusty Parish's untimely death. After he walked his client to the door, he sat back at his desk and signed into BIAChat. Putting his thoughts into a new post, he began writing about Parish, his life in the Marine Corps, the accident that took his parents' lives, and their comrade's death. He wanted the squadron to know that he planned to take possession of their former rifle team member's body. He knew some members of the group could care less that Parish had died, or that he had committed suicide. A few of the team might even have volunteered to help him end his miserable life, but Chandler felt that informing his brothers rested on his shoulders. *Once a Marine, always a Marine*. He knew others from his squadron believed it as strongly as he did.

He spoke at length with his wife, Colleen, about having a military-style burial service. She proposed to Chip that they bring the squad together to honor one of their own. She suggested that a solemn event, such as a funeral, might encourage them to become closer and look out for each other. She followed the efforts of veteran and first responder support groups noting the positive response from the public and members of the military community. Colleen had appeared passionate about those efforts. She told her husband that she hoped the feeling of comradery might infect members of their unit. She even mentioned that Chip might start with General Vance and garner his support, that through his office he could influence the entire squadron.

Chip liked the idea. He agreed that having Parish's funeral and burial services at a Veterans Administration cemetery could bring the team together. It might give the men a chance to renew friendships and to bury past differences.

Planning the event came down to timing and Chip had no idea when, if at all, the medical examiner might release Parish's body to him. He intended to call the M.E.'s office every day so that he would have as much notice as possible. He needed to give his former Marine Corps brothers the lead time necessary to arrange time off from jobs and to make travel arrangements. Many of the squad members lived within hours of Screven County, Georgia, but others, like Jeff Grumen from Ohio, lived further away, and likely would need to fly in for the services.

He stared at the keyboard of his computer, thinking about how to frame his post, making sure the message got across that they should plan to attend Parish's funeral but that they should also keep any animosity for their deceased brother under wraps and out of the public eye. For some, that might be the bigger challenge.

Chandler looked up and stared at the ceiling for a moment, then covered his face with his hands. He took two deep breaths, rubbed his face, then returned his stare to the keyboard. He typed two words, *Dear brothers….* He hit backspace until the words disappeared. He drew a blank, his mind working in slow motion, as if drunk, or fatigued. One more shake of the head and he started typing again.

Hey brothers, most of you know by now, but in case you haven't heard, Rusty Parish passed away this past week, most likely Wednesday or Thursday, September 8 or 9. The medical examiner declared the cause of death to be a drug overdose. We all know well about Rusty's struggle with alcohol in his last year on active duty, but I personally don't recall him ever being involved with drugs. He confided in me that he would never use drugs because of his brother's death. I know you might be skeptical, but I hope you will at least give him the benefit-of-doubt.

Regardless, Rusty did not have any living relatives that I know of. The medical examiner's office has been unable to locate a next of kin. If they don't find a family member and nothing else happens, Rusty might be buried in some no-name potter's field, his legacy lost forever.

We can't let that happen to our brother.

I have contacted the medical examiner and asked if I can take possession of Rusty's body. I have contacted the Veteran's Administration requesting that he be buried in a veteran's cemetery. We have two here in east-central Georgia. If all goes as I hope, he will be buried at the Georgia Veterans Memorial Cemetery north of Glennville. I don't know yet when his body will be released, but, at the earliest, I suspect that it will be sometime later in the week. Please keep your calendar's free late next week. As soon as I have a confirmed date for possession and interment of our brother, I will contact each of you. Colleen and I can assist with travel arrangements. If the cost of travel or lodging is an issue for any of you, contact me directly and we will help you.

*My cell number is listed under my profile. I hope we can
all get together to honor Rusty with a proper burial.*

Chandler took a deep breath and hit the 'Post' button. He watched as his message appeared on the screen in the next available space in the chat room. Within minutes, two members responded with a thumbs up: Rayshon Mack and Brandon Pierce. He knew Mack would like the idea but had doubts on how many others would join in. He signed out of the chat room and shut down his computer, thinking that he would check again later in the evening, giving others the chance to sign in and view his post.

His wife entered his office and stopped short. Her shoulders slumped and her expression changed to a sad face.

"Do I really look that bad?" he asked.

Her lips curled into a forced smile. "Not bad, just…I don't know…worried, like you already know this isn't going to turn out well."

"It's just that Rusty wasn't exactly the most popular guy in the squad, even before he started drinking and raising hell about the drone strike. I mean, we all took our oath seriously, but Rusty took it to a whole different level. Then he just fell apart. Like somebody flipped a switch and he dove off the deep end. I always worried that he would crumble from putting so much pressure on himself, trying to make sure he didn't end up like his brother. In the end, it looks like he did just that."

Chip looked up at his wife, who appeared deep in thought. For a moment, her face contorted into a pained expression. She noticed her husband studying her and shook her head.

She said, "Sorry. Just took a mind trip back to that hellhole."

"I understand. That was a tough part of both our lives – all our lives. Maybe being there and losing his parents made Parish flip out. We'll probably never know."

Colleen smiled and took the few steps to her husband. She sat in his lap and kissed him lightly on the lips. After several seconds, she pulled back and whispered, "Let's work together and make sure our switches never get flipped."

He returned her smile. "I like that idea."

* * *

Hours later, Chip signed into the BIAChat and reviewed his post and the various responses. Positive responses jumped to ten. That left at least fourteen more who either had not seen the post yet, were on the fence deciding whether to attend the funeral, or just ignored the post.

With her husband's focus on the chat site, Colleen retreated to their huge master bedroom. She sat on the edge of their perfectly-made-up-king-sized bed. Her light body sank into the crème-colored comforter. She looked around at the walls adorned by framed pictures with a tropical theme: palm trees, palmetto bushes, and sandy beaches skirted with bright blue waters. She smiled as she thought briefly of their honeymoon to the big island of Hawaii, when they were amazed by the widely varied landscapes. She shook her head, scattering the pleasant recollections.

Using her personal cell phone, she dialed the number for Moska Aziz. After just one ring a woman's voice answered, "Colleen, so nice to hear from you."

"Hi Moska. I can't talk long, but I wanted you to know that Chip posted the initial invite to Parish's funeral, but we don't have many details yet."

"That's fine. I'll start making calls, try to drum up support. I know this is important to your husband, but it's even more important for us. Do you have any details at all?"

"Only that Parish's body might be released at the end of the week. Chip is working on that. He says he's going to keep calling the medical examiner, so I think we'll know something soon. He already told them Rusty didn't have any living relatives and that he and Mack were the closest thing to family Rusty had."

There was a brief silence, then Moska said, "That's good, very good. I'll put a bug in the General's ear, make sure he's on board."

At the mention of Vance's name, Colleen tensed. She closed her eyes and tried to think of anything else but her time under his command. She said, "I know he'll be supportive, especially if he can get some news coverage at the funeral. Bastard."

"Focus, Colleen. Let's take this one step at a time."

Colleen took a deep breath. She knew Moska was right. The plan had been in the works for a long time. Now that the end was near, her personal anxiety jumped, putting her nerves into overdrive, even around Chip. He was such a calming force in her life, but the next week would pose a challenge, even for him.

Moska asked, "Colleen, you still there?"

"Yeah, I'm here. What do you need me to do?"

"Just keep your husband focused on getting the funeral arrangements set and let me know the details as soon as possible. And Colleen, chill out. Everything will work out just fine. You can trust me on this."

More deep breaths. Colleen quietly answered, "Okay, okay. You're right."

The call disconnected. More deep breaths. Then a voice startled her.

"Sweety, who were you talking to?"

Chip was standing at their bedroom door holding a beer. He looked surprised by her reaction.

Colleen forced a smile and replied, "Michelle Workman. She works for Vance. I met her back in Kandahar."

After taking a sip of beer, raising his eyebrows, and looking at the bedroom ceiling, he asked, "Do you think she can help us with getting Vance behind Rusty's funeral?"

Colleen relaxed some and smiled. "Yeah. Yeah, I do."

Chapter 8

Moska Aziz savored the flavor of her second glass of *pinot grigio*, her favorite wine. The fruity flavor melded perfectly with cubes of baby Swiss cheese and miniature multigrain crackers. She smiled as the early evening treat calmed her nerves in advance of the upcoming telephone call. She had rehearsed the remarks she planned to make over and over in her mind. She licked her fingers, then wiped them on a napkin, inhaled deeply through her nose, held her breath for several seconds, then exhaled through her bright red lips. *I'm coming for you.*

"What are you drinking, Mom?"

The young voice brought a smile to Moska's face. She had not heard her nine-year-old daughter enter the large living-room carpeted in a deep-piled, light beige. Moska turned and faced her daughter, admiring the youthful face, an image much like her own as a pre-teen growing up in Kabul, Afghanistan. A blanket of love for her young daughter enveloped her emotions even as another feeling emerged at the perimeter, attempting to chip away at the joy of being this olive-skinned beauty's mother. She resolved she would not let forces beyond her control affect her feelings for young Mina. She would always love her daughter unconditionally. Moska knew in her heart and mind that she must separate the events that led to the gift that Mina had become to her, and the circumstances that made her birth possible.

"Mina. Come sit with me."

Moska smiled at her daughter whose natural, cheerful smile displayed a mouth full of bright, perfect teeth. The child usually had her nose in her Amazon Kindle or a book, displaying a brilliance Moska had never seen before in a preteen girl. Most of her daughter's American friends spent their days texting back and forth, or watching some TV program targeting young girls on the latest fashions and beauty aids. While Mina had many friends and easily warmed up to children her age, she tended to shy away from texting and gossip. When her friends began picking at others' appearance and personality traits, Mina tried to politely steer the conversation away from the mean taunts. If the conversation remained guttural, she quietly withdrew from the aggressors. It was a trait that Moska considered a miracle in her daughter.

Moska replied, "I'm drinking wine. White wine, to be precise. Would you like something to drink? And no, you can't have any wine." She smiled, knowing her daughter had no interest in adult beverages.

In her usual, polite response, she said, "No, thank you. I just finished some water. If I want anything else I can get it." Her face twisted up such that Moska knew her daughter had something profound on her mind.

"Okay, young lady, out with it. What are you thinking about?"

Mina closed her eyes as if deciding whether to tell her mother her secret.

Moska smiled and coaxed, "If you want to talk, just talk. I won't bite, I promise." She took another sip of wine.

Mina looked at her mother and without hesitation asked, "Why aren't you married?"

Moska nearly spit wine across the room, the question taking her by total surprise. She picked up a napkin and touched it to her mouth, catching just a dribble of wine that had escaped her lips. She knew her daughter possessed a brilliant mind, quickly evaluated situations, and exhibited a natural talent for calculating solutions to problems. She noticed her surroundings and asked questions, sometimes non-stop, to the point where Moska asked her to slow down and take a breath. On some level, she knew the day would come where Mina would want to know about her father, his identity, if he was alive, and why he did not live with them.

Moska believed her daughter to be too young to understand the true story of her father. Mina Aziz had never asked about why she and her mother lived alone, or why the only person who came to visit, besides her own friends, was Aslam Sayed. Mina appeared conflicted as if she had been giving this a lot of thought. Moska did not want to reply with some off-the-cuff, flip response, so she said, "Well, first I have to find the right man."

"Is Aslam the right man?"

Moska frowned, "Oh, no. No, no, no. Aslam is a long-time friend, a good friend. But he isn't the right man for us."

"How will you know who the right man is?"

Moska paused, then smiled and looked directly into her daughter's eyes. "First, I must find a man who loves us. He must love both you and me. Second, he must be a good man, a good provider, a man who makes enough money to make sure we have everything we need to keep us happy and healthy. And he must treat us with respect."

"When will you find this man?"

Moska laughed, then noticed the serious look on Mina's face. She stopped laughing, but maintained a bright smile.

"My sweet, sweet girl, you can't put a timetable on such matters. When I find love, I will know it, and you will know it because this man will make us both happy. He will make us feel like we have no worries."

Mina smiled, her mother's explanation appearing to satisfy her curiosity. But she asked one more question. "Will the man help fix your pain?"

The question confused Moska. She asked, "What do you mean 'my pain?'"

"You know, the pain in your back. I see how hard it is for you to bend over, like your back is stiff. I hear you grunt, like you can't twist your back. Maybe you can meet a doctor who can fix that for you."

Yes. Young, observant Mina did not miss much and this worried Moska. She would have to use caution when talking on the phone to Aslam about their plans. Young Mina must never know the truth about what happened in Kabul.

Moska forced a smile then said, "Maybe. We shall see what

Allah has in store." She smiled at her daughter then asked, "Any more questions?"

The young girl shook her head, her straight, dark hair brushing against her shoulders.

"Then give your mom a hug and get back to whatever you were doing." With a laugh, she said, "And try to not worry about me getting married. The right man will come along. Maybe even a doctor. Now give me that hug, because right now, it's just you and me. Always remember, no matter who comes along, you and me, we're inseparable."

She held out her arms to her daughter. Mina smiled and moved next to her mother. Closing her arms around Moska's neck, she whispered, "I love you, Mom."

"I love you, too, sweetheart." They held the embrace for several seconds, then Mina disappeared into her room.

Moska took a deep breath and wiped her eyes of the tears before they could roll down her cheeks. She shook her head, shifting her thoughts away from her daughter to a person who fit the category of definitely *not* 'the right man' – Carmine Russo.

Slowly, and with great effort, she rose from the couch, tried to stretch the stiffness from her back, then picked up her cell phone. She clutched it tight for a moment as she again, in her mind, rehearsed the speech. She smiled, but there was anger behind the smile as the plan began to meld. Despite Aslam's fears, she knew it would work.

She moved into the den then out the sliding glass door onto the back patio. The early evening sun, just above the horizon, projected an orange glow onto the clouds. The heat remained oppressive even as dusk approached, but that mattered little to Moska. She now focused her full attention on former Marine Corps Lance Corporal Carmine Russo.

* * *

The chirping sound, coupled with a vibration in his pocket, alerted Carmine Russo of an incoming call on his cell phone. The call would have to wait. He had two bulky boxes in his hands as he made his way into the Dollar General store northeast of Statesboro, Georgia, at US Route 301 and Clito Road. After several seconds, the chirping and the vibration stopped. He continued with his delivery duties, placing the boxes at the end of a counter beyond the new self-checkout station. As he waited for the store shift manager, his phone came to life again. With a frown, he reached into his pocket and looked at the display, thinking that it must be the FedEx dispatch center looking for someone to work a few extra hours that evening. But the screen displayed '*Restricted*' so he let the call go, again without answering.

It took several minutes for the shift manager to accept the delivery. As Russo returned to his truck and put it in gear, his phone chirped and vibrated again. The same message appeared. He decided to answer and find out the caller's identity.

He put his truck back in park and answered, "Russo."

A husky female voice said, "Corporal Russo, Captain Workman calling from General Virgil Vance's office. The general wanted to ensure that members of his squadron were aware of the passing of Private Randall Parish."

Russo, surprised by the call, especially at this late hour, replied, "Yes, Captain, I heard. Why the call?"

"The general has assigned Charles Chandler to ensure a proper burial for Private Parish. He would also like for all members of the squadron to attend the services. If you are able, of course."

Russo rolled his eyes. Of all the members of their squadron, Parish's funeral ranked last among those he thought the general would support. He wondered if Jeff Grumen knew about Parish's death. Most likely yes. Russo knew that Rayshon Mack and Chip Chandler kept in touch with Parish even outside of the BIAChat site. Mack had tried to get Parish on the straight-and-narrow, mentoring him, helping him get civilian jobs, but that apparently had not kept the troubled Parish from succumbing to his self-destructive personality.

"Corporal Russo, are you still there?"

Russo broke out of his thoughts and said, "Yes. What is it that the general wants?"

"Service arrangements are not yet finalized, but they are most likely to be held at the Georgia Veterans Memorial Cemetery near Glennville, Georgia. The general is counting on your support by being present at graveside. I will forward the specifics to you when they become available."

"I'll see if I'm available."

Russo, about to disconnect the call, heard Workman say, "General Vance is counting on your attendance, Corporal. Remember, Parish was one of us."

The last line seemed close to an order and made Russo cringe. In a voice nearing defiance, he said, "I will do my best."

He swiped the disconnect icon ending the call. He had no intention of honoring that bastard, Rusty Parish. If Parish had stayed around in the service much longer, he would have blown up everything, and Vance knew it. Why show support for this chump in death?

The sound of a horn broke Russo from his thoughts. He started his step van and headed onto highway 301. He had one more delivery before finishing his deliveries for the evening.

* * *

Moska Aziz listened to the connection go dead. She smiled while watching the location icon move southwest along Highway 301. The RFID tracker worked perfectly. She would soon pick up the second device that Aslam Sayed had placed on Russo's car. She smiled as the plan appeared to come together, one piece at a time.

Chapter 9

Peden's call with Rayshon Mack bore little in the way of new information. The former Marine Corps corporal spoke candidly about his time in service, his relationship with his men and his superiors, and the deep unease he felt when Private Rusty Parish lost his cool during the drone strike ten years ago. According to Mack, the mission was straight forward. His squadron had been tasked with laser-targeting a building on the edge of Kabul to guide a hellfire missile for a precision strike.

He described in detail – Peden believed a little too much detail over an unsecured cell phone – how he verified the coordinates on the laser guide for Sergeant Grumen. He had no way of knowing why they targeted the structure. He just made certain the laser readout matched the coordinates on the sheet of paper that Grumen showed him. He assumed that Grumen knew as little about the target as he did.

From his own time in the Marines, Peden knew this to be typical of support operations. You received an assignment with an objective and you carried out your assignment, no questions asked. When each unit carried out its piece of the plan - known only to the command's top brass - they achieved the prime objective of the mission.

While Peden spoke with Mack, Megan performed records searches on the former Marine corporal. In the records to which she had access, she found nothing that would cause her to question his integrity. In fact, Mack maintained a spotless, if not outstanding, record for his time in the corps. He had been recommended for advancement multiple times. His squadron lieutenant had even endorsed the recommendation he be placed in officer candidate school, even though Mack did not have the required college degree. The only blemish, if one could call it that: Mack refused to take the test for advancement to sergeant. He stated, as recorded in his personnel file, that he intended to leave the Corps at the end of his enlistment and, with a limited number of available test slots, he did not want to prevent someone else from advancement.

With the call on speaker, Megan listened in. So far, she had no questions, but recorded the names Mack had mentioned during the call, all of which were on the list provided by Chip Chandler. While Mack did not say anything negative about anyone in his squad, he did note that many, if not all the men in his unit, commented about Rusty Parish's actions during and after the drone strike. Mack also stated Parish's consumption of alcohol accelerated after a confrontation about the strike with his sergeant, Jeffrey Grumen.

Early in the call, Peden had established that they should use first names. Peden asked, "So, Ray, do you know why Parish raised a scene after the strike?"

"No. After the missile hit, Rusty completely lost it. I was laying right next to Sergeant Grumen when we heard Rusty yelling his head off, running towards us. He kept saying, and I quote, 'You hit the wrong house.' I don't know why he believed that, but he yelled it over and over. Grumen kept his cool, in my opinion. He got Rusty to get his head back on straight. I mean, his outburst put us all in jeopardy. A couple of the guys admitted to me that they got real nervous. He was loud and sound travels a good-ways out there in the mountains around Kabul."

"Any personal opinion why he believed the strike hit the wrong house?"

"No, sir, I don't. But he was adamant. Even after Grumen ordered him to stand down, he got in Grumen's face and threatened him that he planned to go over his head and report his grievance directly to Chandler. I mean, he was possessed. To Grumen's credit, he got Rusty to calm down enough to safely move the teams back to our transports. But Rusty did a slow burn, staring at Grumen the entire way, like, for over an hour. It was intense. I tried to talk with him afterwards, but he just clammed up about what made him go off the rails."

Peden thought about Mack's description for a few seconds, then said, "This might be a stupid question, but did Parish have any special clearance that would have allowed him to know facts about the strike that you or even Grumen would not know?"

"Peden, it's not a stupid question, but no, Rusty didn't have any special clearance. He didn't even know anyone with that level of clearance. He had no way of knowing the target or the objective of the mission or the reason we were ordered to mark that particular target. Hell, even Grumen and I didn't know the reason, until we heard it on some overseas news channel."

"I understand that you and Chip Chandler stay in touch. When you heard that he also had concerns about the strike, how did you react?"

"My reaction? I was out on patrol the next day with a new set of orders. I didn't hear about Chip's concerns until a week or so later. I didn't have a chance to talk with Rusty either, but when I got back to camp, I heard that the squad persuaded Rusty to drop his beef with Grumen. You're a Marine. You know, your brothers, especially the men in your squad, can be very convincing."

Peden raised his eyebrows, knowing the type of influence brought to bear by Parish's fellow squad members. When you relied on the men around you for your life, you made sure every person in your squad "had your six," meaning you covered their back and they covered yours.

He did not ask how the squad convinced Parish to drop his issue with Sargeant Grumen, but wondered if Grumen put anything negative in Parish's file.

"So, Parish dropped his complaint about Grumen, but did Grumen take further action against Parish?"

"He threatened to, but in the end, I don't think he did, but I'm not sure. Grumen … I don't want to gossip … but he had some personal issues around that time. He confided in me that he might have to leave the Marines at the end of his enlistment. His wife … she wasn't handling the military wife lifestyle very well."

"He was leaving the Corps to do what?"

"He had a job lined up with his father-in-law. He said he planned to move to Ohio. Sure enough, he did. I've only heard from him through BIAChat.”

“BIAChat?”

“Yeah. It’s a social media site, just for our platoon. Got about forty or fifty members. Grumen is one, but he doesn’t engage in the chat much. Kind of hangs and watches what everyone else is saying.”

Peden rubbed his chin, thinking about what Rayshon Mack had told them. He and Megan knew most of the information he provided so far from Chip Chandler. Peden heard Mack say, “You still there?”

“Yeah, Ray. Who else, besides you, did Parish confide in?”

There was a short stretch of silence on the line, then Mack said, “Nobody, really. When we were in camp, the guys would play poker or rummy. Some guys from up north would play euchre, but Rusty never joined in. He sat away from the crowd and read books or listened to music. Classic rock. Some of the younger guys made fun of him, but nothing serious. Rusty took it alright … until he started drinking heavy. Then everything pissed him off. Got in guys faces, wanting to fight. It came to blows once, but the squad kept it under wraps. Everybody chalked it up to blowing off steam. It was late in our deployment, so we were all getting antsy to get the hell out of there and come home.”

“Who did he fight with?”

“Cassidy Miller. A new guy to the unit, but he’d been a Marine for quite a while. I never got to know him well. He wasn’t there long enough.” A stretch of silence ensued. Peden waited because he believed Mack had more to say, then Mack spoke, “He was a private, but he had been a corporal. He’d been busted for drinking a couple times. The command had him on a last chance letter. I read his file and it sounded just like Rusty’s case. Miller tried to use himself as an example to Rusty, that he should get his stuff together. Rusty, being half in the bag, took exception. They exchanged punches. Four or five of us stepped in and broke it up.

“Thing is, Rusty and Miller were civil after that. Not chummy or anything, but I saw them a few days later talking, kind of privately. He never said anything to me about what they said, but he seemed to calm down just a bit after that day. Drank less. Didn't stop, mind you, but wasn't openly drunk after that. A few days later, Cass transferred out and Rusty headed home."

"Did you ever hear from Miller again?"

"No. Never learned where he transferred. Never heard another word about him – until now."

Peden looked at Megan to see if she had any questions. She shook her head slightly.

When Peden asked if Mack had anything else to add, the former Marine hesitated several seconds before saying no. Something may have been on the tip of his tongue, but he did not want to say anything negative about his brothers in the Corps.

Peden closed the conversation by giving Mack his phone number and stating that if he had anything to add, or if he remembered anything, regardless of whether he believed it to be insignificant, to contact him.

After the call, Peden turned to Megan. They discussed her take on the call. She told Peden that there was nothing negative in Mack's service record and that he appeared honest and forthright.

Peden said, "Rayshon Mack is the kind of Marine I would want at my side during a conflict of any kind. A real standup guy."

Megan nodded. She added, "He has an outstanding record and he obviously didn't want to say anything to tarnish the image of his fellow Marines." She paused, then continued, "Let's talk about the call list. Maybe we should change the order a bit, based on what we just heard."

"What did you pick up that I obviously didn't?"

"Two names stood out to me. Just a subtle change in the tone of Mack's voice."

Peden thought back to the interview. One name was obvious – Jeffrey Grumen. Parish believed that Grumen erred in targeting the structure that had been blown to pieces. But what did a private know that a sergeant did not? Chip Chandler knew because his interpreter lived in the building, but Chandler had not been present during the strike. Why did Parish believe that they had destroyed the wrong building?

Peden broke out of his deep thoughts to find Megan staring at him.

"You had your thinking cap on a little too tight. Did you put any of the pieces together?"

Peden raised his eyebrows at Megan's question. "Nope. But can you tell me how a private knows something that no one else in his squad knew?"

"No, but if we figure that out, I'll bet it leads us closer to whoever killed Private Parish."

"So, you agree that it wasn't suicide by overdose?"

"Yes, I agree. You don't just decide one day to kill yourself by intentional overdose. Parish, a non-drug-using Marine, would've used a gun."

"Pretty cold. But probably true." A moment of silence ensued then Peden asked, "What changes do you want to make to the call list?"

Megan twitched her nose. "I think we should move General Vance to the top and ask him what he remembers about the strike. See if his version varies from Chandler's and by how much. It might be telling hearing the same story from two different perspectives."

"Should we wait to hear what Vance has to say before making any further changes to the call list?"

Her stare gave Peden his answer. Her expression screamed *obviously.*

Peden thought for a moment then said, "I think we should try to find Cassidy Miller."

Megan hitched an eyebrow up in a questioning look, as if asking *Because…?.*

"Because guys don't normally get pulled into a regiment that is headed home, unless he's going with them. His showing up like that doesn't fit."

Chapter 10

After the call to Rayshon Mack ended, Peden and Megan discussed what they knew about Randall Parish's death. More to the point, they highlighted what they did not know. Adding this new player, Private Cassidy Miller, to the cast of characters only muddied the waters of an already vague set of circumstances surrounding the drone strike, the strife within the ranks, and Parish's untimely demise. Peden made a note to ask Chip Chandler what he knew about Miller and why he was not on the list of rifle team members.

Two questions that stuck out in Peden's mind: did the strike really take out the wrong target, and, if yes, how did Parish know that the wrong target had been hit, but Rayshon Mack and Jeffrey Grumen did not.

The silence between Megan and Peden grew to nearly five minutes when Peden's cell phone chirped. He looked at the display and saw Chip Chandler's number. He looked at Megan and said, "It's Chip."

"Hmm, this should be interesting."

He answered as Megan looked on, "Hey, Chip."

"Hey, Peden. Just calling to see if there's anything new."

Peden hesitated before answering, deciding what information Chip should know and what should be held back. Peden looked at Megan who eyed him closely. She mouthed "speaker" at him, so he said, "Chip, Megan Moore is here. I'm putting you on speaker."

"Okay, Peden. No problem."

Once on speaker, Chip said, "Hello, Agent Moore."

"Hello, Chip. Please, call me Megan."

Peden broke into the pleasantries. "We spoke to the medical examiner in Screvn County. Even though he declared the death an accidental opioid overdose, he admitted to us that

Parish didn't exhibit any of the hallmark signs of an addict. In fact, the level of opioids in his blood may not have killed a habitual user. On the other hand, his liver showed signs of long-term alcohol abuse. Parish was not long for this world unless he stopped drinking, cold turkey."

"That fits with what Rayshon and I said."

Peden took a deep breath. "I agree, you were both right. It still doesn't prove that Parish didn't commit suicide by overdose. But other factors don't support an intentional overdose. Megan and I saw where the two fishermen found his body. Nobody knows how he got there. He didn't drive. There was no vehicle anywhere in the vicinity. The deputy we spoke with said that he could have hitchhiked. That seems unlikely. Who hitches a ride to a remote location to kill themselves, unless the location holds some personal significance?"

Megan remained silent. She let Peden steer the conversation, hoping that Chip might say something that would add to the meager amount of accumulated information.

Peden continued, "The deputy found Parish's wallet in his pants pocket. He had his South Carolina driver's license, some money, and a couple credit cards. Megan and I think we can rule out suicide and robbery-gone-bad. That pretty much leaves murder by lethal injection. But why would somebody want to kill Parish, especially if it's related to the drone strike? That's a long time to hold a grudge."

"I agree. If somebody in the squad still had a beef with Rusty, they knew they could have just waited until he died from alcohol poisoning."

"Or any number of alcohol related causes."

"Yeah."

Peden took a drink of water then said, "That brings me to something that we just learned. Rayshon Mack said that Parish got into a fight with a guy shortly before your unit was ordered home. Private Cassidy Miller? He said the guy was only with the unit for a couple of weeks, right before your unit was shipped home. He wasn't on your list of team members. What can you tell me about him?"

Peden and Megan heard him mumbling to himself, as if thinking allowed, "Cassidy Miller, Cassidy Miller … hmm, name doesn't ring any bells."

Over the phone, they heard a female voice ask, "What is it, babe?"

"Colleen just came into the kitchen. Let me ask her."

Before Peden or Megan could object in case they wanted to ask Colleen Chandler in an interview away from her husband, they heard him ask his wife, "Hey, sweetheart, do you remember a guy in the squad named Cassidy Miller?"

About twenty seconds of silence ensued. Both Peden and Megan waited out the lull in the conversation, straining to hear how she would respond. Finally, she said, "I don't recall anyone in the squad by that name. It's pretty unique, so I think I would have remembered since I handled all the transfer paperwork for everyone under Vance."

Into the phone, Chip Chandler said, "Did you hear that, guys?"

Megan nodded, then Peden said, "Yeah, Chip, we heard. We'll check back with Rayshon and see if he remembers anything more about this Cassidy Miller character. Maybe he was with a different squad."

"Could be. Let me know what you find."

"Yeah, Chip. Will do."

Peden looked at Megan who shook her head, no, meaning that she had nothing to further for Chip. He asked, "Do you have any other questions for us?"

"No, Peden. If I think of anything, I'll call. We'll talk later, I'm sure. Bye, Megan, Peden."

The call disconnected. Megan's expression did not change even slightly. Peden asked, "What's on your mind?"

"How does a squadron leader and an admin in charge of personnel's paperwork not know about a private in their command? Especially if that person fought with someone the entire team had an issue with."

"I wonder if Chip and his wife are telling us everything they know."

Megan said, "I wonder if they're telling each other everything they know."

* * *

Chip disconnected the call with his friend, Peden. He sat at the kitchen table, alone. Colleen had exited the house through the patio door to the pool. Chip had no other clients to see for the remainder of the afternoon and his wife planned to work on her tan. Since leaving the Marine Corps, Colleen remained in top physical condition, exercising twice each day in their private gym, then taking laps in their pool for twenty minutes to cool off. She worked-out with such ferocity that Chip wondered about her motivation. He had once asked about what still drove her to exercise with a vengeance. She responded that she wanted to stay in shape, live as long as possible, and to keep him happy. While her response and apparent motives pleased him, he thought that there might be more to her drive than her health and marital harmony.

He had no complaints about their life together. The pristine appearance of the house, her cooking, her healthy, but subdued social life, proved to be positives in their marriage. Especially their sex life, which was a workout all its own. Her aggressive style between the sheets mirrored her workout routines: exhausting, but highly satisfying.

What started out as a call inquiring about progress on the cause of death for Rusty Parish turned into a quandary for Chip. Hearing that he had been right about Parish's cause of death did not surprise him. It would certainly not surprise Rayshon Mack, either. Peden's matter-of-fact delivery of his and Megan's suspicions that Rusty had been murdered fit with, even reenforced, what he believed from the moment he heard the news. Someone with ill intent had killed their Marine Corps brother and that did not sit well with Chip.

But what had Chip scratching his head about the phone call was Colleen's reaction to hearing the name Cassidy Miller. The instant she heard the name, her face paled, and she drew a short, involuntary breath. He watched as she attempted to cover her reaction, feigning deep thought, but Chip knew his wife too well. He sat, deep in thought about their time in Afghanistan just prior to their return home. Turmoil within the squad filled every day with tension. Chip spent his down-time monitoring the mood, talking with squad members, gauging their reactions to the drone strike without bringing attention to his motives. Most of the squad saw right through his inquiries. Vance had assigned him and two rifle teams to a special assignment. Parish had not been part of the assignment and remained at the camp. The two teams patrolled an area where Taliban fighters set up a site with the ability to launch rocket propelled grenades into the Marine base. The patrol lasted ten days without success. No activity described in the mission order turned up.

Chip often wondered about the intention of that assignment. Many of the men sent out on patrol had accosted Parish because of his outburst during the drone strike. Vance may have wanted to keep his Marines busy, to lower the tension and cool tempers within the rifle teams. He never learned of the incident between Parish and Cassidy Miller.

Now he wondered what his wife really knew and why she had such a reaction. Now was the time to find out.

Chip strode out through the French doors that lead to the swimming pool. The bright sun added to the pleasant seventy-degree temperature. Colleen glided through the water with smooth, slow strokes, pacing herself, which indicated to Chip that she planned to do about twenty laps or more. Chip joined her in her swim once each week, but he preferred running and moderate weight lifting to swimming.

He walked back into the kitchen and grabbed two bottles of water, then took a seat beside the pool, continuing to admire his wife's physique. Ten minutes later, Colleen noticed him and stopped her routine in mid-lap. She made her way to the ladder closest to her husband and climbed out, dripping wet, breathing deep, looking sexy in her tight-fitting one-piece swimsuit.

Chip tossed her a towel, at first, smiling. Slowly, his

face turned serious. He noticed Colleen's expression change as she dried off, starting with her head, working her way down to her taut legs, passing the scar on her left hip from the bullet that put her in an admin position for the remainder of her career.

Standing up straight as she wrapped the towel around at her waist, she asked, "Why the glum face? You think I'm getting fat or something?"

His smile returned. "No, not at all. No complaints in that department."

He stood and handed her a plastic bottle of cold water then his smile disappeared. He hesitated before speaking, gathering his thoughts about how to broach the subject. She seemed to anticipate the coming topic of discussion and said, "Cassidy Miller. Am I right?"

He took a drink of water and nodded, keeping his attention on her eyes, looking for any signs of deceit. There were none.

She relaxed as all emotion drained from her face and body. Her eyes drifted away from his, looking at patio furniture, the outdoor bar, then up into the bright blue sky. Her shoulders sagged, not in defeat, but resolution.

"I destroyed the transfer paperwork for Miller at the direction of his boss. My instructions included forgetting that Cassidy Miller ever set foot in the camp. Even Vance knew nothing of his arrival or departure."

"You should have told me."

Colleen walked to one of the patio chairs and sat. "When, Chip?"

"When I came back from that sham patrol. Before we boarded the plane home. When we got home. I don't know sweety, but I should have known that some new guy was in my platoon. Especially one who made waves."

With her left hand, she swiped wet hair straight back from her forehead and gave her husband a serious stare. "Honey, we weren't married then. We weren't even dating. I don't mean to sound harsh, but you were just another platoon leader. One of several." Her face twisted into an anguished look. "I was directly ordered by a one star to do what I did and never speak of Miller again … not ever. At first, I didn't know what to do, then I figured it best to follow those orders. To this day, I have no idea why he was there. I just knew that order came from someone with more brass than Vance, and I wasn't wading into that crap."

Chip sat and leaned back in a patio chair. He nodded at his wife and, with a forced smile, said, "You did the right thing. The only thing you could do back then. Somebody's got to figure out why Cassidy Miller ended up in our platoon."

Collen raised an eyebrow at her husband, nodding in agreement.

Chapter 11

With Megan still at his desk, Peden dialed Rayshon Mack's number. Mack picked up on the second ring. "Mr. Savage. What can I do for you, sir?"

"Hi, Ray. The first thing you can do is call me Peden and knock off that 'sir' stuff."

"Okay, Peden. I can do the first name but 'sir' is in my blood. That one might be tough."

Peden smiled, knowing from his years in the Marine Corps how the use of 'sir' became a natural part of any response in discussions with practically anyone. "Just so you know, Megan Moore is with me and you're on speaker."

"Yes, sir. I mean, okay. Hi, Ms. Moore, ma'am." Megan rolled her eyes, not bothering to admonish Mack for the formality.

Peden moved right to the crux of the call. "We just spoke with Chip Chandler and asked him about the fight between Parish and Cassidy Miller. He said he didn't remember Miller at all." He paused to let Mack think about that. "During the call, he asked Colleen if she remembered him and she also said no. Can you think of any reason why they wouldn't remember someone from the platoon, especially in light of the tension surrounding Parish and the fight?"

Mack stayed silent for a moment. When he spoke, his words carried a tone of caution. "Cassidy Miller didn't come in with a splash, until the dust-up with Rusty. We all assumed that he wanted to be left alone and with our short-timer's attitude, we let him be. Everybody was walking on pins and needles, partly because of Rusty's attitude, and because our time in country was short. Nobody wants to get killed in their last few days over there. Breaking up the fight was the only interaction most of the platoon had with him. Shortly after that, he disappeared and we were headed home."

Megan asked, "When you say 'disappeared' what do you mean?"

"Exactly that. One day he showed up, grabbed an open bunk, gave Grumen a copy of his paperwork to let him know he'd been assigned to Rifle Team Charlie. Grumen let me know. Then, a day or so before we boarded a transport for the states, he disappeared. Him and his gear. Gone."

Peden asked, "Did Grumen let you know anything about his stint with the team?"

"No, sir. I mean, no."

"Did anyone else ask where he came from or why he was assigned to your platoon?"

"Not that I recall. Some of the guys tried to talk with him, but he kept quiet, kind of reclusive. Being older with a rank of private, most of us figured he'd been busted for something. When he didn't talk much with anyone, we left him alone."

"Until his fight with Rusty?"

"Exactly. Even after that, everybody gave him space, left him be."

Peden looked at Megan. She shook her head. Peden said, "Thanks, Ray. If we think of anything else, we'll call."

"Yes, sir." He paused. "Sorry. Old habits…"

When the call disconnected, Peden looked at Megan, who appeared to be deep in thought. Even more now, he believed that they needed to do some research on Cassidy Miller. Lee Sparks' database search skills came to mind. As he opened his mouth to suggest using Sparks, Megan said, "You need to get Lee digging into Cassidy Miller, see what we can find out about this guy. If he has a disciplinary record, it shouldn't be too hard to figure out why he ended up a private."

Peden looked at her and grinned. "Are you suggesting that we do an illegal search into military databases?"

"No, Peden. I'm suggesting that whatever you find, you use that information to get to the bottom of Rusty Parish's murder. How you get there, that's up to you."

Megan stood, grabbed her purse, and headed for the door. She didn't turn around, but waved over her shoulder.

As soon as the door closed behind her, Peden picked up his cell phone and hit speed dial for Lee Sparks. Lee answered on the second ring.

"Afternoon, Peden."

"Hey, Lee. You busy?"

"Nothing I can't put aside for a fat payday."

Lee Sparks contracted with Savage Investigative Consultants on a wide array of computer related services, some of which tiptoed on a thin legal line. Lee had to face it: sometimes he just hacked into databases to which he had no legal right. He always advised Peden on which side of the line his requests fell. In return, Peden left Lee to make the decision on whether to proceed or if the legal trouble might place the risk to his career and freedom above the value of the available information.

Peden told Lee the story about the drone strike and Parish's actions immediately after the strike. He described the tension at the camp centered around Parish in the aftermath, and Parish's subsequent death. When Peden got to the point where he, Megan, and others believed the death to be murder, not suicide, Lee stopped him.

"Hey, Peden, where are we going with this?"

Peden took a deep breath then continued, telling the story of Cassidy Miller and the altercation with Rusty Parish and his subsequent disappearance. Then he got to his instructions for Lee.

"I need for you to do a search on this Cassidy Miller character. We know he was in the Marine Corps in September, 2011. He transferred into the platoon, got into a fight with Parish, then transferred out. The problem is, the person who should have known about his transfers says she doesn't remember a guy named Cassidy Miller. That's why we need to dig up as much information on him as possible."

Sparks mind was already formulating a plan. What databases should he begin with, how should the search terms be set, what kind of security should he expect to encounter? After a few seconds of silence, he asked, "I suppose you need this information yesterday?"

"As soon as you can get it, my man. If you find something of consequence, send it right away. Once you think you've gone as far as you can, send me the whole package. Checks in the mail."

"I'll keep you updated."

* * *

Frustrated after three hours of searching, Lee Sparks pushed his chair back from his keyboard and looked up at the white ceiling, trying to focus on the rosebud pattern of the drywall, just to give his mind a break. Seldom did he ever come up empty with his searches, but when he did, he doubled down on his efforts and the redirection usually paid off.

Not this time.

Lee had searched numerous Marine Corps databases, including those from bootcamp, various military schools, deployments, disciplinary records, and discharges, both honorable and less than honorable. He found no references to anyone named Cassidy Miller.

Knowing that Navy Corpsman deployed with Marine Corps units, he expanded his search to include Navy Corpsman records. The expanded search netted a blank. He found similar names in his searches, but none close enough within the date range that would place these personnel anywhere near Afghanistan at the time of Miller's assignment to Chandler's platoon.

Lee stood and headed towards his kitchen to grab a beer and something to eat when his cellphone rang out in a musical ringtone. He had been running numerous database searches for over three hours and had nothing to show for his work. He figured Peden wanted to know what he had found so far. But when he looked at his cell phone's screen, it said *restricted.* Sparks frowned, then answered the call.

"Sparks."

A baritone, business-like voice asked, "Mr. Sparks, why are hacking into databases to which you have no legal authority?"

Lee was taken aback. Not only had he performed his searches covertly through complex paths, he had firewalls in place to prevent tracing programs from following the source of his searches back to him. If this person tracked him down, they had superior skills, indeed. Since Lee hacked government databases, this could spell serious trouble. He had to think fast before responding.

"You must have the wrong number."

Sparks listened for a split second then disconnected the call. Immediately, his phone chirped again, the same message of *'Restricted'* appeared. He let it go for a few seconds, then answered, "Sparks."

"Mr. Sparks, if you hang up on me again, you will only add to your already serious situation. Listen to me, and listen good. Cease all searches for Cassidy Miller, whether they be from military databases or otherwise. If you do not heed this warning, you may face serious charges. I won't list them now, but trust me, hacking a federal database is the least of your worries. Am I making myself clear."

"Yes, but who are you and who do you work for?"

"You just do as you're told. We already know who you're working for. Give Mr. Savage our regards."

The call disconnected. Sparks just stared at his phone, dumfounded. He sat in his chair, thinking about his next move. He had already hit a dead end on his searches, so it would not be too difficult to comply with the caller's demand. He planned to call Peden to inform him of the lack of results anyway. Since the caller already knew he worked for Peden, Lee had no reason to contact him covertly.

He hit the stored number for Peden on his cell. Peden asked, "Hey, Lee, what do you have for me?"

"A boatload of trouble and nothing good."

* * *

Lee's tone left no room for levity. He described the call from the unnamed person from an unnamed organization, but who most likely worked for one of the many alphabet-soup federal law enforcement agencies with serious resources and superior IT talent. Sparks's talent with computers ranked exceptionally high relative to even the best hackers in the world, but he used those talents for good and never profited personally from his electronic adventures. Being caught in the middle of a database search had never happened to him before, so he knew the folks who detected his probes to be as good, or better than he.

Sparks continued, "On a more negative note, I did complete all the searches I could think of for Cassidy Miller and came up empty. Either the military purged his records, or the guy never existed. I'm leaning towards the latter."

"Ray Mack said the guy was real. He helped break up a fight …" Peden stopped in mid-sentence, putting pieces together as he spoke. "You think Cassidy Miller may have been planted in the platoon?"

"Yeah. Yeah, I do. But I've got no idea why. Not even a clue."

Peden's mind shifted into overdrive. He knew that Rusty Parish's death sat at the fringe of something bigger. But how much bigger?

"Thanks, Lee. I think you should take the caller's advice and back off the searches. We'll talk, soon."

* * *

After Spark's call, Peden decided to call General Vance. He wanted to compare Mack's, Chandler's, and Vance's versions of the strike. He punched in the number from the list provided by Chandler. The phone rang five times before switching to voice mail. Peden hung up and hit redial. Vance answered on the second ring.

A gruff, loud voice said, "Vance."

"General Vance, my name is Peden Savage. I'm looking into the death of …"

"Randall Parish. How did you get this number?"

Peden saw no reason to try to hide the source so he said, "Chip Chandler."

"This is a private number for official Marine Corps business. Parish was a civilian at the time of his death. I'll deal with Chandler later. What do you want Mr. ..."

"Savage. Peden Savage. I'd like to get your version of the events surrounding the drone strike on September 11, 2011."

"That information is classified. You don't have a need to know. Good-bye."

"General, Please, do not ..."

Vance had disconnected the call.

Chapter 12

Megan had left Peden's office just three hours earlier after Rayshon Mack swore to the existence of one Cassidy Miller. Peden had hoped to leave her alone for the remainder of the evening. He would have if not for the troubling call from Lee Sparks. He pondered what agency had the IT resources to detect Lee's probes into their databases and why they had not sent a team to arrest him immediately. Sparks mentioned that the caller knew Peden had directed the searches, so why had they not contacted him to determine the reason he ordered his technician to perform the searches in the first place? Regardless, contacting Megan about this turn of events could not wait. She needed to know about the incident and he wanted her opinion on the whole affair.

Megan answered his call on the first ring. "Pedee, I just left not three hours ago. This must be bad."

Peden's dark tone imparted the serious nature of his call, "Yeah, it is."

He needed to choose his words carefully, making sure Megan did not have direct, recorded knowledge of Sparks' activities. She knew his searches were, at times, close to legal boundaries but she could not be linked to them in any way, through direct or indirect communication.

"First, Lee didn't uncover any information on Cassidy Miller. It's as if he never existed. He certainly was never in the Marine Corps. That's bad news, but after he finished his searches, somebody called him ordering him to cease and desist."

A moment of silence filled the line, then Megan asked, "When you say 'somebody,' what exactly do you mean?"

Peden, his voice laced with anxiety, replied, "Lee said the caller, a man, would not identify himself or what agency, if any, he worked for. He also said the guy knew that I had ordered the searches. How would they know that? How could they know that?"

"Did Lee get a phone number on his cell?"

"Nope. Just the word '*Restricted.*' " He tried to do that thing where you can dial star something or other, but he said that didn't give him any results. I think we're dealing with one of the Fed spook agencies ... no offense."

"None taken." The silence on the line stretched for nearly ten seconds then Megan finally said, "I think we may have stumbled onto something larger than a former Marine's murder. Do you know if Lee had active searches on databases at the time he got that call?"

"No, he didn't. He said he had finished all the searches he could think of and planned to take a break when the call came in. He said the guy meant business, no nonsense. He had a threatening tone, though he never made a direct threat."

"At least they didn't break his door down ... or yours. If it was a federal agency and they wanted to bust Lee or you, they probably would have taken the time to gather more information, establish all the necessary pieces for a search warrant, then raid Lee's and your offices. Just me thinking out loud here. I think they might want you to back off so you don't screw up whatever it is that they're doing. It's what I would do under similar circumstances."

After Megan paused, Peden had to agree that her thoughts made sense. But how could the death of a Marine Corps Private – a former Marine Corps Private – be related to an investigation by an unidentified federal agency, if the caller even belonged to a federal agency?

"Why now? Why did a search for Cassidy Miller raise any red flags for some agency? It must relate back to the drone strike and Parish's actions. Or did Parish know something that he shouldn't have known? Is that even reasonable to raise that question after all these years?"

"Pedee, I think I need to have a chat with our boss. I'll give him a heads-up on this change. I think he'll have some words of wisdom for us."

"Do you want me in on the call?"

Megan thought for a moment then agreed that he should participate. "You have more direct knowledge of what this mystery caller said to Lee. Roland's probably eating dinner right now. Give me about fifteen minutes and we'll do a conference call."

Roland Fosco, Megan's direct supervisor, had been Peden's boss at the FBI. Fosco had been instrumental in helping Peden set up his investigative services business as repayment for Peden remaining silent on a potential scandal within the FBI's Savannah, Georgia office. Fosco kept his promise to deal with the issue quickly and quietly and Peden's business thrived, making it a win-win for all involved: except for the fired and disgraced agents no longer employable in law enforcement.

After the call disconnected, Peden stood and headed for the kitchen at the back of his office to grab a beer and the other half of a sandwich that had been in his refrigerator. At 6:40 p.m. his stomach growled. When he reached the refrigerator, he opted for a bottle of cold water along with the sandwich, thinking that he needed to keep his head clear. Returning to his ancient desk, he sat, leaned back, and stared at the ceiling, mentally arranging pieces of a puzzle to which he had no final picture for a guide. *This is like working on a puzzle with missing pieces. Then pieces from another puzzle get dumped on the table.*

He opened the wrapper for the leftover combo sub sandwich and took a bite. He started thinking about the drone strike, Parish's reaction to the attack, Grumen's rebuke, and the altercation with the mysterious Cassidy Miller. Ten years later, Parish is killed and Chip Chandler wants to honor him with a military funeral. Maybe Chip's insistence that the platoon honor a guy who at one time put the entire platoon in danger rubbed someone the wrong way. But how would any of the platoon members know of Sparks' searches? And why would those searches elicit such a strong response from someone monitoring military databases? 'Strong' didn't fit. 'Odd' seemed better. Maybe he and Lee should expect a stronger response soon. But why would Lee be warned to back off versus be raided for illegally hacking a Department of Defense database for someone named Cassidy Miller? Or, more to the point, who claimed to be Cassidy Miller? *Who is this guy?* Apparently, Cassidy Miller had never been a Marine. Maybe he never existed and if he never existed, why did a guy with a fake military identification show up in Afghanistan and confront Parish?

His head began spinning with all the loosely related bits of data. He finished his sandwich and downed a long gulp of water. Then he picked up a stack of blank three-by-five note cards and began writing a single piece of information on each card. He had a dozen cards filled out when his cell phone chirped. Megan.

"Hey, Megan."

"Peedee, I'm bringing Rollie into the call."

After a moment, Roland Fosco said, "Peden, how are you?"

"Hey, Roland. I'm fine. Just reading the tea leaves, trying to make sense of this pile of information."

Megan jumped in, "I filled Roland in on the call to Lee and everything we have related to Parish's death. I'll let him tell you what he thinks."

After a few seconds, Roland Fosco cleared his throat. "First, I agree with you and Megan, that you've stumbled upon something much bigger than a former Marine's death. I am going to make some calls and see if I can find out what organization has concerns about the, uh, inquiries you've been making."

Peden did not miss the tone of Fosco's comment and the placement of the pause. Fosco knew very well about Sparks' computer knowledge and capabilities. He wanted Peden to know that Sparks should be more cautious in the future.

"One thought: the Marine Corps falls under the Department of the Navy. The law enforcement arm with jurisdiction is NCIS (Naval Criminal Investigation Services). They aren't a large agency, but they have highly skilled investigators, including IT technicians. Just a thought."

Peden's eyebrows shot up in surprise. He had not thought about NCIS. He said, "Good point, Roland. All this started with a scuffle at a Marine Corps camp half a world away. Any idea what crime they might be investigating?"

"No idea, Peden. But I bet it isn't murder, at least, not a recent one. I'd keep digging, but I'd watch where I put my shovel. You might just hit a landmine."

Silence filled the line for several seconds. Then Fosco said, "Megan, keep me informed of your progress and any significant changes. I will let you know what I find out from my end. Peden, I have officially put Megan in charge of the FBI's investigation into this matter, whatever it is. This is off the books for now. Both of you, proceed with caution."

Peden replied, "Yes, sir. Thanks Roland."

Megan added, "Thanks, Roland."

After Fosco disconnected from the call, Mega asked, "Pedee, you still there?"

"Yes, ma'am."

"I didn't say anything but that tidbit about NCIS makes a lot of sense. I don't know why we didn't think of that. Maybe there's just too many moving parts and too much time difference from the start of this to where we are now."

"I was thinking about that before you and Roland called. It occurred to me that Randall Parish somehow knew the wrong house had been hit by the drone strike. I don't know how, but what if he knew? What if some higher-ups knew it, too, and heard about Parish's fit after the strike. Maybe those higher-ups sent Miller in to get in Parish's face and find out what he knew."

"That's a lot of 'what-ifs' and 'maybes.' But I like how you're thinking." A pause. "Do we have information on who was killed in the drone strike?"

"I don't. I didn't think to ask. I mean, this started out trying to determine if Parish really committed suicide by overdose. This thing is growing bigger by the minute."

Megan sighed. "I'll find out what I can. Lee doesn't need to have any more spotlights shined on him right now. Mack said they killed some high-level Taliban and Al Qaeda leaders. That should be easy to find."

"You would think so. Let me know if I can help."

Megan said, "I'll call you later, Pedee."

"Hey, Megan, wait a second. I don't think I should let Chip or Ray know about the call to Lee. I have a feeling someone is holding out on us. Somebody knows more than they're letting on."

"I'll let you decide on how much you should let them know."

When Peden disconnected the call, he looked back at his index cards. He shuffled the stack and randomly placed the cards around his desk: just a bunch of data-points spread out before him. He put both elbows on the desk, clasped his hands under his chin and reviewed the information. No great revelations leapt off the cards, so he began to arrange them by timeline. Then by person. Still nothing.

There's got to be a connection. We're missing some big pieces.

Chapter 13

The back-and-forth banter on the BIAChat social group started with civility where most members agreed to attend Rusty Parish's funeral. Some even offered their assistance with expenses for the service. As Chip Chandler scrolled down the screen, he watched the wave of posts and believed that the support from almost all his former platoon members would sway the few, most ardent, and vocal opponents of the plan. His hopes blew up in smoke when Jeff Grumen initially voiced his displeasure which quickly grew to anger. Chandler believed that Grumen could have kept his feelings to himself and just not shown up at the service. Instead, he decided to air his grievances openly in several posts to the group.

Grumen: I can't believe this crap. I'm stunned. How can we openly support Parish after what he did back in country? His actions could have gotten us all killed, for no reason. He disobeyed a lawful order to mind his post and help carry out our mission. We should have given him a beat-down. Then he should have been thrown out of the Corps on his ass for what he did. And I think many of you agree with me. You're just going along to get along. Grow a pair!

Carmine Russo agreed with Grumen.

Russo: I'm with Sarge on this. Why in hell would we honor this guy? He betrayed us, he disgraced his uniform, getting drunk all the time, getting in everybody's face. This is BS. Why should I – WE – support his ass??

Several other members began to post retorts at the same time, most in support of Parish, stating that the change in his personality and behavior happened after he had received news of his parents' sudden deaths. They empathized with him experiencing that hardship on top of their already stressful situation in the Afghan desert. One member mentioned that he understood the stress all Marines faced, but Parish's challenges went beyond those of others. Grumen responded by asking how anyone of them could know the outside stresses faced by any of their fellow Marines. They just made excuses for Parish.

As the discussion continued, the harsh level of the rhetoric jumped several notches. Members typed in all caps with exclamation points, then the name-calling started: wimps, pussies, and worse. Insults heaped on top of angry words escalated until Chandler had enough. He began to type a post asking for everyone to cool it when General Vance entered a post ordering everyone to stop. Two posts showed up after the Vance's order, but Chandler suspected that they had already been executed before Vance demanded a stop to the discussion. Chandler held his breath, waiting for a follow-up from the general. It did not take long.

General Virgil Vance rarely participated in discussions on BIAChat because enlisted men comprised the largest segment of members. But for this occasion, at Chip Chandler's urging, he posted his support for the ceremony, strongly expressing the need to formally honor their brother and fellow Marine. Hearing the gutter-level of some remarks, Vance apparently felt he needed to put a stop to it and remind his fellow Marines of the brotherhood they all shared, even after release from their active-duty commitment.

Vance: Maybe you've been out for a while, maybe you haven't. We are all Marines – all of us – and Randall Parish was our brother. No man left behind. He wasn't perfect – not one of us is - but we honor, support, and fight for each other to the end, even after our official commissions or enlistments are over. I can't order you to be in Georgia to support our fallen brother, but I hope you remember who you are and who Parish was – a Marine. I will be there for him, as I will be there for each and every one of you. Oorah!

Chandler read the general's message. He hoped it would sink in and convince the vocal holdouts to drop their openly negative comments. If they chose not to attend, so be it. But the message clearly came through. You are a Marine first and foremost. Act like it. Be there for your brother.

Multiple posts responded – *Oorah!*

Chandler waited for fifteen minutes. No further entries popped up in BIAChat. Either Vance's message worked, or Grumen and Russo chose to let it go.

* * *

Dusk approached by the time Chip Chandler signed out of the BIAChat room. His gloomy mood matched the dark office area making it difficult to see the computer's keyboard. He sat back and thought about the exchange between members of the platoon. He had hoped for a smooth discussion. But he realized that several of his Marines still bore deep resentment at what Parish had done the day of the strike with complete disregard for the safety of his brothers. He knew that many found the memories impossible to erase and Parish's actions unforgivable.

Chandler thought it best that he burn-off some energy and hopefully clear his head. He donned swim-trunks and dove into the pool. Colleen had already showered and dressed in a white tank top, powder blue shorts, and flip-flops. She sat in the lanai drinking a rum and coke. watching her husband as he had watched her earlier.

It was not like Chip to let his emotions get the best of him, so when he passed her heading towards the pool with his brow furrowed, she returned his look with a concerned glance. He thought it might be a good idea to stop and talk about the heated exchange on social media, but he believed he needed to calm down first.

Early evening had arrived, the pool and the surrounding area bathed in bright lights, backdropped by the dark night sky. Chip threw his towel on a lounge chair and dove into the shallow end without hesitation. Getting into a rhythm, he began his even, smooth strokes, breathing in a set pattern, gliding through the water with ease. The workout would be evident to the muscles in his arms and chest once he completed his goal of thirty laps.

The primary source of the angst that caused Chip to need a dip in the pool came from the bickering between his old platoon members. One purpose of having the funeral, at least in Chips eyes, had been to bring the platoon together, to share stories, to help some members get past the mental anguish that gripped their brains. Some suffered PTSD (Post Traumatic Stress Disorder). Others simply longed for the comradery a tight-knit group, like a Marine Corps Rifle Team, provided. Chip understood the need, though he had not personally suffered from such afflictions.

When the discussion in the chat room began to fall apart, as comments became insults, his frustration level rose quickly. He wished he could ask several of his team members about Cassidy Miller and what they remembered about him. General Vance most likely did not know anything about Miller, and he did not want to raise the topic in a group setting.

As he made the turn for his third lap, his wife's admission that she really did know about Miller began to irritate him. What other secrets did she have? According to her, she had been ordered by a general from outside of their chain of command to keep information about Miller strictly to herself. They had not been dating at the time. In fact, it would be nearly a year later before they began dating. Should it have come up before Parish's death forced it to the surface? Maybe, maybe not.

After thirty laps, he slowed at the wall in the shallow end where he began, feeling the welcome tightness in his upper body, particularly his chest and shoulders. During the final ten laps, the calming effect of the workout helped clear his mind, but as he hopped out of the water and reached for his towel, thoughts of the argument in the chat room came right back.

* * *

Colleen watched her husband as he dried off, noticing the furrowed brow return. She worried that her revelation about Cassidy Miller might harm their relationship. A strong urge to approach him and talk more came over her, but she thought it best to wait and let things settle between them.

She had signed into BIAChat and followed the comments from Chip's platoon members, the tone of the discussion not surprising her at all. She understood why several members were upset, even more than her husband, but she could not reveal their reasons to him … yet.

* * *

Moska Aziz smiled. Monitoring the posts of the Marine platoon in BIAChat pleased her, but also caused concern. Most platoon members planned to attend Parish's funeral. She had hoped Grumen and Russo would make the trip, but suspected that they had good reason not to attend. There are many ways to overcome such obstacles. The pair could be dealt with separately from the others, which might provide a higher level of satisfaction for her and Aslam.

Her thoughts shifted to Aslam Sayed. *What should I do about him?* She needed his skills to complete her plan, but his demeanor - acting like a trapped rat every time they met in public- drew far too much attention. She did not want to meet with him in private. He had the attitude of most men with similar Muslim upbringing, that women held an inferior position in life compared to men. She could tell that he did not like taking orders from her. Each time they met, his attitude of superiority jumped up a notch, even though she had to remind him to remain calm, act normal, fit in with his surroundings.

She could not help but compare Aslam with his older brother, Amir, who had been killed in the explosion from the drone strike. Amir had been the man of her dreams, a visionary for the future of Afghanistan. He had imagined a country free of war and aggression from other nations. He had written down strategies to slowly westernize Afghanistan while appeasing religious leaders. He believed that the tribal communities of the country could come together and form a government body that worked for the common good. He also believed in a country that would embrace peace while establishing an economy that worked for the people and created a military force capable of repelling invaders. His hopes and dreams evaporated in a literal cloud of smoke.

Every time Moska thought of Amir and his untimely death,

her resolve grew to exact revenge on the men and women who killed him, and essentially, destroyed her life. They had killed Amir and his sister - Moska's best friend – and almost everyone in their family. Only Aslam survived, though he suffered severe injuries.

It pained Moska that Aslam would make himself expendable by his words and actions. His public displays of fear drew too much attention. Once they carried out their plan, she believed that his fear would grow. There would be no way to calm him, therefore he would become a danger to her and her daughter, Mina. She felt sad that she must protect her daughter from Aslam. Mina's heart would be broken when the time came that he would no longer visit and Moska had to make up a plausible reason why.

Chapter 14

Centreville, Virginia - the perfect location for employees of the federal government in and around Washington, D. C. to buy a home and raise a family. Eastbound Interstate 66 made the drive into the metropolitan area relatively easy. With MATA's (Metropolitan Area Transit Authority) planned expansion of the trainlines out to Centreville and beyond, any federal employee would be wise to include the area as a relocation option. Virgil Vance and his wife, Evelyn, made the decision to purchase a beautiful brick home with a three-car garage in the growing area just after he achieved the rank of Brigadier General. He believed that his assignment to the Pentagon would guarantee, as much as any military assignment possibly could, that he would remain in the Washington, D. C. area for the remainder of his career.

Vance's wife agreed with the decision to buy in Centreville. Nearby Manassas, Virginia, being her childhood home, she knew the area well. Her father had retired from the Marine Corps, so her parents were elated when she met and married Virgil Vance, an up-and-coming Lieutenant. Her sister had warned her that marrying Vance held many disadvantages, among them, his time deployed overseas. But the larger issue came to pass when Vance arrived home from his third deployment in Afghanistan. He spent most of his time at the Officer's Club, drinking with his Marine Corps buddies instead of coming home to his wife. The loneliness hurt, piercing her heart, turning her emotions from that empty feeling into bitterness.

Her sense of isolation grew even more when she heard rumors that her husband left the club with young ladies, some young enough to be his daughter. She thought about hiring a private detective to have him followed, but instead decided to go out with wives from the neighborhood. Over time, she found her own one-night-stands. She kept her cozy, married life intact and enjoyed the company of interesting, younger men.

Word finally found its way back to Vance that his wife had cheated on him. He would not have been angry, except that her dates were usually at public places before heading out to a hotel or to the men's homes. When he confronted her, she threw it back in his face, called him a hypocrite, and let him know that so long as he played the field, she would do the same. They settled into an uncomfortable norm, acting like a married couple in official, social situations, morphing to cohabitating singles the rest of the time. He had asked her to use discretion in the company of her dates, to which she replied that he should have thought about that before he decided to cheat on her.

Tuesday morning at 8:15, Evelyn Vance received a call from Moska Aziz. The young woman had become friends with the general's wife over the years. Moska listened to Evelyn's sob stories, providing Vance's wife a shoulder on which to cry. Their bond grew as she assured the distraught woman that the pain of her husband's infidelity would fade as she focused on her own romantic trysts and any other interests that she might have. Not only did her prediction turn out to be true, Evelyn Vance enjoyed her new lifestyle to the point where she could care less about her husband's extra-marital affairs.

Evelyn had her phone on speaker in the master bath as she applied the day's makeup. The calls from Moska always perked up her mood as they chatted about her most recent "date" and the fun she had with a vibrant young man.

"I'm telling you, Moska, James – he goes by James, not Jimmy or Jim – was so full of himself. He should have gone on a date with himself. He talked about his car and his money, which came from the family business, all night. In other words, he's mooching off his daddy's success. But he was polite and not too bad in the sack."

Moska made a point to sound surprised at Evelyn's confession of her sexual exploits. "Girl, you are so bad. Let's back up. Where did he take you for dinner?"

For the next twenty minutes, the two women talked about Evelyn's night on the town. They giggled together like a couple of high school girls as Evelyn gave her a moment-by-moment replay of the evening's events. As their call continued, the details grew steamier. At one point, Moska yelled "oh my god" so loud that Evelyn feared that her husband might hear them.

Evelyn heard the heavy footsteps of her husband coming down the hall and, into the phone said, "I've got to run. The hotshot is coming."

"That's alright, dear. I'll talk with you tomorrow, unless you're too tired to talk."

They both laughed as they disconnected the call.

Virgil Vance entered his wife's bathroom. They had not shared the same bathroom, much less the same bedroom, in many years.

"You didn't have to hang up from your little boyfriend just because I'm here."

Evelyn looked at her husband's reflection in her mirror and smiled, a look of mischief covering her face. "I haven't had a 'little man' in quite some time; probably the last time I slept with you, dear." She looked back at her own reflection then asked, "What brings you into enemy territory?"

Virgil still shook his head at his wife's attempt to belittle him. Being used to her cutting comments, he ignored her sarcasm and said, "We will probably have to fly down to Georgia to attend a funeral for one of our Marines. It looks like Thursday or Friday."

"When you say we, you mean you and me? Is this some kind of formal event that requires me to be there?"

Vance's condescending smile at one time would have had the desired effect of making her feel stupid, but those days were long gone. Now she just ignored them, waiting for the message behind the façade. When he did not get a rise out of her, he said, "Yes, it is an official event: the funeral of a Marine veteran."

Evelyn Vance knew the commitment it took to be a Marine wife. Few civilians could possibly understand the hardships endured by the military family. She had tremendous respect for Marines and their families. In a less snarky tone, she asked, "Who?"

In an equally solemn tone, he said, "Randall Parish." He cleared his throat and continued, "Rusty had a difficult time transitioning to civilian life. He fell on some hard luck and just couldn't figure out how to get it together. He never asked for help, though one of our fellow platoon members tried like hell to help."

"I'm sorry, hon." And she truly was sorry. She felt a heaviness in her heart at the loss of any Marine because she knew that the family of that service member would suffer. She did not know that Parish had no family left, but that did not matter.

She took a deep breath and turned to her husband. "I don't think you really need me on this trip. I'm not sure what I can do in Georgia that I can't do from here. None of your Corps brothers will care if I'm not there so long as you're there."

Vance's face turned serious. He really did not want his wife on the trip but believed that others would have their wives with them. Being the senior man at the ceremony he believed that Evelyn should be at his side. In a voice that, in retrospect, he thought to be too harsh, he said, "Just pack and be ready to go by mid-Thursday. I'll get your ticket." Vance's voice rose, showing his impatience with her attitude. "All you have to do is act like my loving wife, show empathy towards others for their loss, and try to not solicit any of the attendees. Can you just do that?"

Showing a bit of anger, she practically yelled, "You've got a lot of nerve. You started this whole damned .... Nevermind." She took several deep breaths and said in a monotone, "If you can keep your dick in your pants, I can play my part."

Vance shook his head as he turned away from her and said quietly, "Thank you. Good God."

Evelyn turned back to the mirror and started to break down, but she caught herself with several deep breaths and a shake of her head. *How did it come to this? God, this sucks.* She continued to apply her makeup, thinking of the trip to Georgia and who among the other wives might be there. She had not seen any of them in years. *I know. Colleen Chandler. I'll give her a call first. She's probably been in touch with some of the wives.*

She forced a smile and looked herself over in the mirror again. The lines were getting harder and harder to coverup, but overall, not bad for a woman her age. She could still get younger guys in the sack - not much of a bar to clear. She blew herself a kiss with her newly made-up lips.

Walking out of her bathroom to her spacious bedroom with her phone, she found Colleen Chandler in her contacts and hit the call button. Colleen answered on the second ring with a cheerful, "Evelyn, good morning. How are you?"

"Living my best life, dear. And you?"

"Staying healthy, working with Chip, as much as he'll let me."

Evelyn did not waste time on pleasantries and jumped right to the point. "I heard that Chip is running the show on Randall Parish's funeral and that he wants as many of the platoon at the funeral as possible."

"Yes, that's true. He's hoping to use the gathering to soothe some hard feelings. He knows … we all know that Parish's actions over there made a lot of the guys angry, especially those on that mission."

Evelyn let a silence drag on for several seconds then said, "I think the guys were right to be angry, but your husband's also right to try and get everyone to let the past stay in the past, especially with Parish's passing. I mean, he's dead, there's no changing what happened."

Evelyn waited for a response, but none came. She continued, "Are you accompanying Chip to Georgia?"

"That's the plan."

"Do you know if any other wives or spouses are planning to attend?

Colleen had to think for a moment. She had not asked Chip about how many spouses might attend. Having some of the wives there might force the tension level down. "I'll have to ask Chip. I honestly don't know."

"Can you ask Chip to let Virgil know? He wants me to attend with him, but I don't want to be the only woman there. Of course, if you go, I wouldn't be, but it would be nice if others joined us."

Colleen knew of the current marital situation with the Vances and understood why Evelyn might not want to make the trip and be the only female in a sea of men. On the other hand, she might meet one of the general's subordinates and have a go. *Wouldn't that be a hoot?*

"Either Chip will contact your husband, or I'll call you back. It probably won't be until tomorrow, at the earliest. Assuming we're both there, we'll have to get together for a drink, just the two of us."

"I'd like that, dear. Bye, and stay healthy."

Chapter 15

The sun had risen to just above the horizon, the light filtering through the trees on West Liberty Street in Savannah, Georgia, streaming into the office of Savage Investigative Consultants. Sitting at his desk at 8:30 in the morning, Peden noticed the unwelcome distraction of floating dust particles glistening in the sunlight. Something poked at the back of Peden's brain, tapping, trying to break through, but the thought lacked any semblance of clarity. Too many pieces of information floated around in his brain, like the dust particles in his office. No links, no pattern, just particles, or in the case of the investigation, bits of data.

He just finished his plate of scrambled eggs, bacon, and hash browns, along with his second cup of coffee, whose lingering aroma filled the space. After dropping the dirty dishes in the dishwasher, he returned to his desk with a fresh cup of brew. While eating, he pondered the growing list of questions that needed answers. If the pieces of Chip Chandler's puzzle linked in any way, he and Megan had a lot of work to do. He needed to decide what key piece of data he might use as an anchor to which he could begin tying other information. He pulled the stack of three-by-five cards from his desk drawer and began laying out his previous notes, trying to imagine where events could be linked. It would be a long, tedious day.

A dozen cards had notes. On one card, *Drone strike on terror leaders.* On another *Parish reaction – wrong house.* Another - *Parish alleged suicide.* Still others – *Parish not a drug user*; *coroner saw no evidence of drug use*; *C. Miller altercation with Parish*; *C. Miller unknown to platoon except Rayshon Mack*; *Colleen Chandler admin for platoon*; *Sparks cannot find C. Miller*; *Sparks told to stop searches for C. Miller.*

Peden noted that Cassidy Miller's name popped up on many of his cards. How can a man who does not exist come up so many times? Could he have been part of a covert operation? Why else would no one know about his brief stop in Chandler's platoon? Certainly, the platoon's admin clerk would know of transfers in and out. Why had Colleen told her husband that she had no recollection of Miller? Was she lying? If yes, what possible reason would she have to cover up her knowledge of Miller being there?

He placed a blank three-by-five card in front of him on the desk and wrote, *People who knew of Cassidy Miller.* Below the statement he scribbled five numbered blank spaces. In the first space he listed Rayshon Mack. Then he made a mental note to find out who else knew of Cassidy Miller.

One more thought occurred to him: Cassidy Miller confronted only Randall Parish. Why no one else? Was it because of Parish's caustic personality? His drinking? What possible connection existed between Miller and Parish? Could the mysterious Cassidy Miller be Parish's killer ten years later?

Using a blank card, Peden wrote *Missing link-Parish to Miller.* On another blank card he wrote *Was it really the wrong house?* He mumbled to himself, "If we hit the wrong house, Rusty, how did you know?"

"Know what?"

Megan Moore's voice cut through the silence in Peden's office. He looked up as the front door to his office closed behind his former FBI partner. She took a seat in front of Peden's desk. He did not bother asking her if she would like a drink. She scolded him in the past that she knew her way around his kitchen and could take care of herself.

Peden returned Megan's serious look. "Private Parish. If we bombed the wrong house, how would he have known? That kind of intel didn't filter down to the grunts. You received orders and you did your job."

"What makes you so sure they bombed the wrong house?"

"I'm not sure. I *think* they bombed the wrong house. Chip told me they bombed the wrong house. His interpreter and his family lived in that house ... according to Chip. He wanted an investigation into the bombing, but the official report declared the mission a success. It would be nice to know the targets names. Most likely, that is classified at some level."

Megan remained quiet, contemplating Peden's train of thought. As she opened her mouth to speak, her phone chirped. Holding her phone, she said, "Rollie," then swiped across her phone's screen.

"Hi, Roland."

Peden watched as Megan listened to her boss. He could not tell the nature of the conversation - good news or bad - because Megan's expression rarely changed. He would just have to wait until she either ended the call or put Fosco on speaker.

After a full minute of listening, Megan said, "I'll relay this to Peden and Lee. Anything else?"

A brief silence before she said, "Thanks, Roland. We'll call if anything breaks."

With the call disconnected, Megan said, "Rollie made some agency-to-agency calls. Officially, no one knows anyone named Cassidy Miller."

"Officially?"

"Right, officially. But when he finished his call with his counterpart at NCIS (Naval Criminal Investigative Services) in King's Bay, he received an anonymous call saying that his inquiries were making some folks nervous. If we keep poking around, looking for Cassidy Miller, we might step on some high-level toes. The caller wouldn't identify himself or what agency he represented, but he strongly suggested that the FBI back off. He mentioned you by name."

"You mean, Rollie is ordering me to stand-down?"

"No, Peden. The caller said that you needed to order Lee to stop the database searches for Miller."

Peden's eyebrows shot up in surprise, then came down into a frown. Clarity flooded in. Some agency sent an agent under the name Cassidy Miller to dig up something at that Marine camp. Parish's murder must have some connection to Miller's visit, but they just did not have enough information to determine what.

"Some anonymous caller from an anonymous agency ordered Rollie to tell me to back off. Again, is Rollie ordering us to stand-down on the murder investigation?"

Megan looked straight in Peden's eyes. "No. He wants us to continue what we're doing, just stay out of the *federal* databases. We need to figure out another way to find Parish's killer."

Silence filled the office as the two began pondering just how they might continue the investigation with these new restrictions. It made an already difficult investigation even more challenging, but Peden knew they had been in tough situations before. They just needed to dig deeper, but more quietly. He would contact Lee Sparks and change his marching orders, but first he and Megan needed to agree on a new approach. As he muddled through the news from Fosco, he looked at Megan, seeing her concentration. He knew she would formulate the beginning of a plan that they both would massage. His next actions included contacting the platoon members to whom he had not yet spoken. The list included Colleen Chandler, Jeff Grumen, Carmine Russo and a few others.

Megan broke the silence. "You call Lee and tell him to continue his searches, but he must stay out of any federal databases. I think the official term is "shall" stay out of federal databases. Also, have him look for newspaper and magazine articles for stories about terror leaders killed on September 11, 2011. If their mission to kill Taliban and Al Quada leaders was successful, that should have made the national news here in the states. Politicians love to brag about stuff like that. Weapons-based drone technology made headlines back then."

Peden nodded in agreement.

Megan continued, "Your old buddy, Chip, didn't believe the suicide story about Parish. You think he might have more reason to doubt that Parish took his own life; that maybe something from back in Afghanistan – bad blood between a couple Marines – might have swayed his opinion?"

Peden looked up at the ceiling, thinking of his calls to and from Chip. The last time they spoke, Peden wondered about his hesitancy in answering the question about Cassidy Miller. More to the point, he wondered about his wife's lack of knowledge of a Marine in their platoon. Could that have been what had tickled his brain before Megan arrived?

"I'm calling Chip and Colleen back. Everything points back to this Miller guy and we can't even verify that he exists, except by Ray Mack's account. I'll call Mack and a couple other guys from the platoon. That should finish the call list from Chip. Maybe they can shed some light on this Miller guy."

Megan pushed a strand of blond hair behind her ear, again in deep thought. When she shifted in her chair, she said, "You need to be awfully careful, Pedee. If someone from a government agency knows you by name, that your employee is performing *database searches,* meaning 'hacking into' private, possibly classified information …."

"Say what you mean, Megan."

"We might be dealing with folks who might have already killed once. If this mystery person had anything to do with killing Parish, we need to watch our backs."

Peden took a deep breath, then nodded. He knew Megan's instincts to be spot on. Extra precaution – good advice.

Megan stood and headed for the door. Without another word, she left, allowing Peden to make his calls. First up – Lee Sparks.

Lee provided no new information for Peden, but the frustration level in his voice spoke volumes. He took the news of a change in direction without argument. After all, Peden paid his salary. He let Peden know that he would begin the search for the names of the assassinated leaders right away and hoped to have results later in the day.

Next, Peden called Jeffrey Grumen, former Marine Sargeant and squad leader for the rifle team that targeted the house hit during the drone strike. Rayshon Mack told Peden that Grumen handled Parish's outburst professionally, and kept the rifle teams safe. He expected to hear the same story directly from Grumen.

After just one ring, a clear, confident voice said, "Davidson Construction, Grumen."

"Jeff Grumen, my name is Peden Savage. I'm calling …"

Grumen spoke before Peden could finish, "About Rusty Parish. I've been expecting your call. What do you need to know?"

"I'll get right to it. Do you have any reason to believe that your team targeted the wrong house on September 11, 2011?"

"No, sir, Mr. Savage. First, let me say that there is no way that I would know for certain, even if we did hit the wrong house. But we had coordinates in our orders. Rayshon Mack and I verified those coordinates on the sighting scope, then we relayed that we had the target marked. Simple as that."

"Do you have any reason to believe that Parish knew information that would make him think you bombed the wrong house?"

Grumen laughed bitterly, with absolutely no humor behind it. He said, "Private Parish had no idea what the mission entailed except his job - guard our northern flank with about a dozen other Marines. His actions in the field surprised the hell out of me." Grumen paused, but continued before Peden could ask another question. "Frankly, Mr. Savage, I think Parish's drinking caught up with him to the point he could barely function. He should have been written up and court-martialed then dishonorably discharged. But somebody went soft on him. Were you a Marine?

"Yes. I served just before the towers went down, then I joined the FBI."

"Then you know the drill. You follow orders. You do your job. You don't ask questions. Parish couldn't do that."

Peden waited a few seconds, then asked, "Did you know a Marine private named Cassidy Miller? He joined your platoon for a brief time just before your platoon came back stateside."

Peden waited as the silence grew. Finally, Grumen said, "No. Never heard of him."

"I'm surprised, because Rayshon Mack said that Miller and Parish scuffled in their quarters and that you helped stop it. You sure you don't remember?"

"Yes, sir, I'm sure. I remember everything about Parish during that time period. I'm sure I would have remembered somebody named Cassidy Miller."

Peden said, "Mr. Grumen, thanks for your time. Keep this

discussion between you and me."

"Yes, sir."

With the call disconnected, Peden wondered why everyone came down with a case of amnesia regarding Cassidy Miller.

Peden then dialed the number for Carmine Russo but no one answered. Frustrated, he went back to his three-by-five cards, adding a new card: *Cover-up?*

Chapter 16

Sitting at his home-office desk, Chip Chandler's brain worked overtime on Tuesday morning, September 14. The overcast morning sky only helped to darken his mood as he thought about events going back over ten years. Growing up in Sevierville, Tennessee, a career in the Marine Corps had been his life's dream. His father, also a former Marine, served during the Vietnam War. A strong brute of a man, he earned numerous medals for valor and injuries sustained during his time in country. The elder Chandler's body shrank from two-hundred-twenty pounds to nearly one hundred pounds when he succumbed to lung cancer before Chip turned sixteen. Chip's mother advised him to stay out of the military, believing that a similar fate awaited her son, but Chip believed otherwise and could not wait to finish college and pursue his dream of being a Marine Corps officer.

Less than six years after receiving his commission, his attitude soured considerably. After returning home from his second deployment, one with high tension and much personal, internal conflict, Chip strode into his commanding officer's office and submitted his paperwork to resign his commission. After receiving a gruff, five-minute dress-down from his boss, he reasserted his desire to resign, turned and left. As he walked out his commanding officer's door, he bumped into a female Marine officer heading into the same office. Apologizing for his inattention, he looked up and recognized Captain Colleen Temple. He smiled, and at a loss for words, stared at her. She broke the brief silence, saying, 'Fancy meeting you here. What brings you to the big guy's office?' He replied that he submitted his letter of resignation from the Corps. She smiled, extended her hand to show him her resignation request. He warned her that the boss might not be in a good mood, receiving two resignation letters within moments of one another. Chip got his wits together and asked Colleen out for a drink. They married six months later and have been inseparable since that chance meeting.

Thinking back over the several years of their marriage, Chip realized that he and Colleen never fought. They did have serious discussions about money, family, children, even religion, but neither raised their voice above a normal conversational tone. They thoroughly enjoyed each other's company and trusted each other without question – until now.

Colleen's revelation that she knew about Marine Private Cassidy Miller's presence in the platoon and that she had been ordered to keep even his existence to herself made Chip wonder what else she may have kept from him. Her explanation that they did not even know each other well at the time seemed plausible and there was no reason to discuss the situation before now. The murder of Rusty Parish brought all the drama, tension, and animosity of their time in Afghanistan to the surface. Things that should have remained buried in the past somehow exploded into full display. The nasty discussion in the BIAChat room exposed the deep mental wounds and subdued anger that his Marines harbored against one of their own.

He had hoped Rusty Parish's funeral might help the healing process for men exposed to situations no one should be forced to endure. But it appeared the fanfare only ripped away scar tissue and lay bare the anguish beneath the surface, suppressed by time and distance from the incident. He questioned if his idea of the platoon's support of Parish at the funeral might be ill-conceived.

Movement at his office door caught his attention. Colleen stood in the doorway, leaning against the wooden frame, holding mugs of coffee in both hands. A quizzical expression across her face, she looked at Chip as if waiting to be invited in.

"You're going to let my coffee get cold if you don't come in."

"How do you know it's coffee and how do you know it's for you?"

"It has to be for me 'cause I kicked your boyfriend's wimpy ass and sent him packing."

A smile came across her face as she slow-stepped to his desk, bringing his coffee around to his side. She set both mugs on his desk then bent down and kissed him full on the lips. The kiss was soft, sensuous, and long. When Colleen pulled back slowly, looking at her husband with alluring eyes, in a soft, sultry voice, she whispered, "This coffee's gonna wake you up, but that doesn't mean we can't go back to bed." She kissed him again, this time with a touch more passion.

After a moment, Chip pulled away, looked into his wife's eyes, and said, "You drive a hard bargain, and I hate to throw cold water on this moment, uh, but I have a client coming any minute."

The doorbell rang and broke the spell. Chip asked his wife, "Can you answer the door? I have to calm myself so I can function properly."

With a quick kiss on the lips, she whispered in a taunting manner, "I'll get the door, but remember where we left off."

With a soft touch to his cheek, she left his office and headed for the front door to welcome one of their clients. Chip took a sip of piping hot coffee and sighed. He hoped he could keep his thoughts straight during his meeting. His client's net worth exceeded twenty-five million dollars. He shook his head and, with a smile, stood to greet the casually dressed, elderly gentleman. As the man entered the room, Chip saw his wife blow him a kiss over the man's shoulder. Chip's smile grew, knowing that his work day would end on a positive note.

* * *

The meeting lasted until 11:30 in the morning with the wealthy client bragging about his life, fortune, home, cars, and business. Chip mentioned numerous times that another client would be arriving soon without specifically telling him to leave. That would have been rude. Colleen saved the day when she called Chip's phone and told her husband to put the call on speaker. When he did, Colleen said, "Chip, your next meeting is scheduled to start at 11:40. Do you need me to ask your next client to reschedule? They just called and they're on their way."

Chip looked at the gentleman who shook his head and, with a smile, said, "No need. I have a lunch date at Ironclad. My grandson should be finishing up a round on the links by then. He wants me to meet his new girlfriend. Looking for my approval, I guess."

After another five minutes delay, where his client thanked him for the fine job keeping his fortune growing, the man left. Chip watched as he pulled his Mercedes Benz onto Route 17 south. After locking the front door and taking a deep breath, Chip headed to their bedroom. A sheet of paper on their bed caught his attention. He walked over and picked up the note which said, "Turn around." When he did, Colleen stood in the closet doorway wearing nothing but a tiny pair of red panties and a mischievous smile. Chip eyed his wife's body from head to toe. He tried to speak, but his mouth had dried.

Colleen said, "Lunch is on me … literally."

* * *

After forty minutes of intense lovemaking, Chip should have been in a post-coital fog, but instead, his mind turned to all the ugliness on the BIAChat discussion. His mood did not go unnoticed by his wife.

"Not the face I was expecting to see," she said, propping herself up on one elbow, looking into his eyes.

"I can't get this whole Parish thing off my mind. I mean … the comments about the funeral, the negative attitudes … sure, what he did … he screwed up. But that's all in the past. If guys don't want to support sending him off with military honors, I can understand that. Just don't show up. How tough is that? But to drag the guy down before his funeral …?

He turned to face his wife as she stared back, her face a mixture of concern and empathy, apparently at a loss for words. She rested her head on his chest and slowly rubbed his stomach. Chip could not concentrate on her attempt to calm him and clear his thoughts of the upcoming funeral with all the drama that might occur. At this moment, he was not sure the ceremony would happen at all. With the dissension among the platoon members and the fact that he did not know when, even if, Parish's body would be released to him, the timing alone might derail his plans.

Finally, Colleen spoke, "Listen, sweety, if it is meant to happen, it will. If it isn't as perfect as you envisioned, then it wasn't meant to be. You're doing everything you can to make sure Rusty gets proper recognition for his service to his country. That's all you can do. Right?"

Chip looked at his wife, kissed the top of her head and said, "Thank you. You're right. I'll keep trying to make it happen. I know some of the guys will appreciate it." He paused as he slid his hand down his wife's back. "After we get dressed, I'm calling Vance to get him to try one more time to convince the holdouts to participate and to tone down their comments."

Chip noticed when he said Vance's name, his wife tensed momentarily, then relaxed. He wondered why, but did not say anything. He kissed her head again and slid a finger lightly up and down along her backbone. She shivered and moved as close to him as possible, purring her approval. They stayed in bed another hour before showering and dressing for the afternoon.

* * *

While Colleen showered, Chip called General Vance's office, hoping to have a few minutes of the general's time. Vance's office assistant told Chip the general would call when his meeting ended, which should be about twenty minutes. Twenty minutes later, almost like clockwork, Chip's phone chirped just as Colleen walked into his office. She sat in one of the client chairs, watching her husband with dreamy eyes.

"Colonel Vance. Thank you for returning my call."

Colleen could hear only one side of the conversation as Chip asked Vance for his help with getting the troops on-board for the funeral. She heard the muffled sounds as Vance responded and watched Chip closely for his reaction. After a few more minutes, Chip ended the call.

"He said he would call Grumen and Russo personally and tell them to knock off the public comments about Parish. He would tell them he expected that they attend the funeral. Whether it would do any good, he did not know. They were no longer in the Corps, so orders no longer applied, but he said he would do his best."

She smiled at him and said, "That's why I love you so much. You don't do anything half-way."

Chip smiled at his wife, but it lacked conviction. He wanted to ask her why she tensed when he mentioned Vance's name earlier. He suspected that she held something back from him during their discussion, but they enjoyed such an intensely satisfying day so far, he did not want to spoil it. There would be plenty of time to pursue his questions over the next few days.

Chapter 17

The beautiful, sunny morning had Lee Sparks in a good mood, despite the call from some unknown bullies the previous day. He showered, ate breakfast, read his newsfeed on the computer, and initiated several data searches for Peden. With the air conditioner off, he opened all the windows to allow fresh, cool air into his condominium. The scent of fresh pine and an array of flowers from the neighbor's yard freshened his living and work space, all by the work of mother nature.

Sparks' three computers purred away, churning through data from major news outlets. True to his new marching orders, he avoided hacking into any government databases, agreeing with Peden that they should try to avoid antagonizing the unidentified caller. One search looked for a list of terror leaders from the Taliban and Al Queda. He believed that acquiring a list of enemies of the United States of America from the middle east would be an easy task. At least, it sounded easy. In reality, mining the data required specific parameters to narrow the inquiry so the search would get the desired results, not just a list of common middle eastern men's names. His frustration jumped a bit after the first search failed. Then a second search timed out due to too much data being retrieved. Finally, he managed to narrow the parameters adequately so that the search returned the desired results. Having the list for reference would be an important part of identifying the terror leaders targeted in the drone strike. The list held over five hundred names, all spelled in such a way that Sparks wondered if he would be able to decipher the information. He shook off his negative thoughts and reminded himself that continuing to narrow the parameters would direct the computer to do all the hard work.

As he monitored the screens crunching through the searches, he thought about his inability to find this Miller character. Concluding that Cassidy Miller must be a cover name, he wondered how he might set up a computer search to identify the man who assumed the Cassidy Miller identity. After realizing no starting point existed, he abandoned the idea that his computer could provide an answer. He then thought there must be a traditional method to identify and locate Miller. Surely records existed that logged his arrival and departure to and from the platoon. Someone maintained those records. He knew the information could not be electronic because he already performed all the data searches. Peden must have thought about the human trail already, but it would not hurt to ask him.

As he picked up his cell phone, the computer search for news stories dinged, indicating a completed search. Sparks sat at his desk, reviewed the on-screen information, and clicked a few keys to display the results. *Bingo*!

One story appeared in the New York Times. Two short paragraphs describing a drone strike in Afghanistan that purportedly killed a Taliban Leader and an Al Queda leader. The story, titled *Terror Leaders Killed* in a font not much larger than that used in the body of the article, took up very little space. Buried in the lower right corner of page ten in the front section of the paper, it must have gone largely ignored except for avid readers of the Times. The names, Taliban leader Mawlawi Abdul Badri and Al Queda leader Abu Al-Madani, meant nothing to Lee. He initiated another search using their names. Within minutes, several news articles displayed, detailing the terror activities over the lives of the two leaders. All the articles predated September 11, 2011, the date of the drone strike.

Clear pictures of Badri displayed in the articles, showing a man with crooked, stained teeth, and a sneer on his gray-bearded face. The man's dark eyes looked evil to Sparks, even in a picture.

All pictures of Abu Al-Madani were blurry, grainy, and out of focus. The man's bearded face, even in the low-quality photos, appeared scarred and angry. One picture displayed an evil smile with several missing teeth.

Sparks thought for a moment about what he planned to tell Peden. He figured that he and Megan would want to know about the names of the leaders killed in the strike and his belief that no computer search would yield what they wanted to know about Cassidy Miller. He picked up his cell and hit speed dial for Peden, who answered after the first ring.

"Lee, my man, what have you got for me?"

"Hey, Peden. A couple of things. First, the two leaders killed in the drone strike are Mawlawi Abdul Badri and Abu Al-Madani. Badri is Taliban, Madani is Al Queda. They both were leaders on the military side of their respective organizations. The articles say Madani was more militant, more aggressive. The only article I found about the success of the drone strike was in the New York Times, buried on page ten. It didn't get much fanfare."

"Interesting, but at least we know the strike really happened and they supposedly hit the right building. That doesn't explain Parish's actions after the strike: why he believed they hit the wrong house, and why Chip also believed it."

"You're right about that. There has to be more to the story, but maybe Parish didn't know as much as he thought."

Sparks paused, thinking Peden might have more to say on the subject. When the silence dragged on for a few seconds, Sparks went on, "Anyway, the other thing. The computer searches aren't going to get us anything more about Cassidy Miller. If it is a fake name, maybe part of some covert op, no search, even in federal databases, will get us what we need, and you barred me from those databases anyway. You might want to ask the platoon members more questions about that."

"Thanks, Lee. Megan and I figured as much. We planned to head down that path today. Let me know if you find anything interesting about our dead terrorists. It just throws more puzzle pieces into the mix. Nothing seems to be coming together in this mess."

"I'll keep digging."

With the call disconnected, Sparks began reading the articles about the dead terrorist leaders. Both men participated directly in attacks on U.S. interests in the middle east and other countries around the world. Both had a hand in setting up training camps in countries hostile to the west. One article named successors to the two men. On a whim, Sparks copied the names of the new leaders and initiated a data search of news articles. He stopped the search and removed the date restriction so that all stories with these new names would be searched. He looked back at his other computers with searches in progress, noting that they still churned, no indication that they neared completion.

He yawned and stretched, rubbed a hand over his close-cropped hair and headed for the kitchen, planning to brew another pot of coffee. When he opened the cupboard door where he kept his coffee and filters, he heard his computer ding. His recent search completed already.

Shaking off the messages from his brain for more coffee, he made his way back into his office and looked at the monitor displaying the search results for the new terror leaders. A counter informed Sparks that over twelve hundred stories from a wide variety of news sources contained the names of the men who replaced Badri and Al-Madani. He took a deep breath, thinking about the best way to sort the results and make the most efficient time reviewing relevant information on the terrorists. He decided to sort the stories by news outlets. Then he would begin reviewing the stories by major news outlets. The twelve hundred stories came from just over one hundred news outlets or syndicated organizations, such as the Associated Press and Reuters.

Sparks brought up the first article from the Associated Press. The article appeared in multiple major newspapers across the country and included pictures of Badri's presumed successor and several of his subordinates in the Taliban. The story described an attack on a military outpost where half a dozen western contractors were killed and their bodies mutilated. The writer, Brandon Wilson of the Associated Press, described the mutilations as barbaric.

Sparks moved on to other articles about the Taliban, but most contained repetitive stories written by Wilson. It appeared that many of the news outlets believed the reporter to be an expert on the Taliban and other splinter groups. Sparks performed a quick search on Brandon Wilson. A short story by the Associated Press, published by many major news outlets, announced the horrible, tragic death of Brandon Wilson, describing him as a brave, top-notch journalist, dedicated to his profession. He died from carbon monoxide poisoning January 2021, just eight months ago.

After becoming bored by the repetitiveness of the articles, Sparks moved to smaller news outlets and magazines. The basic information in these outlets appeared to be similar, but the reporting had a partisan leaning, attempting to appeal to one political ideology or another. The target audience became obvious the further he read into each article.

These articles had more pictures of Taliban and Al Queda members performing atrocities from simply beating women exposing too much skin, or killing bound and blindfolded enemy combatants, on their knees in front of a mass grave. Each of the pictures had dates and the name of the photographer. Most of the blurry photos had been taken from a distance while others appeared remarkably clear.

At first, Sparks focused on the victims of the atrocities: men whose crimes no one would ever know, committed only in the minds of the Taliban victors. To them, a court of law did not matter. The death sentence came from one of the religious or military leaders, many times being the same person.

He shifted his focus to the Taliban men carrying out the executions. Their actions appeared to be mechanical, mindless, void of any emotion. Just another chore. The next set of pictures displayed women with shovels, brought in to bury the men. Were these women the new widows? Were they forced to bury their husbands?

Angry, Sparks moved to the next series of pictures, concentrating on the faces of the men with guns. About eight men carried out actions directed by two other men. The two leaders appeared to point and give orders to the others. That is when something caught his eye.

"It can't be."

He looked at the date of the picture and the photographer credit. March 21, 2016. Photo by Harlan Wilson – Associated Press. The picture was not the best quality, but Lee Sparks thought he was looking at a picture of Mawlawi Abdul Badri who had supposedly been killed in Kabul, Afghanistan in a drone strike on September 11, 2011.

Chapter 18

Jeff Grumen stared at the half-empty bottle of Jack Daniels Black Label No. 7, giving up the fight to avoid taking another shot of the dark liquor. His resolve disintegrated well over an hour ago. He thought the pressures in his life would ease once he left the Marine Corps. After all, what could be more stressful than facing an armed enemy hiding in the hillsides along the narrow dirt paths they called roads in that God-forsaken country, Afghanistan? That idea fell apart when his father-in-law hired him into the family business, expecting that his military leadership background would translate directly to being a foreman at Davidson Construction. Not only did Grumen have to learn the ins and outs of commercial construction, the politics of being inserted into a workforce that already functioned like a well-oiled machine frustrated him. As a foreman, he immediately drew the ire of men who were in line for promotion to the foreman position, but now, due to their age, had little-to-no-chance of taking charge of their own construction crew. They did not blame Grumen for ruining their future opportunity at promotion, but he became the target of their disdain. Their animosity hung in the air every day.

While the men and women who worked for Davidson Construction respected his service to the country, they knew it would be a long trek bringing Grumen along, helping him learn the finer points of the business. His natural instincts were to give orders that he expected would be followed. Learning that private sector employees did not follow orders like Marines came as a surprise. Two of the company's more senior men pulled Grumen aside and tried to explain that the civilian world did not work that way. They told him that employees make suggestions on ways to do things better. He should give their comments consideration, at least until he learned the business better. Lacking the experience in the construction world meant that he might have to rely on the knowledge and proficiency of his crews. That did not sit well with him, causing frustration and more than a few near-physical altercations. Grumen still worked out daily, keeping his body in top physical condition, his frustration with his job prompting him to work that much harder. He knew hand to hand combat and might have seriously hurt any of his fellow employees who might be foolish enough to challenge him, but the situations defused as cooler heads prevailed.

Now, sitting alone in his basement "man-cave" in Hilliard, Ohio, Grumen stewed and drank. He thought he might have been better off staying in the military. Surrounded by Marine Corps memorabilia on one wall, Ohio State Buckeyes on another, three professional grade gym machines at one end, and an eight-foot tournament-sized pool table in the center of the room, his pickled brain churned. Should he have divorced his wife and let her follow through on her threats to leave him and take their daughters with her? He poured another shot of black label and downed it in one motion. The longer he wallowed in his pity, the more he detested the position she put him in; either leave the Corps or lose her. He already lost her to her family anyway. Little more than a hired hand given a token position in her father's business, he felt less in control of his life with each passing day. He had more control back in Afghanistan when he shouted out orders to his men and they were carried out without question. *The civilian world should run more like the military. There'd be fewer wimps and we could put this country back on track. Everyone respected me back there, except those two; punk-assed Parish and that wimp, Russo. They should have kept their mouths shut.*

Grumen's brain focused on Carmine Russo, the guy who tried to act like he supported him, but just wanted to cover his butt for the many mistakes that he made back in country. He followed his sergeant around like a puppy dog, waiting for a chance to show his loyalty. He did not sit quite as high on Grumen's shit-list as Parish, but not far below. The guy just did not know when to keep his mouth shut.

Once again, he filled the shot glass to the rim and sucked down the brown liquid, finishing by slamming the shot glass on the coffee table. The bang reverberated around the basement like a gunshot. He heard steps moving quickly on the floor above, expecting his wife, Cora, to open the basement door at any moment, to check on her husband.

As if on cue, Cora called down to him, "Honey, are you all right? I heard a loud noise, like something fell over."

Grumen wanted to tell her to go screw herself and stay the hell out of his space, that he was fed up with her crap; and screw the rest of her family, too. Especially her dad. Pulling him into his company so he could have his little girl close by. *Screw him. Screw the whole bunch of 'em.* If the last two shots of Jack Daniels made their way to his brain, he might have told Cora exactly what he thought of her and the family business. But some of his senses remained intact.

In a slightly slurred, gruff voice, he replied, "Everything's just fine. Just … just thinking about work."

"What was that loud noise?"

She questioned his answer. He told her everything was under control. Why couldn't she just leave him alone?

"I tipped over a …" he looked around the room looking for something that might make a loud noise, but not be of concern. "a pool cue. I accidentally kicked it with my foot and it hit the concrete. I'm fine. I'll be up in a bit."

A few seconds passed where he knew she listened for anything that might cause concern. Then he heard the door to the basement close and her footsteps return to where she had been before he slammed the shot glass down. He grunted then looked at the bottle. He struggled to sit forward in the comfy chair - his chair - in his man-cave. He deserved this private space. Why did she violate his privacy? Anger began to bubble up in his mind as he leaned forward to reach for the bottle. He picked up the shot glass and began to pour when his cell phone belted out a ringtone.

"Shit. Who the … just leave me alone."

He looked at the screen – *Restricted*. He swiped the red handset to disconnect the call before it began. He turned his attention back to the bottle, but his cell phone rang again. The same message came up on the display. *Maybe it's one of the guys about the funeral.*

He swiped the green handset, put the phone to his ear, and in a gruff, slurred voice said, "Yeah?"

A sensuous female voice that he did not recognize said, "Jeffrey, how are you?"

He paused before answering, fighting the effects of half a fifth of whiskey, trying to place the voice. He asked, "Who is this?"

"You know me, Jeffrey. We met many years ago. Don't you remember?"

His mind already in a fog, he could not place the voice. He asked, "Where did we meet?" He paused as the last two shots began to take effect. He sat back in his chair, still holding the cell phone to his ear.

"You're starting to remember now, aren't you? Listen, someone wants to say hello."

As Grumen waited, the room began to move, swirling. He grabbed the chair's arm with his free hand, but that did little good. The alcohol began to outpace his ability to stay in control. He heard a tiny voice over his cell phone.

"Hi, Daddy."

Daddy? Who the hell is this? Did Cora have one of the girls call me? But the voice sounded nothing like his daughters. They were in their teens. This voice sounded younger.

"Who is this?"

"It's me, daddy. You remember me, don't you?"

Slurring his speech heavily now, he growled into the phone, "Little girl, I don't know who you are, but I ain't your daddy. You got that?"

The woman's sensuous voice replied, "That's not very nice, talking to your little girl like that. All she wanted to do was wish you well. She wanted to ask you if she could come see you."

Grumen, losing what little control he had, shouted into the phone, "Who the hell are you?"

"Don't worry, Jeffrey. We'll meet again soon enough. Good night."

Into the phone, Grumen shouted, "Don't you hang up on me, you bitch. Who are you?"

He listened to silence, then noticed the woman disconnected the call. He turned to throw his cell phone across the room when he noticed Cora standing at the bottom of the basement steps, staring at him as if he were a madman. She looked directly at the half empty bottle of whiskey, then turned, and ran upstairs.

Grumen fell heavily back into his chair and passed out.

* * *

Moska Aziz smiled at her cell phone after disconnecting the call to Jeffrey Grumen. Pleased with her performance imitating her young daughter's voice, she set her phone down and walked into her condominium from the patio. Nine-year-old Mina sat at the kitchen table reading the last few pages of a book, a fresh glass of water sitting within arm's length. Moska smiled at her brilliant daughter, knowing Mina had become self-sufficient in so many ways. She still needed her mother, but in just a few years, that would change. The time would come when her friends would be the most important part of her world, but for now, Moska savored the time she could spend with her little girl.

"What are you reading, sweetheart?"

"It's a mystery. Nancy Drew."

"Wow. Tell me about it."

Mina began to describe the story to her mother. As she described the way the story began, Moska's mind wandered to the tasks that lay ahead for her and Aslam Sayed. There could be no mistakes. She could not leave her precious Mina an orphan. She heard Mina's voice and refocused on her child's description of the adventures of Nancy Drew. She smiled, but the smile held a twinge of sadness knowing that her need for revenge might cause her to lose her daughter forever.

Chapter 19

Chip Chandler waited patiently on the phone. He had called the Optim Medical Center and requested to speak with the Medical Examiner, Dr. Daniel Erin. After spending over ten minutes navigating their electronic call operator – *If this is an actual emergency, hang up and dial 911. For office hours, please press 1, for directions to our facility please press 2 ...* - When he finally spoke with an actual receptionist and asked to speak with the Medical Examiner, she informed him that Dr. Erin might be as long as half an hour. Chip explained to the woman the reason he needed to speak with Dr. Erin and said that he would wait.

And wait, he did. After twenty-five minutes of poor-quality elevator music filled with static that repeated after one minute and twenty-two seconds – yes, he timed it to the second - another receptionist came on the line and said, "Dr. Erin will be with y'all momentarily."

Two minutes later, Dr. Daniel Erin came on the line and asked with more than a touch of attitude, "How can I help y'all Mr. Chandler?"

"Thank you for taking my call, Doctor. I'm calling about Randall Parish and when I might be able to take possession of his body."

"Linda did mention we have a very busy schedule today, right?"

"Yes, in fact she did, and I told her I would wait until you had a break."

With a sigh that sounded more like impatience and a moment of silence that followed, Chip felt like the medical examiner planned to wait until he would give up and call back some other time. Dr. Erin gave in and said, "Just a moment, please. I'll have to retrieve his file and do a very quick review of where we stand."

The line went silent while Chip waited. *At least I don't have to listen to the nauseating music.* In less than a minute, Dr. Erin came back on the line. "Mr. Chandler, we're still waiting to hear whether there are living relatives who might claim Mr. Parish's remains. Until we have exhausted all avenues, we can't release the body to y'all. If there is anything else ..."

Chandler expected as much, but he wanted to pin down exactly when the doctor's office would complete their search since he already knew they would never find any living relatives for Parish.

He cut Dr. Erin short. "Doctor, I can appreciate the need to follow procedures and the law, and I'm not asking you to ignore those requirements, but I'm working with the Veterans Administration to schedule a funeral in a veteran's cemetery. We have potentially dozens of people, his former platoon members, coming to honor him and many of them need a specific date range to make travel arrangements. Do you have a date when your search might be complete?"

A lengthy silence ensued, the only sound, the pounding of computer keys. Finally, Dr. Erin replied, "I believe that if we do not hear anything by the end of the day, today, we can refer Mr. Parish's case to the Board of Distribution of Cadavers. They meet Friday at 9:00 in the morning. I sit on the board and assuming we receive no information on next of kin, the board would certify that y'all can claim the body then."

Dr. Erin turned the call back over to his receptionist who briefly reviewed the procedure for taking possession of a body and how to get Parish's remains to whatever facility would handle preparation of the body for burial. The entire process seemed laden with red tape. He wondered how anyone ever made it to their final resting place.

Chandler thanked Dr. Erin's receptionist and told her he would be in touch. In turn, she said that they would keep Chandler informed when the board finished with Parish's case.

With the call complete, Chip took a deep breath and looked at the clock. He initiated the call nearly an hour ago. At least now he felt closer to the point when he could schedule Parish's funeral. He looked up the number for the Veteran's Administration cemetery in Glennville, Georgia, and punched in the digits on his cell. Expecting an automated selection menu, a man's voice with a strong southern accent surprised him.

"Glennville Veteran's Cemetery. Cecil Parsons. How can I help y'all?"

"Uh, yes. My name is Charles Chandler. I'd like to schedule the interment of a Marine veteran. What do I need to do to make that happen?"

"Umm … when did you need for the deceased to be interred?"

Chip thought for a moment then replied, "Would it be possible for next Friday, September 23?"

"Well, that depends. We need to have y'all fill out the proper forms. We'd need a copy of the deceased veteran's DD-214 and a death certificate. There are a few other requirements. For instance, a funeral home must prepare the body for burial. Will the remains be cremated or buried in a casket? Don't answer. Most of this is covered on the form. Are y'all a relative?"

"No. I'm his former platoon leader. I'm working with the Screvn County Medical Examiner to take possession of the body. Mr. Parish, the deceased, has no living relatives."

There was silence on the line for several seconds, then Cecil asked, "When will the body be released to ya?"

"Possibly as soon as this Friday."

Chandler could hear the rattling of keys on a keyboard. Then Cecil said, "Since y'all are not a relative, y'all'll need the ME and the Board of Distribution of Cadavers to certify by affidavit that y'all have taken possession of the body and we'd need a certified copy of that document. I would also suggest that y'all line up a funeral home right quick to take care of the body's preparation for burial. I can give y'all the names of a couple local funeral homes that might be willing to slip y'all in. That might help speed up preparation of the body so that y'all can meet next Friday's target."

"Thank you … uh … what is your name?"

"Cecil Parsons. I run the cemetery here. It's a small operation. It's just me and a couple part-time guys. All three of us are retired veterans, so it's more of a sense of duty to us than a job."

"Thanks, Cecil. I appreciate this."

"Before ya hang up, let me get y'all's email address and regular address and I'll send y'all copies of all the forms y'all'll need. If you have questions, y'all should have my number on y'all's cell phone. Y'all're calling from a cell phone, right?"

"Yeah. I've got it. Thanks again."

With the call disconnected, Chandler shook his head. A lot of work laid ahead just to take possession of Parish's body with the load of required paperwork. A busy slate of appointments for his business awaited him in the coming days. Most of those could be rescheduled, but some of his clients may not like it. Regardless, he took this task upon himself and he swore he would see it through. Parish would get a proper military burial. He felt he owed him that much.

He quickly reviewed what he learned this morning and felt confident that the funeral and interment would take place on Friday, September 24. The next step – contact the platoon members via BIAChat. He hoped that the exchange would be less contentious than the previous session.

Chandler sat in front of his computer and opened his email. His eyebrows shot up as he noticed two new emails from the Georgia Veterans Memorial Cemetery in Glennville. One appeared to be a standard email thanking him for contacting the office. It also provided introductory information about the cemetery such as phone numbers, email addresses, and a website for people asking questions. The second email had four attachments. Chip decided to wait to open the forms and, instead, opened the BIAChat room app.

After signing in, Chip posted a brief message stating that he planned to lock in Randall Parish's funeral date for Friday, September 24 at the Georgia Veterans Memorial Cemetery. He hoped to schedule the funeral service for the morning. After waiting a few minutes, he added a new post with his plans to contact the closest veteran organization and invite them to participate with a color guard. A brief search revealed the American Legion Post 168 in Hinesville, Georgia to be the closest veteran support organization to the cemetery in Glennville. He also asked for volunteer pall bearers from the platoon. He finished with a personal appeal to his brothers that they wait one more day to make travel and lodging arrangements to ensure that the proposed date is set. He just wanted to give everyone a heads-up regarding Parish's funeral arrangements.

After posting his last remarks, he watched as a dozen members posted short remarks in support of attending the services, with two volunteering to be pall bearers. He took a deep breath and crossed his fingers that the positive comments would continue. He waited fifteen minutes more but no more posts were added. He would check later in the day, figuring that many of the platoon worked normal daytime jobs.

So far, so good. He signed out and headed for the kitchen, hoping to make loaded scrambled eggs, grits, and coffee. When he arrived, Colleen sat at the kitchen table eating yogurt, toast, and coffee.

He asked, "Mind if I join you?"

"Free country, Marine."

He smiled and poured himself a cup of coffee and began the task of making his breakfast. To Colleen, he said, "It looks like the funeral will be a week from this Friday in Glennville. From what I saw on the maps, there's no good hotels in Glennville, so we're probably going to have to get a block of rooms in Hinesville, Georgia. It's about a thirty-minute drive to the VA cemetery. They have an American Legion post there. I'm hoping we can get a color guard from the post for the funeral."

"When will you know for sure about the date?"

"I have several forms to fill out and get to the ME in Screvn County, then they'll release the body. With a little luck, and some hustle on my part, it looks like this Friday. Seems like a lot of red tape just to get a guy buried."

Still looking down at her yogurt cup, she said, "Let me know what I can do to help."

Chip wanted to say '*The first thing you can do is tell me what you're not telling me.*' But he held his tongue, thinking that the appropriate time would come, but right now did not feel right. Too many tasks on his plate and he did not want to take his mind off the objective: give Private Randall Parish a proper military burial.

Chapter 20

The new day started out overcast darkening all the rooms at Savage Investigative Consultants in the Bird-Baldwin House. The weather forecast called for sunny skies early then scattered thunderstorms later in the day. The humidity had risen from the previous day's moderately dry conditions, promising that any work activities outside would be a bit more laborious.

Peden Savage had just finished getting dressed when his cell phone vibrated. He looked at the display, saw Lee Sparks' name, and quickly swiped across the screen. He hoped Lee had good news regarding the searches for certain, dead terror leaders, and Cassidy Miller.

"Hey, Lee. What have done to earn your paycheck today?"

"Good morning to you, too, boss. While you were sleeping your life away, I ran all kinds of database searches ..."

Peden interjected, "Not in any government databases, right?"

In a mockingly staccato, military voice, he replied, "Yes sir, those were my instructions, sir." He shifted to a normal tone. "I found something that will change your mind about the drone strike. At least I believe it will."

After a brief silence where Sparks hoped Peden would beg for the information, he said, "You know those dead terrorists who were killed in the September 11 strike?"

"Yes?"

"Well, at least one of them is still alive."

Silence filled the line until Peden said, "Come again?"

"Let me back up. I found a very short news article about the drone strike - the 'successful drone strike.' The story had the names of two terror leaders: Taliban leader Mawlawi Abdul Badri and Al Queda leader Abu Al-Madani. I also found articles about the attacks that both of these guys had been involved in against western assets – military bases, oil refineries, ships – throughout the middle east. These guys were near the top of the leadership in their respective organizations. It makes sense that our government and others wanted them dead.

"Then I found a picture dated March 21, 2016, by an Associated Press photographer. The photo isn't real good quality, but I'm sure one of the guys in the picture is Mawlawi Abdul Badri, the Taliban leader supposedly killed in the September 11 drone strike."

Peden's mind raced. Could Sparks be mistaken? Lots of men from the middle east have similar physical characteristics; dark beards, sun-parched skin, wearing a turban. Maybe the picture simply resembles Badri.

"Peden? You still there?"

"Yeah, Lee. Are you absolutely sure, 'cause this changes a whole lot of our assumptions. I mean … official reports say this guy is dead. If he's not … what about the other guy, Al-Madani? Is he still alive?"

"I only found a picture of Badri. If Al-Madani is alive, he's staying off the grid. Badri's been lying low, too. No one has raised any questions about him."

Silence on the call extended for more than twenty seconds as both men processed the ramifications of a terrorist, once thought killed in a military operation, now being alive and well. Peden thought back to Chip Chandler's first call to him about Randall Parish's death, describing his actions after the drone strike. Chandler and Parish emphatically believed they had bombed the wrong house. The brief newspaper account that Sparks described lacked any detail, even less than Chandler had described to him. The news organization would not have printed the story without a press release or some form of confirmation, from the Pentagon … or would they? There did not appear to be a reason for the military to put out false information about a drone strike, especially with the military touting the use of drones as an emerging technology. They would want to announce their successes and keep failures from the press.

"Hey, Lee, send me a link to the article and the picture associated with it. Can you also find this Harlan Wilson and send me his contact information?"

"Already on its way, brother."

Peden smiled to himself and said, "You keep this up and I might give you raise."

"Hah. Like I haven't heard that before."

* * *

Peden called Megan Moore and relayed the information that he just received from Sparks. He also told her about his call to Jeffrey Grumen, who declared he never heard the name Cassidy Miller, and that he obviously held contempt for Randall Parish. As usual, she showed no outward reaction to the news. She asked Peden what he planned to do next.

"If Lee is right, and I have no reason to believe that he isn't, then it is possible that either Abdul Badri escaped the drone strike before the explosion or . . ."

Megan finished for him, "They hit the wrong house. If that is true, it takes us back to the big question: how does a private know details about a drone strike that his team leader and others up the chain of command didn't know?"

Peden added, "And if Badri escaped the strike, did Al-Madani also escape and where is he now? Does our government ..."

Peden stopped mid-sentence, realizing that the requests for Lee, Peden, and Megan to stop searching for Cassidy Miller might be directly tied to an investigation into the drone strike.

"Pedee, you're thinking that these terrorists are alive and that's the reason some unknown federal government organization wants us to back off? We might just turn over the wrong rock?"

Peden's brain tried to gather the puzzle pieces and arrange them in a logical order. If what Sparks said turned out to be true, then the government's intervention made sense.

There may be numerous logical explanations, but this one piece of data allowed him to connect several seemingly unrelated events. Other questions came to mind. Did the government also suspect, or know, that these two terror leaders cheated death? If yes, did someone kill Randall Parish to shut him up for good so he did not screw up their investigation? Would a government agency take such drastic actions? What good would it do to kill a man discharged from the military almost ten years ago? Even if he did talk, who would believe him?

Peden said, "I'm not sure that they're alive, but Lee thinks at least one of them survived the attack. We have to get a good look at that picture and compare it to photos of Badri. Remember, it's only one picture and Lee said it wasn't the best quality. We sure can't go to the FBI lab for help on this. So, we're on our own, unless our boss can get us some help covertly."

Megan took a deep breath, then said, "I'm not sure where he would take this. He did say for us to keep digging and Lee did stay out of official government databases, so he followed orders. Let's go talk with him before we go any further."

"Good plan. We'll look at the pictures ourselves." Peden paused, then said, "I wonder who has the authority to declare that a strike is a success, and who has the responsibility to declare that the targets were actually killed?"

"Might be a good question for Roland. But let's get with Lee first. Call him then call me back when you have a time for us to meet."

* * *

Peden and Megan walked into Lee Sparks' impressive home office. Multiple computers and other electronic devices emitted a low hum and produced heat they felt as soon as they walked in the door. Lee sat at one computer station rapidly tapping away at a keyboard. As he did, a large monitor's screen changed multiple times in just seconds. Sparks turned and welcomed his guests.

"Hey, guys. If you want anything to drink, you know where the fridge is."

They both shook their heads and waited for their host to finish what he started. Within seconds, Sparks stopped typing, stood, and walked to a copier, picked up several sheets of paper containing pictures and text. He handed two sheets each to his guests.

"The picture on the top left is the one that caught my eye. The one on the right is a stock photo of Abdul Badri from the Associated Press. That picture has been featured in lots of magazines and newspapers around the country." Sparks paused, allowing them a chance to look at both photos. After they looked up, he said, "Notice the facial discoloration on the right side of Badri's face, at the front edge of where his beard begins. At first, I thought it was a birth mark, but then I read a news article where he had been injured - burned, actually - during a battle in Iraq. That happened around the time he turned sixteen."

Sparks paused as he watched Peden and Megan look from one photo to the other. Peden's eyebrows raised as if seeing the similarity of the facial injury in both shots, though taken from different angles.

Lee continued, "There are tons of middle-eastern men with similar features, but this mark is unique. Even in the grainy picture, you can see the shape of the burn. It kind of looks like West Virginia with that spot that sticks out."

Peden and Megan both looked closer at the picture. They strained their eyes to see any detail in the grainy photo. Though the general shape of the mark did vaguely resemble the mark from the stock photo, Peden did not believe they could make a positive identification based solely on the mark.

He asked, "Have you contacted the photographer? Maybe he knows who the guy in the picture is."

"I thought I'd leave that to you, boss."

"What's his name?"

Sparks handed a slip of paper with a name, address, and phone number. "There you go."

Peden asked Lee's permission to call the photographer from Lee's office. Lee replied, "No problem."

Putting his cell phone on speaker, the three gathered around a table, waiting. After the third ring, a quiet, male voice with a southern accent answered, "Hello?"

Peden asked, "Harlan Wilson?"

"Yeah, this is Harlan."

"Mr. Wilson. My name is Peden Savage. I'm a consultant with the FBI. You are on speaker phone. I am with FBI Special Agent Megan Moore, and my IT specialist, Lee Sparks."

After a brief silence followed by a deep breath, Wilson asked, "Okay. What's this about?"

"We're calling about a photograph that you took of the Taliban executing a man in Afghanistan several years ago. It's been published in a number of news outlets."

An extended silence ensued. Peden asked, "Mr. Wilson, are you still with us?"

"Yeah, I am. I'm just wonderin' why, after all these years, the sudden interest in that photo."

Peden and Megan looked at each other, not quite understanding Harlan Wilson's response. Peden spoke, "Well, we were wondering if you knew the names of the Taliban fighters in the picture."

Another, shorter pause ensued, then Wilson said, "That's what the last guy asked, almost word for word."

Megan jumped in, "Mr. Wilson, are you saying that someone recently called about this photo?"

"Call me Willie, everybody else does. Next, to answer y'alls question, yes. A guy called me yesterday around noon and asked if I knew the identity of the guys in the picture. They were interested in one guy in particular - the guy with the mark on his face."

Peden and Megan were stunned. Megan asked, "Did the caller identify himself?"

"No, he didn't give me a name. He wouldn't answer any questions, but he sounded like a fed, like he worked for the

CIA or FBI, or some other secret agency from the government."

Peden asked, "What makes you say that?"

"Because he acted like he didn't have to follow the law, like I should just give him anything he asked. He even threatened me. Said if I didn't tell him what he wanted to know, I'd be real sorry." There was another pause. "Y'all don't work with this guy, do ya?

Megan answered, "No, we don't. In fact, we'd like to find him."

Lee jumped in, "Did he have a baritone voice that sounds like he should be on the radio?"

"Yeah, he did. How'd ya know?"

"He called me and threatened me the same way."

Harlan Wilson spoke, an edge in his voice, "I'd like to talk with y'all, but it has to be face-to-face in a public place, like a restaurant. My brother worked for the Associated Press as a staff writer. He wrote about Afghanistan, Iraq, the Taliban, Al Queda, and our involvement over there. He died under suspicious circumstances. I don't want to join him."

Megan said, "Name the place and time and we'll be there."

Chapter 21

Aslam Sayed sat at a table in the basement level of his apartment in Richmond Hill southwest of Savannah, Georgia. He lived slightly over three hundred yards from Moska Aziz, though he seldom saw Moska and her daughter Mina. She insisted that they not meet about business at either of their residences and that they minimize the time they spent at each other's apartments. Aslam visited her apartment many times, though most visits were after dark. She would not permit him to stay late to avoid talk amongst their neighbors, and she did not want her daughter to assume that a love relationship existed between the two. She told Aslam that the less they associate in their community, the better. She said that Americans were suspicious of anyone with middle-eastern physical traits, especially in the south. Aslam reminded her of the many times she accused him of exhibiting paranoid behavior. She responded that her actions were far from paranoid but part of a proactive measure to keep anyone from assuming they were part of a terror cell. Moska hid her heritage well, using makeup and her wardrobe to blend in with college-aged women. Aslam stood out in a crowd with prominent middle-eastern features even though he dressed casually in blue jeans and golf shirts. She told him many times that he could pass for a Latino, but her assurances did not convince him. One look in the mirror reenforced his concerns.

Since he lived alone in the modest two-bedroom apartment, it would be a stretch believing that he belonged to a terror group, a church group, a book club, or a group of any kind. He never entertained guests. In fact, he never allowed anyone in his apartment. The only foot traffic that darkened his door carried boxes marked with logos from Prime, FedEx, UPS, or food delivery services. He picked up mail from the communal mail boxes at the edge of the parking lot about two hundred feet from his front door. Since mail delivery to his complex usually occurred late in the afternoon, he waited until dark to collect what typically amounted to bills, junk, and parts for his projects that he ordered on-line. He seldom encountered or spoke with any of his neighbors. His English was passable midwestern when he concentrated, but when nervous, his Afghan accent seeped through. When hungry, he ordered out and had his meals delivered. He spent all his time alone in his apartment working on the task assigned to him by Moska.

Moska. He hung his head as he thought of her. Aslam, Moska, and her unborn child, Mina, were the only survivors of the bombing of his family's home. Fate intervened in such a peculiar way. She walked outside because her morning sickness overwhelmed her. He survived because he followed her, checking on her well-being. Amir had not been so lucky, perhaps seconds behind Aslam to check on Moska, standing in the doorway. Then all hell rained down on the Sayed family home, which exploded into small chunks of stone and dust, killing them all - except Moska and Aslam.

Moska. Just the thought of her raised his anxiety level. So arrogant, she believed herself to be superior to him even though he possessed the skills that she needed to execute what she called 'her plan.' She liked to take credit for the plan, but it really originated in his mind. Yes, she did have suggestions that improved the chances for success, and she kept her cool in public. *But it is my idea, my plan. If we fail, I will be the one who pays the ultimate price.*

Aslam thought about his dead brother, Amir, the one who had high hopes for his country. His hope that Afghanistan would one day return to the peaceful destination for tourists looking for historic and religious sites and artifacts. He strongly believed that the Afghan people would capitalize on their cultural centers, the sites that scientists studied. Amir Sayed had contacts with political and religious leaders. He worked diligently to convince those leaders to sit down together, to form a strong central government, one that could form a military with the might and weapons to protect its citizens. He dreamt big, and advocated big for the Afghan people. He could see the future in his mind and tried to instill that vision in the minds of others. Everyone listened to Amir. Though many disagreed with his vision of an ideal future for Afghanistan because of religious ideology or centuries-old tribal disputes, they at least gave him an audience and listened to his words, logical and full of hope. Even those who disagreed with what he believed to be the ideal future for his country, still believed Amir to be a leader. Many had hopes that his ideas could take their country out of the war-torn dark ages to a modern, self-directed country.

Amir. Everyone listened to his older brother. Just three years Aslam's senior, Amir's visions and intellect stood far above his and even their father's. Aslam wished he could have been more like Amir. Moska clearly loved him and had her sights on him as her future husband. When Amir spoke, Moska stared, mesmerized by his words, like a love-sick puppy. When Moska became pregnant, he wondered if Amir fathered her child. He doubted that his brother would be so foolish to impregnate his younger sister's best friend. The shame that such an act would bring upon the family would knock him from the pedestal of influence that he held. No, Amir did not father the child, though he did have his heart and mind set on eventually marrying Moska.

Aslam snapped out of his thoughts as his phone wailed the *Adhan*, his morning call to prayer. He looked up from the project on his desk to the picture of the inscription known as Mohammad, the Messenger of God. He grabbed his prayer rug, spread it on the floor in the middle of the room, knelt, faced east, and, in total concentration to Allah, recited his prayers. He asked for no guidance or clarity of thought, just peace of mind and a steady hand as he worked on his project.

After completing his prayers, Aslam sat back at his desk and looked over the schematic, verifying the wiring that he had already completed. He picked up the prepaid cell phone and punched in the number to another phone. The sheen of sweat appeared on his forehead. His mind raced, reviewing the wiring diagram in his mind. No sense delaying further. Watching closely, he hit send. An audible click sounded from the device on his desktop. The visible spark made his body jerk. His broad smile lit up the room as his improvised explosive device passed the first test.

The ringtone from his cell phone made him jump. He shook off the tension, laughing to himself at his nervous reaction. He looked at the screen – Moska.

"Hello, Moska."

"Aslam. You seem pleased with something. Should I ask?"

"Things are going as planned. There is nothing to worry about."

Moska said, "I wish that were true. The discussion in the chat room isn't going so well. It looks like a few of the men will not attend the service."

Aslam remained silent for a moment, remembering that he told Moska that getting all the platoon members together would be a challenge. She replied that they would make it happen.

He replied, "Do we know who?"

"Jeffrey Grumen and Carmine Russo. So far, all the others answered that they would make the trip. I don't think we should make any assumptions yet, but if they plan to skip the service, we'll have to make other arrangements for them – especially those two. The other key figure is Vance. So far, he will be there. In fact, he is encouraging the entire group to attend. He may yet convince Grumen and Russo to put aside their personal grudge and make the trip, if for no other reason, to show solidarity.

"Regardless, I think we should make alternative plans for those two. If anyone else backs out, we can take care of the others in the same manner."

This time Moska remained silent until Aslam asked, "We know where Russo lives. How about Grumen?"

"He lives in central Ohio, a suburb of Columbus. He has a wife and two daughters. The girls are young teens. He works for his father-in-law."

"Give me his address. I will do some research."

"Use caution, Aslam. We are very close."

Aslam did not like Moska's tone, her treating him like a child, like he did not know the stakes of his work. His work, if discovered by the American government, would mean prison … or worse. He feared for his safety anytime they met in public. He told her that they should meet in the privacy of his apartment, but she refused to listen. Maybe she feared that he would accost her once he closed the door to his apartment. He did not believe her excuse that they should not meet at their residences because of racism against Muslims. Millions of their Muslim brothers filled the cities of the United States. Their federal law enforcement agencies could not keep track of known cells of freedom fighters. *That is the true name for the many who fight to eradicate American and Zionist influences in the middle east.*

He replied, "I am always careful, Moska. Don't treat me with disrespect. I am not a child."

He could almost see Moska rolling her eyes at his rebuke.

She replied, "I meant no disrespect. We are very close to completing our work. Once we finish, we can decide where our efforts are best used. Just finish your work and get those plans together. Let me know what we need to do, just in case.…"

Aslam said nothing further, hoping to avoid an all-out argument. They needed each other at this final juncture. They lived among their common enemy. No sense directing their anger at each other.

"Good day, Aslam."

"And to you."

Chapter 22

Peden cleared the lunch dishes from his desk and spread the three by five cards out in no particular order. He added several new cards with the names of the terrorist leaders and the atrocities they committed against American troops around the globe. He added a card with the name of the photographer from the Associated Press who snapped the photo of Mawlawi Abdul Badri which purportedly showed him alive long after the 2011 drone strike. He honed in on the card with the statement *Parish reaction - wrong house.* Peden's logical mind began to lean towards believing Parish, that he somehow knew they destroyed the wrong house. Based on Lee Sparks' research, at least one the supposed targets of the strike survived – if the photo could be confirmed.

As Peden finished spreading the cards around, Megan called with flight information for their trip to Knoxville, Tennessee. She planned to pick him up in just over an hour. The flight would take them from Savannah-Hilton Head International Airport to McGhee Tyson Airport south of Knoxville on a small jet chartered by the FBI. A Waffle House restaurant sat to the north of the airport. Harlan Wilson agreed to the meeting place, the location being convenient for him. They would have their meeting and head right back to Savannah. With luck, they would be back before 9:00 p.m.

As Peden reviewed the cards on his desktop, one card stood out - the one with the Parish's reaction: *Wrong House.* He said to Megan, "I have to contact Chip Chandler again. This thing about Parish knowing they bombed the wrong house sticks out like a giant weed on a golf course fairway."

"Why would Chip know anything about how Parish came to have that bit of information?"

"I don't know, Megan, but somebody knows a lot more than they are letting on. I think the only one who isn't holding back in Ray Mack. He seemed to be straight with us from the start. I thought Chip was, too, but I don't know. Maybe between him and his wife, Colleen … I don't know."

"Finish your thought. Chip came to you about Parish. Why would he hold back now?"

"Well, he's married to the person who should have known about Cassidy Miller and she claims to not remember him at all. How likely is it that you don't remember a guy named Cassidy Miller? A guy who fought with Parish, who was in the spotlight at the time."

Peden shook his head, thinking that his old friend started out wishing for something, but it got messy faster than he could control the unfolding events.

"Pedee, you call Chip. See if we can meet with him. In the mean-time, we have a flight to catch. Be ready to go in … fifty minutes."

"Yes, ma'am. I'll be ready, ma'am."

The call disconnected. Within seconds, his cell phone sounded with the death march ringtone that he designated for his ex-wife, Susan.

He and Susan wrangled through a bitter divorce and still engaged in antagonistic, hateful rhetoric. They have not held a civil conversation in years, since before the actual divorce. Their two college-aged girls hated the ground he walked on even though he provided the financing for their college tuition and living expenses, including parties. The subject of nearly every call Susan made to Peden involved money for the girls because they had maxed out their credit cards on food, clothes, ride-share fares, and concert tickets. She called him every disgusting name she could think of and invented a few of her own. He toyed with the idea of letting the call go to voicemail, then figured he might as well answer. Swiping across the screen he said, "Hello, Susan."

In an uncharacteristically cheerful voice, Susan said, "Hello, Peden. I'd like to ask a favor."

Peden hesitated before answering with a tentative, "Okay. Ask."

"Kaitlin is engaged and she would like for you to meet her fiancé."

Peden remained silent. There must be a catch. Kaitlin's most recent call to Peden, several months ago, had been filled with hatred because Peden refused to pay off her credit card. He tried to explain to her that she needed to take more responsibility for her spending. The discussion went down-hill from there.

Peden replied with a drawn-out, "Okay."

"Well, will you do it?"

Peden's senses prickled, knowing that some trap awaited him – usually a money trap. "Susan, I hate to sound skeptical, but why?"

"Why what?"

"Kaitlin hates me. Why does she want me to meet her fiancé? And isn't this kind of sudden? I didn't even know she had a boyfriend."

Susan sighed into the phone so loudly that Peden thought he could feel the hot air on his ear. "Why can't you just be reasonable and meet the kid? Your daughter is in love. He seems to be a nice guy."

"Susan, why don't you have Kaitlin call me and ask? Why do you have to be the go-between?"

"Jesus, Peden. Why do you have to be such an ass about everything?"

Here we go. "Susan, I'm in the middle of something. Have Kaitlin call."

"Yeah. The middle of that Megan Moore bitch."

Peden hit the red handset ending the call. Peden thought *That went better than most.*

He turned back to the cards on his desk and stared. *Parish reaction – wrong house.*

Peden picked up his phone, found Chip Chandler's number and hit the green phone symbol. He picked up on the second ring.

"Hey, Peden."

To Peden, Chip's voice sounded tentative, almost cautious, like he expected his call, but did not necessarily want to receive it.

"Hey, Chip. I wanted to give you an update on where we stand. This thing is getting a little weird. We can't find anything on this Cassidy Miller character. Have you and Colleen talked about that anymore?"

Peden heard Chip take a deep breath, maybe reluctant to talk about it, maybe nervous about what he would say. Or maybe he knew that he needed to come clean about what he knew. Peden was not sure what to expect.

Chip finally said, "Colleen swears she doesn't remember anybody named Cassidy Miller. Neither do I. I called a couple of the guys. The only one who remembers the guy is Ray."

"Chip, how is that possible? If Ray remembers the guy because of the fight, somebody else has to remember, or your guys are lying, trying to protect someone … or something."

Chip took a defensive tone, "Look, Peden, I'm the one who asked you to dig into this. I want to know what happened to Parish. He was a brother and he served his country. He deserves better than being unceremoniously dumped in the ground."

"I agree, Chip." Peden paused, not sure if he should divulge certain facts that he knew. He felt he needed to give Chandler something that might push him, break down the wall that kept him from opening-up.

"We need to know how Parish knew that we bombed the wrong house. How did he get that intel? How did we hit the wrong house?"

Peden purposely used 'we' to let Chandler know they were on the same team.

Chandler's silence dragged on. Peden let him think. After nearly twenty seconds, Peden said, "You know something, Chip." It was a statement, not a question. "I can tell. What is it?"

"Not over the phone, Peden. When can we meet?"

"Tomorrow morning. Just you and me. What time and where?"

It took a few more seconds, then Chandler said, "The Waffle House off I-95 on Route 76. Can you make 9:30?"

Waffle House two days in a row. That might be tough, but they served more than just waffles. "Sure, that'll do, but let's make it 10:00."

With the call disconnected, Peden drew in a deep breath, looked at the ancient ceiling tiles in his office, then back down at the index cards still scattered on his desk. He realized the Rayshon Mack's name kept coming up as a central figure in the drone strike, the fight involving Cassidy Miller, and Randall Parish's life as a civilian. He believed that Mack told him everything he knew, or at least believed he knew. Peden thought that, if he gave Mack a few more details about where they stood with the investigation, it might jog his memory. Even as he thought about what he might ask Mack, he thought it would be worth a try. *Nothing ventured, nothing gained.*

He picked up his cell phone and punched in Mack's number. Ray answered before the second ring.

"Mr. Savage, sir. What can I do for you?"

"Hi Ray. You can start by calling me Peden."

"Right. I know you told me that before. Tough habit to break, sir … I mean Peden."

Peden plowed right in. "Ray, when Parish and Cassidy fought, what can you tell me about who saw it and who intervened."

"I did, and a couple others guys. Let me think. I remember Carmine Russo and Danny Ames. Then Jeffrey Grumen stepped in when Parish threw a punch at me. It was wild and missed, but it would've hurt."

"I spoke with Grumen. He said he never heard of anyone named Cassidy Miller."

"Well, that's a damn lie. He talked with Miller after the fight. He listened to Miller's version but wanted to write Rusty up. I talked him out of it. I don't think he put anything in his file."

Peden thought for a moment before replying. Why would Grumen lie about knowing Cassidy Miller? It was a minor dust-up. Stuff like that happened all the time during deployments. Guys missed home, families, wives, and kids. They poked fun at others and sometimes raw, exposed nerves are touched. Sometimes, brawls started for no reason at all, except to blow off steam. On long deployments, tensions built up and needed an outlet.

This seemed to have deeper roots. Everyone involved had been discharged. What possible reason would these men have to hide their knowledge of the identity of a Marine from over ten years past?

"Ray, has anyone approached you about keeping quiet about Cassidy Miller?"

"No, sir ... I mean, Peden. No one."

"Okay. Okay. If anyone other than Megan or me ask you about Miller, you call me right away. You got me?"

Mack remained silent for a split second, then said, "Should I be worried? I mean, Parish is dead and you sound ... I don't know – concerned."

"You just let me know if anything starts feeling weird to you. Okay?"

"Yes, sir."

He did not correct himself this time.

Chapter 23

The smooth, eventless, flight from Savannah-Hilton Head International Airport to McGhee Tyson Airport near Knoxville, Tennessee, took less than an hour in the FBI's Gulfstream G450. Except for the pilot and copilot, Peden and Megan had the sleek aircraft to themselves. Once they reached the cruising altitude of forty thousand feet, the pilot told them to help themselves to the full bar and snacks located just behind the cockpit. They both nodded politely but did not avail themselves of the amenities except that they each drank from a bottle of water while they discussed their notes on the Randall Parish case.

The local FBI office arranged for a rental car in Knoxville which Megan drove out of the airport grounds north onto U.S. highway 129. She was pleased that she remembered her sunglasses as the cloudless afternoon reflected sunlight off every chrome and light-colored surface. The temperature hovered near eighty degrees with no indication of a change to the weather in the five-day forecast. They drove less than a mile and made a left turn onto Judson Drive, then an immediate right into the Waffle House parking lot, where a half dozen cars sat close to the front entrance. Megan chose a spot facing Judson Drive which allowed them to look for Harlan Wilson through the windows of the restaurant as they approached the front entrance. They spotted him sitting at a booth at the far right, front corner of the building, watching them as they walked through the parking lot.

Wilson, who held a glass of soda that appeared to be half-empty, stood when they walked towards the booth. He was shorter than both Peden and Megan at five-feet-six-inches tall. He kept his hair cropped close which accentuated the retreating, scaly scalp on either side of a peninsula of sandy-gold hair. His skin indicated that he spent a lot of time outdoors in the sun. His thin face and nose reminded Peden of a rodent. A Tennessee Volunteers ball cap sat on the table. He did not smile, his expression all business. Megan matched his expressionless face as she extended her hand and shook Wilson's and said, "Mr. Wilson."

Wilson smiled and, in a deep southern accent, said, "I thought we already established that y'all can call me Willie. Everyone else does."

"Right, Willie. Call me Megan."

"That makes y'all Peden, am I right?"

Peden repeated the handshake greeting and said, "That's right. Thanks for meeting with us." Wilson motioned to the booth with his hand. They sat and moved around the circular table, spacing themselves equidistance apart.

An older woman with salt and pepper hair wearing a waitress apron approached and asked for their drink orders. Peden and Megan both ordered coffee, Megan's with cream, Peden's black.

When the waitress retreated Peden started the conversation. "I read about your brother's death. You said he died under suspicious circumstances. The stories I read seemed to dismiss the idea of foul play. Can you tell us why you suspect different than the official account?"

"First, I hope y'all don't mind, but I'd like to see some ID. It might be over the top, but I need to be careful."

Megan and Peden did not hesitate. Megan showed the photographer her official FBI credentials and Peden showed him his Georgia-issued Private Investigator's ID. Wilson read both for several seconds, then nodded his head.

Wilson's eyes shifted from Megan to Peden, to the parking lot and back to Megan. He took a deep breath to calm his nerves, but kept his voice steady, "Okay. My brother. We both worked for the Associated Press. He started before me and helped me get in the door a couple years later. I was twenty-three at the time, he was twenty-five. I loved the work since it was exciting, a real adventure, traveling 'round the world, doing what I loved. I've been to places many times most people'll never see once, except through my pictures. We was never assigned the same story. I don't think it was an official policy, but our bosses told us they wanted our total focus on our assignments. They figured if we worked together, that we might get distracted if somethin' happened to one of us."

He took a deep breath, looked out the window again. Peden and Megan remained silent, giving him time to collect his thoughts.

He took a deep breath, then continued, "When I took that shot of Abdul Badri, I didn't know it right away that this guy was supposed to be dead. After I did some research on the subjects in my photos, I knew it was Badri. I didn't know what to do next, who I should contact, letting them know what I discovered so I sat on that for a while. Then I thought what better way to raise the issue to the right folks in Washington than to get a reporter involved? So, I called my brother, Brandon. He started lookin' into it and told me there's a real story - a big story - there. That was a year ago this month."

Megan jumped in, "Your brother has written many stories about Middle Eastern conflicts. I read several after we spoke yesterday. The articles don't appear all that controversial. It sounded like good journalism to me, pretty straight forward, no embellishment of the situations. Just the facts."

"He was honest and fair in his writin'. Like y'all said, just the facts, no opinion, one way or another. He wasn't a real political kind of guy. When he started his research on this Badri guy, he got a couple calls for him to back off. I think it's the same guy who called me."

Peden said, "The guy with a deep, radio voice."

"Yup."

Megan asked, "How did your brother die?"

The waitress brought their coffees and asked if they would like menus to which they replied no. She thanked them, smiled, turned, and left them alone.

"Carbon monoxide. His furnace 'malfunctioned.'" He used finger quotes to drive home what the authorities told him.

"Exhaust poured into his house while he slept. The local fire marshal did an investigation and found the exhaust piping clogged with what he called 'a bird's nest.' But birds don't build nests in the middle of January in Kentucky. When I heard that he died, I went to his house and had the fire marshal explain it to me. He said he couldn't explain it 'cause he'd never seen that kind of blockage before. When I asked him if he really found a bird's nest in the pipe, he said it wasn't exactly a bird's nest, but that he had to check off somethin'. He didn't want to talk to me much. I asked a couple more questions that he couldn't answer, then he just cut me off and left."

Peden's face tightened to a frown. He thought *The guy with the radio voice must be working for someone who wants this whole story to disappear. If he works for the U.S. government, this has to be an off-the-books operation.*

Megan must have been thinking down the same line. "Willie, did you follow up, in any way, on your brother's death and what you suspected?"

"I went to my boss and told him what I just told y'all, that somethin' wasn't right here. He said he would talk with the higher-ups, but he told me that it didn't go anywhere. I asked if they would assign an investigative reporter to it to at least satisfy my concerns. They said no. So, any investigation died before it ever got started."

Peden asked, "Do you still work for the Associated Press?"

"Yes, and no. I'm no longer directly employed by the AP. I run my own photography company, but I do some contract work for them. They're payin' me more now than when I worked directly for them."

"You said your bosses didn't do any further investigation into your brother's death, but did you look into it, on your own?"

Wilson paused and looked out the window to the parking lot, then rubbed his chin, thinking how much he should tell anyone associated with the federal government. He turned to Peden, "Yeah, I did. I called his camera-person. She had been assigned a short job in Washington, D.C. the day before he died. The assignment lasted two days, but it really wasn't much of a job. The AP had people with her skills who could've done the job without sending her on that junket. When she returned to Kentucky, she found his body. She thinks he was set up."

Peden's face tightened again as he rubbed his eyes. He wondered how far the tentacles reached of whoever pulled the strings. Megan's expression did not change, her expression as stiff as a statue, the serious eyes looking at Harlan Wilson.

She said, "Mr. Wilson – excuse me, Willie - you have our sincere condolences. I believe you should be extremely cautious in whom you contact about your brother's death and the fact that Abdul Badri is alive. Someone wants to keep a tight lid on anything related to Badri. We don't know who or why, but at least two people are dead. I believe your brother was murdered because he asked the wrong person questions about Badri."

Harlan Wilson's face tightened and he drew in a deep breath as he considered Megan's warning, wondering whether he might be next on someone's hit list. Peden believed that his mind must be trying to process why his brother had been killed and by whom.

After a moment, he opened his mouth to speak, then closed it as more thoughts collided. With his hands folded on the table, he shook his head slowly, then rubbed his face with both hands. Finally, he said, "Do y'all have any idea who killed my brother?"

Megan answered, "Probably the same person or persons who killed a former Marine named Randall Parish. We have a lead and a name, but the name is bogus. We're trying to find the guy but so far, no luck. We seem to be running into the same roadblocks as you. Some guy with a deep voice trying to chase us off."

Wilson looked from Megan to Peden and asked, "Is there anything I can do to help?"

They looked at each other, then back to Wilson. Megan said, "Not right now, but if we can think of a way for you to help, we will call you."

Peden chimed in, "How would you like to cover the funeral of a Marine Veteran?"

"I mean, I'm between jobs right now. I don't have anything lined up until the first week in October. When would ya'll need me?"

"Next Thursday and Friday, Glennville, Georgia, at the veteran's cemetery. Maybe the night before as well."

"Y'all tell me how I can help. Anything I can do to find out who killed Brandon, I'm on board."

With that, the meeting ended. Peden and Megan headed for the rental car. Wilson remained seated at the booth in the Waffle House.

Back in the rental car, Megan asked, "What do you have in mind?"

"I think he should take pictures of the attendees at Parish's funeral, and see if anyone is watching from the perimeter of the cemetery or parking lot. There seems to be a lot of interest in his death. There's got to be more to this than we're seeing."

"Pedee, you are the master of understatement. By the way, I hear congratulations are in order."

"What do you mean?"

"Your daughter. I hear she's engaged to a really nice guy and Susan wants you to meet him."

"Are you tapping my phone?"

"I've got friends, Pedee."

Chapter 24

Thursday morning came early for Peden. The sun, yet to break the eastern horizon, painted the wispy clouds a light pink. The day would start comfortably enough, but promised to be unseasonably hot and humid.

Already showered, dressed, with breakfast finished by 6:50 a.m. he scratched the top of his head after reading a fifth article by Brandon Wilson. This piece focused on the United States extended military presence in Afghanistan and the growing reluctance among U.S. citizens to support maintaining that posture. The constant and endless stream of television ads asking for donations to support soldiers who had lost limbs, been severely burned, or sustained traumatic brain injuries, cast a negative pall on the psyche of the population even as the generosity of Americans poured millions into the coffers of those organizations. The ads put faces and names to the injured men and women and pumped their images, personalities, and stories right into the living rooms of everyday Americans. Over time, the ravenous hunger for revenge for the attacks on September 11, 2001 turned into an overwhelming desire to end support for foreign wars, especially those that involved U.S. military troops. These seemingly endless conflicts permanently altered or ended the futures of thousands of the finest young men and women in the country. Far too many made the ultimate sacrifice. Sentiment opposing foreign aid continued to grow against the backdrop of missteps by military leaders, and a growing concern over caravans of immigrants breeching the United States' southern border.

Peden found all five articles to be straight forward news without political leaning to the left or right. Prior to reading the news articles, he had read Wilson's bio written by two writers who rated journalists and news agencies. The bio praised Wilson for his no-nonsense, non-political style, noting that

Wilson had won several awards from both liberal and conservative think-tanks for his journalistic professionalism. Impressed, Peden wondered why any government agency would target him, and, as his brother Harlan suspected, murder him.

Peden's concern for the safety of his closest friends and colleagues had grown rapidly over the previous twenty-four hours. Lee Sparks appeared particularly vulnerable. He had no security except outdoor cameras and door locks protecting him from thugs who may, or may not, be employed by some agency of the federal government. That they could not identify the people or agency posing the threat worried Peden. He wanted to believe that the person with the deep media voice did not belong to any official agency, that they acted of their own volition. As of now, he had no proof, one way or another. He had to find a way to put a name to the voice and then affiliate that name to an agency, or exclude them from the same.

He picked up his cell phone and hit the speed-dial button to call Lee Sparks, hoping that his late-sleeping, technical guy had already risen for the day. As the phone rang, he looked at his watch; 7:06am. *Way too early for Lee.*

To Peden's surprise, Sparks answered on the second ring sounding wide awake.

"Hey, Peden."

"I'm trying to reach Lee Sparks. Did I dial the wrong number?"

"Very funny. You're so technically challenged you're probably calling me on a rotary landline phone. I've been up since around five. This mess with Cassidy Miller, Badri, Brandon Wilson - my mind's racing. Anyway, this is your dime. What's up?"

"It's about this case. I'm concerned. With Brandon Wilson's death and the circumstances, I think we need to take some extra precautions. I think some defensive actions are in order until we know what we're up against. Is there a way you can set up something to record all our cellphones' incoming and outgoing calls?"

Lee remained silent as he thought about his boss's request. He said, "Yeah, I think I can do it. I've got some gadgets that will do the trick. When you say 'all' you mean you, me, and Megan?"

"Yeah. Exactly. Are they small enough to be portable, unnoticeable to someone looking at us while we use our phones?"

"Yeah, yeah. Basically, it's an attachment that would fit right on the phone. It looks like one of those things that the kids use for holding the phone between their fingers."

"I've got no idea what you're talking about, but I'll take your word for it. Where would the recording be stored?"

"I can have the calls sent to a server pretty much anywhere you want; even multiple places so we have a backup."

Peden thought to himself and smiled. He loved Spark's solution. "Let's do it. How soon can you hook this up?"

"This morning if you like."

"I'd love to, but I have a meeting in Florence, South Carlonia, in a couple hours. Can you stop by when we get back into town? Megan will be with me. I'll try to convince her that this is a good idea and that she should do it, too. I have a couple other people whom I'd like to have set up as well, but I have to convince them that it is in their best interest to do it."

"Okay. With this gadget, I can program them and show you where to attach the device on any phone. If you get them to go along, you could attach them and I'd check to make sure it records and stores the calls. I'll start on the programming right away. See you later today. Just call when you're about half an hour out."

When the call disconnected, Peden used the bathroom, grabbed a cup of coffee, and headed for his blue Tahoe. Once seated in the driver's seat he announced his destination into his cell phone to get directions. Then he set the phone in his cup holder. He used voice command to call Megan Moore who picked up on the first ring.

"Morning, Pedee."

"Hi, Megan. I'm on my way. I should be to your place in a few minutes."

He told her about his fear of the unknown caller and relayed Lee's plan to record phone conversations. She asked if the device could be turned off so that personal calls would not be recorded. Peden replied that he did not know, but they could ask Lee. Twenty-five minutes later, Peden and Megan cruised up I-95 north in Peden's Tahoe.

Megan asked, "What's the plan with the recording devices?"

Peden's jaw tightened as he cruised along the interstate at eighty miles per hour. Even at that speed, cars sped past him as if he were standing still. "I hope we won't need anything that we record, but these threats have me rattled. If we get this guy's voice recorded, maybe Lee can use some voice recognition software and track him down. I was worried when the threatening calls started, but knowing that Brandon Wilson may have been killed, we have to do some counter measures, go on the offensive … somehow."

Megan remained silent. She stared at the road ahead without a sound. After a full two minutes, she asked, "What if Rollie can provide some technical support from Quantico. Do we trust that my counterparts aren't involved in the cover-up?"

Megan's use of 'cover-up' surprised Peden. He did not believe that the FBI had skin in the game, but that feeling did not approach one-hundred percent confidence. He put the question right back at her, "Do you?"

"Completely certain? No. But we have to trust someone. We can't fear every alphabet soup government agency. There are way too many. Even if we narrow down the likely players, you're still looking at dozens of intelligence agencies; the CIA, NSA, NCIS, and on and on. That's if *any* agency is behind the calls. This could be a lone wolf deal."

Peden's tension ticked up another notch. He hated not knowing the face of his enemies. He especially hated being told to stop something by someone who refused to identify themselves, someone who expected blind compliance, which pointed to one of the haughty spook agencies.

Peden thought for a spell as he settled in to the rhythm of the drive. He wondered if Parish's death, the drone strike, Cassidy Miller's arrival in Afghanistan, and the recent threats to Lee Sparks and him were directly tied.

Megan confirmed his suspicions by saying, "Everything about Parish's murder goes back to the drone strike and the events that immediately followed. Too many people knew about Cassidy Miller and are lying about it. We need to shake that tree harder."

Peden nodded, which meant he must be deadly serious during his next meeting with Chip Chandler.

* * *

Colleen Chandler could feel the muscle tension as she glided through the eighty-eight-degree water in the pool. The early morning workout on the treadmill and rowing machine, followed by twenty laps in the pool, helped direct her mind away from the upcoming funeral. She wished she could avoid the gathering altogether. She held little interest in seeing anyone from her former platoon, even though she had limited contact with most of them while in country. She especially wished to avoid General Vance, the person to whom she reported and the person with whom she dealt with on a daily basis back then. Seeing him would certainly dredge up painful memories.

At the completion of her twentieth lap, she stood in the shallow end of the pool looking towards the eastern sky where the sun had yet to break above the horizon. Clouds illuminated with bright oranges and reds painted a spectacular picture, like a forest fire above a distant tree line. The crisp, seventy-degree temperature felt good on her wet skin as she took deep breaths and stretched her arms over her head. A pine scent from the trees that surrounded their property filled the morning air. She closed her eyes and continued with slow, deep breaths. With her workout complete, she took some time to think about the events from ten years ago that set more recent events in motion. Dread crept into her mind as she came to terms with the fact that nothing could stop the coming confrontations. She hoped that her marriage could survive it knowing that certain revelations would test her husband's commitment to her.

"Penny for your thoughts?"

Chip's voice startled her. She had not seen or heard him step out onto the lanai by the pool. She forced a smile as she kept her arms stretched high over her head.

"Just enjoying the morning, the beautiful sky, the fresh air. Great for a workout. You want to join me?"

Chip admired his wife's body as she continued to stretch. He wished time permitted him to take a swim. Her movements were so fluid and sensuous that he felt like a voyeur staring, but he could not divert his eyes. A wicked smile lit his face, his thoughts drifting, tempting him to join her, but his morning schedule would not allow it. He shook his head to clear his carnal thoughts, which dragged his mood down. The topic he needed to raise with her before leaving for a meeting would be difficult. It might even escalate into an argument.

"I wish I could, babe, but I have a meeting this morning in Florence."

Colleen frowned and lowered her arms. She read his face and knew that bad news lay on the horizon. The truth always seemed to find its way to the surface and this truth would reveal damning secrets that she previously thought would remain buried.

Feigning ignorance, she asked, "Do we have a rich client in Florence?"

Chip's steely glare let her know that he knew her question to be disingenuous. His silence stretched until Colleen said, "This is about Rusty. You're meeting your buddy Peden Savage, right?"

Chip took a deep breath then asked, "What else aren't you telling me about that day, about Rusty, about Vance?"

At the mention of Vance's name, she tensed, then recovered as best she could. He pressed on, "Why do you react whenever I say his name, Colleen? What happened back there?"

Colleen stood perfectly still, the droplets of water now chilling her skin. Her mind raced as her brain ran through the options of responses. She could tell Chip about the several times Vance tried to make passes at her, or the time that he actually pinned her down on his desk, pulling at her uniform buttons. Private Parish saved her from being raped by pushing Vance away from her. After that day, Vance never tried to get physical with her, but he kept up the crude comments that always made her wary and uncomfortable around her commanding officer.

"Nothing happened Chip, not that Vance didn't try. Maybe he would have forced himself on me if our time over there hadn't ended." Tears formed in her eyes as she repeated, "But nothing happened."

She didn't answer his other question: *What else aren't you telling me?*

Chapter 25

As Chip Chandler drove south on US Route 17, his confrontation with his wife just twenty minutes earlier pushed his anxiety to high gear. That he left her at home without finishing their discussion bothered him immensely. He told her that he planned to tell Peden that she lied about Cassidy Miller and would explain her reasoning for lying. She retorted that it would do no good to reveal that information now, that the past should remain in the past. He told her that the truth would come out, sooner or later. He reminded her that they still had no idea why Parish was murdered. She continued to argue, even beg him, to keep her lie just between the two of them, but he cut the air with his hand, indicating the end of the discussion. He turned and left without another word.

Now, as he played their argument over and over in his head, he felt badly about the way it had spiraled out of control, but he knew he could not keep the lie to himself. He also wondered why Colleen remained stubbornly adamant about keeping her knowledge of Cassidy Miller a secret. For the first time in their six-year marriage, he wondered if she held even more secrets, and if so, what did he really know about his wife?

His mind shifted to Randall Parish. He hoped to finalize funeral arrangements with the cemetery tomorrow but he still had no word from the Screvn County Medical Examiner for release of the body. He contacted the Glennville Funeral Home and received a tentative date for processing Parish's body for interment. If all went as Chip hoped, the funeral would be held next Friday, one week from tomorrow, at the Glennville Veterans Cemetery. Nearly a dozen forms awaited completion before he could send them to the appropriate agencies, then get them delivered to the cemetery at least twenty-four hours ahead of the planned burial time. Colleen offered to help with the forms, but Chip wondered if she would still be willing after this morning's confrontation.

He thought about calling his wife to clear the air and apologize for allowing the tension to escalate, but changed his mind, believing that it might lead to extending the fight, defeating the purpose. She looked at his plan to reveal her lie as a betrayal. How could he go against her wishes and reveal her secret to Peden? He could explain it away as simple as not remembering the name among the thousands that she handled. He knew that it would not fly. Peden knew how transfers worked in the military, and in Afghanistan. He saw it and lived it.

Now on Interstate 40 west, north of Wilmington, North Carolina, and sun at his back, the rest of the trip should have been relaxing. But the urge to call his wife remained. Before today, they never left each other in anger, the feeling being foreign to him. He hated the tension between them.

* * *

Colleen Chandler's emotions ranged from anger to fright. She thought back to the day she received the call from General Clark – he called himself General Clark anyway. He ordered her to not divulge any knowledge of Cassidy Miller. He threatened her with all manner of negative consequences if she even hinted to anyone that she knew Miller existed. The call convinced her that it was in her best interest to remain silent. To emphasize that fact, before his departure from the base, Cassidy Miller himself, made a visit to her quarters to threaten her that all hell would break loose if she hinted that he ever set foot on the base. Normally not one to back down from a challenge, the directness and tone of the threats convinced her to keep the secret to herself.

Now, ten years later, the secret put a chasm between her and her husband. She violated the order to remain silent, but that order expired with her resignation of her commission. But did that matter? Miller's voice reverberated in her brain, the threat as fresh in her memory as when he gruffly whispered the words in her ear. *Tell no one, ever.*

She nearly picked up the phone to beg her husband one more time to keep her secret, but she knew the call would have no effect. Chip would tell Peden of the lie and no amount of begging or pleading would change his mind.

Should she call Evelyn Vance and tell her? Or Moska Aziz? But neither of her friends knew of her dilemma. They would be of no help.

She concluded that the secret would come out. Hopefully Chip's friend, Peden would use discretion in whom he told. Maybe Chip would ask that of Peden and the secret would remain in a small, but growing, circle.

Right. Like that ever happens.

* * *

At 10:25 with the bright morning sun coming through the windshield directly in front, Peden pulled off the highway at exit 157 southwest of Florence, South Carolina, and veered right towards the towering Waffle House sign. Nearly an identical structure to the restaurant where they met Harlan Wilson just yesterday afternoon, Peden parked just as Megan had, facing the road. As they approached the restaurant, Chip Chandler opened the front door and welcomed them. He wore a frown overlayed with a forced smile.

"Peden. Agent Moore."

"Call me Megan, please. Let's keep this informal. Okay?"

"That's good for me, Megan."

He looked at Peden and said, "I thought this meeting was between the two of us."

"I changed my mind. I thought I might need support."

Chandler raised an eyebrow at that. A waitress, who could have been the twin sister to the waitress from yesterday's visit to the Waffle House in Tennessee, seated them at a table about as far from the front door as possible. They ordered three coffees. Chip asked for a short stack of pancakes with sausage.

When the waitress left, Peden looked at Chip with a dead-serious stare and asked, "Why did you lie to me about Cassidy Miller?"

Chip's jaw dropped as if he might argue, then closed it as he rubbed his face with both hands. He remained quiet for nearly a full minute, in deep thought, either deciding what lie to tell to cover the previous one, or what part of the truth he should reveal. When he looked at Peden, he said, "You know Colleen kept records for the platoon. After she recovered from being shot, she was assigned to Vance as his personal assistant. She shuffled paperwork, kept records on everything, including personnel. Hated the job, hated Vance, hated not being able to go on patrol. Basically, she wanted to get back with her former team and do her job."

Peden interrupted, "She knew about Cassidy Miller ... and so did you." He paused to let that sink in. "So, why did you lie to us ... lie to *me* Chip?"

Chandler shot back, his temper rising at Peden's challenging and accusatory tone, "I had no clue about Cassidy Miller. Until you brought it up, I never heard the name before. She was ordered to forget about him including destroying all records associated with his transfer in and out of the platoon."

"Did Vance order her to do that?"

Chandler paused, looked around the restaurant, then looked Peden in the eyes and toned down his retort. "No. He didn't. That order came from outside our chain of command. She was threatened with all kinds of repercussions if she told Vance or anyone in the platoon. Hell, I didn't even know that she'd been directed to do it until the other night; Tuesday night, to be exact. I confronted her when she lied to me while I spoke with you on the phone. I knew she was lying, but I couldn't say anything to her while I talked with you. I couldn't think fast enough to make sense of it."

Megan just watched Chandler while Peden grilled his friend and former Marine brother. She analyzed his facial expressions, body movements, the tone of his voice.

And she believed him.

Megan jumped in and asked, "Chip, when Colleen confided in you, did she tell you who ordered her to silence?"

"Yes and no, not by name anyway. She just said the call came from a one-star, a general. His orders were sharp and to the point. She feared her career was in jeopardy if she didn't follow orders to the letter. After that call, she didn't hear anything more about it, so she thought she was in the clear. When she resigned her commission, she never gave it another thought … until now."

Peden asked, "Any idea how this relates to Rusty Parish's death?"

Chandler took a deep breath and let it out again. He started to speak then stopped and rubbed his face. He inhaled a second time, then said, "Parish knew we targeted the wrong house because he'd been to the house the week before the strike …with me."

Both Peden and Megan looked astonished. Peden shook his head as if clearing any thoughts, then said, "Come again?"

"The house belonged to the family of my interpreter, Amir Sayed."

"Who else knew that you hit the wrong house?"

"Vance. And Colleen, but she didn't know until I stormed into Vance's quarters and read him the riot act. He threatened to bring me up on charges. I didn't care. We killed my interpreter and his family! After I'd calmed down, he assured me he would investigate the incident, file a report up the chain and see what the brass wanted to do about it. See if they could find out where the bad intel came from. Vance showed me the report he planned to send … but he never sent it. Colleen saved a copy. He sent a different one that declared the mission a success. Says we killed two top terror leaders, one from the Taliban and one from Al Queda. He lied."

Megan said, "Abdul Badri and Abu Al-Madani."

Chip's surprised face looked almost comical, except for the serious nature of their discussion. Megan continued, "We know that Badri is alive but we're not sure about Al-Madani."

A light sparked in Chips eyes. "Somebody's trying to find out who screwed the pooch on that drone strike."

Peden took a deep breath, his face still showing the anger that he had been kept in the dark by one of his own, the person who brought his attention to the rapidly expanding situation.

Chip said, "I've gotta talk to Colleen again."

Chapter 26

After Peden and Megan left Chip sitting alone in the Waffle House restaurant, he pushed the plate of sausage and pancakes aside, his appetite gone. He could no longer smell the aroma that had earlier enticed him to order one of his favorite breakfasts. With his face in his hands, he pondered the dilemma he and Colleen now faced.

After ten years, a government agency still monitored events related to a military action in Afghanistan that everyone - almost everyone - in the United States believed to be long forgotten. The report on the strike declared success. It should have closed the books on the mission. But now, Peden and Megan determined one of the targets identified as killed in the strike was alive and well. If Peden and Megan's resources determined the strike failed, then certainly many federal agencies have arrived at the same conclusion.

Chip knew that Grumen and his rifle team destroyed the wrong house, and in the process, killed his interpreter. They literally murdered Amir Sayed's family. He knew it the day after the strike and should not have been surprised that the men targeted in the attack would be alive, still carrying out terror actions against the United States and their allies. He hoped that Badri and Al-Madani died over the years in other battles or by natural causes. That at least one of the terror leaders remained alive carrying out military – no, terror – activities spelled bad news for the United States and its allies. It might well come back to haunt him and his wife.

The waitress approached him and asked if something was wrong with his breakfast. He replied that he just lost his appetite. She asked if he wanted a to-go box. Without looking up, he just shook his head. She nodded and, seeing that he lapsed into deep thought, retreated to the kitchen.

Chip thought about the men who told his wife years ago to remain silent about Cassidy Miller. Were these same men now in pursuit of information about the strike? Had they murdered Randall Parish, or did his murder bring new focus on their mission? What did they hope to find? Rifle teams from his platoon carried out the mission, though he had not been directly involved. Were they searching for the person who submitted a fraudulent report? If so, he knew the answer to their question. Colleen possessed the proof that he wrote the true account of the mission and that the man in charge of the Marine camp, then Colonel, now General Virgil Vance decided to can that report and send his own version of events. He did not remember where his wife put the copies that she made of both reports, but believed it to be locked in their safe at home.

The urge to call his wife gripped him, but he stopped short of picking up his phone. He wanted to tell her face-to-face about his meeting with Peden and Megan. He needed to see her expressions as well as hear her words. Up until this past Monday, just three days ago, Colleen had followed her orders to the letter to remain silent about Miller. She never told him a single detail of the order, even though it had come from outside her chain of command. He understood her genuine fear of repercussions if she divulged the directive to any of her superior officers within her chain. He also now understood why she abruptly resigned her commission. Now that Chip knew the facts, it seemed knowledge of Miller and his placement in their platoon spread quickly because of Peden's inquiries. Chip wondered if Colleen bore any responsibility to remain silent once she resigned her commission. If any fingers pointed towards Vance, he certainly would redirect those fingers at his wife. That she held onto those reports might just save both their asses.

Peden had paid for Chip's breakfast and their coffees and left a generous tip before he and Megan left. Chip threw an extra twenty dollars on the table. He felt badly about the way he treated their waitress after the meeting broke up, so he hoped the extra money would make up for his coarse attitude.

He walked out to his Cadillac, started the car, and turned the air conditioner on max cool. The morning sun blazed in the cloudless sky. Tension and heat caused sweat to break out on his forehead and temples as he thought about all the pieces of this rapidly changing situation. He wondered, not for the first time, if getting the old platoon together might be a mistake.

He headed east on US Route 76 through downtown Florence. As he reached the eastern outskirts of town, his cell phone sounded. He looked at the screen. The Optim Medical Center number displayed.

He answered, "Chandler."

"Mr. Chandler, this is Andrea Wills from Doctor Daniel Erin's office. He would like a word with you if you have a moment."

"I'm driving, but I can talk."

"I'll put the doctor on."

Chip waited for nearly two full minutes before Doctor Erin picked up the phone. He said, "Mr. Chandler, sorry to keep y'all waiting."

"No problem, Doctor."

"As y'all believed from the start, we've been unable to locate any living relatives for Randall Parish, therefore I am going to recommend that his body be released to y'all at tomorrow morning's meeting of the Cadaver Distribution board."

"Thank you, Doctor. I am …"

Doctor Erin cut him off, "Y'all understand that there are still numerous procedures that must be followed. We have to fill out several forms and y'all must present us with an affidavit …"

Chip cut in saying that he had several people helping him with the process. He tried ending the call by thanking Dr. Erin with as much false bravado as he could muster. This being a pivotal moment, he did not want to slow things down by being less than gracious with the man who could throw a wrench in the process.

"What time should I call your office tomorrow, doctor?"

"We should be finished with our meeting by around 10:00. If y'all call about 10:15, that should give us time to give Andrea the signed paperwork. She can also help y'all with the rest of the process, at least as it applies to our requirements. I'm sure y'all'll have a few more hoops to jump through before it's all said and done."

Again, Chip thanked Doctor Erin and disconnected. His emotions banged around his head. On one hand, the pending release of Randall Parish's body put many activities in motion, requirements that he could not delegate, unless his wife offered to assist. He could now let his Marines on BIAChat know they should make travel and hotel arrangements for next Thursday and Friday. Before that, he needed to contact the Hampton Inn in Hinesville and set aside a block of rooms for those planning to attend the funeral.

The Screvn County Funeral Home moved to first place on his call list. He would ask what forms they needed to take possession of Parish's body from Optim Medical Center and what they needed to pass the prepared body on to the veteran's cemetery. Every step of the process required at least one form – in most cases, more than one – to make the transfer of possession for Parish's body legal. Timely handoffs remained a top priority for Chip to ensure that he did not have thirty to forty former marines travelling to Georgia for no reason.

Even with all the distractions associated with Parish's body, Chip's mind came back to one thing; some unknown person or agency wanted answers on a ten-year-old mission. The answers might tear his marriage, and the life he and Colleen had built, into tiny pieces.

Chandler pulled off the road into a country diner and turned off the car's engine. He dialed the number for the Screvn County Funeral Home and spoke with their administrator. After twenty minutes, SherylAnn – 'one name, no spaces' – Gentry advised him that they work with the medical examiner's office regularly and they would be happy to accommodate his schedule for an interment next Friday. They would make any needed schedule adjustments to accommodate timely preparation of the body for burial. She explained the forms that they needed prior to taking possession of the decedent, but that could be accomplished by email and digital signature. That would make the forms part of the process more efficient. It put Chip's mind somewhat at ease.

Still sitting in the parking lot of the diner, he hit the saved number for the veteran's cemetery. The call connected on the first ring. Apparently a slow day for Cecil and his part time crew.

"Georgia Veterans Memorial Cemetery. Cecil Parsons. How can I help y'all?"

"Hi Cecil. Chip Chandler."

"Mr. Chandler. I was hopin' to hear from y'all soon. How can I assist y'all this fine day?"

* * *

By the time Chip finished with his calls to the funeral home and cemetery, he received commitments from both that the funeral service for former Marine Corps Private Randall Parish would take place on Friday, September 24. The lengthy calls and the helpful guidance of SherylAnn and Cecil gave Chip confidence that the funeral plans might come to fruition. He thought about the details as he cruised north on Highway 17 less than fifteen minutes from his home in Holly Ridge. He began to feel the tension ease now that a big part of the plan fell into place.

One issue could now be considered under control just as other problems began to blossom. With dread, he thought about facing Colleen with the news that at least one terror leader of two who everyone believed killed in a drone strike was alive. She could be implicated in falsifying a report related to that "successful" strike.

Though he empathized with her reasoning, the fact remained that someone in the jungle of federal agencies had an active investigation into the strike. Or at least it appeared that way.

* * *

Reaching home mid-afternoon, Chip announced his arrival at the mudroom door. Colleen came in from the Lanai wearing a sun dress, looking beautiful as ever. A tentative smile adorned her face as she looked her husband over, hoping to find him at ease, hoping that he changed his mind about revealing her deception to Peden. She could not gage his mood, one way or another.

"So, how did it go?"

He looked up at the ceiling, searching for the words that he needed without causing alarm in his wife. He took a deep breath, then said, "We've got a lot to talk about. Let's get a drink and sit."

A few minutes later, Chip had his laptop computer at the kitchen table, natural light shining in through the window. With her help, he spent the next hour filling out forms and electronically signing them on-line to make sure Randall Parish's remains moved as quickly as possible through the bureaucratic maze so that he could be buried with honors at the Georgia Veterans Memorial Cemetery on Friday, September 23, at 9:00 a.m.

With the task complete, Chip closed the laptop, turned to his wife and said, "We've got a big problem. Somebody in some spook agency knows that the report for the drone strike was falsified. I sure hope you kept copies of both reports."

Colleen's face drained of all color. For a moment, Chip's heart sank. Then she nodded and said, "I did. They're in the safe in a sealed envelope. I haven't touched that envelope in years." She took a deep breath, tears came to her eyes, and she asked, "How deep is the shit we're in?"

"I guess it depends on a couple things. Who wants to know and do we have enough evidence to point the finger away from you and me?"

Colleen stood and moved to her husband, sat in his lap,

and hugged him tight. Chip could feel the fear and tension radiate through his wife's sobs.

Chapter 27

Chip and Colleen Chandler spent most of late afternoon discussing their situation with the drone strike reports. As the sun streaked into the kitchen through their lanai, fueled by their anxiety, they poured several rum punch drinks. As the liquor began to lighten their hearts, passion took hold. Light touches turned to petting and sensuous kisses, then to unabridged passion. As they embraced and the heat climbed, they quickly made their way to their bedroom, casting off clothing along the way. If Chip harbored concerns over the strength of their marriage, Colleen did everything in her power to assuage his fears. Over the next hour, she reaffirmed that they were in this together for the long haul, no matter what. They stayed in bed long after their passion subsided and held each other, their hearts and minds melding into one.

Knowing that they possessed an ironclad defense against accusations of deceit, they spoke of their next moves should agents come to their home and question them regarding the strike. Colleen suggested that they make additional copies and put the reproduced documents, Chip's original report and the falsified report by Vance, in a safe deposit box at their bank. She also suggested that they give copies to someone they trust. Chip suggested Peden Savage as one possible choice. Colleen raised an eyebrow asking if he knew Peden well enough and if his partner, Megan Moore, an FBI agent, could be trusted. Chip did not reply, but seemed deep in thought. They remained silent for a while, gathering their thoughts, holding each other, their bodies feeling good and right against each other. Their silence and light embrace had a calming effect, and they fell asleep.

* * *

Chip's phone sounded, waking them both. He viewed his cell phone's screen, disappointed that an NRA solicitation call interrupted their time together. He swiped the disconnect button on his phone, ending the call before it began. With the sun just above the horizon, light streaked in around the edges of the curtains, casting the room in multiple, subdued colors. Knowing they could not stay in bed forever, they showered together then dressed.

Chip smiled at the memory of their late afternoon in bed, but he could not keep thoughts of the coming tasks from his brain. With most of the forms completed for the transfer of Parish's remains, he told Colleen that he needed to sign into BIAChat and get the word out about the time and date of the funeral and the details for hotel arrangements. The Hampton Inn gave him a code that arriving guests should use to get the special room rate. He wanted to tell them when they should arrive at the hotel in Hinesville in hopes that the group could get together Thursday evening for a toast to their fallen brother. Colleen kissed him lightly, but her lips lingered before she pulled away. The tension between them had melted away over the past hours leaving an attraction which they found hard to break, even for a short time. Finally, Colleen stood and retreated towards the kitchen.

"Hungry," she asked?

"Yeah. Did you have anything in mind?"

With a wry smile she said, "Yes, but I need food, too. How about Island Wok. You want your usual?"

"You know me too well. I'll be in the office. Call me when it gets here. If you want to join me while I type out the info, come on in."

As Chip moved into his office and opened his laptop computer, he heard Colleen ordering their evening meal. He signed into the BIAChat room and, over the next twenty minutes, keyed in the information about the funeral. He left out any hint of begging or coercion. He figured that anyone opposed to attending had already voiced their grievances and made up their minds whether to attend or not. He just hoped that the few who were most vocal with their opposition would either cave in and join their brothers in the get-together or just remain silent and not show.

His final entry asked that they contact him either in the chat room or by using a direct message of their plans. He needed a count of attendees so that he could inform the hotel of the number of guests to expect. He took a deep breath and hit enter, setting the funeral service for Randall Parish in motion.

* * *

Aslam Sayed smoothed out the wrinkled instruction booklet on his workroom table. The papers looked like a well-used owner's assembly manual for a riding lawn mower or a new gas grill. The manual had been sent to him from a contact overseas, one with a specialty in explosives. He reviewed the wiring diagram one last time. He tested the trigger device at least a dozen times and worked out two minor issues. The cell phone trigger now worked consistently for six consecutive tests.

That part of the project complete, he turned the pages of the manual and moved on to the next steps. Every step required perfect execution for the device to work properly. The test of the triggering device, while crucial to its successful operation, held no significant danger to the technician during the assembly and verification process. The next steps of the operation could not be tested without catastrophic consequences.

He looked over the warnings momentarily then scanned the steps needed to complete this phase. The instructions for these next steps listed multiple warnings with skull and crossbones on either side of the text. As he read down the page, the need for the warnings became clear.

He looked at the boxes on his workbench that he received from a mail-order service from one of the big box home improvement stores: nails, metal washers, and screws. On a shelf above the work-bench he read the labels on cans that sat side by side. They contained explosive chemicals, both liquid and powder form. He had never assembled an improvised explosive device before, but he watched numerous videos from a thumb drive, also sent by his overseas connection. While watching the videos, his confidence that he could build the destructive devices easily enough boosted his confidence. It looked easy. But thinking through the tasks, reviewing the instructions, and assembling a bomb…that elicited waves of doubt.

Anxiety swept through his body, thinking about the task ahead. He decided to take a break to calm his nerves before reviewing the procedure one more time.

As he stood, he took a deep breath and looked at his handy work. Just like the times he and Moska were out in public, his eyes bugged out as if in fear, his brain in overdrive, thinking that an army of agents from the U. S. government would crash through his door at any moment. His mind drifted, thinking that, if he were raided now, he would be hauled away to a top-secret prison and tortured for information. He turned towards a mirror and noticed the look of terror on his face. The chill that gripped him made him shiver from head to toe.

Then he thought of Moska Aziz. He hated Moska more each day, the closer it came to exacting revenge on the men who killed his family. She kept pressure on him to make sure he finished his project on time. She had not yet shared the details about the time and place for their attack, but he knew it would be soon. '*You have little time to spare. You must be ready,*' she would tell him, urgency in her voice, as if he did not know the consequences of not completing the project. She acted as if she alone had an ax to grind. Certainly, she suffered physical pain. Her back would never fully recover. The attackers also killed – vaporized - her best friend. But Moska's best friend was his baby sister. They both owned a share of the coming revenge.

He looked in the mirror again and saw exactly what Moska told him. He looked like a scared middle-eastern man with a massive chip on his shoulder. The anger notched up, mixing with the tension and fear, causing a toxic mix of emotions. His whole body began to shake with anxiety. He wanted to confront Moska, grab her and show her the man she could not see in him. Nausea welled up in his stomach. He ran to the bathroom and wretched three times, though nothing but bile came up. Sweat poured from his face as he moved to the sink, leaning against the vanity. He looked in the large bathroom mirror and now saw a pale face, sweat rolling down his forehead, temples, and cheeks. Turning on the cold water, he splashed his face, then dried it with a toweled, taking sucking, deep breaths.

He sat on the closed toilet seat and continued with deep breaths to calm his anxiety. He knew he needed to take a break from his project. He could little afford to make a mistake during the next steps. Miscues at this stage held deadly consequences.

* * *

Moska Aziz smiled as she read Chip Chandler's entry in the BIAChat room. Several quick responses gave the entry a thumbs up and positive responses that they would attend, some with and some without guests, spouses, or significant others.

"The more, the merrier," she said quietly to herself. She would monitor the chat room for another hour, then exit the site and return later in the evening to see who, and how many men and women would attend the festivities.

As she continued to review the comments, a guitar strum ringtone caught her ear. Aslam Sayed. She smiled as she swiped across her phone's screen.

"Aslam. How is your project coming?"

A grunt preceded the answer, as he cleared his throat. A moment of silence filled the connection, making Moska believe that the call disconnected. Then Aslam cleared his throat again and asked, "What, no 'How are you, Aslam?' No, 'Good evening. It is good to hear from you.' Why can't you ask about me? It is always the same with you, Moska."

She shook her head, wondering why Aslam took such a harsh tone with her. Was it as she feared, that, despite his claims to the contrary, he could not handle the pressure to complete his project? From the start of her quest after arriving in the United States, she believed that she should build the IED and leave Aslam to lesser tasks, but he assured her that he could and would handle the project. He boasted that his overseas connections would provide the knowledge and guidance to build a high-quality explosive device. He convinced her back then, but now her confidence in him waned.

In a calming voice, she asked, "Aslam, why the attitude? I simply asked about your progress. I meant nothing by it. You sound tense. Are you having technical problems?"

In a staccato retort, he said, "No, Moska. Everything is moving forward according to plan. You tell me when and where and it will be ready."

"Good. Do you need to take a break, get out for dinner or just to relax before continuing? We have time, that is, if you think you are ahead of schedule."

She could hear his deep breaths as if he tried to maintain control of his emotions. His lack of response gave her pause. She wondered if she should risk a visit to his apartment, but did not wish to leave her daughter alone. When he did not answer, she said, "Let's go out for breakfast in the morning. Mina and I will meet you at your apartment around 8:00. We can walk to the diner. No shop talk, just to eat."

Aslam replied with a short, "Fine." The call disconnected.

Moska wished that her plan did not hinge on Aslam's success.

She whispered a short prayer to Allah.

Chapter 28

Evelyn and Virgil Vance sat across the dinner table at their home in Centerville, Virginia. With the sun below the horizon, darkness reigned outside. The chandelier hanging above the dinner table illuminated the Vance's dining room. Their strained conversation held only one genuine topic – Randall Parish's funeral arrangements. The general read the entries from Chip Chandler in BIAChat, and believed that he must be an example to his Marines, both current and former, that he would attend the festivities. If an active-duty general could make the time to pay his respects to a fallen brother, then they could all follow his lead.

Evelyn pushed her food around her plate, taking only nibbles. She had no appetite for her dinner, for the upcoming funeral, or for her husband's bullshit. She did not want to go to Georgia to attend the funeral of a Marine whom she believed to be a drunken drug addict who either killed himself or died in a drug deal gone bad. The idea that her husband now supported honoring this man and encouraging – no, coercing – his former men to do the same stood out as contrary to everything she thought her husband believed in. He should have stood by this man in life instead of putting on this charade of a ceremony in death. She knew nothing of the purpose of the gathering, but it certainly had nothing to do with honor.

Over the past three days, she voiced her reluctance to join her husband, sometimes in a loud, aggressive manner. This afternoon, she decided to tone down her opposition to the trip and simply avoid the topic altogether. She resigned to the fact that her husband wanted her there which ended conversation on the subject. She would accompany him whether she liked it or not and she planned to do everything in her power to make sure he understood that she wanted no part of it.

Virgil finished chewing on a piece of filet mignon and washed it down with whiskey and water. He cleared his throat and said in a tone so low that Evelyn could barely hear, "Chandler posted the schedule for the funeral. We should be in Georgia by mid-afternoon, next Thursday. I'll make the arrangements."

She did not look up and said nothing. She took her own drink and swirled the vodka around, the ice clinking on the sides of the cocktail glass, then took a gulp, nearly finishing off her drink. She stood and headed for the bar to fix another.

Virgil said, "Fix me another one, please."

"Fix your own damn drink. I'm going into the office."

"Why the hell do you have to be that way? Why can't we just talk?"

Evelyn looked at her husband as if ready to shoot him with poison darts. The glare alone expelled an invisible venom meant to maim the general. She said, "You really have the guts to ask me that? You destroyed our marriage. You and your big, bad military career that you've thrown in my face for nearly as long as we've been married. When did you stop loving me, Virgil, the moment you said 'I do'? Did you think you were trapped for the rest of your life?" Her voice rose in volume and intensity. "My mom warned me that there would be times that I would be tested, that I might have to be tolerant, that you might be tempted because of your position." She took a deep breath and dove in, shouting. "You used me, Virgil. You're nothing but a pig. A big, egomaniacal pig. Your dick is bigger than your brain, and that isn't saying much. It's going to cost you."

The general pushed his chair back and hissed, "Lower your voice. The neighbors'll call the cops."

She shouted, "Good. Maybe you can brag to them what a big man you are, and how your little wife just doesn't understand that you need younger women to feed your ego. You lousy bastard."

She finished mixing her drink. Grabbed it, as nearly a third of the liquid spilled over the top onto the hardwood floor, and headed from the dining room down the hall to their home office. She did not look back. The door slammed and she locked it.

Vance shook his head, walked to the bar, and freshened his drink. Then he took a shot glass and poured a straight shot and downed it in one, swift motion. He took his drink and headed for the den near the back of the house. He had just reached his recliner when the doorbell rang.

"Jeezus, what now?"

Setting his drink on a coaster on the table in the den, he headed for the front door. The doorbell rang again just as he reached for the handle. Before opening the door, he looked out the peep hole and saw a man in a dark suit. He frowned, then opened the door and looked the man over. Nearly bald with sharp facial features, the man wore no identifying patches or any indication that he might be law enforcement, a salesman or a deliveryman. A bulge on his right side indicated a hidden sidearm.

Vance asked, "Can I help you?"

In a baritone voice suited more for a disc jockey, the man said, "Sir, we heard raised voices. Is everything alright?"

Vance wondered why, if the neighbors had complained, a plain-clothed man stood at his door instead of a Centerville police officer. Besides, they responded much too quickly for a patrol officer to respond to a complaint. He and his wife just finished the boisterous jousting moments before. Not enough time passed for a concerned neighbor to call to 911. To Vance, the man looked like a federal agent, or a police investigator. He looked over the man's shoulder and noticed a dark sedan parked at the curb with the engine running and the parking lights on. He directed his look at the man, an uneasy feeling coming over him.

"Everything's fine … Mr. …"

"Detective Gordon, sir. We're in the neighborhood on an investigation and I heard the arguing. I thought I'd check and see if anyone needed assistance."

"Like I said, Detective, we're fine. My wife and I are just having …a disagreement. She's just not happy with me right now. You know how these things can go. We'll keep it down."

"Alright, sir. I understand. You have a good evening."

The detective turned and headed down the walkway to the driveway and to his car. Another man sat in the driver's seat looking towards the house. Vance closed the door and turned to see his wife glaring art him. Mascara streaked down her face from her red, puffy eyes. She wore a nightgown and held a freshened drink. If looks could kill ….

* * *

An hour later, Evelyn Vance held her cell phone to her ear, waiting for Colleen Chandler to answer. After three rings, she heard Colleen. "Hello, Evelyn."

In a slurred voice, Evelyn said "Hi, sweetie. I hope your night is goin' better'n mine." She did not wait for a response. "Virgil's such an ass. He's been houndin' me about this trip. I told 'im that I want no part of it, but he insists that I go. We have to keep up 'pearances, ya know."

Evelyn polished off six drinks over the past two hours on a nearly empty stomach. The booze made its way into her system and removed any filters that her brain might normally have in place. She spoke in a loud, angry tone and had no concern if her husband could hear her. "He keeps sayin' that this is about honor and duty and country. That's a load-a-crap. I know it. He knows it, too."

"Evelyn, I'll be there. Maybe we can get away from the guys and have our own get-together. I know Chip will want me to be with him for at least part of the time, especially at the toast the night before and the graveside ceremony, but the rest of the time we can get away from the crowd."

Evelyn said, "That might at least make it tolerable."

There was a silence for several seconds that seemed unnatural. Finally, Evelyn asked, "Do you know if any other wives are comin'? I woun't mind seein' a few of the ladies."

"Chip is supposed to look in the chat room later this evening. He heard from over a dozen guys from the platoon who said they are attending. I can let you know tomorrow. He should have a better count by then."

"Colleen, you're such a darlin' young lady. Chip? He's a lucky man. He's lucky to have ya. I mean that."

Colleen knew that the alcohol affected Evelyn's tongue. She asked, "Are you going to be alright tonight?"

Another drawn out silence eventually turned to quiet whimpering. Then Evelyn said in a shaky voice, "I'll be fine. You jess make sure you're there. Okay?"

"Okay, Evelyn. You get some rest, now. We'll talk tomorrow."

Evelyn disconnected the call. Colleen wondered just how badly the Vance's relationship had crumbled. She knew the general chased women over in Afghanistan, she being one of his unsuccessful pursuits. And she heard rumors from some of the Marine wives at official gatherings since she came back to the states. Evelyn appeared quite drunk during the call. Colleen hoped she would keep quiet about plans for the coming week. That might be a problem; one that would blow everything apart.

Colleen thought about calling Moska Aziz, but what would she tell her? Evelyn got drunk? Hardly news to either woman. Best to just keep talking with the general's wife and make sure she keeps her act together through next week when they would all get together for the one last bash.

Chip walked into the den and asked, "Hey, babe, how about a few laps in the pool?"

"I'd love it. Is this a suits optional swim?"

"Umm, maybe we should wear our suits for the swim and shower afterwards."

Colleen stood in the lanai and pulled her blouse over her head, removed her bra and panties and walked towards her husband.

"I've got my suit on."

Chip looked at his wife from head to toe and said, "Suits optional it is," and began to remove his shirt.

Within minutes they embraced in the middle of the pool, exploring each other, kissing passionately. Without taking a lap they moved out of the pool, down the hall, and back into bed. After an hour, they were fast asleep in each other's arms, exhausted from their workout.

Chapter 29

Peden stepped out of bed, stretched, yawned, and rubbed his hands over his face. He looked at the novel on the night stand that he had not touched in days then picked up his charging cell phone. A bright display against a dark picture of the Savannah Riverfront at night read 6:32 a.m., Friday, September 17. The early morning sun had yet to breech the horizon east of Savannah. The hour-by-hour forecast graph on the display called for a moderately cool start to the day followed by a gradual heat build-up. By mid-afternoon a temperature near the high eighties would make the day uncomfortable for all except those few souls who loved torturous heat.

The schedule for the day included a visit from Lee Sparks who would load the recording device on his cell phone. He planned to have the device installed on their way back from their meeting with Chip Chandler, but Sparks became unavailable. He received a call from Savannah State University to look at an issue with computers in the forensics lab. Megan promised to stop in early and have the same type of gadget placed on her business phone. Lee assured her that she could disable the recorder for sensitive calls. She trusted Lee so gave the go-ahead for the installation. Lee set up his own phone, with perfect test results.

During a breakfast of coffee, cashews, and a bagel with cream cheese, Peden reviewed the Savannah Morning News. No glaring headlines grabbed his attention. One week ago, Randall Parish's body turned up on the shore of the Savannah River in Screvn County. Reading the paper this morning reminded him about the story that held scant details about fishermen finding Parish's body and the phone call from Chip Chandler that followed. He filled in the missing information on Parish, plunging Peden into an investigation that seemed to expand with each new detail. There were so many moving parts to the story he felt he needed to ground his mind with some basics.

He removed his three-by-five index cards from his desk drawer and placed them on top of the newspaper. He added data to several blank cards including Chip admitting Parish knew about the wrong house being hit and the reason he knew. He wished that Chip had provided that bit of information up front. He and Megan wasted precious time trying to figure out how and why Parish might have known about the botched strike. He added a line on another new card- *Who killed Parish and why?* Then another – *Who killed reporter Brandon Wilson and why?*

Did Parish have any documents that might implicate someone in the strike? Did Parish know or contact Wilson? How would he know to do that? Peden shook his head. He did not see a connection. But what if Parish had some kind of document in his trailer? Who stood to be exposed if the truth about the strike was revealed? Could someone from one of the federal agencies have ordered the strike because they believed Chandler's interpreter work for the Taliban or Al Queda? Chandler trusted Amir Sayed completely, but U.S. soldiers had been shot by Afghan soldiers many times; men supposedly vetted. Afghanistan existed as a country, but could more be likened to a collection of tribes. Deep seeded divisions within the populace, both political and religious, were far too many to track.

Peden wondered if anyone cleaned out Parish's trailer yet. He would call Rayshon Mack and see if he noticed anything when he walked through the trailer looking for his friend. He and Megan could search Parish's home, see if they might find something overlooked by the sheriff's office.

Megan walked in as he gathered his cards. She said, "Hey, I was thinking that maybe we should look through Parish's trailer. See if he had any documents or notes, or even a diary. Somebody killed him for a reason and they tried to make it look like a suicide. What do you think?"

Shaking his head, amazed that they were on the same page, he replied, "That's a great idea. Why didn't I think of that?

"Oh, and Lee will be here for our phones. He said it would take less than five minutes each, then we can head up to Fairfax."

Megan said, "Contact the Sheriff's office in Allendale County to let them know we'll be searching the trailer. Call Rayshon Mack and pick his brain a bit. See if he noticed anything when he walked through the trailer. With those two deputies drawing down on him like they did, Mr. Mack might have been startled and may have forgotten what he saw. It's been a week now, maybe he'll remember something."

"Another great idea. I'll start with the sheriff. We can call Ray on the way up."

Lee Sparks strolled into Peden's office holding a plastic shopping bag in one hand and what looked like breakfast from a fast-food restaurant in the other. He greeted them with a little too much cheer.

Peden asked, "What are you so perky about?"

"Well, Peden, I think we might have found our second terrorist, Abu Al-Madani, alive and well. What's even better is he's in custody in Britain."

Peden's jaw dropped.

Megan's face did not change, but Lee knew he had surprised her. She asked, "How did you find this nugget?"

"Megan, it's called hard work and persistence. A friend of mine whom I will not name, sent me a document that described his arrest. Al-Madani set up a cell in London and planned to take out a main section of the Tube at rush hour. He and three others were apprehended as they loaded up their gear for the attack. They also picked up several documents that outlined other operations in the planning stage. Major coup."

Megan asked, "When did this happen? I never heard a peep about it."

"It happened last year. It sounds like they kept it compartmentalized and buried deep, for some reason. They didn't want word of this guy's capture known. Usually, the feds like to make headline news about stuff like this, but mum's the word on this one."

Megan looked up as if looking for answers written on the antique ceiling tiles. Peden spoke up. "Maybe there's an ongoing operation that our friends, the ones who keep harassing us, don't want exposed. Déjà vu?"

Megan looked at Peden then Lee. "Makes sense. It fits. We're possibly tapping on the door to the same op."

The three remained silent, looking at each other. Finally, Peden said, "Let's get these things put on our phones. Lee can test them and we can hit on the road. We have a long drive ahead."

* * *

Installation and testing of the recorders went quickly. Lee set up three separate storage locations for the devices that did not require action by Peden or Megan. The data automatically downloaded to the hard drives that Lee designated. The files saved and remained active until manually removed. Sparks planned to make a backup of each dataset every forty-eight hours for insurance. If some government hacker figured out how to locate and delete the original files, they would at least have the backup data.

With Megan in his Tahoe's passenger seat, Peden drove north on Highway 17 towards Hardeeville, South Carolina to pick up highway 321 towards Fairfax, South Carolina, and Randall Parish's trailer. The drive would take approximately an hour and fifteen minutes. Megan called ahead to the Allendale County Sheriff's Office and spoke with Deputy Walter Aims, explaining to the deputy that they would like to search Parish's trailer. He said he recently visited the trailer and it would not be released to the owner until Megan gave him the okay. The deputy did not ask what they might be looking for. He would meet them there, give them access, and wait outside while they performed their search. The owner expressed that he would like to get Parish's possessions out so he could get a new renter.

Aims told him their investigation was not complete, but it would not be much longer.

They arrived at the trailer by 9:50. Deputy Aims opened his cruiser's door and greeted them on the rough gravel drive as they exited the Tahoe. After introductions, Aims handed Megan a key and used his hand like a game show host, indicating that they should proceed. He walked back to his airconditioned cruiser and sat in the front seat. The temperature had risen by mid-morning, but remained comfortable.

Megan handed the key to Peden who looked at the steps, assessing whether the aged and brittle-looking wood would support his weight. Megan stood back, waiting until Peden unlocked the door and pulled it open.

The heat from the trailer's interior caused Peden to take a step back. He looked at Megan and said, "Wow. I'm going to open the back door and a few windows. It's like a blast furnace in here and it stinks."

Megan nodded and looked around the neighborhood. She noted the identical trailers and the lack of trees on the block. She walked around the perimeter of Parish's trailer and noticed the undersized window air conditioner. No sound came from the unit which either died trying to keep up with the heat or was switched off. As she reached the back of the trailer, Peden opened the back door. If a back porch ever existed, it had been removed. She looked up at Peden who had sweat pouring from his forehead. She shook her head and continued her journey. When she arrived back at the trailer's porch, she entered the living room. Peden finished opening all the windows he could. The temperature in the trailer remained elevated, but a breeze brought the temperature down from near hell to just below blast furnace.

Peden said, "This might sound sexist, but why don't you start in the kitchen. I'll start in the bedrooms."

She crooked her eyebrows, then said, "Fine."

Peden headed down the hall past the first bedroom with the stack of dirty clothes. The pile reeked, fermenting whatever toxic mix of bacteria existed in the stack. He kept moving past the bathroom, which emanated an equally foul smell, and stepped into Parish's bedroom. He swept his eyes over the room, taking in the ceiling, the walls, the decrepit dresser, and the open closet doors. The bed sheets were strewn in a haphazard pile. Peden did not want to guess the source of the odor emanating from the bed. He reached into his pocket and pulled out a pair of vinyl gloves, wishing he brought a rubber overcoat to cover his arms.

He started with the bed, lifting the mattress, finding nothing but several dead roaches and a well-worn porn magazine. He moved to the dresser, opening each drawer, rifling through the scant contents, looking at the underside of each. Moving to the floor, he looked for any loose carpeting, again finding nothing but dead roaches and spiders. Even these vermin could not take the heat.

He moved to the closet. The only thing on the bar was a mixture of a dozen empty plastic and wire hangers. The shelf above the bar sagged but not from the weight of any objects – it was empty. Made of press-board, it had just given way over the years. He looked at the ceiling in the closet. It did not appear to have been disturbed. He looked at the floor where a pair of work boots and a pair of tennis shoes lay as if tossed from across the room. Dirty, gray tube socks stuck out from the top of the boots. He kicked the boots to the other side of the closet and noticed one corner of the old, worn carpeting appeared wrinkled and loose. Reaching down, he grabbed the corner of the carpet and pulled up, revealing a wood panel, approximately eighteen inches by twelve inches that did not match the rest of the wooden floor. A one-inch hole in the panel gave Peden pause. He thought about putting his finger in the hole and pulling up, then remembered that spiders love dark spaces. He reached into the sheath on the side of his belt and pulled out his Leatherman multipurpose tool – like a Swiss Army Knife on steroids. He opened the pliers and used it to pull up on the panel. He stepped back and looked at the papers stacked in the box under the floor in the closet. He took a deep breath, happy that he used his Leatherman, as the black widow

spider just sat there in its web above the stash of documents.
He yelled, "Megan, I think I need your help."

Chapter 30

The stack of papers removed from Randall Parish's trailer included official documents, loose notes, and a spiral notebook that Parish used as a journal. Before they separated the stack of papers into multiple piles for review, they crushed three spiders and a handful of other insects which they could not readily identify. Megan's face rarely showed emotion, but she gritted her teeth as she slapped at the unwanted bugs with a fly-swatter. Peden grabbed a roll of paper towels to help clean up the multi-colored splotches.

One-by-one, they lifted each sheet off the main pile, wiped it down with a slightly damp paper towel and did a quick scan to determine the subject. Three types of documents were evident as they continued their review: personal records, such as Parish's DD-214 (his discharge papers), the spiral notebook and other handwritten papers with no official purpose, and official documents outlining orders and operations. Peden and Megan knew that a Marine private should not have documents such as these as many were marked "Confidential," the pages outlined in red. Even though "Confidential" rated at the low end of the secrecy scale, these papers should have been kept in a locked file cabinet and should never have been copied or removed from a military installation.

Once sorted, Megan said, "I'll review the 'Confidential' stack, you start with the personal notes."

Peden just nodded and moved the spiral notebook and other papers in front of him. He began with many of the loose papers. Some were short notes with no dates or timeframe. "Call Ray" on one scrap and "Talk with Ray" on another were scrawled in barely legible handwriting. On another folded sheet of paper, the letters C.T. were written on the outside. He unfolded the sheet and saw a note. *I saw three SOBs do something today. It is no wonder these people hate our guts. Talk later.*

Peden leaned back in his chair, thinking *Who is C.T. and did Parish ever send the note?* He placed it aside and moved to the next folded sheet with the initials R.M. on the outside. He opened it and read, *Ray. The new guy's bustin' my chops over what we talked about last week. Who does he think he is? He's a private like me. He keeps pushing me. I'm not talking behind anybody's back, but this might get bad. You know who I'm talking about, the guy's voice carries like a loud speaker.*

Peden closed the sheet and said, "Hey, you should read this. Let me know what you think."

He handed the paper over to Megan who took it and read the page. When she finished, she said, "Based on what we know, it sounds like he's writing to Rayshon Mack and talking about Cassidy Miller. What are you thinking?"

"That's exactly what I think. If we carry it a step further, it appears that he is describing Miller having a loud voice. He doesn't say baritone or radio voice, but …"

"You're thinking that Cassidy Miller might be the guy who's calling you and Lee?"

Peden thought for a moment then asked for the paper back and reread it. He looked back at Megan, nodded, and said, "Yeah. Yeah, I am." He remained silent for a moment then continued, "I wonder if he ever sent this note to Mack? If he did, Ray left out some details about the squad's encounter with Miller. Let's keep going. Maybe some holes will get filled in."

Peden read and put aside three more sheets containing mostly scribbles on them, then found a sheet with 'R.P.' in neat handwriting on the front. He opened it and read *You need to stay away from that guy. Something's up with him that isn't right. Just stay away.*

Peden looked at the handwriting – neat and precise, like a clerk, feminine. Even though the other note appeared to be headed for Rayshon Mack, he did not believe it to be Mack's handwriting. The only female he knew to be stationed at the camp was Colleen Chandler, Chip's wife, Vance's assistant. Then he thought about the first note to 'C.T.' and he wondered if Colleen Chandler's maiden name started with a 'T.'

A multipage document drew Megan's full attention. She appeared to read the same words over several times. His curiosity piqued, but he held his tongue. If she found something of interest, she would tell him in due time. He picked up the spiral notebook and opened it to the first page. The dated entries ranged from a few lines to nearly full pages.

The first entry, dated March 7, 2011, stated *Been in this God-forsaken country for months. It's hot and dry, then cold and dry. Our missions take us out in the desert and back, up and down mountains. We haven't seen a single enemy. What the hell could be so important that we're here? WTF?*

The next entry, dated March 13 – *We finally saw some action today. Ran up on some rag-hat assholes. They tried to ambush us, but we got the best of them. No casualties in our team but we killed five of them before the rest scattered.*

The next seven pages consisted mainly of entries covering three months by a bored Randall Parish, until June 1, two days after Memorial Day. *Our first female Marine showed up for duty today. She's an officer, Colleen Temple. She's in charge of a squad, three rifle teams. Seems competent. Some of the guys are already saying she won't hang. We'll see.*

Colleen Temple. C.T. Coincidence?

Another entry caused Peden to stop and read the details. *June 15 – Captain Temple and five rifle team A members were on a routine mission when Temple got shot in the ass. It wasn't serious. Didn't even get shipped out for recovery and rehab. But she did get assigned to desk duty. Vance's assistant. She is not a happy camper.*

An entry dated June 27 grabbed Peden's attention. *Me and Hunter stood guard while Captain Chandler entered the house of his interpreter on the outskirts of Kabul. He stayed in the house for a long time. When he came out, he seemed pissed. We asked him why, but he just told us to head back to the Jeep. We drove back to camp. He never said anything more about the meeting but it might be about the Afghan girl I saw getting roughed up last week. Didn't hear anything more about it but we were ordered to stay away from the city for a while.*

He was about to read on when Megan cleared her throat and said, "Listen to this. Jeffrey Gruman wrote this disciplinary report on Parish. The report is on an official-looking form. It describes what Parish did the day of the drone strike. It's pretty harsh, suggests that Parish should be fined and confined to barracks for three months, then dishonorably discharged. There's a note attached from Gruman saying that he didn't submit it yet, but would hang on to it and see how Parish reacted."

"What's the date on the report?"

"September 12, 2011, the day after the strike." She picked up another paper and said, "Here's another report. Talks about Parish's drinking and insubordination. Again, not signed. This one's dated August 27, before the strike. Looks like Parish was already skating on thin ice."

"His journal is some pretty good reading. Puts a timeline to many things and says things that we didn't know about."

Megan put up her hand as she read the next paper, this one outlined with a red border. She said, "This is the official order to support the drone strike. It's marked 'Secret.' It gives the exact coordinates for the strike and the time the team needed to have the laser in place. September 11, 2011. It doesn't say who the target is. It also doesn't leave room for interpretation. Pretty straight forward."

Megan flipped to the next document. It looked like an exact copy of the previous order. She almost skipped the page when her eye caught something out of place. She flipped back to the previous document and looked closer. Then she held both pages side by side. Peden thought he saw her expression change. She faced Peden and said, "The target coordinates are different on the order. I think one might be the original order. Somebody changed the target coordinates on the other."

Peden looked shocked. He thought how this information might link together what they already knew. If someone from a federal agency with had a stake in the success of the mission knew Parish possessed these documents, it might be a motive for murder, but only if they could retrieve the evidence. If that someone was guilty of altering an order, they surely would not kill Parish without first finding these papers. Was Parish trying to bribe someone, maybe make a big score to put himself back on solid financial ground? From what Rayshon Mack told them about Parish, he did not appear to be smart enough or stable enough to pull off a plan like that. But why did he keep them? Was he holding them for someone else?

The bigger question: why would someone change the strike coordinates on a mission of such importance? The opportunity to take out two terror leaders with one strike did not present itself often. Did they receive information that the meeting place changed at the last minute? These were questions for the camp leader, then Colonel, now General Virgil Vance.

Peden asked, "Any theories on why?"

"No, but let's keep going. Maybe the answer is in here somewhere."

Peden turned his attention back to Parish's spiral notebook. After August 2, the entries leaned towards being a bored Marine in a hot and dry desert camp. Then he came to August 27. *Grumen wrote me up, or at least, he said he did. He brought the paper to me, waved it in my face, and swore he planned to submit it in the morning. Tagged me as a drunk, but what the hell else is there to do in A-effin'-ghanistan. I told him to go ahead. My whole family is dead. I got nothin' to live for.*

On September 10 he wrote *We're heading out in the morning to support a strike. Can't say more. All hush-hush and shit. Screw this place.*

The next entry skipped to late October. *We're finally heading home. This place can kiss my ass, especially those bastards, Miller and Grumen.*

Peden flipped back a couple pages. It appeared that Parish made no entries from September 11 through the end of October. He frowned at the inconsistency. He held the notebook up and noticed indentations in the last page that did not appear to match the writing from the previous page. Peden believed Parish may have torn out a sheet or two from the notebook. But why?

He said, "I think I might need Lee to do a little tech work on this notebook. There's a big gap in the timeline. Maybe he can do some of his magic for us."

Megan's full focus remained on the sheet of paper that she held in her hands. After a full minute of silence, Peden turned back to the spiral notebook. He flipped the page when Megan said, "Here." She handed him the paper she had been reading.

Peden read the transfer paperwork for Private Cassidy Miller, sending him to a different camp in Afghanistan. The transfer coincided with the date that Chip Chandler gave Peden for Chandler's platoon to transfer back to the states. The words "Destroy" and "Burn Pit" had been written diagonally across the page.

Peden looked up as Megan watched for his reaction. She said, "Somebody wants Miller to remain a ghost."

"More like a 'spook.' How in hell did Parish, a private, get hold of these documents? Somebody helped him … or unwittingly gave him a death sentence."

Megan, in a rare change of facial expression, raised an eyebrow.

Chapter 31

After disconnecting the call with Moska Aziz, Aslam Sayed strode into the kitchen, filled a glass with ice water and downed it as if it might be his last drink on earth. He raised his arm to hurl the glass across the room, then stopped. Taking deep breaths, he lowered the glass to the counter and closed his eyes, whispering a prayer for guidance. He wondered if, despite his bravado to Moska, that taking on the task of building the IED might be beyond his capabilities. Yes, he watched numerous videos on the subject which guided any technician through the construction of such a device. Even a person with limited knowledge of chemicals and explosives could do it if they followed the instructions to the letter. It looked simple in the video, even with the warnings of death and destruction should one make mistakes – check that – a mistake. The thought made him shiver as the chill ran down the length of his spine.

An instruction video was one thing. Watching someone on a computer monitor assemble a bomb made the process seem so simple. But performing the task, handling explosive materials, mixing those ingredients in the proper proportions, that took steady hands and nerves of steel. Just standing in his kitchen thinking about those crucial steps made his anxiety jump, his stomach making its way into his throat. He now wondered, even doubted, that he could successfully build the device. Then he wondered about the handling and storage of the bomb until needed to implement their plan. When the time came, he would transport the bomb to the final location while keeping it hidden from everyone. Concealment was important, especially in a country where every middle eastern man drew suspicious eyes. He remembered the look on his face in the mirror earlier and thought, *Especially one who looks like you, Aslam.*

His mind shifted again to Moska Aziz, the woman who thought herself superior to him. No doubt, with an ax to grind, her anger and thirst for revenge held no higher place than his. The Americans killed his entire family. His parents, his brother, Amir, and his young sister, Zahra died at the hands of the American made bomb.

Zahra. My sweet sister Zahra. Moska's best friend. She died in a fireball when the bomb demolished our home. Only a crater and rubble remained. Not a single whole body remained of his family. He never saw the aftermath of the explosion; only second-hand accounts, nearly a year after the blast. He and Moska had laid outside the house and were transported to a hospital in Kabul. An American soldier mistook Aslam for his brother, Amir, and directed that he and Moska be transferred to the military hospital in Landstuhl, Germany. That action saved his and Moska's lives, and allowed them to be relocated to the United States. Ironic that American soldiers killed his family, yet saved his life. A nurse told Aslam that a soldier had visited him in the hospital once in Germany, but he did not remember the visit. He was in a coma and wrapped in bandages for weeks after the blast. When he came out of the coma, the doctors and nurses kept calling him by his brother's name. At the time, he couldn't remember his own name, much less the names of his family.

The first name he remembered – Moska. He saw her sitting unnaturally ramrod straight in a chair next to his bed. Purple and yellowed bruises covered her face and neck. She had difficulty speaking, her words soft and unclear, as if her mouth was stuffed with cotton. When he spoke her name, tears came to her eyes and she said, "Amir, you are awake."

He barely remembered that moment. Confusion clouded his mind. Why did she call him Amir? He tried to protest and correct her, but she shook her head and said, 'Don't speak. Save your strength. We will talk later.' The image of her struggling to stand up from her seat, even with the assistance of two hospital staff, gripped him as he thought back on that moment.

Aslam sat at his kitchen table, still thinking about their stay in Landstuhl. It would be months before they both healed sufficiently to walk on their own without assistance from a nurse or other hospital staff.

During this time, Moska told Aslam about the bombing of his parent's home. *They are all dead. You are the lone survivor.* She told him that they, the military, believed him to be Amir, his brother, an interpreter for a military officer named Chandler. They did not know his true identity and he must not let them know about their mistake. It would be their ticket to America. Then they could make plans to punish those who destroyed their lives.

Aslam played along. Luckily, the officer named Chandler never came back to the hospital. A nurse passed a note to Aslam one day. Chandler wrote that he hoped his recovery would be complete and that they might meet again one day. He apologized for the mistake made by his country.

Mistake. He called the murder of his family a mistake. Aslam fumed, but with Moska's help, he remained calm and kept up the ruse. Aslam and Moska made great progress in their recoveries.

Then the meetings started. Military personnel spoke with them about relocating to the United States. They were eligible for assistance to assimilate into the U.S. because of the aid they leant the United States military.

Aslam smiled then and his current rage turned to a smile now. His recall of his and Moska's journey calmed him. His confidence returned. He knew he could finish the project and he would finish the project in plenty of time. Revenge surged through his veins providing new fuel to get back to work.

For you Mom and Dad. For you Amir. And for you Zahra.

Allah be Praised.

* * *

After knocking and hearing Lee yell to 'come on in,' Peden walked into Lee Sparks condominium holding a plastic bag. After a brief greeting, he handed the bag to Sparks who removed the spiral notebook. Peden explained it appeared at least one page had been removed from the notebook, but the impressions from the missing page were evident on the other pages.

After Peden showed him where he suspected the pages appeared to have been removed, Lee gave the papers a cursory look and said, "You're right. It's pretty clear that pages are missing and I can look at it, but this isn't my type of work. I think you need to take this to a crime lab. They have the tools where I think they could make short work of this."

Peden frowned. He and Megen discussed this very topic before Peden left his office. "Couldn't you just give it a look to see if you can make out the indentations?"

"Yeah, I could. But I don't want to do anything that might damage the indentations. I just don't have the tools, and anything I do further degrades what is there. You know what I mean?"

"You can't just shine a light across the paper and see the shadows?"

Lee looked at Peden as if he was a difficult child. He said, "I can do all kinds of things, but the prudent thing for a professional investigator would be to take it to a crime lab and have them use the most efficient method to lift the information … without damaging the original paper."

Peden moved his mouth back and forth and looked up at the ceiling as if the decision were written there. Finally, he looked back at Lee and nodded. "You're right. But that means we have to trust the FBI lab and I'm not sure we can."

"We don't have to take it to the feds. I've used private labs before. There are a couple close by." Lee held his finger to his chin as if thinking about local labs who could do the work. Then he snapped his fingers and said, "How about Savannah State University? They have a Forensic Science program. Maybe one of their professors would be willing to help. They might want to use this as an example of actual case work in their classroom."

"How good is the program and do you know anyone who might be willing to help?"

Lee smiled and replied, "Yeah. Yeah, I do. The lady's name is Min Li. She's brilliant."

"Can you call her and ask if and when she might be able to fit us in?"

Lee punched in the cell phone number from memory. Peden did not ask just how close a friend Min Li might be.

* * *

Min Li, a tenured professor and Doctor of Forensic Science at Savannah State University, agreed to perform the analysis right away. She finished her classroom work for the day and told Lee to bring the notebook over. When Lee and Peden entered the laboratory, she greeted Lee with a bright smile and a handshake that lasted far longer than professional courtesy required. They held eye contact as they exchanged pleasantries. Finally, Lee turned to Peden and introduced him as his employer and the owner of Savage Investigative Consultants. Min smiled and nodded in Peden's direction.

She turned back to Lee, still smiling, and asked, "So you want to find out what secrets the missing paper holds?"

Lee replied, "That's it. We want to maintain the integrity of the original page and I told Peden that you would be the best resource for that."

Min nodded again, still smiling. While she and Lee continued to talk about the paper, Peden tried to guess Min's age. She stood just under five feet tall with short black hair and smooth, tanned skin - typical of Chinese nationals. She might weigh under 100 pounds. She kept her hair in a bob style just above the shoulders, and her glasses were larger than necessary, almost like those in a caricature. When she spoke, her voice did not fit with her image. Nearly baritone, it projected with perfect midwestern English and not a hint of a foreign accent. In a classroom setting, Peden believed she would command the attention of her audience.

Lee handed her the notebook and the three moved towards a workstation with a stainless-steel surface. Min gestured to a machine on top of the work area. She said, "This is an Electro-static Detection Apparatus. We'll use this to find the text from the missing page. It's pretty easy to use, but it takes a few minutes to set up and run. The good thing about this device is it is a non-destructive test, meaning the sample paper from where we will lift the information remains undamaged.

As they watched Min set up the machine, Peden looked around the lab at numerous workstations. His glance came back to Lee as his technical guy watched in fascination as Min ran through the setup procedure. He smiled, noticing that the professor used a manual and followed every step. Finally, she turned the power on and watched as a viewing screen displayed a white image. While they watched, the image began to show dark lines in different locations on the screen. After several minutes, the screen filled with written notes. Peden recognized the barely legible scrawl that matched Randall Parish's handwriting.

Peden asked, "Can the content of the screen be printed?"

"Yes. How many copies would you like?"

Peden thought for a moment. He could make copies at his office so he said, "Just two of each page."

"So that will be eight sheets in all."

Peden looked quizzically at Dr. Li, "Eight sheets?"

"Yes. As you'll see, there are two pages missing with writing on the front and back of both pages. You will notice in a minute that the machine recognized four sets of indentations. Based on what I see in the notebook, the print from all four sets of indentations matches the writing in the notebook."

Peden's eyebrows shot up, now glad that they had come to a specialist.

After ten minutes with the Electro-static Detection

Apparatus and five minutes of Lee and Professor Li making small-techie talk, they left the lab with the promise that they would have the finished documents by Monday morning. They left Professor Li's office disappointed that they did not have the papers in hand but believing that the documents would bring more light to their investigation.

Chapter 32

After a long and rewarding day at the lodge, Rayshon Mack sat at his office desk, a place he rarely spent much time. The setting sun left the room dark. He switched on his overhead light so he could see his computer's keyboard. Earlier in the day he guided a group of four hunters from Greenville, South Carolina, on a deer hunt beginning at 6:30 a.m. Three of the four men bagged bucks, one with a healthy, twelve-point rack. The fourth man did not even take a shot. He explained that he just wanted to get away from his wife for the day. The other three joked with him, saying he was talking about their mom. Everyone laughed. The men went home happy and Ray earned a large tip for his excellent work. They showered him with compliments on his skills in the field.

He smiled, thinking back on the day's work as he hit a few keys and opened his email account. He looked at his email almost every day. Typically, over ninety-five percent of incoming emails were junk and he deleted them. He performed this ritual after coming home from the lodge and taking a long shower. He usually ate a light dinner with a glass of water, avoiding any sugary drinks. Tonight, he opted for a beer because of the upcoming trip to Georgia and his heightened anxiety level.

After deleting the junk from his email account and reviewing the three legitimate emails, Ray logged into his BIAChat account. He scanned the most recent responses from his fellow Marines. Surprised by the many positive responses, he noted two exceptions that stood out; Jeffrey Grumen and Carmine Russo. He shook his head, first in disappointment, then in anger. He expected Grumen's reaction, but Russo had no ax to grind with Parish. Russo got along with Parish as well as anyone else in the platoon, more so than most of their fellow Marines. Why he now loudly voiced his opposition to the ceremony that Chandler arranged surprised him. The more he read, his anger pitched up another notch.

Ray knew Russo played this game before, back when they were stationed in Afghanistan. Russo would sit back and watch an argument begin, then he would jump in on the side of the most senior man in the discussion. In the chat room, Grumen held that position among enlisted men. Chandler and Vance were in on the chat, but Vance rarely joined the fray. Chandler usually waited until the discussion cooled. Then he would join and try to offer a way to calm overheated emotions. This last time, Russo saw the opening to support Grumen and he jumped in, even though Ray knew Russo did not even like their former sergeant.

He decided right then to call Russo and give him a little piece of his mind on the subject. He hoped he could keep his cool during the call. That might be tough given Russo's penchant for verbal jousting.

Mack rarely called any of his Marine brothers, except for Chip Chandler. He looked up Russo's number in the BIAChat directory. After he found the number, he took a deep breath, then another and dialed. Russo picked up on the third ring.

In his booming New England accent, he nearly yelled, "Ray, my man, how are you?"

"Hey, Carmine. I'm good. Well, I'm okay. I was planning to buy you a beer next week in Georgia, but I see that you're not planning to be there. What's up with that? I thought you and Parish were good."

A brief silence followed, then in a slightly toned-down voice, Russo said, "Yeah, well, we kind of had a falling out after the, you know, when he lost control on that mission, then the fight with that Miller guy. I just sorta wanted to keep my distance after that. You remember that. Right?"

Ray did not miss a beat. "That's not how I remember it. You were one of the guys who talked to Rusty even after that. He acted like he wanted everybody to leave him alone, but you hung in there, watched his back. I remember because Rusty even told me that you and me were the only ones who didn't bust his chops over that – at least among the enlisted guys. Cap gave him a little support, but he couldn't get too close, being an officer and all."

Russo's loud, Boston accent and attitude notched up a little. "That ain't right, Ray. I rode his ass after that. I told him to pull his head outta his ass 'cause the rest of the platoon wanted to beat his ass. He always drank, but he didn't even try to hide it after the strike. That one guy, Miller, even jumped him and threatened him. Remember? That was weird, 'cause Miller wasn't even on the mission."

Ray grew tired of hearing Russo make himself out to be some kind of watchdog while at the same time trying to distance himself from Parish. Ray thought *You can't have it both ways.* At the same time, he wanted to get him to agree to make the trip to the funeral. He figured he might be able to play Russo's own words against him.

"So, Carmine, you had his six back then, why not now? Why are you bad mouthing him in the chat room? Before he died, Rusty told me he appreciated you're trying to help him. He had serious issues and you still hoped he could stop drinking or at least control it. He appreciated your help. I know he would appreciate it if you did him one final good turn. Be there in Georgia for him, brother."

An extended silence followed. Russo finally spoke. "I'll have to put in for vacation at work. This is really short notice. I don't know if I can pull it off."

"You can always play the 'I'm a veteran' card. Companies are bending over backwards these days to support us. They might be afraid to deny it, especially if you tell them the reason for needing the time off."

Russo said, "I'll be there, Ray. At least I'll do my best."

"That's all we all can do, brother. Thanks. Your first drinks are on me."

"Thanks, Ray. I'm looking forward to seeing you, bro."

* * *

After completing the call with Carmine Russo, Mack hit the speed-dial button for Chip Chandler. He wanted to let his captain know he swayed Russo to attend Parish's funeral with greater than ninety percent confidence. It turned out being much easier than Mack anticipated. He feared that Russo, with his Bostonian attitude, might pull his in-your-face posture up and fight it, just for spite. He did not know why Russo relented and decided to show, but, with less than a week to go to get time off from work, he was confident that Russo would make every effort to be there.

On the fourth ring, Mack moved to end the call when he heard his captain's voice. "Hey, Ray. You packed yet?"

"Hey, Cap. Not yet, but I travel light. It won't take long."

"Great. What's up?"

"I wanted to let you know that I spoke with Russo. He changed his mind and he's making the trip to Georgia. I also told him to knock off the negative BS in the chat room."

Chandler seemed genuinely surprised. He asked, "How the hell did you do that? He talked like no one could convince him to make the trip; almost as obnoxious as Grumen."

"Yeah, well, Jeff's got good reason to hold a grudge, way more than the rest of us. I think Russo might have been feeding off Grumen's anger. Russo's brave so long as he's got backup. He talks a good game, but one-on-one, he's kind of a wimp." Mack smiled to himself.

Chandler remained silent for a few seconds. "I'm a little nervous about this whole get-together, Ray. I know the guys are planning to be there, but more than a few do have legit reasons to be pissed at Parish, even in death. I hope everyone keeps their cool. I know I'm looking forward to reconnecting with a everybody."

"Don't worry, Cap. The guys respect you. I know many of them are looking forward to seeing you and your wife. How is she, by the way? She's coming with you, right?"

"Yeah. She'll be there. It looks like many wives and girlfriends will be there. You bringing anyone?"

"Who, me? Oh No! No, no, no. I'm staying out of that game."

"Nobody special in your life?"

"Yeah. About five different ones."

They both laughed.

Chandler said, "Thanks for taking this on, Ray. You didn't have to and it removes one of the two big naysayers."

"I can take a run at Grumen if you like."

"No. Maybe he'll come around on his own when he sees that Russo changed his mind."

Ray laughed and said, "That's wishful thinking, Cap, but stranger things have happened."

"We'll see you in Georgia, Ray. And thanks again."

"You got it, Cap."

* * *

When the call to Chandler disconnected, Ray thought back to his call with Russo. Something seemed off with Russo. Usually loud and brash, through most of the call he remained calm and in control. Ray could be intimidating. His size alone impressed most people, but the way he handled people's verbal interactions commanded respect without him being overly aggressive.

During their time in Afghanistan, Russo's personality always came across as loud, overly confident, and arrogant. Mack just believed it to be his heritage, his upbringing in Boston. He knew a few people from that part of the country and they all exhibited a similar larger-than-life, in-your-face attitude. Ray could not remember a time when Russo did not fit that stereotype – except on this call. He wondered what might have tempered his reaction to Ray's request.

Then he remembered Russo talking about the scuffle between Parish and Miller. Russo said something about it being related to the strike and Parish's actions in the field, but Miller transferred into the platoon after the strike. He wondered why Miller confronted Parish. He did not remember anyone talking about it afterwards. He just knew Parish seethed with anger when they were separated. By the time Mack and others had intervened, the two combatants were fighting, not talking. Later in the evening, Parish drank extra hard and passed out in his rack. Miller left the tent and disappeared until his next assigned watch. Just days later, Miller transferred out and the platoon prepared to head home.

Ray signed into BIAChat to see if Russo let everyone know he changed plans. He read down the comments of others letting Chandler know they planned to attend. The most recent entry – Carmine Russo. *I plan to attend. I will be alone.*

Ray smiled. Just then his cell phone rang. The club manager asked if he could come in an hour early.

"Yeah, I can do that."

Chapter 33

Lee Sparks worked late on Friday into the early evening. He liked to wrap up the week by setting up any long-term database searches to run over Saturday and Sunday on one computer while virus and malware scans ran on the others. That freed up his late evening and early morning hours to watch old television reruns. He loved the classics like *Daniel Boone, The Lone Ranger, Gunsmoke,* and *The Rifleman.* He considered these shows to be masterpieces of early television.

At 8:00 p.m. he popped a bag of popcorn in his microwave and headed to the living room when his phone rang. The screen displayed the message *Restricted.* He ignored the call and the ringtone went silent … but not for long. The second time the ringtone sounded, he answered, "Sparks."

After a brief silence, a booming voice caused Lee to hold the phone away from his ear. The man with the baritone voice belted out, "I thought I told you to stop looking into Cassidy Miller."

Lee moved the phone close to his ear again and said, "No, you didn't. You told me to stop searching in federal databases. You also threatened me, that I'd be arrested. I haven't …"

Baritone man cut him off, "Listen, smart guy. This isn't a game and I'm not playing with you. You're stepping into some very serious shit here! Now back off!"

Without thinking, Sparks asked, "Who the hell are you? You haven't identified yourself or your link to any law enforcement agency. Why the hell should I listen to you?"

Baritone man boomed, "Because if you don't, you'll find yourself in a jail cell! This is way bigger than you and your buddy, Savage, understand! Cease and desist!"

"I'm almost impressed with that last comment. It almost sounds like a real cop. This is still the United States.

I've got rights." He waited for a response. When none came, he asked again, "Who do you work for and what authority do you have to force me to stop my legal searches?"

In a calmer, toned-down voice, the man replied, "Listen, Sparks. I'm trying to keep you from getting hurt. That's all. Since you won't listen, just understand that whatever happens next is on you and your employer."

"What the hell is that supposed to mean?"

"Randall Parish had rights, too. Look what happened to him."

"Sounds like a threat."

"I'm just the messenger and I'm warning you. You're a small-time tech, Sparks. You don't want the full force of the government coming down on you for something you're clueless about. Just back off."

Lee remained silent as he contemplated his next words. He came this far, so he decided to keep going. "You know who I am. I have no idea who you are, what agency you're with, why you're trying to strong-arm me. So, until you give me something, I'll just keep doing what I'm doing."

"You've been warned. Just so you know, Parish was warned, too."

The phone went silent. Sparks took a deep breath. That last line sent a shiver down his spine. It left him wondering if he might be in danger. He would contact Peden and let him know about the call, but before he did, he wanted to see how successfully his recording device captured baritone man's threatening call. He opened the program and looked at the list of calls captured to date. There had been several. The last entry on the list showed nearly four minutes, which seemed about right for the call from the baritone-voiced guy. He double-clicked the file which launched an audio-play program. When the program's home screen displayed with the file already cued, Lee hit play. The booming voice of the caller filled the office, the quality of his voice better than what Lee heard over the phone. He listened for nearly a full minute before hitting the stop button.

Sparks rubbed his hands over his face as he took a deep breath, then hit the speed dial for Peden. As the phone rang in his ear, he looked at the digital clock on the computer screen. 9:40. Peden should still be awake. He answered on the third ring.

"Hey, Lee. You caught me getting a snack before I head for bed. What's up?"

"I have something for you to listen to. It's a call from our mystery man. He's not a nice dude."

"Lay it on me."

Lee played the entire conversation before getting back on the line with Peden. "What the hell is going on? He sounds like a Fed, but he won't come clean on that, and that last bit about Parish being warned - that sounded like a threat. Would a government agency kill a U.S. citizen, a military vet?"

Sparks waited for several seconds. Finally, Peden said, "I don't know, Lee, but I have to let Megan hear this and it can't wait until morning. Let me see if I can get her on the line."

After a full minute of silence, Peden came back on the line. He asked, "Megan, you there?"

"Yeah, Pedee, I'm here."

"Lee?"

"Here."

"Okay, Lee. I briefed Megan. Go ahead and play the call again."

The three listened to the call without interruption. When the digital recording ended, Megan said, "Get a copy of the recording to me with instructions on how to play it back. Roland needs to hear this. Still no clue who this guy works for?"

Lee responded, "Nope, not a clue. You heard me ask and he just ignored me."

Peden interrupted the conversation and said, "I've got an incoming call. Restricted. Maybe radio-voice thinks he can fare better with me. Stay on the line. I'll try to tap him in live."

Peden tapped a few keys on his phone, then, before he could say anything, all three heard the booming voice that matched the one they just heard on the recording. "Savage, I couldn't get through to your tech guy, so I'll try again with you. You need to call him off his inquiries into Cassidy Miller. This isn't a request."

Peden remained silent for a few seconds, then said, "It might be more effective if we knew who gave the order for us to stop."

"What is it that you don't understand? This is a matter of national security and you're wading into a serious situation! Lots of people could get hurt. I'm trying to avoid that!"

Again, Peden let seconds tick by. He hoped the caller would get the message - he needed to give them something - a good reason why they should stop. When the silence dragged on, Peden said, "Look … what's your name?"

The caller remained silent.

"Okay, play it like that. We have an investigation into Randall Parish's murder. We understand it goes back to his time in Afghanistan. We also know the strike might have been botched. Sound familiar?"

This time, baritone-guy said, "We'll handle it from here. You have to stand down. It goes way beyond the murder of a Marine."

"So why don't we work together? We can tell you what we have and you can tell us the purpose of the operation."

"That ain't gonna happen."

"Can you at least tell us what agency you work for?"

"Jeezus! No! No, I can't! You just don't get it!" They heard the caller take a deep breath, then he continued in a more controlled tone, "This isn't your business. Look, I tried to warn you. Either back off now or I can't guarantee your safety."

Megan had been quiet during the exchange. She spoke up now. "Are you Cassidy Miller, or is that one of your aliases?"

Peden had not expected Megan to say anything and was surprised when she did.

"Who's asking?"

"I asked first."

"You must be Megan Moore, FBI Special Agent out of the Savannah, Georgia office."

"And you must be Cassidy Miller, ghost private who has never been in the Marine Corps, among other covert names, I'm sure."

The caller must have come to a decision. He said, "Look, I'll meet with you, Agent Moore. Just you and me. I can only convey a little information; enough, I hope, to get you to understand that you and Savage have got to back off."

Megan asked, "When and where?"

"Tomorrow morning, 7:30 at the Waffle House on Ogeechee Road, just off five-sixteen bypass."

Peden thought *What the hell is it with Waffle House?*

Megan answered, "Fine."

Peden texted Lee and asked if he could verify the caller had disconnected. Sparks replied yes, only the three of them remained on the line.

Peden said, "Megan, are you sure you want to meet him alone?"

"Of course not. We're both going and I'm going to ask Rollie for backup, just to be in the area in case it hits the fan. But I don't think it will. This is a dark op by either CIA, NSA, NCIS, or some anti-terror group. I think they're after whoever screwed up the thing in Afghanistan. They have two terror leaders who are supposed to be dead and it's only by luck they have one of them in custody. I think they need a head on a platter and they can't allow the guilty party to see it coming. That's the reason they want us to back off."

Lee had not said a word during the entire call but now remarked, "Megan, you can use your phone to record your conversation with this guy. I'll show you how to set it up. You can be recording right before the meeting."

"You read my mind, Lee."

As the three were about to disconnect the call, Peden said, "I have another call coming in. It's Harlan Wilson."

Megan said, "Keep us on and answer."

A moment later, the southern drawl of Harlan Wilson came on the line. "Sorry it's so late, Peden, but I got another call from the guy with the deep voice. Y'all know the one I'm talkin' 'bout, right? He got pretty loud on the phone, said I need to stay away from y'all."

"Hey, Willie. I got a call, too. So did my computer guy. We're meeting him tomorrow morning. Maybe we'll find out why he's telling us to back off."

"Well, I'm not too keen about gettin' hassled. Makes me want to keep diggin', ya know what I mean?"

"Willie, I'll call you after our meeting and let you know what we find out."

"That'll be fine."

Peden asked, "You still planning to be in Hinesville Thursday night?"

"Wouldn't miss it. Y'all want me to be covert about takin' pictures and videos and stuff? I can stay away from the crowd and still observe everything. I can stay in touch by phone."

"I think we'll need to talk before Thursday. When is a good time for me to call you?"

"Peden, y'all can call me anytime, day or night. Let me know what this baritone guy says. Maybe he can shed some light on why my brother was killed."

"We'll ask him, Willie. Anything else?"

"Nope."

After the call disconnected, Peden asked Megan and Lee if they had anything to add. They both replied 'no.' But Peden had a question for Megan. "Do you plan to ask this guy if he knows anything about Wilson's brother's death?"

"I hadn't planned on it, but I do now. I'm calling Rollie and asking him again if he's hearing any chatter from his counterparts at NCIS or other agencies. If this thing is as serious as the guy says, Rollie's got to be hearing something, even if they're only rumors."

Chapter 34

Peden poured a fresh cup of coffee to help wash down the remnants of a breakfast of eggs, grits with sausage, and wheat toast when Megan strode into his kitchen. She grabbed a coffee mug from a kitchen cabinet and poured herself a full cup. She did not add anything to the strong brew and took a sip from the steaming mug. She sighed as she looked up at the ceiling. It was just after 7:00 a.m. Plenty of time remained to make the ten-minute drive to the Waffle House on Ogeechee Road southwest of Savannah's historic district. Baritone man said for Megan to come alone, but Peden would be joining her and Lee Sparks would be listening, recording the conversation.

Megan asked, "Why didn't you wait and get breakfast at the restaurant?"

"They can't make sausage and grits like mine. Besides, I didn't want to have a mouthful of food when talking with this guy, whoever he is. We both need to stay focused on what he says."

Megan nodded. "I spoke with Rollie last night. He's been calling his counterparts. None of the other agency heads he knows have heard a peep about a special op having anything to do with old military campaigns, terrorists, or recent murders. If there's something going on, it's being held close to the vest. He's made a couple calls on our behalf, all related to Parish. He said he can't keep making inquiries or his contacts are going to get seriously suspicious about what the FBI is doing, looking into this obscure death."

Peden walked his dirty dishes to the sink, rinsed them, and placed them into his dishwasher. "Do you think the CIA or NSA is trying to track down Abdul Badri?"

"I don't think so. This feels more like an internal thing."

"Meaning …?"

"Okay. Our focus has been on the murder. We're trying to find out who killed Parish. Miller's only touch point for this – his fight with Parish over ten years ago. We're just trying to find out who 'Miller' really is. How does that trigger any agency to believe that our simple inquiries would trample on their op? Would they assume we have more information than we really do?"

"Maybe they know we have information, or that Parish had information that we might come across. We're still waiting on those missing pages from Parish's notebook."

"Yeah. I wish we had them in hand for this meeting."

Megan nodded in agreement, then asked. "Ready to go?"

"Yeah. You head out. I'll leave about a minute behind you. When we get to the restaurant, how do you want to play this?"

"Let's see where he's seated. Since I'm going first, I'll get seated across from him, whether it's a booth or a table. If he's in a booth, you sit on the same side as him, kind of blocking his exit. See how he responds."

"Sounds antagonistic. But it will probably rattle him a bit, seeing that we can play hardball, too."

She nodded. "I'll do all the talking until you see a spot to jump in."

Peden nodded. "Finish your coffee. We'll get going, separate cars, right?"

"Yep. You park away from where I park. We'll go in from different directions."

Peden smiled. *Devious.*

Without another word, Megan headed to her green Honda Accord.

Peden finished his lukewarm coffee and followed moments later.

* * *

Peden pulled into the parking lot of the restaurant on Ogeechee Road. A feeling of déjà vu hit him, this being his third visit to a

Waffle House in three days. The building, parking lot, even the surrounding commercial area appeared eerily similar, like a cookie-cutter version of the other restaurants. As he pulled into the parking lot, he noticed Megan's car about eight spaces in from the road, across from the restaurant's main entrance. Peden opted to drive further towards the back of the building and parked directly behind the building. He waited a full minute before he exited his car and headed towards the main entrance. As he walked past the first windows, he casually glanced through the glass and saw Megan and a man, whose face he could not see, seated in a booth next to the last window. Megan took the seat facing the back of the restaurant. She did not even move her eyes in his direction.

When Peden entered the building, he made a right turn towards the booth where Megan and a stern-looking man were seated. As he approached the booth, a man stood from a table near the middle of the dining room and stepped into Peden's path. The man's close-cropped hair and physical build screamed *former military*. Wearing a light sportscoat over a golf shirt, and highly polished shoes, he appeared relaxed, comfortable with confrontations.

Peden said, "Excuse me."

The man said nothing, but did not move. About two inches taller than Peden, several facial scars let Peden know he had previously been in physical scuffles.

Peden leaned forward towards the man and quietly said, "You move or I'm going to make you cry like a little girl in front of your partner."

The man smiled as if he liked a challenge, but remained stubbornly in Peden's path. A waitress behind the counter noticed the two men and stopped pouring the two cups of coffee on the counter near the service window. The few other patrons remained oblivious to the tension between the two men.

All four of them knew they had broken the agreement that Megan and 'Miller' would meet alone. Peden looked around the left arm of the man standing in his path and said, "Megan, it looks like …"

Without warning, Peden reach out with his left hand and grabbed the man's right twisting in a way that bent his thumb and wrist at a painful angle. The man went to his knees and tried to swing his left hand at Peden's jaw.

The other man sitting across from Megan smiled and said, "Sid. Let Mr. Savage pass. We don't need the police here."

Peden eased the pressure on 'Sid's' thumb and said to the man, "We're not going to have a problem here, are we Sid?"

He grunted, "No."

Peden let go of the thumb and allowed him to step aside. As per his and Megan's previous discussion, Peden slid into the booth next to the man who smiled and said to Megan, "I like your style."

Megan's expression did not change. "Let's start with a name. You already know who we are and probably a whole lot about us. We don't know anything about you."

The man's smile evaporated, seeing that Megan meant business. He looked at 'Sid' and bobbed his head to the side. 'Sid' moved back to the table where he sat before confronting Peden.

"Myles Cassidy."

The waitress who observed the confrontation walked cautiously to the table and asked if Peden and Megan would like menus. Cassidy already had a coffee and a small plate with toast or English Muffin crumbs. Peden said, "Two coffees, black. Thanks."

When the waitress moved out of earshot, Megan said, "Sounds like another alias. Is that your real name? And is that Myles with an 'I' or a 'y'?

Myles replied with a slight smile, "It's close enough. With a 'y' and you want to know why we're asking …"

Megan cut him off. "What agency?"

Myles looked at her like she just asked him to solve world hunger. He remained silent.

"Myles, this is going to be a short meeting and not real productive if you keep this attitude up. What agency are you working for?"

Cassidy took a deep breath, then looked defeated. He came to the realization he would have to give them something. He surmised Megan had little patience for cat and mouse games. He said, "NCIS. We're full time." He nodded towards his partner 'Sid'. "Myles Cassidy is my real name. I'm the special agent in charge of an investigation into the several botched military operations in Afghanistan and elsewhere in the middle east. The one involving Parish was dormant for about nine years - until he turned up dead."

Megan pressed on, "What clued you in to Peden's technician performing searches on your alias?"

Cassidy did not miss a beat. "We placed electronic flags on any searches using my undercover name as the keyword. There were other flags as well, but when your man, Sparks, did his searches, we had flares going off in the various databases we had flagged. Sparks is pretty good. If we hadn't had the warnings built in, we'd have never known about his mining."

"So, what are you investigating? What's the angle for your op?"

Cassidy shifted in his chair. He clearly did not want to divulge the depth of his investigation or the ultimate goal.

Megan did not wait for an answer and said, "We know the wrong house was bombed. We also know the targets, Abdul Madri and Abu Al-Madani are still alive. One of them is in British custody. The other is out plotting against us. You must also know that, yet, you continue to investigate. So, Special Agent Cassidy, who's your target?"

The look on Cassidy's face would have amused Peden had the circumstances been less serious. He watched as the NCIS agent's defenses seemed to melt away. It may have been an act, but Peden believed that they were about to learn new information that might fill in the holes in their own investigation.

Cassidy said, "General Virgil Vance. He was in charge of the camp when the failure occurred, but worse, we believe that he intentionally falsified a report regarding the results of the strike. Randall Parish's death came to our attention the day after his body was discovered. Since then, we've been implementing a plan to question the key participants in the strike, but Savage's tech guy got us side-tracked."

Megan remained silent for a time, maintaining eye contact with Cassidy. His story sounded legitimate but holes remained as to why NCIS waited until now to reopen the investigation or why they paused it at all.

"Special Agent Cassidy, why did you confront then Private Parish ten years ago?"

"I was assigned to the platoon as a plant to gather information. I tried to get in good with Lieutenant Temple, figuring if I could sweet-talk her to gain access to sensitive files. It didn't work. The guys in the barracks talked about Parish and his reaction in the field and that he drank heavily. They were worried about him. I figured I might be able to exploit his drinking problem. That didn't work either. My presence and inquiries ended up drawing more attention to myself, so we shut down that angle. We didn't make any headway with anyone at the camp, so we backed off; maybe try a different approach. Before we could get everything ready to go, the platoon received orders for home. We remained active for about ten months after the incident, then the decision was made higher up we should back off the investigation, but not close the file. It's been dormant ever since – until now."

Megan looked at Peden, letting him know she planned to give Agent Cassidy some of the information they collected and he might not agree. But ultimately, she made the call.

She turned back to Cassidy and said, "Agent Cassidy, it's your lucky day. We have copies of some documents that you might need in your investigation. We're waiting on a few more, but so far, it tells a very disturbing story."

"Agent Moore, I'm all ears."

"I think this conversation should continue in my office Monday morning, for security reasons."

"Agreed."

She continued, "One last question. Do you know why a reporter by the name of Brandon Wilson was killed?"

Cassidy didn't hesitate, "I heard about Wilson's death. The coroner on the case signed it off as carbon monoxide poisoning - an accident. We have reason to believe that he may have been killed as part of a cover-up."

Megan glanced at Peden. She had some thoughts, but preferred to keep them to herself – for now.

Chapter 35

Chip Chandler finished his morning exercise routine, including twenty laps in the pool. He showered and ate a breakfast of black coffee, eggs over easy with bacon and wheat toast, all before 7:30. Colleen slept in until 7:00. Chip heard her in the pool, gliding along on her way to her normal thirty laps, the first leg of her morning ritual. Right after he downed two vitamins and a protein drink, he sat in his office and signed into the BIAChat room. He reviewed the comments on the upcoming gathering in Hinesville, Georgia; just five days to go. He took a deep breath, trying to keep a positive attitude. The application opened.

As he reviewed the many entries, the number of affirmative responses pleased him, especially the one from Carmine Russo. In a positively worded entry, Russo explained his change of heart, not mentioning any coercion by others. He sounded contrite in his explanation and spoke positively about seeing his bothers at the lounge the night before the funeral services. Several platoon members responded they were looking forward to having a beer with him as well.

Almost every platoon member from ten years ago planned to attend the gathering on Thursday night and the funeral on Friday with two exceptions. Wesley Brookins and Jeff Grumen posted that they would not attend the gathering Thursday night nor would they be at the funeral the following morning.

Brookins explained that he and his father planned a trip to a remote area in South Dakota to hunt elk. The trip was scheduled nearly five months earlier at a significant cost, already paid in full. This would be their last trip together as his father, also a former Marine Corps enlisted man, had less than a year to live after being diagnosed with a rare form of cancer. His dying wish; to have a two-week-long hunting trip with his only son. Brookins passed along his condolences with hope that everyone would enjoy the gathering, despite the solemn occasion.

Grumen, on the other hand, left a short and disrespectful final entry. He repeated his disdain for the entire idea of having a military funeral with honors. He would not attend the festivities and act as if he honored someone who did not deserve it. *Parish dishonored and disrespected us all by his actions. He can rot in hell for all I care.*

Chandler wished he could remove or hide Grumen's remarks, but he believed it best if he did not respond or take any further actions aimed Grumen. He noticed there were no follow-on comments to Grumen's remarks, which Chandler believed to be a good sign.

Still, it rankled him, Grumen's bashing of a fellow Marine. He decided to call his former sergeant and confront him directly, out of view and earshot of the other platoon members. After finding his cell number, Chandler dialed and waited for four rings until Grumen answered.

"Hey, Cap. A little early on a weekend for a social call."

"Jeff, you and I both know what this is about." He took a deep breath and continued, "I read your last post in the chat room. You know, it's been ten years since you and Parish had your run-in. Why can't you drop it now? What gives?"

Chandler heard Grumen take a deep breath, apparently measuring his words even though he did not hold back with his BIAChat remarks. After a moment where Chandler heard nothing but breathing, Grumen said in a voice that sounded annoyed, "Look, Cap, you weren't there. You didn't see and hear Parish, how he put all three rifle teams in danger. He acted like a madman, waving his arms, shouting at the top of his lungs, acting crazy. If I hadn't shut him up, hell, we might all have been killed. As it was, I thought we were all in danger."

"I know we've been through this, but what was he yelling about?"

"Hell. He screamed we bombed the wrong house. The coordinates were right in the orders. We targeted the building specified in the order." As he spoke, his voice became louder, the anger creeping up with each passing second. "You can verify it with Ray Mack. He looked at the laser and the order and made sure they matched. We watched the targeted building get lit up, then Parish went nuts."

They rehashed the same discussion from ten years before, shortly after the bombing. Grumen and Chandler both knew the wrong house was destroyed because Chandler made it clear to Vance and the platoon brass his interpreter lived in that house. Grumen said back then, ten years ago, he had no idea how the order specified the Sayed house be bombed, and he maintained ignorance even today.

"Listen, Cap, I know this is personal to you, about your man, Amir, but we had no way of knowing beforehand. How Parish knew, I have no idea."

Chandler knew. Parish went to the house with him one day when he spoke with Amir. He never told anyone until just a few days ago when he told his wife, Colleen.

"Jeff, you still haven't explained why you can't just go along to get along. It's not like you have to claim you and Parish were friends. Hell, everybody knows you hated his guts."

Grumen's answer came out hot and harsh. "Cap, there is no way I'm going to Georgia. Like I said, Parish can rot in hell. It still pisses me off that you guys are honoring him with full military honors. He was a disgrace to his uniform and to his country. He should have been tossed out immediately after I reported his actions to you and Vance. I still don't know how he received an honorable discharge. Hell, he was drunk half the time in country … an Arab country. You know how the brass frowns on that."

Chandler did know. He also knew that many Marines broke the rules related to alcohol. Most received an official verbal reprimand which meant a negative write-up made it to their personnel record, while others just received a stern warning without any official action.

"Nothing I can do to change your mind?"

"Absolutely not. Save your breath."

Grumen disconnected the call without so much as a goodbye, or even a 'go to hell.' Chandler looked at his phone in disgust. He hit the speed dial number for Virgil Vance's private cell phone.

Afte a single ring, in a voice that sounded winded, Vance said, "Hey, Chip. What's up?"

"You out running this morning, General?"

"Yeah. Taking it easy but trying to make it four miles. I have a set path I take. Easy terrain on streets and walkways. But you didn't call to check on my workout routine."

Chandler drew in a deep breath and said, "I just spoke with Jeff Grumen. He'd bashed Parish in the chat room again. I just wanted to call and see if I could change his mind. He's adamant about staying away and he still won't stop his rants in the chat room. Would you to call him, see if you could change his mind?"

The general drew in a series of long, deep breaths, then said, "Sorry. Just trying to catch my breath. Look Chip, Grumen won't change his mind and the more we try, the worse his comments will get online. Let's just count our victories and be glad that his negative rants didn't infect the rest of the guys."

Chandler hoped Vance would take up the cause. Grumen might accept a strong suggestion from a general versus a captain. But he agreed. Time to be thankful so many of the platoon would attend and the funeral and services came together at all.

He wiped his forehead and said, "General, I agree. I'll leave Grumen alone. He'll have to deal with his own conscience over the years."

"By the way, Chip, did anybody need financial help to get to Hinesville?"

"Yes, sir. I helped buy some plane tickets and paid for several rooms for a couple guys. It wasn't too much."

"Let me know how much and I'll cover the costs."

"Not necessary, sir. We're good."

"If the situation changes, let me know. I'm glad to help. You did a hell of a job, pulling this together. I'm proud of you and the rest of the platoon."

"Thank you, sir."

* * *

Moska Aziz smiled as she read the latest BIAChat entry by Chip Chandler. She hoped someone could convince Jeff Grumen to attend the ceremony, but he seethed with anger even at the suggestion he put aside his hate for Randall Parish. She figured things might work out this way, and put together a contingency plan to deal with Grumen or any of the others who refused to attend the services. Grumen, like the others, would not go unpunished. She need not hurry, just in case he changed his mind, though she felt confident Grumen's refusal to attend anything related to honoring Randall Parish would stand. A drive to Columbus, Ohio, and back would take over sixteen hours by car. Add two hours to deal with Grumen and several hours for meals and rest, that left plenty of time to attend the festivities in Hinesville.

Her spirits were lightened by this new development. This way, she could see his face and the anguish he would feel deep inside as he watched the person closest to him suffer as she suffered. She could taste revenge as the time grew closer to dealing with those who killed her best friend's family; and the man whom she hoped would be her husband. Violently, they stole her innocence and her future. Now they would pay. The years passed slowly, but now the time drew near. Her physical pain would always remain with her, but revenge would ease her mental torment, and her suffering would come full circle.

She wondered if she should call Colleen Chandler and let her know that she would be out of town for a few days. She decided Chandler could find out about Grumen like the rest of his platoon. It did not matter. In five days, the scales of justice would once again be balanced.

Chapter 36

Virgil Vance, alone in his basement 'man cave' office, surfed television stations looking for a decent college football game since Navy enjoyed a bye week. Except for the light emitted by the flat panel TV, the large space remained dark. A cocktail glass with ice and what remained of two fingers of his favorite liquor, Jamison Black Barrell Irish whiskey, sat on the table within easy reach.

He stopped clicking at the pregame show for the Ohio State versus Tulsa game. Seeing the Buckeyes helmet on the desk in front of the four network analysts made him think about Jeff Grumen. He remembered the sergeant bragging about attending The Ohio State University and how they possessed the most dominant football program in the nation. Then he thought back to comments left by Grumen on the BIAChat group regarding the upcoming funeral and Chip Chandler's request that Vance contact him and set him straight. He told Chandler they should ignore Grumen. The former Sergeant being the only vocal holdout probably worked to their favor. As long as no one else picked up his negative rhetoric, they should consider it a victory and a positive sign for the coming week's gathering. After some silent consideration, Chandler agreed.

Vance hardly noticed the pregame discussion leading up to the kickoff. He was not thinking about the funeral and the get-together the night before. His mind had been consumed by the possibility that he might be promoted to lieutenant general. Three known opportunities existed based on announced retirements, and rumors circulated that Congress planned to expand the number of lieutenant general positions by three. A good chance existed he would fill one of the positions. Among his peers at major general, several confided in him they planned to retire as well, narrowing the number of available candidates able to advance. He had been schmoozing his senators, their staff, and his superiors, hoping that his name remained prominent among the eligible candidates.

The one area he needed to address concerned his wife's public behavior. Over the course of their marriage, he tried his best to keep his many affairs hidden from her and the public. On the other hand, Evelyn seemed less concerned about his public image. In fact, she used her marital infidelity to punish him as payback for his adulterous conduct. She did not want to get even. She wanted to take her husband down a notch, but without affecting her own standard of living. If he really wanted this promotion - and he did - he needed to impress upon her that her lifestyle could take another step up if he made lieutenant general. Pay raises at this level of service were substantial, as were retirement benefits, including his future pension. As a major general, the compensation offered a very comfortable retirement. Advancement to lieutenant general would put Vance in an exclusive club. He understood the promotion would be a huge boost to his income and, more important to him, his ego.

He just settled on watching the Buckeyes game when his phone rang. He thought *What does Chandler want now? I told him to let it go.* When he looked at his phone's screen, the message *Restricted* displayed. He ignored the call and let it go to voice mail. After twenty seconds, his phone rang again with the same message on the screen. His curiosity overrode the urge to ignore it again. He swiped across the screen and barked, "Vance."

A sultry, smooth, female voice said, "Good afternoon, general. I hope I'm not interrupting anything important."

Vance paused before answering. He could not place the voice and believed that it might be a spam call. He barked into the phone, "Lady, whatever you're selling, I'm not buying. Goodbye."

Before he hung up she said, "You should listen to what I'm about to tell you. It may affect your promotion. I know how much that means to you."

She cooed the words more than spoke them. He frowned, wondering how she knew he might be in the running for one of the three-star-general posts. Only a relative handful of people knew of his ambitions, and most of those were with his senator's office, or were close friends and colleagues.

He growled into his phone, "Who are you and what do you want?"

"Oh, I love it when you show me how tough you are, such a big man. No wonder you've come this far. You know how to put people in their place. I like that in a man."

"I'm hanging up now."

"You haven't even heard my reason for calling."

"It can't be too important. You won't even identify yourself."

She laughed into the phone, then said, "You know me. At least, you did. I think you'll find this call among the most important of your career. You see, I know what you did in Afghanistan. Everything you did. What a shame it would be if all those – how should we say it – scandalous acts came to the public's attention. You could probably kiss that promotion, and your career, goodbye. Don't you think?"

He tensed and hesitated before answering as he thought back ten years prior. He shook his head, believing no one could possibly know anything about his time in country. After a long, uncomfortable silence, he said, "You don't know anything because there's nothing to know. You shouldn't spread lies. It could come back to bite you."

He disconnected the call without another word. Then he began to recall his time at the little camp south of Kabul.

How could anyone know?

* * *

Moska Aziz heard the silence on the line when Virgil Vance disconnected the call. She laughed out loud feeling self-gratification at making the arrogant, conceited general squirm. Before long, she would have her ultimate victory. Her life would not change except she would know that the men who changed her life completely would be punished.

Mina heard her mother's laugh as she walked into the room and smiled. She said, "Is it a joke you can share?"

Moska tried to not look surprised at her daughter's entrance. She forced her laughter to continue and said, "I'm sorry sweetheart. I just thought of something that tickled my funny bone. It's nothing. You are a little young for what I was thinking."

"Mom, I'm nine. I'll be ten soon."

Moska smiled. Her daughter indeed had grown up fast … too fast. Remembering she had only fifteen years on her daughter, it pleased her they lived in a country where resources were plentiful, education of school aged girls was not only promoted, but required by law. She hoped Mina would be able to take advantage of those laws, of their lifestyle change from life back in Afghanistan. A tragic event in Moska's life made this opportunity for Mina possible. She remained bitter about the circumstances, but grateful for her daughter's sake.

Mina kept her eyes on her mother as Moska came out of her deep thoughts and asked, "You're smiling, but why do your eyes look sad?"

Moska admired her daughter's perceptive mind. She would have to be much more careful during her conversations with Aslam and Colleen Chandler. Mina must not know of coming events.

* * *

Virgil Vance stood, grabbed his tumbler of whiskey and headed to the wet bar along one wall of his basement. As he thought about the troublesome call from an unknown woman, he wondered what she might know. If certain details of events half way around the globe came to light, even if only in rumors, it could derail his chances for a third star on his lapel. It might even end his career. The military thrived on rules and order. Any behavior which caused the ranks to doubt those in leadership positions must be removed and replaced immediately. Controlling weapons of mass destruction, or even a military force capable of rapid deployment and overwhelming offensive dominance could only be accomplished if everyone trusted and followed the orders of those in their command structure. Distrust could not be allowed to manifest itself in the ranks.

As he poured his third Jamisons, Vance thought of those in a position to reveal any secrets from some ten years prior. The names made for a very short list. One name stood out among the short list - Lieutenant Colleen Temple. He did not believe her to be privy to details surrounding certain events, but she did interact with the men in the platoon regularly; maybe a little too frequently. Vance knew she held a great desire to get back in the field with her rifle team. She hated riding a desk. He also knew she hated him, but like many commands, Vance's superior ordered him to keep her behind a desk and out of harm's way stating *The last thing the military needs right now is a dead female officer.*

Thinking about others who might know too much, he wondered if Carmine Russo ran his loud mouth to friends at some bar, bragging about his time in Afghanistan. He regularly drank just enough to make his already overbearing personality a step above arrogant. Could he have spun a tale a bit too close to the truth to the wrong crowd? Russo always walked a fine line between truth and fiction. When called on it by others, he would back off his claims – at least when not too drunk.

Then there was Jeff Grumen. Vance regretted he allowed Grumen some latitude in the boundary between officer and enlisted personnel. Under the guise of having security while Vance travelled to Kabul, he and the former sergeant became friends, even shared a drink or two when away from camp, a risk Vance now knew he should have never taken. But being away from home and away from your family opened doors that normally would remain shut. It weakened the moral compass. What could go wrong? Who would know? They were half way around the globe in a country as primitive as existed on the planet. Between the United States and Russia, the constant war pushed Afghanistan even further back in time.

When Grumen produced a bottle of his favorite whisky, then Colonel Vance could hardly turn it down. One shot turned into four, then more. The colonel could not recall the rest of the day and early evening.

Time to make the call.

He punched in the number for Jeff Grumen's cell. He answered after the third ring.

In a slightly slurred voice Grumen said, "If it isn't the mighty General Virgil Vance. I can't say I'm happy to hear from you."

Vance and Grumen did not part ways on good terms. When Vance awoke the day after the drunken trip in Afghanistan, the general regretted he let a mere enlisted man cause him to stray from his long-term plan. Of the few people with dirt on Vance, Grumen had a front row seat.

"I just got a call from some bitch who claimed she knows about misdeeds from ten years ago. She wouldn't tell me her name or what she knew or who put her up to the call. You have any ideas on that?"

When he responded to Vance's question with anger fueled by five beers already under his belt, he barked, "Who the hell do you think you're talking to, Vance. I'm not one of your lackies. Not anymore. You've got some balls accusing me of talking." He paused, but before Vance could answer, he said, "Why don't you call Russo?"

Vance nearly shouted back, "I planned to call him, but you came to mind first. For good reason."

"Look, I don't have time for your shit. I'm doing something far more important than worrying about your tainted career. I'm watching the Buckeyes. Don't call again, ya self-important prick!"

Grumen ended the call. Vance sat looking at his drink, then downed it in one smooth motion. His anxiety ticked up another notch, not knowing the source of some unknown woman's threat.

This is not good.

* * *

The Buckeyes game became a blur as Grumen thought back on the day in Afghanistan when he, Vance and Russo drank a whole bottle of Jamison's. They ate very little before their trip to Kabul, hoping to have a little fun, touring the city. They barley remembered getting to the outskirts of town before taking notice of people walking around the marketplace.

I never should have trusted him. Biggest mistake ever.

Chapter 37

Aslam Sayed worked on the final step from the instruction manual; sealing the seams of the galvanized pipe to the pipe caps. Even with the temperature in his condominium at sixty-eight degrees, as he applied the adhesive, tension sweat from his forehead ran into his eyes. His hands shook as he moved the tube around the circumference of the pipe. It took all his concentration to keep moving at a steady pace allowing him to apply an even coat of sealant. The instructions stated that, while applying the sticky substance, the technician should make the application in one smooth, continuous motion, thus creating a good seal. Though the instructions stated this step in the process posed little danger, he still feared the least misstep would send him on a premature journey to meet Allah. With the final bead of adhesive applied, he picked up a rag and wiped the sweat from his brow and temples as he took a deep breath. He stepped back and smiled. He would wait before calling Moska to allow his nerves to calm. He did not want her to hear any tension in his voice.

Aslam looked around the workbench. No extra parts lay scattered on the tabletop. The surface remained clean and free of dust and debris of any kind. He picked up the manual he had used for the past month and slowly, methodically reviewed the steps while thinking about his actions during the construction of the improvised explosive device. It took nearly forty minutes to complete his review. As he read the final step, he smiled, confident he completed every step to the exact specifications called for in the pages of the booklet. He even connected the throw-away cell phone, though it remained powered down. *Time for a celebration.*

He dialed Moska's number and waited. After three rings, she picked up and said, "Aslam, I'm surprised to hear from you this late. How is the ….” She stopped and said “How are you?”

He bristled at Moska's near misstep, knowing that she nearly questioned his progress on the project. She quickly recovered. After their last tense exchange, he hoped she would become more personal when they spoke, and less business-like. With Moska, it appeared she held little interest in him. Outwardly, her entire personality, her entire being, centered on vengeance. She called it justice, and he agreed. When their plan succeeded, justice would be delivered in spades. But what about after they completed their task? Where would they go next? Would she and Mina leave Georgia? The United States? Where would they go? *Will I be welcome to go with them?*

“Aslam, are you still there?”

“Yes, still here. I am fine … better than fine. I may even celebrate tonight.”

He wanted to tell Moska the good news about their project - his project. He planned to stretch out the call a bit more before he proclaimed his triumph for completing the device that would punish the Americans for their crimes in Afghanistan. This major step proved his commitment to their cause. He hoped it would endear Moska to him. In his mind, she owed him that much.

She asked, “Tell me, Aslam, what are you celebrating?”

He let the silence build to what he hoped would be a climactic pronouncement, then proudly said, “The project is complete. We can deliver the device when and where needed.”

Moska replied in a cheerful voice, “That is fantastic news.” She paused then said, “Have you verified all the steps? You are certain that it will work as described?”

Immediately, his attitude changed and he nearly shouted into the phone, “Of course I did. I walked through the manual, step-by-step, making sure I did everything with precision. I am certain it will function as advertised.” He took a deep breath, then in a voice filled with anger and hurt, he said, “Why do you question my abilities? Do you think I am an imbecile, unable to read and perform simple tasks? It is like a cook book. Any fool could do it."

As soon as the word 'fool' passed his lips he regretted it. He believed that she would seize on his own words and turn them against him. To his surprise, she replied, "Aslam, you have done well. We have plenty of time to finish preparations for the trip to Glennville. But something has come up and we have a more urgent matter to tend to. We must make a trip north and take care of a problem that has emerged."

Aslam frowned. "What is it?"

"I can't talk about it over the phone and tonight I have to find someone Mina can stay with for three days. I will pick you up tomorrow morning at 7:30. Pack a bag. We will talk about it in the car. We will have breakfast before we leave but plan to be away for several days. When we get back, we will have plenty of time to finish our business."

They made plans to eat at a local diner the next morning, then disconnected the call. Aslam raised his head and smiled, proud of his accomplishment. In the end, Moska would also be proud of him and see him in a different light.

She will see me as a great man and reward me.

* * *

Moska smiled when she disconnected the call with Aslam. *He said fool. He must have read my mind. I'm surprised he completed his task without blowing up the neighborhood, and himself; like the dummy used by the ventriloquist comedian. Aslam, the dead terrorist.* She stifled a laughed, hoping Mina did not hear her and ask questions.

She called a friend with a daughter in Mina's class at school. The woman, a devout Catholic, treated Moska and Mina with such kindness that she believed it would be no problem getting the woman to agree to watch her daughter for a few days.

"Hi Pattie, I have a huge favor to ask. I hate to ask on such short notice. Could you watch Mina for three days?"

The woman seemed alarmed and asked, "Oh, Moska, is everything alright?"

"Yes, and no. I have to visit a friend in Indiana who is having health issues and I need to go see her. I don't want Mina to miss any school this early in the year."

"Oh my. I'm so sorry for your friend. I'll say a prayer for her. I'll have to check with my husband, but it shouldn't be a problem. Mina is so well behaved, I'm sure he'll agree to it. And Jenny will be so happy to have Mina over. I'll call you after Sean gets home from work."

"Thank you, Pattie. I appreciate it so much. Let me know if it is a problem. I'll make sure Mina has everything she needs for school and after."

"That would be wonderful, Moska. I'll call in a little bit."

When the call disconnected, Moska smiled. She felt confident her friend would be able to convince her husband to allow Mina to stay over. She thought of options if it did not work out, but believed alternatives were not necessary.

Next, she performed an inventory of the tools she needed for the job in Ohio. Her body tingled all over thinking ahead to Monday. Revenge would start early.

* * *

Chip Chandler monitored the BIAChat multiple times on Sunday morning through early afternoon. The incoming comments slowed. Everyone with travel plans to Hinesville announced they made their reservations. Two men had contacted Chip directly asking for assistance which he provided with no strings attached. He assured the men that no one else would know. On Monday, he would contact the funeral home and make sure that they were on track to have Randall Parish's body ready for interment. He wanted to get the schedule of transfer for the body so there were no slip-ups.

He decided to call General Vance and provide an update on the plans. Before he could punch in Vance's number,

Colleen walked into his office. She leaned over his shoulder and kissed him on the cheek.

He turned, smiled, and asked, "What was that for?"

With her face inches from his, she asked, "Do I need a reason?"

"Not at all." He continued to smile at her, wondering if she might sidetrack him from his call. He turned towards Colleen and stood, leaned over, and kissed her lightly on the lips.

When he pulled back, she said, "You keep that up and we won't get a thing done this afternoon."

He turned his head slightly and lifted an eyebrow. He said, "You started it. How about if I make my call and I'll meet you in the den. We can decide where we want to go from there."

"How long do you plan to be on the phone?" As she asked, she ran her hands down his chest, then back up to his shoulders.

"Umm, it won't be long at all."

"Good. I hate to waste an afternoon waiting around just thinking about … well, you fill in the blanks." She turned and walked towards his office door, swinging her hips with just a little more sway than usual.

Chip picked up his glass of ice water and took a big gulp. He said to her retreating form, "Don't get too comfortable."

Damn.

He turned back to his desk and punched in the number for General Vance's cell. Vance picked up on the second ring.

"Chip. Anything new?"

"Nothing new but I wanted to let you know that I plan to call the funeral home and the cemetery tomorrow and make sure that everything is on schedule."

"Good, good."

The sound of the general's response made Chip think he had been drinking a bit, but being Sunday, he suspected Vance's calendar was clear. He knew the general wanted to get that third star so he believed that Vance might be taking a chance drinking even with an open schedule. With worries of his own, he did not need to add other's concerns to his list.

Chip asked, "When are you scheduled to arrive in Hinesville and are you staying at the Hampton Inn?"

There was a delay in Vance's answer, then he said, "I'll be there Thursday morning just before noon. I'd like to be there in time to greet everyone. I know there might be a few of the men who arrive earlier."

"Will Evelyn be accompanying you?"

Another pause. "Yes, she's looking forward to it."

His last line sounded as unconvincing as one could get. Colleen told him that the general and his wife were experiencing some 'tension' in their marriage. Chip accepted his statement without further comment.

Vance asked, "And Colleen?"

"Yes, sir. She will be with me. She feels strongly about paying her respects."

Chip thought about Colleen's remarks regarding advances the general made back in Afghanistan. He remembered the look on her face when they spoke about it. He tensed, thinking back to what his wife told him about Vance's aggressive behavior.

When the silence dragged on, Chandler said, "General, thanks for your help in making sure that this didn't fall apart. Your post in the chat room sealed the deal for many. I appreciated that and I know they did, too."

"My pleasure, Captain. See you in Georgia."

"Yes, sir."

Chip disconnected and thought about the call. For some reason, his thoughts about Vance and Colleen bothered him now more than in the past. If one innocent comment from Vance about his wife bothered him, he wondered what other emotions this get-together might stir up in others. He hoped everything would go off without a hitch. The more he thought about the gathering the more his anxiety notched up.

Chapter 38

Moska Aziz smiled as she and Aslam Sayed strode along Heather Ridge Drive in Hilliard, Ohio. Looking east through the trees, they barely caught glimpses of the capital city's downtown buildings. At 9:30 in the morning, the sun's angle cast shadows of mature trees across the road. The seventy-degree temperature felt cool, their being used to the eighty-plus temperature and high humidity of Georgia.

Moska reminded Aslam multiple times to relax, smile, and maintain a casual pace so their walk in the upscale subdivision would not draw attention. *So long as we fit in and appear as though we belong, no one will take notice.* They turned a third corner putting distance between them and the parked rental car, then watched the house numbers. Again, Moska told him to smile and slow down as his face took on the nervous, terrified look of someone being hunted. He forced a smile, but it looked so unnatural that Moska shook her head in dismay.

Finally, the house at 2745 Heather Ridge, the home they were looking for, came into view. It looked exactly like the house they viewed on the travel application they used before leaving Georgia yesterday. Maple trees with high, full canopies provided shade to the nicely maintained home. In fact, all the homes in the area sported neat, well-manicured lawns, and a few late model cars. Most of the residents in this upper-middle-class neighborhood were apparently at work. That played well for the two visitors to this peaceful community.

They turned onto the sidewalk and climbed the two steps to the front door. Aslam shifted the backpack to his left shoulder. Moska rang the doorbell. They had no idea who, if anyone, would open the door. If no one answered, they would come back later in the day and try again. Moska's finger hovered near the doorbell again when she heard footsteps approach the door from the inside.

When the door opened, a pretty, blond woman in her thirties answered. She asked through the screen door, "Can I help you?"

As they rehearsed, Moska would do all the talking. She would pretend to be a candidate for Hilliard City Council and ask that the residents sign a petition to get her on the November ballot. They would have a petition form on a clipboard and a pen that did not work. They hoped that Mrs. Grumen would invite them in while she looked for a working pen.

With a vibrant smile and a confidant tone, Moska said, "Hello. My is Michelle Workman. I'm running for Hilliard City Council and I was hoping that you would sign my petition."

Cora Grumen smiled back, seemingly impressed with the young woman. She quickly glanced at the man with her. Her brow furled but she immediately turned her attention back to Moska and said, "It is nice to see younger people interested in politics."

Moska's smile beamed bright. She handed the clipboard to Mrs. Grumen. When the pen would not write, Cora tapped the pen on the clipboard and said, "Your pen isn't working. I have one in the kitchen. Please come in."

Once inside, Aslam closed the door behind him. When Cora Grumen disappeared into the kitchen, he placed the backpack on the floor, unzipped the bag, and removed a syringe, which he held behind his back. When Cora returned from the kitchen, she signed the petition and handed the clipboard to Moska. When she did, Moska grabbed her left wrist and pulled the unsuspecting woman off balance. She fell to the floor where Aslam straddled her and plunged the syringe into her neck.

Cora Grumen, shocked by the attack, thrashed her arms and tried to role on the carpet, attempting to fight off her attacker. The more she fought, the weaker she became as her strength faded away from the injection of Rohypnol. It took only minutes for the drug to take full effect.

Aslam and Moska both took deep breaths, thinking about the next steps in their plan. After a moment's rest, Moska said, "Pick her up. I will find the master bedroom."

Twenty minutes later, Cora Grumen lay face-up, spreadeagle, completely naked, tied by her wrists and ankles to her bed. Her pale skin shown in sharp contrast to the dark bedspread on which she laid. She had yet to stir from her drug induced slumber.

While Aslam prepared Cora Grumen in bed, Moska searched the house for the woman's cell phone. She found it in the kitchen, on the table near a magazine. She swiped across the screen which displayed the apps. She tapped the phone app, then Cora's contact list. Jeff's cell occupied the first position. She smiled at how well their plan proceeded.

As she entered the bedroom, she noticed Aslam staring at the woman's naked body, lust evident on his face. When he heard Moska enter, his cheeks flushed with embarrassment. He backed away as the woman began to stir.

Moska said, "Put a gag over her mouth. Do not make it too tight, but tight enough that she cannot scream." She remained silent for a moment, then said, "And Aslam, you cannot rape her. We must not leave evidence that can be traced to either of us. Do you understand."

He shot her an angry sneer. "I'm not an idiot, Moska. Do not treat me like one."

She held his stare for a moment, then looked away.

Twenty minutes later, Moska stood over the naked, gagged, and incapacitated Cora Grumen. Her eyes bulged and moved rapidly between Moska and Aslam. Her body shook with fear, not knowing what these two home invaders were up to.

In a soothing voice, Moska said, "We are not going to hurt you. We need for you to do something for us. If you do exactly as we say, you will go free unharmed. Do you understand?" She hoped that Aslam would not say anything or role his eyes and give away Moska's bold-faced lie.

Cora Grumen nodded, though her eyes remained wide, bulging with the emotions of a woman who feared for her life. She shifted her gaze to Aslam, then back to Moska, perhaps pleading to have the man leave her room and allow her some modesty. Moska ignored the woman's pleading, thinking back to the humiliation she suffered. This woman would soon know why she found herself in this predicament.

Again, in a soothing voice, she said, "I am going to make a call to your husband. When he answers, you will tell him that he needs to come home immediately. When he asks why, you tell him to just come home. It is an emergency. Do you understand?"

Cora's body tensed, sensing that her husband would be walking into a dangerous situation. With no other options, she nodded.

Moska said, "You understand that if you do not do exactly as I said, Aslam will kill you, after he has his way with you. There is no need for that, am I right?"

Cora again nodded, fear emanating from every fiber of her body. She glanced quickly at Aslam who was wide-eyed, standing at the foot of the bed, salivating over every inch of her body.

Moska nodded as if asking if she was ready. She nodded back.

Moska told Aslam to remove the gag from Cora Grumen's mouth. As he approached, her eyes widened in horror. She feared he would not stop with removing the gag. When he untied the gag and removed it, she took deep, sucking breaths. Aslam could not help himself and he ran his hands over her breasts. She shrieked and twisted away as much as possible, but could not move far enough to escape his hands. With a scowl on her face, Moska pushed him away from the woman.

As he resumed his position at the foot of the bed, Moska said, "Remember what I said. Ready?"

She nodded, keeping an eye on Aslam who continued to stare at her exposed body. Moska hit the contact button for Jeff and let the phone ring once, then twice. When Grumen answered, she held the phone up to Cora's ear.

With a stern face, Moska stared at the bound woman and nodded. She heard Jeff Grumen say *Hi Sweetheart.* Cora remained silent until Moska pushed the phone against her face hard.

Cora said in a voice laced with fear she did not have to fake, "Jeff, I need you to come home, right now!"

"But, honey, I'm kinda …"

"Right now, Jeff!"

Moska disconnected the call before either Grumen could say another word. She turned to Aslam and told him to gag her once more. Once he finished with the gag, she tossed a prophylactic on the bed and said, "Do with her what you want, but leave no evidence."

Cora Grumen screamed as hard as she could against the gag, all to no avail. Her muffled screams could not be heard beyond the walls of the second-floor bedroom.

* * *

Jeff Grumen called his foreman and advised him that he needed to take off for the remainder of the day. He explained that his wife called about some emergency at home. He said it with a nonchalance that made his foreman laugh, like he just heard an inside joke about wives in general. He told Jeff that he need not worry about work. He would handle whatever came up. Jeff thanked him and headed for his F-250 pick-up truck.

Fifteen minutes later, he pulled into his driveway. Nothing looked out of place. He wondered what might be serious enough for his wife to call him away from work. Maybe the kitchen faucet dripped, or the dishwasher would not start, or one of a hundred other minor household issues that could wait. But he left the Marines for this life. He would make the best of it.

He walked in the front door and, in a booming voice, said, "Cora. I'm home. What's the problem?"

When he got no response, he wondered if she might be in the master bathroom upstairs. Maybe the toilet would not stop running. He marched up the stairs and yelled again, "Cora. I'm home. Where are you?"

When he walked into the master bedroom, he saw his wife tied, spread-eagle on the bed. In a panic, he moved quickly towards her. He noticed her eyes dart to his left and his senses went into alarm mode. But it was too late. He felt a sting as a syringe punctured his neck. He turned to see a man, much smaller than he holding the empty vial. He jumped at the man and punched him in the jaw. He moved to attack him again, but began to feel as if someone tossed a weighted net over him. After several seconds he collapsed to the floor, unconscious.

When he awoke, he tried to move, but his arms and legs would not respond. He tried to talk, but a gag covered his mouth. His eyes began to focus as his mind cleared. He looked down and saw the zip ties restraining his arms and legs to a chair at the foot of his bed.

Cora.

He looked up. He was shocked to see a man's butt moving up and down. Then he noticed a woman's legs on either side of the man's.

Cora.

He tried to break free of the zip ties to no avail. His eyes watered, a helpless feeling flooding his body and mind.

He heard a woman's soothing voice. "You feel helpless, don't you, watching another man do as he pleases with your wife … your wife. There is nothing you can do. Do you remember my voice, Sergeant Grumen? Do you remember me? Do you remember taking your turn raping me in Kabul after you and your friends kidnapped me from my neighborhood, my home? Would you like to know how your wife feels now?"

Again, he tried to break free, but the influence of the drugs they had injected into him still drained his strength. He stopped trying and watched as a strange man he never met abused his wife. Tears rolled down his face as he wondered whether he or Cora would live to see their children again.

When Aslam rolled off the bed and stood, he smiled, then laughed at Grumen. He put on his clothes and stood by the bed, giving Cora Grumen's breasts another squeeze - just because he could.

Moska picked up a knife that looked exactly like the knives carried by Marine Corps infantrymen. She held the knife and admired it, watching the light shimmer off the blade.

She looked at Jeff Grumen, then at his wife. She said, "Not only did you rape me, but you killed my best friend's family." She nodded at Aslam. "His family. You are going to know how that feels during the last moments of your life."

Grumen's eyes bugged out of their sockets and he screamed against his gag as Moska lifted the knife above Cora Grumen's chest. She turned and smiled as she plunged the knife straight down, then repeated the motion half a dozen more times.

Cora had stretched her bounds as far as she could, but she could not escape a single thrust of the knife. The blade pierced her heart multiple times as her chest flooded with her blood.

"That was one wound for each of Aslam's family members."

She set the knife down, wiped her hands on the bed sheet, then picked up a pistol. She asked, "Do you recognize this weapon?"

Grumen, through tear-clouded eyes recognized the pistol as his gun. He slumped over in the chair, realizing what was to come.

"Look at me! Look – At – Me! You did this to me! You made me what I am! Look at your wife! You did this to her!"

She picked up a piece of paper with a typed note. She held it in front of him. "Here is your good-bye."

He read the suicide note with his name at the bottom, then sobbed into the gag.

Moska Aziz lined up the muzzle of the gun to his temple and pulled the trigger. Before they left the home, they cleaned up, removed the ties and gags, placed them in a plastic grocery bag and left the house. Within minutes they were on Interstate 270 heading south.

Chapter 39

At 7:20 Monday morning Peden sat with Megan in her office in downtown Savannah, Georgia, sipping coffee, waiting for Lee Sparks to call. Spark's friend, Professor Li had promised to deliver the recovered pages from Randall Parish's journal. Despite the significant volume of information already gleaned from the documents retrieved from Parish's trailer, they believed the missing journal pages would answer many questions for the time after the strike until the platoon headed for home. They both finished their breakfast, Peden a large everything omelet, Megan a tiny, low-fat yogurt. They did not know what to expect from the documents, but they hoped the information would fill in more of the missing pieces of their investigation.

They did not expect to hear from Lee Sparks until later in the morning, so Peden raised an eyebrow when Megan's phone rang. Her assistant, Shanique King, did not start her day until 8:00, so Megan answered the call.

"Savannah FBI office, Special Agent Megan Moore speaking."

Roland Fosco, Megan's boss, said, "Good morning. Is Savage with you?"

"Yes, he is. Should I put you on speaker?"

"Yeah. You both need to hear this."

After Megan hit the speaker button, Fosco's voice filled the office, "Hey, Peden."

Peden acknowledged Fosco who continued, "Your investigation is raising eyebrows at some pretty high levels in the federal investigation's community. I just finished a call with Marlene Harris and Bill Campo. They're my counterparts at NCIS in Jacksonville, North Carolina. They have jurisdiction over the southeast. Without going into a lot of detail, our investigation crosses both of their territories. Seems that they have concerns. You're treading into a sensitive situation."

Megan jumped in, "Rollie, are you going to ask us to stop?"

"No, not at all, Megan. On the contrary, you are to work with their agent, Myles Cassidy, and make sure we don't foul-up their efforts, which are coming to a head soon."

Megan took a deep breath. Not one to take orders from anyone outside of her chain of command, she asked, "Are you expecting that we allow NCIS, and Myles Cassidy, to take the lead on our next move?"

Fosco's voice took on an intense, but not angry tone, "No, Megan. I expect that you and *Myles*," he stressed the NCIS agent's name, "will exchange information that each of you can use in your respective investigations. From what my counterparts told me, our agencies have differing objectives, but it involves the same principals. You should be expecting Cassidy at your office this morning. He has been instructed to be as forth-coming as I am directing you to be. If he is not, you call me. I'll call Jacksonville and we'll make sure we all understand each other. You good with that?"

Megan looked at Peden. He nodded. She then answered, "Yes, sir, we are."

"Good. I'll leave you to it."

With the call disconnected, Megan looked at Peden. She said, "You heard the boss. Cooperate. I guess we better share our document stash with them."

Peden nodded then said, "It would be nice to have those papers from Professor Li before Cassidy gets here."

"Or not."

Peden smiled just as the phone rang. Megan answered, "Savannah FBI office, Special Agent Megan Moore speaking."

Megan did not expect a baritone female voice to be on the line and say, "Good morning, Agent Moore. This is Doctor Min Li at Savannah State University. I have some documents for you."

Megan glanced at Peden and mouthed Dr. Li. "Wonderful, Doctor Li. Can I send someone over to pick them up?"

"Not necessary. I can have one of our students bring them to your office."

Megan raised an eyebrow. The papers contained critical information for their investigation. Megan believed that a chain of custody had to be maintained. "Dr. Li, if you don't mind, I'd rather have Lee Sparks pick them up."

This seemed to please Dr. Li. She said, "That would be great. I always enjoy seeing my good friend, Lee."

I'll bet you do. "Please address the envelope to me and have Lee sign something when he takes possession. And Doctor, thank you for your work on this. We very much appreciate your taking this on right away."

"It was my pleasure, Agent Moore."

Almost immediately after the call disconnected, Megan's phone rang again. Lee Sparks said, "Sounds like I'm playing courier."

"How did you find out so quickly?"

"The recording device on your phone. I happened to be checking the recordings on file when the call from Min came in. I'll get over there as soon as I finish breakfast."

"Great, Lee. See you in a bit, and Lee, you don't have to rush. I'll explain later."

"But you do want the package today, right?"

"Yes.

"Okay. Maybe I can talk with Min for a bit."

The phone disconnected. Megan's intercom sounded. Shanique King must have arrived. She said, "Megan, Special Agent Myles Cassidy and Agent Sidney Pattelli to see you."

"Good morning, Shanique. Send them in, please."

Peden moved to a spot behind and to the left of Megan's desk as the two NCIS agents entered Megan's office. Patelli carried a briefcase in his left hand. Megan moved to the front of her desk and shook each agent's hand. Peden did not move or make any effort to be cordial. She motioned to the visitor's chairs in front of her desk and asked if either cared for coffee or water. Both shook their heads in the negative and sat. Patelli placed the briefcase on the floor between them as he gave Peden an angry scowl.

When the door to her office closed, Megan jumped right in, "I understand that we're to cooperate with each other, even though our investigations are separate and have different objectives."

Both men nodded without a word, so Megan continued, "The way we'll proceed is I will give you a piece of information in our possession and you will then reciprocate by giving us something. Any questions?"

Again, both men nodded, but remained silent.

Megan said, "Good. We have the document, the order to Vance's command that clearly shows coordinates which target a home in Kabul where two terror leaders were to meet. We told you this Saturday when we met. We also have the exact same document, same revision number, with different target coordinates. The original order had not been rescinded. Someone altered the order."

Agent Cassidy said, "We need to see both documents."

Megan opened a manila folder on her desk and handed Cassidy both documents. He looked them over slowly, reading the details contained on each page. He looked at Megan and said, "I'll need to confiscate these. They contain confidential information."

Megan shrugged her shoulders and said, "Okay. Your turn."

Cassidy nodded and Patelli placed the briefcase on his lap, opened it, and extracted a folder which he handed to Cassidy. He placed the folder on the edge of Megan's desk and leaned forward. He pulled a stapled stack of papers from the folder and handed it to Megan. Several multicolored Post-it notes extended out from the body of the stack. Megan did not look at the report, instead waited for Cassidy to paraphrase the content of the papers.

Cassidy said, "This is a certified copy of the official report from then Colonel Vance on the drone strike of September 11, 2011. In it, Vance claims they achieved the objective of the strike successfully. Both targets had been neutralized." He paused, then said, "We received a different report from another federal agency within a few days, claiming Vance's report was in error. Both targets turned up outside Kabul … alive and well." He paused again, looking for Megan or Peden to react. When neither did, he continued, "NCIS put together an operation to find out what went wrong. We quickly discovered we destroyed the wrong house. Our goal is to find out how that happened and who is responsible for falsifying the report."

Megan asked, "Are you sure someone intentionally falsified the report?"

"We have reason to believe it was. When I confronted Parish ten years ago, I asked him why he went crazy after the strike. He said, and I'm paraphrasing now, 'That son-of-a-bitch killed them on purpose.' When I asked who, he stopped and looked at me like I might be in on some plot to get him. I knew I had to back off. We were getting loud and physical and other Marines were jumping in to separate us."

Peden asked, "Did Parish say anything about being in possession of highly classified documents related to the strike?"

Cassidy drew in a deep breath, the exhaled, "No. Did he have other documents … other than the ones you just showed us?"

Megan looked Cassidy in the eyes with a steely gaze and said, "Yes. We have copies of several documents and a journal." She paused, then added, "For an alleged drunk, he kept meticulous notes."

Megan handed a copy of Parish's journal to Cassidy. He took a minute to read over the notes, paying particular attention to the pages leading up to September 11, 2011 and the day after. He paused when he noticed the gap in dates from the day after the strike until the day Parish's platoon departed

Afghanistan. He looked at Megan and asked, "Where's the rest of it?"

Megan said, "We're having those pages recovered by a forensic scientist. We hope to have them soon. Someone removed the pages from the spiral notebook that Parish used as a journal. We don't know who removed them or why."

Cassidy's look showed a hint of mistrust. He nearly smiled, then said, "You'll let us know immediately when you get them, right?"

With a straight face, Megan said, "Of course. Now tell us what you did learn from Private Parish."

"Nothing. A few days after that altercation, I took one more crack at him, tried to make out like I wanted to apologize and make nice, but he didn't say a word. Gave me a glare and walked off. He still didn't trust me."

"And you didn't pursue him?"

"No. Rayshon Mack – you know who he is, I'm sure – pulled me aside and told me to back off. He wasn't nice about it. Remember, I played the part of a disgraced private. Corporal Mack outranked me and I couldn't blow my cover."

Peden asked, "Whom do you believe falsified the report declaring the strike a success?"

Cassidy took a deep breath then said, "We believe the report was falsified by Vance. We also believe he may have had a hand in Parish's untimely death."

Megan did not react, but Peden's eyebrows shot up. "That's a serious charge. Why would Vance do anything like that?"

"We suspect that Parish may have been blackmailing Vance, threatening to turn over the falsified report to a major newspaper. Parish was near destitute. He could have used his knowledge of the report to extort money from Vance."

Peden's doubts were etched on his face. Before he could ask another question, Megan jumped in. "Did you know Parish had copies of these documents before today?" She waved a hand at the folder on her desk.

Cassidy hesitated, then said, "No, but we figured he must have had something on Vance."

Peden asked, "Any phone records with calls from Parish to Vance?"

"We're working on that."

Megan said, "Sounds like a veiled 'no.'"

"You got any better theories?"

"Not yet. We're working on it."

Cassidy tapped his partner on the arm and said, "Let's go."

He turned to Megan and said, "Let us know when you have those pages in hand. We'll let you know when we have the phone records. We good with that?"

Megan stood and reached her hand across her desk. The agents shook. Finally, Peden stepped forward and offered his hand to Sid Patelli, "No hard feelings."

Sid turned and left without a word.

When they were gone, Megan said, "I don't like Vance for Parish's death. He has too much to lose."

Peden replied, "I agree."

Chapter 40

An hour after NCIS agents Cassidy and Pattelli left Megan's office, Lee Sparks hand delivered the envelope containing the recovered pages from Randall Parish's journal to Megan. Lee's good mood radiated from his face and body language. Whatever the friendship between Lee and Professor Min Li, Peden believed it to be good for his friend's overall outlook on life. He never saw his technical-go-to man so relaxed and comfortable. He hoped the relationship with the professor, whether professional or casual, would continue.

Megan invited Lee to stay while she and Peden reviewed the contents of the missing pages, but he declined, stating work awaited him at his home office. At Megan's request, he closed the door behind him when he departed her office. She wasted no time in opening the envelope, breaking the seal Doctor Li had applied, and making copies before looking at their content. She laid one set on her desk and handed the other to Peden, who immediately began reading from the first page.

Parish's log read:

September 11 – We just got back from our little road trip on the outskirts of Kabul. Either we screwed up big-time or someone knows something more than they're letting on. I might be on the next transport out of here, cause I got in Grumen's face. He knows he screwed up – unless we bombed the wrong house on purpose. How messed up is that? When Chandler finds out we destroyed his interpreter's house, he's gonna go ballistic. I don't know how anybody survived. If they did, they're gonna be messed up for life.

September 12 – Sgt. Ass-wipe Grumen wrote me up. Said he was gonna make sure my life was a living hell until they bounced me out of the Corps. This write-up and the one from back in August just might be all they need to bust me out.

Screw 'em. I got nothing to live for, so why spend the rest of my life in this hell hole? Send me home. Maybe I'll cold-cock that bastard before I go.

September 15 – Just got back from a two day/overnight patrol. I think they just wanted us outta here for a few days to let things cool off within the squad. I was glad to get away from this bullshit. Mack's been talking with me, trying to get me to cool down. I told him I'll cool down when I get out of this outfit. Only a few months to go even if I don't get busted out sooner. Makes no difference to me.

Peden noted that several days passed with no new entries, then on September 19, a long entry took up a page and a half. The handwriting appeared rougher. Parish appeared agitated or drunk, but definitely angry. As Peden read the passage, he believed anger to be the primary cause because the content indicated a confrontation with a new member of the team; a guy named Cassidy Miller.

September 19 – This new guy, Miller, keeps busting my chops over the strike. Says he wants to know how I know so much about it, that we bombed the wrong house. Wants to know why I freaked out. He says guys like us, we shouldn't know shit about details like that, we should just follow orders. I don't know this guy from Adam, but he got me so mad I yelled at him that we killed that family on purpose. I shoulda kept my mouth shut, but he kept at me. Everyone in the squad eyed us 'cause he's got a loud voice that carries even when he tries to be quiet. Anyways I yelled when he kept badgering me. I gotta get outta here before this whole thing blows up. We destroyed Amir's family so they could keep their secret. Bastards!!!

I'm getting little bits of information from my buddy. C.T. says they're keeping a lid on information sharing. Sounds like we're trying to cover up or somebody's ass is gonna get toasted. My bet is on Vance, Grumen and Russo. I think they caused a problem in town when I saw them a few months ago. Right after that, Grumen wrote me up and kept threatening me. He's right. I'm drinking. Some of the other guys are, too, but I guess I'm leading the way. Yahoo! I'm drinkin' now. So screw 'em. Screw 'em. Screw 'em.

All I need is the right documents to get 'em all back, which I will do, mark my words. I really just want Miller to leave me alone.

I know C.T. is scared, too. She wants so bad to get back in the field, but that isn't gonna happen. Rumor is we got about two weeks left in country, then we're heading home. It can't come soon enough.

Peden took a deep breath wondering about whom Parish had written and what secret they kept, most likely to this day. It must have been a whopper to cause all this commotion ten years later. It could possibly have gotten Parish killed.

He looked at Megan. She focused on her copy of the document as she read the entries. He could not make out any emotion behind her face, which gave him no indication what her impression might be. He read the next entry.

September 21 – Private Miller approached me again today. Tried to suck up to me, telling me he understood what I was going through. He said he'd been busted down from corporal to private a couple times. He said if he screwed up one more time, he was out on a dishonorable. He'd lose his pension. Being a Marine was all he knew. His dad, his brothers, they were all Marines. He'd be disowned by his family. Said he wanted to help me. I told him that I don't have any family left and I didn't care if I got the dishonorable. He tried again to get me to talk about the strike. I walked away. Screw him and his family.

September 22 – C.T. gave me some papers to hold onto. I looked them over last night. I got proof. Those SOBs knew what they were doing. I heard that Amir and his sister's best friend were the only ones to survive the blast. What the hell are we even doing here?

I have half a mind to show Grumen the proof, but he'd get the documents from me and then I'd get written up for having classified documents that I have no right to. C.T. said she would get them from me when we got stateside. She's thinking about taking them to someone above Vance. I told her she was throwing her life away 'cause they'd find a way to blame her. For now, I'm hanging on to the papers. Maybe I'll burn them when we get home.

Home ... I don't even know where that is.

Peden felt the gloom and doom conveyed in the handwritten notes on the page. Parish's whole life evaporated when his parents were killed in the accident. According to Mack, the bank sold the family home at auction. Parish would start from scratch when he received his discharge papers. You would think that the military or some veteran's organization would support guys like Parish, keep banks from screwing over military personnel. Civilian organizations began stepping up recently, but for Parish, it was too little, too late. Peden thought *He deserved better. He deserved our help.*

Megan, reading a few pages ahead of him, turned towards him and asked, "Are you to the entry where he claims Vance, Grumen, and Russo raped an Afghan girl?"

Peden's jaw dropped. He asked, "What page?"

"Page 3 near the bottom. Read it and tell me what you think."

Peden flipped the page and read the passage Megan referenced.

September 27 – I just heard from C.T. She said she overheard Russo talking to Grumen. Russo's worried that someone's gonna find out about what they did to the girl. Grumen tried to hush Russo up, but he kept talking as if no one was around. Russo told Grumen, "If I go down for this rape, you and Vance are coming with me. You got it?"

Grumen told Russo that nobody knew about it, unless he ran his big mouth. "Besides, the girl got blown up in the bombing. When they found her, she was nearly dead – probably is by now." Russo told Grumen that he better find out for sure." C.T. said she didn't hear anything else.

Peden looked back at Megan. "I'd bet a year's pay they blew up that house because someone there knew about the rape. This guy, Amir had been Chip's interpreter. His sister's best friend practically lived at their house."

"That's exactly what I was thinking. They tried to destroy the evidence and take out any witnesses, or anyone the young girl told. Bastards."

Peden shook his head, "We need to talk with Chip and Colleen Chandler. I think they know something about why we bombed the Sayed family home. If not, why did 'C.T.' pass documents to Parish. Maybe she thought Parish would be sent home before the rest of the platoon. They could meet up once she got stateside, but something happened and she couldn't make the connection."

"I'll get Chip on the phone right now. Hopefully they're both home."

Peden punched in the number for Chip Chandler. He answered on the second ring, his voice sounding subdued.

"Hey. Peden. Are you calling about Grumen?"

Peden, confused about the way Chip answered, said, "Let me put you on speaker. I'm with Megan."

Once on speaker, Peden said, "You're on speaker. Go ahead Chip. What about Grumen?"

"I was about to go in our chat room and tell everyone. Grumen killed his wife then killed himself yesterday."

Shocked by the news, Peden looked at Megan. Her teeth were clenched and her brow furrowed. They were speechless.

Chip said, "Is that what you called about?"

Peden cleared his throat then said, "No, Chip. But tell us what you know about Grumen's murder-suicide."

Chip went on to describe what he knew, that the Hilliard Police Department believe Grumen stabbed his wife to death then took his own life with a large caliber pistol. He continued saying that Grumen left the Marines at the insistence of his wife. At the time, he held a grudge for her forcing him to make the decision: either her and the family or the Marines. He could not have both.

This turn of events left much for Peden and Megan to ponder, but Peden came back to the reason for the call. "Chip, is Colleen with you?"

"Yeah. She's in the pool. You want me to get her?"

"Yeah, if you don't mind."

Moments later, they heard Chip and Colleen talking as they came back into whatever room they were in. Chip said, "Colleen's here with me."

She didn't say anything, so Peden said, "Colleen, is your maiden name *Temple*?"

She hesitated, then replied in a quiet voice, "Yes."

"This next question … this is going to be …"

Megan jumped in. "What Peden is trying to ask is, did you pass some documents to Randall Parish in the days after the drone strike in Afghanistan?"

There was a long pause. Colleen may have been looking to her husband for help, but Megan jumped back in, "We know you did, because we just read them and the journal that Parish kept detailing the events of those weeks up to, and after, the strike. He said you passed him the documents with the plan that you would retrieve them from him when the platoon arrived stateside."

Colleen decided to own her actions and said, "Yes, I did. I kept copies, too. They're in our safe. I needed them as an insurance policy in case Vance decided to pin his deceit on me."

"Have you read Parish's journal?"

"No. I didn't know he kept a journal."

"Did you ever contact him to retrieve his copies of the documents?"

"No."

Peden said, "Chip, did you know that Amir Sayed and his sister's best friend survived the strike?"

"In a sullen voice he replied, "I knew they survived the immediate blast, but they both were a mess when transported to the hospital. I heard that they made it to Germany. That was the last I heard of either of them."

Megan looked at Peden and motioned across her neck. Peden said, "Chip, Colleen, we'll call again if we learn anything new."

Chapter 41

With the call from Peden complete, Chip turned to his wife, a look of total disbelief on his face. He held his hands palms-up, as if asking her to explain what he just heard over the phone. His mouth hung open as he tried to think of what to say. His mind raced, analyzing everything happening around him: why Grumen killed himself, why he killed his wife, why, over ten years ago, Colleen passed classified documents to Parish. She knew he might be dishonorably discharged and sent home at any time. She risked her entire career, even prison, by taking copies of those documents and passing them to Parish before she resigned her commission. The documents she held in their safe, she must have hidden for months before she left the Marines. But more importantly, she kept all this from her husband. He asked her if she held any more secrets from him. She told him *'no.'* He now knew that to be a lie.

Colleen broke the silence, though tension remained high, "I can explain."

"Explain which part? The part about passing those documents to Parish? The part about your having some kind of relationship with a private who nearly drank himself out of the Corps? The part about Cassidy Miller? Or the part about you being 'totally honest' with me?" He paused then asked, "Where would you like to start?"

His stare burned into her eyes with laser-like focus. Just days before, she swore she held no other secrets from him. One brief phone call laid bare her deception.

Tears formed in her eyes as she began to speak, but she choked and cleared her throat. Finally, she said, "Rusty and my relationship lasted less than one week. He desperately needed help. I stumbled across him one day, drunk, trying to hide from everybody, everything. Maybe even himself. He ranted about hating his life, the Marines, Afghanistan. He told me he thought about killing himself."

She looked past her husband at nothing; just a stare, remembering the episode and the pathetic human being Randall Parish had become. Tears rolled down her cheeks, her chin quivered at the memory.

She continued, "I told him to go back to his barracks and sleep it off, to knock off the pity-party. I tried to get him to remember his training to overcome his personal grief, and get his shit together. After a couple days, it seemed to be working. He would come by my desk and we would take a walk, just talk. Then I crossed the line and let it become personal: a short fling until I pulled my head out of my ass. I knew it would destroy my career. I could be brought up on charges, so I ended it, abruptly. He went off the deep end and began drinking more. Then, a couple days later, his rifle team supported the drone strike. He came to me the next day and … well, you know the rest. I knew we bombed the wrong house. I also knew that Vance falsified the report - the one you wrote - and the original strike orders because I saw both copies; the original and the one with changed coordinates. I needed to protect myself because I knew it would be easy for him to point the finger at me. I felt trapped into protecting Rusty, too. I feared he'd blurt out that I knew about the deceit and about our relationship."

The entire time Colleen spoke, Chip stared at her with cold, piercing eyes. For the first time in their entire time together, he wondered if he could trust his wife, if he could believe what she said. His anger burned from his gut and his mind but his heart wanted to comfort her even as he doubted her words.

Chip asked, "If you ended your relationship, how did Parish get the documents?"

"I ended the personal contact. I could tell he still needed a distraction to get the bombing off his mind. He felt guilty we killed Amir's family. He knew why it happened and he didn't stop it. He kept talking about it, to me anyway. I don't think he confided in anyone else." She paused then said,

"He told me that he couldn't talk with you about it. He knew that Amir and you had become close. He worried what you might do if you knew the whole truth."

Chip's stare softened and he turned his eyes away from his wife.

In a quiet voice he said, "He spoke with me about it the day after the strike. Not the reason for killing Amir's family, but the fact that we bombed the wrong house. That's when I stormed into Vance's office."

"I remember. I tried to stop you."

He laughed with a bitter tone, "I don't even remember you being there. I was so damned mad. I thought we just made a big mistake, that somehow the coordinates got screwed up."

Colleen remained silent. Tears filled her eyes again. Chip watched her. He thought about the lives destroyed; people just trying to live in peace, torn apart by a war that nobody wanted. No one possessed the courage to put a stop to it.

Colleen turned to Chip and said, "When Vance trashed your report, I'd already made a copy of it. I made copies of the strike orders, too. I knew it violated so many rules, but I also knew that Vance wanted this to be one of his great successes, the arrogant bastard. He only cared about his next promotion. I didn't know how to keep the copies hidden. When Grumen burst into Vance's office and yelled that he wanted Parish busted out of the Marines, I thought I might have a way to move the documents stateside and safe … with Rusty. At first, he wanted to take them and rub them in Grumen's face. It took a while to explain the flaws with that idea. Finally, he agreed to take them stateside and hang onto them until we could meet. That never happened … because I fell for you." She looked at him, her eyes pleading for forgiveness. "You changed my life. You saved my life. I was so distraught about the bombing, about the orders from some general that I didn't even know. I felt trapped over in that god-forsaken country. I just knew I had to get out, free myself from this crap. I didn't know what I would do once I resigned my commission. Then, out of the blue, you filled that void."

Chip, torn between his wife's emotional plea for forgiveness and her lie about holding no more secrets, remained skeptical of her motives, both past and present. What he just heard did not fit with the loving, caring, strong woman he knew.

He yearned to hold her, but he kept distance between them until he could sort out his own feelings. He needed to separate the truth from the emotion, which would take time.

She took a tentative step towards him, but he backed away, not yet willing to let his feelings for her cloud his thinking. He said, "I have to let everybody know about Grumen. I shouldn't be long."

He turned and headed for his office. Though he did not turn around to look, he heard Colleen break down in loud, breath-sucking sobs.

* * *

Chip signed into BIAChat. When the home page came up, he took a deep breath and looked at the ceiling. *What to say about Jeff Grumen?* After a second deep breath, he looked at the screen and began to type.

You may have already heard, but from what we know right now, Jeff Grumen committed suicide yesterday. Worse, it appears that he killed his wife before he took his own life. I know many of you were close with Jeff. Please pray for his family, especially his two children. They will need all the support they can get. We'll toast Jeff along with Rusty on Thursday. I don't know if Jeff had pre-arranged any services. As soon as I know more, I will pass the information along. That's all for now.

He hit the 'Post' button and watched the screen. A few responses were posted immediately. He watched his computer screen, but Colleen's image filled his mind. He shook his head. *How could she keep all this from me?*

* * *

Colleen stood in the living room for several minutes after Chip headed for his office. She wiped her tears with the back of her hands then used her fingers to wipe her cheeks. Her mind worked overtime, trying to sort through the avalanche of bad news assaulting her mind. She tried so hard to be the woman Chip wanted, the woman he needed. As soon as she heard that Rusty Parish died by the Savannah River, she knew her life would change. The call from Moska Aziz later that day cemented her future. The plans that Moska announced to her, that she planned to kill Grumen, Russo, and Vance, all but assured that her secrets from a country halfway around the globe would be exposed.

Distraught over her and Chips relationship, her distress turned to anger. She agreed with the plan to punish the three men. They raped an adolescent Afghan girl and left her in an alley. She survived, but would not have survived the ridicule from her people for being a promiscuous whore if they discovered her resulting pregnancy.

She knew Jeff Grumen did not commit suicide. Grumen sealed his fate when he refused to attend Parish's funeral. She knew Moska would not allow Grumen to escape her brand of justice. The Hilliard Police Department would soon announce the real cause of Grumen's and his wife's deaths.

Colleen's face turned red, the heat rising from within. She grabbed her cell phone and headed to their spare bedroom and closed the door. She dialed Moska's number.

After just one ring, Moska's pleasant voice answered, "Colleen. How nice to hear from you."

Her teeth clenched, seething with anger, Moska's pleasant tone pushed her outrage higher. Through quivering lips, she growled into the phone, "I know you had to get your vengeance on Grumen, but his wife? Why? She did nothing to you. Why, Moska?"

In a calm, soothing voice, she replied, "Because he had to know what I felt. He had to feel my pain. The only way to do it was to watch his wife as she experienced what I did."

"Did this somehow cleanse you, clear your conscience, make you better than him?"

"No, Colleen. But I am one-third of the way to justice. You would be wise to stay clear of the other two-thirds."

Silence followed as Moska disconnected the call. Colleen collapsed to the floor, consumed by guilt. She covered her face and sobbed.

Chapter 42

Tuesday morning, September 21, 2011, Peden awoke early and devoured a light breakfast of cereal with milk and hot coffee. As he ate, he thought about the murder-suicide deaths of Jeff Grumen and his wife. Even with Chip explaining Grumen's grudge against his wife and her family, it made no sense he would wait nearly ten years to take out his frustration and anger to such a tragic end. He wrote on a three by five card *Grumen murder-suicide?* He believed a call to the Hilliard Police Department should be his next step in verifying Chip's account. As he finished the last spoonful of the chocolate-peanut butter crunchy bit of heaven his phone vibrated. He looked at the screen. Megan.

"Good morning, Megan. You're up early."

"Peedee, I've been up for hours, thinking about everything that's happened over the last week or so. Have you contacted the Hilliard Police yet? I think we need more details on the murder."

Peden smiled, "I agree. Did you want me to call and make it a three-way?"

"Why not? They should be at work by now, especially with a high-profile murder-suicide on their hands."

Megan waited while Peden retrieved the number and punched it in. After just one ring, a man said, "Hilliard Police Department. How may I direct your call?"

"My name is Peden Savage. I'm a private investigator from Savanah, Georgia. I also have Special Agent Megan Moore, FBI, on the line with me. We'd like to speak with the detective in charge of the Grumen murder-suicide, please." Several seconds of silence passed where Peden could hear the man breathing. He finally said, "Just a moment. I'll ring Detective Cummings."

After just a few seconds, a louder-than-necessary woman's voice came on the line, "Detective Cummings."

Peden went through the same introduction. Megan identified herself as the FBI's special agent in charge of an investigation involving the late Jeffrey Grumen.

Cummings asked, "So how can I help?"

Peden said, "We understand this is being investigated as a murder-suicide. Is that correct?"

Cummings took a deep breath. She appeared to be considering just how much she should divulge to people she had never met. When she spoke, she qualified her statement up front, "When officers first approached the crime scene, the Grumen's bedroom, it looked like a murder-suicide. I'm reluctant to give you too many details, but when I looked at the scene, it became obvious the whole thing had been staged. What I'm going to tell you has to remain between us until all the evidence is processed."

Megan said, "You have our word. If need be, you can verify my credentials with my boss, Roland Fosco."

Cummings said, "That won't be necessary, Agent Moore. Mr. Grumen's wrists and ankles were bruised, indicating he had been restrained. A chair found in their bedroom exhibited fresh scratches around the armrests and front legs. We believe Mr. Grumen was restrained in the chair. We did not find any zip ties but we did notice marks in the carpet at the foot of the bed which matched the chair legs. We believe the chair was positioned there purposely."

Cummings paused and took another deep breath. She continued, "This is important, because Mrs. Grumen appears to have been tied to the bed. Her wrists and ankles were severely bruised, the skin broken in a manner consistent with the use of zip ties. The bed posts had scratches. We're pretty certain she was tied to the bed, spread-eagle, and struggling to get free. When officers found her, she had been stabbed in the chest multiple times. She was naked. Our CSI team lead found evidence of sexual assault. That observation is not definitive. But it fits with our theory."

Peden asked, "Which is what?"

"Mrs. Grumen was tied to the bed and raped then stabbed to death while her husband was forced to watch."

The line remained silent for several seconds while Peden and Megan tried to process this new information. Who would hold such hatred for either of the Grumens to kill them both in such a heinous way?

Cummings broke the silence, "Our medical examiner will perform an autopsy of both bodies today. We're thinking that both of the Grumens may have been drugged."

Megan asked, "Did his coworkers say anything about his demeanor being off, like being distracted, depressed, complaining about his home-life?"

"No. Exactly the opposite. They said he acted just like he did every day. They were genuinely shocked to hear he and his wife were dead. His coworkers said he received a call to get home because of some unknown emergency. When he left, he wasn't in a panic. He joked maybe the toilet wouldn't stop running or something like that. He did tell them he probably wouldn't be back."

Megan asked, "Did any of their neighbors hear or see anything out of the ordinary?"

"We canvassed the neighborhood, door to door. Nobody heard or saw anything. This is a quiet, working-class neighborhood, so most folks were either at work, shopping, or doing house work. Nothing out of the ordinary." Another pause ensued. Then Cummings said, "In Grumen's house, we found a clipboard with a fake petition on it for city council. We think it is possible someone gained access to the Grumen home by presenting the fake petition. Our CSI folks looked for finger prints on the paper and clipboard. They found a couple that might be usable."

Megan said, "I'll send you my official email address. Send me a set of whatever prints you find as soon as possible. We can have them sent to our lab. We'll share our results with you."

"Copy that. Anything that you can share with us?"

Peden said, "This may be related to a murder in Georgia which occurred a little over a week ago. Randall Parish died from a drug overdose which initially looked like a suicide. We now know he was murdered. We think the same people may have committed the murders. We don't have much to go on right now, but your information helps."

"Keep us informed. Things like this don't happen in Hilliard. We don't want it happening again."

Peden and Megan both thanked Detective Cummings and waited for her to drop off the line. Peden spoke first, "Far cry from murder-suicide. Sounds like a revenge killing."

"Agreed. I'll be at your office in ten minutes. We have a lot to figure out here."

Megan arrived at Peden's office nine minutes later. She moved quickly to the seat that normally sat across from his desk. Peden moved it to his side of the desk so that she could see the three by five cards he already set out on his desk. He cleared the normally messy desktop of all clutter before Megan's arrival.

Megan flipped a loose strand of hair over her left ear. She remarked, "On the way over here, I'm thinking about these three murders, and believe they must be connected to the rape of the Afghan girl. We don't even know who the girl is, but I would bet it is either Amir Sayed's sister or her friend. We need to find out if Amir and the girl survived the bombing ten years ago. It sounds like their injuries were severe."

Peden said, "There must be some information on the survivors of the strike. I wish I could have Lee do one of his searches but we've already been put on notice. He can't risk it."

"Yeah. Maybe Myles Cassidy already knows. He's supposed to share information, right?"

"It's worth a try. Let's call him. We can muddle through these cards afterwards."

Peden put his phone on speaker and punched in the number Myles Cassidy provided. He answered with his loud, baritone voice on the third ring, "Savage. How can you help me today?"

"Agent Cassidy. You are on speaker and Agent Moore is with me."

After pleasantries, Peden asked, "Agent Cassidy, we have a couple questions. First, did you receive the phone records for Parish? Did he make calls to General Vance?"

After a brief pause, Cassidy replied, "No. we couldn't find any contact between Parish and Vance. That theory isn't completely dead, but it looks unlikely."

"Okay. On a different matter, do you know if Amir Sayed and the Afghan girl who were injured in the blast survived?"

"As far as we know, they did. We tracked them for a month after their transfer to the hospital in Landstuhl. At first, it looked bleak, but they pulled through the initial round of surgeries so we stopped watching them."

Megan jumped in, "We believe the change in target coordinates is related to the cover-up of the rape of an Afghan girl, possibly Amir Sayed's sister, or her friend. Three U.S. Marines raped the girl."

Peden asked, "Are you aware that Jeff Grumen and his wife are dead?"

"No. When did that happen?"

"Yesterday."

Cassidy said, "How is that connected to our investigation?"

Peden looked at Megan who nodded. He said, "We received the other pages from Parish's journal. He alleges Vance, Grumen, and Russo were the men who raped the girl. This alleged rape occurred several months before the drone strike. We think Vance may have changed the orders to destroy any evidence of, and witnesses to, the rape."

Cassidy remained silent for several seconds. They could hear him breathing over the phone. He finally said, "If all this is true, it puts a few more pieces into place." He changed subject and said, "We're going to Hinesville Thursday. Our plan is to let the burial ceremony take place Friday, then arrest Vance. We'll wait until the crowd clears and do it kind of quietly. We prefer to not disrupt the services for Parish."

Peden said, "That's good of you, seriously. We still don't know who killed Parish. His death is what sent this whole thing in motion. We're planning to be in Hinesville Thursday as well. I think we should try to avoid any contact except by phone."

"I agree. I need to stay out of sight so no one recognizes me. Who knows what a shit-storm would start if one of them yells 'Hey, it's Miller.' We'll stay out of sight until the end. Hopefully Vance will be alone when we arrest him."

Peden looked at Megan but she shook her head, having nothing else to add.

"Agent Cassidy, we'll make contact with you when we're settled in Hinesville. Let us know if you find out more about Amir Sayed and the girl. We'll send you copies of the recovered journal pages by email. Safe travels."

"Will do."

The call disconnected. They began looking at the cards on Peden's desk when his phone sounded. Harlan Wilson.

Peden put his phone on speaker again then answered, "Willie. How are you doing?"

"Fine, Peden. How y'all doin'?"

"Great. You're on speaker and Megan is with me."

"Megan. You doin' okay?"

"Yes, Willie. What can we do for you?"

"Just wanted to let y'all know that I'm headin' for Hinesville tomorrow. I'll get set up and scope out the area around the cemetery and hotel and all. What exactly do y'all want me to do while I'm there?"

Megan replied, "We want you to take pictures of everyone associated with the services for Parish, especially if a person acts suspiciously or if they appear out of place in any way."

"Are y'all lookin' for anyone in particular?"

"Yes, but we don't know what they look like, so this might be a bit tricky. We're looking for a man named Amir and a woman who might be his sister or a friend of his sister's. It's complicated, but if you see anyone with middle-eastern features, shoot and send them to us."

"This sounds like it might be fun."

Peden warned the photographer, "Willie, three people have been murdered already – four if we include your brother. You need to be very careful … and stealthy."

"Y'all got it, Peden. I can do that."

Chapter 43

Wednesday morning, September 22, Peden and Megan sat at Peden's desk trying to arrange three-by-five cards in some fashion that made sense. They laid them in chronological order; difficult because they did not know exact dates and times for some events. They used one card as an anchor and linked others to the central card. That seemed to work better, until the ten-year date gap broke any sensible linkage. Many bits of data did not work to bridge the passage of time. They rearranged them so that characters were central to the layout, then tied events to the characters. Nothing seemed to click.

As they worked, Peden updated the text on some cards, such as the Cassidy Miller cards. They knew his real identity and purpose for being at the camp in Afghanistan. Peden wrote *Yes* in red marker across the card which asked if the wrong house was bombed. But holes or missing links remained in the scheme.

With frustration building, Peden looked at Megan and asked, "Should we reshuffle the deck and start over?"

"It can't hurt. We've been working for hours. I think we need a break, a fresh cup of coffee, and, I don't know, a few more pieces of information."

Peden pulled the cards into a neat stack and stood. The card at the top of the deck displayed *Colleen Chandler steals classified documents*. Peden pondered the card for a moment, then moved to the kitchen where Megan already poured two cups of fresh coffee.

They sat at the kitchen table away from any distractions. Peden opened his mouth to mention Colleen Chandler's deceit when his cell phone sounded the Death March; his ex-wife, Susan. He put his head down and rubbed his forehead. "Dear God, not now."

Megan reached for his phone, swiped across the green handset, then spoke into the phone in a sultry voice, "Not now, Susan. We're busy."

She swiped across the screen and disconnected the call. She didn't smile, but Peden knew she derived some perverse pleasure pushing Susan's buttons, the downside being Peden would face the blowback at some point.

They both sipped coffee in silence for several minutes when Peden said, "Who, of the known players, is at the center of this whole affair?"

Megan thought for a moment then said, "Virgil Vance. He allegedly raped an underage Afghan girl. He falsified orders and bombed a house where the girl lived or visited frequently. He falsified a report about the success of the bombing. That's just what we know about. He may have a hand in Parish's murder, though I'm not sure he had opportunity." She paused then continued, "What if he ordered the murder? What if Parish threatened to expose his secrets?"

Peden turned his head from side to side, trying to loosen the tension in his neck. He said, "Yeah, but remember, Cassidy said there hadn't been any communication between Parish and Vance."

"Parish might not be able to contact an important guy like Vance. Maybe he threatened one of the others involved in the rape: Grumen or Russo. They might have contacted Vance and let him know Parish planned to feed a story to the press. Maybe Parish told one of them about the documents."

Megan raised an eyebrow. Peden could see the wheels turning. She said, "Let's get Cassidy on a phone search for calls between those three. Can't hurt."

Peden swiped his phone and hit the saved number for NCIS Agent Myles Cassidy. He answered on the first ring. "Hey, Savage. What's up?"

"We need to use your resources again. You're on speaker and Agent Moore is listening in."

"Okay. Shoot."

"Two things. Can you have your techs do a search on phone calls between Vance, Grumen, and Carmine Russo? Also, calls involving Parish."

"Already done. There's only two calls between Vance and Grumen. Both are recent, like within the last couple days. Russo called Vance half a dozen times. All the calls were between September 5 and September 15. Four were before September 10, One on September 11 and one on September 15.

"As far as Parish goes, we don't have any calls from him to the other three. He made and received calls to and from Rayshon Mack regularly. He also received calls from a few numbers we haven't been able to identify. We're still working on it."

Peden and Megan remained silent, thinking about the timing of the calls Russo made to Vance.

Megan asked, "Were there any other calls between Vance and Russo before those you mentioned?"

"No, and that goes back to the time the unit returned from Afghanistan nearly ten years ago. Also, Grumen and Russo didn't communicate at all, except one recent call."

Peden walked into his office and grabbed a handful of blank three by five cards. He wrote on one *Calls between Vance/Russo*. He wrote on another *Grumen murders/timing*. Peden wondered if Vance, Grumen, and Russo were worried information about their role in the rape might be simmering to the surface.

Cassidy asked, "What else is on your mind?"

Megan said, "We'd like to let Lee Sparks do some searches in some databases to see if he can figure out where Amir Sayed and the Afghan girl relocated."

"Sure. By-the-way, we determined that the girl's name is Moska Aziz, not Amir's sister, but a family friend."

Megan replied, "That will be very helpful. Thanks."

Cassidy advised Peden and Megan again to not use Vance's name in any database searches. They did not want to spook him before they planned to take him into custody.

With the call ended, they moved back to Peden's desk, coffees in tow.

Peden suggested, "While I call Lee, can you sort the cards out? Do it in some kind of new way we haven't tried yet."

Megan nodded as Peden hit the number for Sparks. He answered on the second ring.

"Peden, I was about to call you."

"Hey, Lee. Lay it on me."

"I just read an article about Marine Corps potential retirements and advancements in the executive ranks. It appears General Vance might be in line for a third star. If any hint of a scandal pops up, he'd be crossed off the list and his career would stall, or maybe be over. Motive for murder?"

Peden replied, "We're looking at that angle. NCIS discovered Vance received a half dozen calls from Carmine Russo in a timeframe suggesting they may have been planning something. It's still a long shot, but the timeline fits."

Peden reviewed the timing of the calls with Lee and the way it fit with Parish's murder. He then changed the subject to Lee performing a search for Amir Sayed and Moska Aziz. He explained the two had been injured in the blast which killed the Sayed family and they had been resettled in the U.S. in upstate New York after their recovery in Germany. Lee said he would move on it right away. The call ended with Peden saying the search for Sayed and Aziz was his top priority.

Peden strolled back to his desk and watched as Megan placed the cards into two stacks, one from events in Afghanistan, the other for recent events. She took the stack with recent events and said, "Would you take these cards and see what you can figure out? I'll look at the others."

She took her stack and moved them to the visitor side of his desk and spread them out, thinking about a unique way to arrange the cards. She looked at one card - *Colleen Chandler fears Parish's stability.*

She looked at Peden, showing him the card, and asked, "What did you have in mind when you filled out this card?"

"Remember she said she feared Parish would be so drunk he might blab his mouth about her taking the documents or rubbing them in Grumen's face? I tried to capture that thought."

Megan pondered his answer for a bit then commented, "Could Colleen Chandler have been in contact with Parish recently and asked for the documents back and he refused, or maybe threatened her?"

"What would he gain by threatening her?"

"Money, revenge for being rejected. I don't know."

Peden pondered her answer. Was Colleen Chandler capable of murder? "Why would Chip report Parish's death if he knew his wife might be a suspect?"

"Maybe he didn't know."

Peden's eyebrows rose. *Food for thought.*

* * *

Lee Sparks made short work of his latest assignment. Having the unique name Moska Aziz made the search for her movements within the U.S. easy. After hacking into the U.S. Department of State Resettlement Tracking database, Lee immediately located her records. After being released from her final checkup at Walter Reed Medical Center in Bethesda, Maryland, she settled in the community of Saratoga Springs, New York. She received a full scholarship to Skidmore Woman's College, but attended classes for only one semester. She left Upstate New York and moved to Richmond Hill, Georgia, just twenty minutes from Peden's Liberty Street office.

The search for Amir Sayed presented a slightly more difficult challenge. Amir Sayed disappeared without a trace while living in Saratoga Springs. Lee altered his search several times but hit paydirt when he entered 'A* Sayed' as the search terms. Aslam Sayed had started using his real name when he moved into the same apartment complex as Moska Aziz in Richmond Hill, Georgia,.

Coincidence? Not a chance.

When Lee called Peden, he answered on the first ring. "Hey, Lee. I just spoke with you a little over an hour ago. I take it you have good news?"

"I expect a bonus in my paycheck. This might be a record of some kind."

"Well, are you going to make me beg?"

"Moska Aziz and Aslam Sayed lived in Saratoga Springs, New York, for a short period of time before relocating to Richmond Hill, Georgia. They now live in separate units in the Sterling Creek Apartment complex on Lullwater Drive. It's about twenty-five minutes from your office."

"Wow. Do you have their unit numbers?"

"Not yet, but you'll be the first to know." He paused then continued, "You know, living where they do, it's only about an hour and a half to where they found Parish's body."

Peden didn't answer for a moment as he thought about the implications of Aziz and Sayed living so close to where Parish was killed and where he would be interred. He said, "It can't be too far from Glennville Cemetery and Hinesville where the ceremony will be held."

Lee, thinking out loud asked, "Could they have manipulated some of this? But how? Could someone with local ties have helped?"

Peden said, "I think I might have an idea who that is."

* * *

Chip and Colleen Chandler rode in silence on their way to the Hampton Inn in Hinesville, Georgia. The five-hour plus drive, adding time for a meal and bath break, would give them an arrival time just after 7:30 p.m. Chip divided his time between concentrating on the drive and thinking about his wife's deception. At times, his anger grew to the point of almost turning to her and yelling that her lies were destroying their future together. He swallowed those thoughts and shifted his focus back to the road ahead, keeping him from saying anything that might drive a wedge into the divide between them.

Heading south in Interstate 95 just after 5:15, Colleen broke the silence, asking, "Hungry?"

Chip cleared his throat and looked out the driver's side window at the passing South Carolina trees lining the interstate. He looked back at the road ahead, gaging the traffic, wondering what restaurants might be at the coming exits south of Walterboro. To the best of his recollection, the choices were limited.

He asked, "What are you hungry for? I hope burgers or a chicken sandwich, because there isn't much else down this way."

"Anything's fine. I'm not that hungry."

"I don't have much of an appetite, either. Maybe we should wait til Hinesville. It's only about another hour and a half."

"Chip, I need to tell you some things, but …"

"But what, Colleen? More lies? More half-truths?"

Colleen yelled, "Lookout!"

Chip nearly rear-ended a slow-moving, beat-up, pickup truck traveling at nearly half the speed limit. He veered to the passing lane just missing the truck and avoiding a car in the passing lane flying along well over the speed limit. He veered back into the right-hand lane and slowed to just above the limit, taking a deep breath, trying to get his heartbeat under control. He looked quickly at Colleen and asked, "Are you okay?"

"I will be. I'm so sorry … for everything."

Tears welled in Colleen's eyes. She wiped them away with the back of her hands and continued, "Let's get off the highway. We're not in a hurry, not tonight, at least."

Fifteen minutes later, Chip took the Hardeeville exit to Highway 17 south. They pulled into a Waffle House parking lot.

Chapter 44

Chip parked at the Waffle House, but they stayed in their Lexus. Both lost their appetites and Colleen looked to be in emotional distress. Her puffy, red eyes punctuated the dark circles under both. She appeared as if she had been slapped in the face.

Chip's tight jaw jutted out, a pronounced cleft showing. Still rattled over the near collision on the interstate, he took a sip of lukewarm water, hoping to ease his tension. After a long drink and several deep breaths, in a commanding voice not used since his time in Afghanistan, he said, "You need to tell me everything, right now, and don't leave out a single thing. Am I making myself clear?"

Colleen nodded, a look of fear and apprehension covering her face. She shivered as she took a deep breath. "Vance tried to rape me in his office back in country. He bent over on his desk, pinned face-down, my pants nearly down to my knees. Parish came into my office to talk when he heard me struggling. He ran into Vance's office and pushed him off me. He asked me if I was okay, then started to go after Vance. I stopped him before he could attack Vance."

"Why did you stop him," Chip asked?

"Because Parish already had three strikes against him. Attacking Vance would have been the final straw. I didn't think about it at the time. I just reacted." She paused. "There's more." She looked around the parking lot, maybe trying to find strength to continue. Finally, she whimpered, "I don't know how to tell you this next part."

"Just spit it out. It can't be worse than what you've already told me."

By the look in his wife's eyes, he knew he was wrong and needed to brace himself.

"The Afghan girl who Vance, Grumen, and Russo raped … I've been communicating with her. I think she and Amir Sayed's brother killed Grumen and his wife."

Chip's mouth dropped open. He searched for something to say, but words would not come.

She continued, "They plan to kill Vance and Russo tomorrow night."

* * *

Thursday, just before noon, Peden and Megan sat with Harlan Wilson for lunch at Melody's Coastal Café in Midway. The restaurant sat near the main intersection in the town just three miles from Hinesville and the Hampton Inn where the toast to Rusty Parish and Jeff Grumen would take place. They hoped to work out a few communications details with Harlan and, for his safety, some restrictions to his actions. For instance, if he noticed something with any possibility of putting the photographer in danger, he should avoid the situation and report it to Peden.

Wilson asked in his southern drawl, "Y'all know this ain't my first rodeo, right?"

Peden smiled, "Yeah, Willie. We know. But this is our rodeo and we like our cowboys to stay safe." He paused then said, "We got a call from one of the men who will be at the gathering tonight. Someone, a middle-eastern woman and man plan to kill the general and one of the other men. We don't know when or where this might take place, but we need you to keep an eye on the grounds and let us know immediately if you see anything out of the ordinary."

"Hell, I don't think there's anything ordinary about any of this, but I know what y'all mean. I got both y'all's numbers saved. Y'all are one click away. Where should I set up?"

They discussed the layout of the Hampton Inn, the lounge, and the lobby. Harlan said he would move around in a stealthy manner and try to not draw undue attention. As they finished their meeting, Peden's phone vibrated. Myles Cassidy.

As Harlan Wilson stepped away, Peden answered, "Agent Cassidy, what's up?"

Cassidy's baritone voice boomed over his cell phone, "Hey, Peden. We're at the hotel, all checked in. We're watching from a couple rooms on the first floor. We have a good view of the entrance to the lobby. We're keeping track of the guests as they arrive. It's early, so we haven't seen anyone except the Chandlers. They arrived last night."

"Yeah. I spoke with Chip about 8:00 p.m. They had just checked in." Peden paused, thinking that he needed to let Cassidy know about the threat to Vance and Russo. "We received information that there may be an attempt on Vance's life sometime today."

Peden went on to describe the threat as best he knew. Cassidy replied they would be on the look-out for the suspects as Peden described them.

Cassidy said, "This is getting to be a real shit-show. Too many moving parts."

Peden replied, "Hopefully, this will be done and over with, peacefully, before midnight."

Cassidy laughed. "Right. Savage, you've got an odd sense of humor. If we were smart, we'd just arrest Vance right after he arrives. It would get messy, but not as bad as it might if we let this play out."

Peden remained silent while he thought about the ramifications of what Cassidy said. If they did allow Vance's arrest, they would most likely never find Parish's murderer, their opportunity would be wasted.

"We have to let this play out. We're close, I can feel it. Keep in touch. We'll let you know what we find."

"Okay. You and Agent Moore be damn careful."

"You, too."

* * *

The gathering in the lounge had been set for 8:00 p.m. Peden and Megan arrived back at the hotel at 2:10 p.m. They walked around the lobby, the lounge, and the surrounding area at the perimeter of the hotel, acting like a couple. Peden thought he might have caught Megan smile, but most likely was mistaken. He observed the arrival of about a dozen men and a few couples who appeared to be there for the ceremony. Neither he nor Megan spotted Harlan Wilson or Myles Cassidy anywhere.

Peden remarked, "I guess Willie's pretty good at his job. I haven't seen a hint that he's here."

"That's a good thing. If we don't see him by 4:00 or so, I think we should give him a call; make sure he really is here."

"Not a bad idea."

As they entered the lobby after completing their final trek around the parking lot, they saw General Vance step up to the check-in counter. Peden ignored the general, looking away, purposely feigning disinterest. Peden looked out to the drive-up covered entryway and saw Evelyn Vance sitting in their rental car. The look on her face showed just how much she hated being in Hinesville, Georgia.

Megan turned to Peden and said, "Dear, they have a rack with pamphlets for local attractions. Let's take a look."

The rack sat right next to the check-in counter. The two of them would have to move to within six feet of Vance. Peden rolled his eyes but followed Megan, who began picking out pamphlets at random, commenting on each attraction. She turned and looked right at Vance. He turned to face her and smiled.

Megan said to Vance, "Is this your first trip to the area?"

Vance looked at her from head to toe, smiled with what Megan believed to be his best seductive glance. He said, "No. I've been to Savannah several times. The historic district is fantastic. Many great restaurants and a couple nice hotels."

"Thank you. We'll have to make the trip into Savannah." She turned to face Peden, "Did you hear that, dear? Savannah historic district. Let's plan a day trip there."

Peden nodded and said, "Whatever you want, sweetheart." He nodded to Vance who turned his attention back to the clerk, but not before he gave Megan one more head to toe appraising look.

As they walked away, Megan whispered to Peden, "Wasn't that fun? He thinks he's God's gift. Ugh."

Peden rolled his eyes then looked at a clock on the wall - 3:50. They headed to their shared room. Time to call Harlan Wilson.

* * *

When the door to their room closed, Peden hit the button on his cell phone for Wilson, who answered on the first ring.

"Hey, Peden. I saw y'all checkin' things out. It looks like about fifteen of the guys from the platoon are here. What did Megan say to Vance?"

"Saw that, did you? Just small talk about vacationing in the area. That's her way of trying to be normal."

"Well, it looked pretty casual to me, so it must have worked. Vance sure has an eye for the ladies. He's checked out every female rear end since he got out of his car. His wife looks like she'd rather be boiled in hot oil than to be here. I saw the Chandlers, too. The Misses looks whipped. She's been crying – hard. She's got makeup on, tryin' to hide it, but it ain't workin'."

Peden took a breath then said, "The Chandlers have hit a rough patch because of this whole affair. Are you snapping any pictures?"

"Taken over a hundred since I got here. Nothing too interesting yet, but the party's just gettin' started."

Peden replied, "Yeah. Some party. Remember what we talked about. Be damned careful. Call me in a couple hours, just to check in; sooner if you see anything interesting."

"You got it, brother."

The call disconnected.

Megan looked at Peden with questioning eyes. He said, "Willie hasn't seen anything too crazy except some blond woman talking with Vance. Said she looked pretty normal in the exchange."

"He sure knows how to stay out of sight. I haven't seen even a hint that he's here. It isn't like this is some jungle with loads of trees for cover. He's good."

"Yeah. Let's hope he can keep it up. What do you want to do for the next few hours?"

Megan struck a thoughtful pose then said, "Before we do anything, call Chip and tell him if he and Colleen see us to not approach us. We need to remain anonymous."

"Oh, like not talking with anyone associated with the platoon, like Vance?"

"Oh, Pedee, you're no fun."

Peden shook his head then made the call to Chip who answered on the third ring.

"Hey, Peden."

"Chip. I see you and Colleen are here."

"Yeah. Colleen's getting a shower, trying to get herself together. She's kind of a mess right now, emotionally, I mean. I've been tough on her, but she deserves it. I don't know where we go from here."

"Chip, once this is over, you and Colleen will figure it out. Right now, we all need to concentrate on this gathering. So, if you and Colleen see Megan and me, ignore us. Act as if you don't know us." He paused, then said, "That reminds me, have you seen Rayshon Mack yet?"

"No. I expect he'll be here anytime though. Carmine Russo's here. Arrived about twenty minutes ago. You won't miss him. Big mouthed Bostonian. Dark hair and perpetually tanned skin."

"We'll watch for him. If you hear from Ray, tell him to call me, but tell him the same thing I just told you. Ignore us. That should be easy for him. We've never met him except over the phone."

"I'll let him know. I've got to go. Colleen's getting out of the shower."

"Okay, Chip. Remember, ignore us and be careful tonight."

"Copy."

Chapter 45

At 7:45 p.m. General Virgil Vance and his wife, Evelyn, stood just inside the doorway of the lounge at the Hampton Inn and greeted members of the platoon and their guests – wives, girlfriends, and just friends - as they entered. He wore an expensive civilian suit with a Marine Corps lapel pin, opting to wear his dress military uniform at tomorrow's funeral services. With a smile, he shook each person's hands and let them know drinks were on him, they should relax and get reacquainted with their brothers. He made no mention of the reason for the gathering, trying to keep the mood light for as long as possible. For her part, Evelyn smiled at each platoon member and hugged their guests. She did eye any handsome males with a smile and a bit more interest than appropriate, but no one seemed to notice, except Peden and Megan. Further into the lounge, Chip and Colleen Chandler repeated the greeting in similar fashion. Many of the platoon members gave Chip a brief hug along with the handshake, tugging on his heartstrings. Colleen worked hard to smile and relax, but her face showed the tension gripping her. She looked around the lounge, fear lurking just below the surface of her face, as if evil might walk through the door at any moment.

Peden and Megan sat at a table in the corner of the lounge, both their seats facing the gathering and the door at the opposite end of the lounge. Maintaining a position where each could react quickly to any threat that emerged, they assessed each person who came through the doors, looking for any hint of aggression.

Anyone could see that this gathering involved military and former military members. A couple sitting at the bar not affiliated with the group openly thanked each participant for their service. They asked why the men and women were at the hotel. When they learned of the upcoming funeral, their faces became somber. They told the bartender to put a round of drinks for the men and women on their tab. When they were told drinks for the gathering had been taken of, they gave a large tip to the staff instead.

A powerful looking black man walked through the door from the lobby. Rayshon Mack joined the gathering. A man further down the bar with a strong New England accent yelled 'Ray' and waved his hands indicating that Mack should join them. He nodded at the man but first approached Vance and his wife, then moved on to Chip Chandler. Ray shook his hand and gave him a tight bear-hug. They smiled at each other, but the smile displayed a touch of sadness. Ray turned to Colleen and shook her hand, then, seeing her face, gave her a tight, but gentle hug. Tears welled in her eyes as they separated. He held her hands for a moment longer, then broke from the Chandlers and moved towards the crowd of men and women further into the lounge. He approached Carmine Russo, shook his hand, and motioned towards the bar.

"I told you, I'm buyin' your first beer."

Russo said, "Thanks, Ray, but it's an open bar."

"Even better," Mack bellowed.

The group laughed. When Ray and Carmine had their beers, they raised their bottles and yelled, "Oorah!"

At 8:10, General Vance used a fork to clang his beer bottle to get everyone's attention. After about ten seconds, the group quieted and Vance addressed the crowd. Peden and Megan listened but kept looking around the lounge, checking the doors.

Peden's phone vibrated in his pocket. He pulled out his cell and looked at the screen. Harlan Wilson.

He swiped the green handset and whispered into the phone, "Hey, Willie."

"Peden, I'm in the main parking lot and there's a skinny guy gettin' out of a blue foreign car. He looks middle eastern. He might be headin' … wait. He's leaning back into the car sayin' somethin' to the driver. Okay. He closed the car door and he's headin' into the hotel."

Peden whispered into his phone, "What's he wearing?"

"Blue jeans, blue denim jacket, bright colored tennis shoes, a Bulldogs ballcap, and he's carryin' a small backpack." He paused then said, "And Peden, he looks scared outta his wits, like everybody's watchin' him. He looks guilty of somethin'."

Peden disconnected the call and whispered to Megan, "Watch for a skinny, middle eastern guy in blue jeans, a blue jean jacket, and a ballcap, carrying a backpack. Willie says he looks scared."

* * *

Aslam Sayed asked Moska to pray with him as they sat in her blue Honda Accord. She said she would, but he needed to take a deep breath and calm down first. This angered Aslam, his nerves already in overdrive. After their dinner at the Denny's restaurant off Interstate 95 he downed two cups of coffee. She warned him that the caffein would send his already tightly strung nerves into overdrive, but he ignored her. Now, his eyes were so wide open they looked ready to pop out of their sockets. The high humidity added to his tension, causing sweat to run down his temples.

She said, "Aslam, you will be fine. We've been over this a dozen times. You calmly walk into the lounge and set the backpack on a chair or under a table and walk out. Walk slowly. Do not rush and do not look around the room, especially like you have something to hide. Smile. Think of something pleasant."

He looked at her with a sneer, "If it is so simple, Moska, why don't you do it?"

"I would, Aslam, but Chip Chandler knows who I am. He's seen my face. He'll recognize me."

"That was ages ago, Moska. What about me? He worked with Amir. He never met me, but I resemble Amir. He might think I am my brother. What then?"

"You just have to keep your head down and make sure you keep the ballcap pulled down over your eyes. Do not make eye contact with anyone."

Aslam took a deep breath and then scolded Moska, "Enough. I will do it. Now pray with me that our mission will be successful."

They prayed briefly, asking Allah to help them avenge the deaths of his family and her best friend. She said nothing of her rape and her thirst for vengeance.

He opened the car door and turned to face her. He said, "When I leave the backpack and return, we can finish the job together. You will see first-hand my commitment to our cause."

He closed the car door and headed towards the hotel, looking around for the police or some federal agents ready to apprehend him. He pulled the Georgia Bulldogs ballcap lower, but not before Harlan Wilson saw the bulging eyes and the fear that radiated from every part of his body.

Moska watched as Aslam moved towards the hotel lobby, shaking her head. He looked like a posterchild for how to identify a terrorist. Her confidence in their success dropped.

She opened an application on her tablet and monitored the screen divided into four views. Three were different angles in the lounge from cameras that they had placed the day before. She easily picked out Virgil Vance and his wife, Evelyn. On another shot, she saw Chip and Colleen Chandler. Finally, she noticed a large, healthy-looking black man whom she did not know. Next to him stood Carmine Russo. A glorious ending to ten years of heartache, anger, pain, and a thirst for vengeance rapidly approached.

She whispered, "Allah be praised."

* * *

Colleen Chandler stared at Virgil Vance as he addressed the former platoon brothers. She did not hear a word he said, her ears humming as her anger ramped up. She thought back to the camp outside of Kabul where this arrogant, self-important ass tried to rape her. Had it not been for Rusty Parish, he might have succeeded. As Vance spoke, he looked around the room, making eye contact with many of the men. Finally, he swung towards Chip and Collen. He briefly looked at Chip, then locked eyes with Colleen. He seemed to sense the hatred emanating from her … and he smiled slightly, not missing a beat in his address. Her loathing edged up even more.

She hoped his speech would end soon. She could hardly stand to be in the same room with the man. Chip looked at her, sensing she approached a breaking point. Despite their earlier friction, he put a hand gently on her back and leaned closer in a comforting gesture, brushing a light kiss on her left cheek. The act helped relieve a little of the pressure building up inside her heart and mind. Tears threatened to pour from her eyes, but she fought to maintain control.

Then she saw a man wearing a Bulldogs ballcap standing at the open door to the lounge. When she saw his bulging eyes, everything else in the lounge disappeared from view. She held her breath, waiting to see what the man did next.

Chip, his hand still resting lightly on her back, felt the sudden change in her body as muscles tensed. Misreading the change, he whispered to her, "Ignore Vance. This will be over soon enough."

As the words left his mouth, the skinny man with the bulging eyes moved into the lounge, his ballcap pulled low. No one seemed to notice him walk past the crowd, trying to stay as far away from the group as possible. When he reached a point just over halfway into the bar, he sat down, removing the backpack, setting it on the seat next to him. He lowered his head as if in prayer, then took a deep breath and stood. He looked directly at Colleen, then at Chip. She looked at Chip and saw the recognition register on his face; a very brief smile, followed by confusion.

* * *

From the opposite end of the lounge, Peden and Megan saw the skinny man with the Bulldogs ballcap and blue jeans enter the lounge. More importantly, they noticed the backpack that appeared to have at least one heavy object weighing down the light fabric. Peden noticed Colleen Chandler's reaction to the man. When Peden stood, his cell phone chirped. He looked down and saw Harlan Wilson's number and answered.

When he swiped across the screen he heard Wilson's voice yell, "Get outta there! She's gonna blow the place up!"

Peden dropped his phone on the table just as Megan leapt to her feet. They headed towards the man who stood just thirty-five feet away.

Before they could take two steps, Colleen Chandler yelled, "Bomb!"

She ran at Aslam. Startled, he turned towards her. With only fifteen feet between them, he did not have time to remove the phone with the bomb's trigger number already keyed in. If he hit the send button, the bomb would detonate.

Colleen launched herself at Aslam and sent him tumbling on top of the backpack. Other members of the platoon turned, stunned by her pronouncement of a bomb in the lounge. They moved towards her to assist in whatever she did.

Aslam struggled to get the phone from his pocket, but Colleen restrained his arms in a bear hug. Chip moved in next to his wife, helping pin the terrorist's arms to his side. The startled man could not move.

Chapter 46

Moska Aziz watched as Aslam sat at the table. She knew he could not just follow her instructions. He had to prove that he knew better than she, that he alone made the decisions for them. *That's what a man does, Moska.* But his decision made no difference. She never planned to let him leave the lounge alive.

Moska pulled up the phone app on her tablet. Reviewed the number that she had already keyed in. She whispered, "Good-bye, Aslam. Allah be praised."

She hit the button and watched towards the hotel, expecting the section of the building where the lounge was situated to be destroyed in a massive fireball and for the blast to shake the ground. She watched, taking pleasure in the moment, the moment of revenge. The death of those who defiled her and killed her love.

She heard the blast, but it did not meet her expectations. The building remained intact. She looked at the tablet expecting the cameras to be destroyed, but she could see that the bomb, though it had detonated, did nowhere near the destruction she and Aslam expected. Men and women still stood, unharmed, though there were some injuries. Through the smoke, Moska saw Aslam on the floor covered in blood next to Colleen Chandler. Two others had injuries but one thing became crystal clear - the bomb had malfunctioned. Aslam had failed.

Moska started the car and slowly headed towards the exit. The last thing she saw at the Hampton Inn was a man taking pictures of her and her car as she turned east onto highway 84.

* * *

Inside the lounge, rapped in Colleen Chandler's arms, Aslam managed to pull the backpack out of the chair. Just before the bomb detonated, he relaxed and smiled, believing he achieved greatness, ready to accept his place in heaven. When Colleen saw his face, she knew she would not survive the blast. She just followed her training and did what she could to protect her Marine brothers. She pulled the backpack tight against her chest.

The bomb exploded as two more Marines dove onto Aslam. In a cloud of smoke and dust, nails, washers, nuts, and bolts flew everywhere, but Colleen Chandler and Aslam Sayed took the brunt of the blast. They both died instantly.

Chip tried to reach for his wife, but the force of the blast knocked him backwards. Small pieces of shrapnel hit him in the arm. The concussive effects knocked him unconscious.

Peden moved a fraction of a second before Megan and took at least three pieces of shrapnel to the right arm and shoulder. Megan, coming up behind him, escaped harm.

NCIS Agents Cassidy and Pattelli ran into the lounge. They first checked on Peden and Megan. Seeing they were not mortally wounded, they turned their attention to Virgil Vance and his wife, who had been standing back, unsure of what to do. Cassidy said to Vance, "General, please come with us."

Vance and his wife, thinking that the men were part of a protection detail, followed the men without hesitation. Cassidy turned to Evelyn Vance and said, "Not you, ma'am. Just the general."

In shock, Evelyn Vance did not know what to do. Being far enough away from the blast, she was not injured, but dust and rushing air from the shock wave left her hair and dress a dirty, disheveled mess. With her husband ushered away, she looked around for someone to help her, but platoon members assisted the injured men and women. Rayshon Mack caught her eye. He must have seen the panic on her face. He noticed two men escorting the general away. He recognized one of the men and thought *Miller? It can't be.*

He approached Evelyn Vance and asked, "Mrs. Vance, are you alright? What happened to the general?"

She broke down in tears as she leaned into Mack's chest. "Two men took him. I don't know where."

Mack put a muscular arm around her, hoping to comfort the distraught woman. After a moment, he looked around the room and decided to get the general's wife out into the lobby away from all the commotion just as the local fire department and EMTs arrived on the chaotic scene.

* * *

Once Vance settled into the back seat of a black Suburban, he thanked them for their quick action to protect him, but asked why his wife was not allowed to join him. The agents looked at each other as if amused, though nothing remotely funny had occurred. With Pattelli driving, Cassidy turned to Vance and said, "General Virgil Vance, you are under arrest for the rape of Moska Aziz. In addition to that charge, you will be charged with falsifying official documents and reports. The charges will …"

Vance yelled, "What the hell are you talking about? I don't have to put up with this shit. I just witnessed one of my Marines murdered. I'm heading back to …"

When Vance tried the door, it would not open. He hollered, "Open this door. Do you know who you're screwing with?"

Cassidy looked directly at Vance with steely eyes and replied, "Yes, sir. We do. We really don't give a damn who you think you are. We'll make sure your wife gets back home safely." He turned and faced the parking lot exit, then said, "Sit back and enjoy the ride, General. We have a long night ahead."

Vance leaned forward and looked down towards his shoes, but all he saw was his career going up in flames.

* * *

Paramedics at the scene of the explosion loaded Colleen Chandler onto a gurney and quickly moved her through the lounge and lobby out to the waiting ambulance. As they moved, a trail of blood drops marked their path. The grim looks on their faces told Chip Chandler all he needed to know. He rode the ambulance with his wife, but she never regained consciousness. It took less than two minutes from the parking lot at the Hampton Inn to reach the emergency room at Liberty Regional Medical Center. Doctor Amos Reems declared her dead-on-arrival at 8:32 p.m. Chip collapsed to a sitting position on the floor near the emergency room entrance with his elbows on his knees, his hands covering his eyes as tears flowed in earnest.

He thought back to the moment he hesitated, thinking Amir Sayed entered the lounge. After looking closer at the Afghan man, he realized that it could not have been his friend and interpreter, but the resemblance was uncanny.

As he sat there, another ambulance pulled up to the bay. A second gurney appeared when the doors to the ambulance opened. The paramedics exhibited no urgency in their movements. Doctor Reems approached the gurney and declared the second person dead.

Chip stood and walked to the dead man. He wanted to spit on his wounds, to somehow defile the man who killed his wife. He tensed as he thought about dragging Aslam Sayed off the gurney to the floor and stomping on his head and his heart, or where his heart should have been.

A third vehicle rolled up to the crowded emergency room bay. The driver and front passenger doors opened. Two men dressed in black sports coats ran to the driver's side back door and opened it. Myles Cassidy and Sidney Pattelli both hollered for help as they reached into the vehicle and pulled a man to the edge of the seat. Chandler watched as a pistol rattled to the ground at the NCIS agents' feet.

Emergency room staff ran to their side as Cassidy yelled, "Gunshot wound to the head. He shot himself. He shot himself. We didn't check him for a weapon. Oh, God. We should've checked."

* * *

A third ambulance arrived at the Hampton Inn by 8:40 p.m. The crowd was herded into the parking lot but instructed to stay to the right of the main lobby entrance. Megan helped

Peden stem the minor blood flow from his arm. Several members of the platoon suffered similar injuries as Peden, but he felt certain that only two fatalities resulted from the IED. Peden looked at the remnants of the pipe bomb. He knew that, whoever had built the device, they screwed something up. For an IED of that size, had it been assembled properly, most of the people in the lounge would have been killed or severely maimed.

Megan said, "You should get to the hospital and have that looked at."

"Later. Did you see Cassidy escort Vance out of here?"

"Yeah. They must have decided to move right away after the explosion."

Peden looked around the lounge at the damage done. The bomb exploded between Aslam Sayed and Colleen Chandler containing the damage from the blast to a fifteen-foot radius. Through the windows, Peden could see that hotel staff evacuated the building

He reached for his phone. Amazingly, when he swiped the screen, it lit up. He hit the button for Harlan Wilson who picked up on the first ring.

Harlan asked, "What the hell happened in there. Y'all should be dead."

"We've been better. But, Willie, right before the blast you yelled that we should get the hell out of there. How did you know?"

"The lady that skinny guy rode with, she detonated the bomb. I saw her with a phone number on the screen on her tablet. I knew she wouldn't wait for her partner to get out. I know how these folks operate."

Peden thought for a minute as Wilson continued talking. He cut Wilson off and asked, "Is the lady still in the parking lot?"

"No. Sorry, but she left right after the bomb went off. She seemed disappointed, then drove off. To her credit, she drove away slowly."

"Did you try to follow her?"

"I tried but got blocked in by emergency equipment. I did get a bunch of pictures of her, the car, and the license plate. I can call the local cops, the sheriff, and the state police as soon as we hang up."

"Do it, Willie. Right now."

"Y'all got it, Peden."

* * *

Chip Chandler saw the body of General Virgil Vance as the medical staff assisted the two NCIS agents in moving the general's body to a gurney. Doctor Reems shook his head in disgust and looked at the clock on the wall: 8:47. He said something to the nurse at his side and walked back into the confines of the emergency room. Other patients, living ones, needed his care.

Chandler's face turned red. He removed his cell phone from his suit jacket pocket and hit the button for Peden Savage. Peden answered on the first ring.

"Peden. Colleen's dead."

Peden took in a deep breath, but remained quiet for several seconds before replying, "Ahh Chip. I'm so damn sorry. I wish I could have …"

Chip cut him off. He said, "Peden, none of this is your fault. There's more. The bomber is Aslam Sayed, my interpreter's younger brother."

"Yeah, Chip. We learned about him yesterday. We thought he might try something at the gathering tonight, but had no idea how or when." He paused before continuing, "He has an accomplice. Moska Aziz, a friend of your interpreter's sister. She was in the hotel parking lot. We're pretty sure she detonated the bomb, then left."

"How do you know that?"

"We had someone watching the grounds, but she escaped in the chaos."

"Peden, Vance is dead, too. He killed himself."

The line remained silent. Peden heard a click as Chip Chandler disconnected the call. He had nothing more to say.

* * *

Peden and Megan approached Carmine Russo. He rambled on in his loud, obnoxious manner about how he could have been killed. When they asked to speak with him, Russo said, "I need to get to the hospital and get checked out."

Megan looked him over from head to toe and did not see a single drop of blood or any evidence of an injury. She said, "We'll make sure you get there, but right now you're going to tell us about something that happened back in Afghanistan a little over ten years ago."

Russo said, "The hell I am. Who the hell are you?"

"My name is Special Agent Megan Moore, and you are in deep shit. We're going to detain you and turn you over to Agent Myles Cassidy when he returns. He's already in a bad mood because a man in his custody just committed suicide."

Russo frowned. He watched as General Vance was escorted away after the blast. His face lost all color and his mouth dropped open. He should have kept his mouth shut, but that had never been a strong suit at any time in his life.

Russo said, "I didn't have nothin' to do with assaulting that girl."

Peden said, "Atta-boy, Carmine. Keep talking."

Russo finally clammed-up and demanded a lawyer.

Epilogue

October 15, 2021
Peden Savage
Final Case Notes and Report
To: FBI Special Agent In Charge Roland Fosco, Atlanta, Georgia Field Office
Cc: FBI Special Agent In Charge Megan Moore, Savannah, Georgia Local Office

Barring a change in circumstances, this will be my final report.

The case to determine Randall Parish's murderer is closed with this report. Randall Parish died from a fatal overdose allegedly administered by Carmine Russo at the behest of the late General Virgil Vance. These two men, and the late Jeffrey Grumen, allegedly assaulted and raped a fifteen-year-old Afghan girl named Moska Aziz around June 2011. The alleged rape was known to these three only until Colleen Chandler (then Captain Colleen Temple) overheard Russo threaten Grumen with exposure if he were accused of the rape.

On September 11, 2011, the United States military ordered a drone strike intending to kill two top terrorist leaders from the Taliban and Al-Queda in Kabul, Afghanistan. Evidence exists that shows Vance changed the orders without authorization and bombed the home of the Sayed family frequented by the young woman with the intention of killing anyone with knowledge of the rape. The only survivors were Aslam Sayed and Moska Aziz. After being relocated to the United States, Sayed and Aziz concocted a plan for revenge against the man who killed the Sayed family and the others who participated in the rape.

Prior to the murder of Randall Parish, an Associated Press reporter, Brandon Wilson, died under mysterious circumstances. While Wilson's death is not part of this investigation, I believe that his death may be related to a story he intended to publish about the bombing of the Sayed residence in Kabul. Vance and Russo communicated several times prior to Wilson's death. Vance's motive - ensure that the story never became public.

It is my understanding that Special Agent in Charge, Megan Moore, will provide additional details about this case in her official report. At this point, the case is closed.

Please see the attached invoice detailing compensation and expenses for the resources provided by Savage Investigative Consultants. It has been our pleasure doing business with you. We look forward to future opportunities where we can assist the Federal Bureau of Investigation.

Sincerely,
Peden Savage
Savage Investigative Consultants.

As Peden hit the print button, Megan Moore walked into his office looking fresh with her usual stone face. She sat in one of the visitor chairs in front of his desk and placed her clutch on his desk.

"Well, Pedee, Rollie is really impressed with you. We started out investigating a suicide and wound up taking down a dirty general, a couple jerks, and a terrorist who wasn't on anyone's radar."

"It all sounds good, but one got away and Russo may never be charged. Any news on Moska Aziz?"

Megan said, "No. She's one smart chick – a real planner. When she left Hinesville, she must have had another car staged. The Liberty County Sheriff's Office found the blue Accord at an abandoned farmhouse northwest of town. She may have had another accomplice, but I'm betting on the getaway car theory."

"Is she someone we should be concerned about?"

Megan looked up at Peden's metal ceiling tiles in his nineteenth century office, contemplating his question. She replied, "I don't think so. Two of the three people who raped her are dead. Plus, NCIS is considering pulling Russo back into active duty to court-martial him and send him to Fort Leavenworth."

"But we killed her friend's family."

"I didn't say we can forget about her, but my bet is that she's satisfied."

"We'll see."

They were silent for a spell. Peden remarked, "I'm happy that Parish's funeral went off on time despite the, uh, interruption. He deserved it. And I haven't heard from Chip since Colleen's funeral. Poor bastard. I should call him, or just drop in on him. He needs support right now.

"Yeah. His life turned upside-down, from living the dream to crap in just over a week."

Peden rubbed his chin then said, "I spoke with him after Colleen's funeral and he could barely think straight – real conflicted. He said to me *I had everything, still do materially, but I'd give away everything to have her back, even after her deceit. God, I loved her – still do.* It's gonna take a long time for him to get over her, if he ever does."

A long silence followed. Megan took a deep breath and said, "I heard Cassidy faced a disciplinary hearing, but just got a slap on the wrist. The fact they picked up the investigation after ten years seemed to temper his boss's actions. I think they went through the motions to satisfy the upper brass. I'm glad. I liked his style."

Peden smiled, thinking that Cassidy's style mirrored Megan's. Two peas in a pod.

The Death March wailed from Peden's cell phone. Susan, the wicked ex.

Peden moaned, "Oh, God. I forgot. I'm supposed to meet my daughter's boyfriend later today."

Megan reached for the phone, but Peden beat her to it. He swiped the red handset to hang up without answering.

Peden said, "I'm already in trouble with her. No sense spoiling my day this early. How about breakfast? Rollie's buying. It's on my invoice."

Megan rolled her eyes as she stood and led the way out of Peden's office.

***

Carmine Russo pulled his FedEx truck to the curb in front of a house in Statesboro, Georgia, that looked abandoned. Shrugging his shoulders, he picked up the package and headed towards the front porch. A female voice emanated from the box.

He clearly heard, "Goodbye, Carmine."

He stopped in his tracks and looked at the package, a confused look on his face.

The explosion rocked the FexEx truck and blew the windows and front door into the house. Only smoking shoes remained where Carmine Russo had just stood.

From the parking lot of a strip mall less than half a mile away, Moska Aziz watched the plume of smoke.

She mused, "If you want something done right, let a female do it. Allah be praised."

She smiled and drove away.

<u>The End</u>

Other PJ Grondin Suspense Novels

The McKinney Brothers Series

A Lifetime of Vengeance - Book 1
A Lifetime of Deception - Book 2
A Lifetime of Exposure - Book 3
A Lifetime of Terror - Book 4
A Lifetime of Betrayal - Book 5

The Peden Savage Series

Drug Wars - Book 1
Flash Drive - Book 2

Non-Series

Under the Blood Tree

Visit www.pjgrondin.com
pjgron@pjgrondin.com

All titles are available in trade paperback and
various eBook formats.

Author Information

Pete 'P.J.' Grondin, born the seventh of twelve children, moved around a number of times when he was young; from Sandusky, Ohio to Bay City, Michigan, then to Maitland and Zellwood, Florida, before returning to Sandusky, Ohio. That is where he married the love of his life, Debbie Fleming.

After his service in the US Navy, in the Nuclear Power Program, serving on the ballistic missile submarine U.S.S. *John Adams*, Pete returned to his hometown of Sandusky, Ohio, where he was elected to the Sandusky City Commission, serving a single term. He retired from a major, regional, electric utility after twenty-six years of service.

Past Sins is his ninth novel, the third in the Peden Savage series. His previous works include Peden Savage novels, *Drug Wars* and *Flash Drive*, A non-series novel, *Under the Blood Tree*, and five novels in the McKinney Brothers series: *A Lifetime of Vengeance, A Lifetime of Deception, A Lifetime of Exposure, A Lifetime of Terror,* and *A Lifetime of Betrayal*.